Buried Ethics

Digging Up Bones
A Greg Webster Series Book

Gerard Michael

Marimac

Dedication

To Marilyn for your editing skills, and most importantly, for your love, understanding, and unending support that set me free.

To my children who prove that constant, never ending, and unconditional love is reciprocal. You are an inspiration for me.

And to Anna for reading my books cover to cover even though the subject matter is difficult for her.

"Light can be found even in the darkest corners of our lives."

-Greg Webster-

Preface

My first novel, Deadly Ethics came about as a result of a conversation I had with a co-worker many years ago. As I created the characters, and told their stories, I became more and more attached to them.

This book had to be written to keep them alive! This band of ordinary people from different walks of life, pulling together for a common cause, pulls at my heartstrings. Their selflessness brings me to an emotional place that causes me to pause my writing so that I may fully absorb and appreciate the moment.

These are stories of everyday heroes armed with nothing more than their generous attitudes and a little instinct. As individuals, they can only do so much but together, they can do anything.

I hope this second book in the series is satisfying and that it leaves you craving the third.

Happy reading!

Gerard Michael

Prologue

There is an expression, "blood is thicker than water." I suppose it's true, at least I've been led to believe it is. It was a term a grandmother used to describe her three adopted children although I was never quite sure what she was implying. Perhaps she was comparing her relationship with her own natural parents to her relationship with her children. She felt a greater commitment to her parents because they were "blood."

Another phrase we hear frequently today is "nature or nurture." Are criminals born that way or is it learned? I had a friend who had eight children, seven grew up to be respected, productive members of society. The eighth did not turn out as well. He believed that no matter what you do as parents, "sometimes a child just grows up sideways."

Some believe our time in the womb can encourage, if not determine our persona. We know that drug addicted babies come from drug addicted mothers and that a smoking mother will likely produce lower birthweight babies. But these examples are truly blood related. The parent ingests and the fetus ingests. Some also believe playing music and singing while pregnant can produce brighter, healthier, and more artistically inclined children.

Greg Webster has witnessed the unthinkable before. As an outsider, he found himself in the center of a horrific crime story. One that he helped resolve. This time it's personal, as he once again finds himself drawn toward the unthinkable. He learns that greed isn't the only cause of poor ethical behavior. Sometimes blood is truly thicker than water.

Chapter 1

"911, what's your emergency?" the operator inquired calmly.

"There has been an explosion," a young man's voice replied, not so calmly. "I understand, are you injured?"

"No, I'm not near the area that blew up," he said.

"Alright sir, tell me your name and where you are," she asked.

"My name is Jared Atell and I'm a student at SUNY Plattsburgh."

"Thank you, Mr. Atell, I'm alerting local authorities right now. Please stay on the line with me."

"Mr. Atell, help is on the way. Please tell me what you saw, what you heard and how you know it was an explosion."
The other end of the line was silent.

"Mr. Atell? Mr. Atell, are you still on the line?"

"Yes, I'm sorry. There were people running toward me and I got a little nervous there for a minute."

"I understand Mr. Atell. I'm going to ask you to try to calm down and just talk to me, okay? Everything is going to be all right."

"Yeah, I'm not sure about that, but I'll try."

"Alright then, tell me what happened please" she said in a calming voice.

"Just before I called you" he started, "I was walking toward the cafeteria when I heard a loud boom. It seemed to be coming from behind me, over toward the science building. When I turned around to face the direction of the noise, I saw a brief, tall flame and then thick smoke rising from the back of the building."

"Did you hear or see anything else, Mr. Atell?"

"No, I just stopped and called you. Then the alarms went off."

"What alarms Mr. Atell?"

"The emergency alarms, you know like fire alarms."

"Alright, Mr. Atell, I have captured your mobile phone number. I'm sure the local authorities will want to speak with you. In the meantime, move as far away from the area as possible and wait for further instructions from the authorities. Thank you for calling 911." She ended the conversation and the call. Jared stood still and faced the smoke.

On the back side of the campus, a black, late model BMW was leisurely heading toward the highway. The driver wasn't worried about being noticed. The fire trucks and other rescue vehicles were all heading the other way, passing him with their sirens blaring.

There were security cameras in the parking lot where he had parked, but he wasn't worried about them either. He was taught to plan ahead.

Chapter 2

It was a perfect late summer Saturday in the hills overlooking the Mohawk River valley. It would be another five or six weeks before the first changes of fall would be noticeable. No one rushed summer in these parts, it was too nice. Sure, fall would bring fresh picked apples and pears along with cooler days, something to look forward to, but not hurried.

This was a big day for the Shands. Their baby girl, Maria, was turning fourteen today. As with every year, John and Sara looked forward to hosting a birthday party for their little girl although they really couldn't call her little anymore.

It seemed impossible that fourteen year ago, they had almost entirely given up on having a child. They could not imagine being childless today. Had it not been for their friend and neighbor, Greg Webster, John and Sara's life together would only be a shell of what it is. At the time, Greg was just an acquaintance of Sara's and an old college roommate of John's.

Greg was working for the state health department at the time and was called to High Falls to investigate a suspicious death at City Hospital. He and John were reconnected as a result of the work they did together to solve the mystery. Greg was the lead guy and John was the part-time house physician on staff at the hospital.

When all was said and done, they had exposed a greed-driven assault on hospital patients that was responsible for up to one hundred-twenty deaths over the course of many years. The head of the operation, was killed in his final attempt to eliminate a patient. His accomplices were snared as well. Some went to prison.

John and Greg became local celebrities, but Greg's part in the story gave him national recognition. At the end of the investigation, Greg was offered the CEO position at the hospital and accepted. He appointed John to the Medical Director position, and they have both been there since, working together to fulfill Greg's promise of a better, patient focused healthcare system.

One of the last victims of the murder spree was a patient named Lorena Nunez who had just given birth. Just days later when the assaults ended, Greg pulled some strings at the health department and found the perfect parents for Lorena's newborn daughter, the Shands. Here they are fourteen years later, ready to celebrate that union again.

"Uncle Greg," Maria shouted as she ran up to give him a hug, "thank you for coming to my party" she exclaimed, holding him tightly.

"Are you kidding?" Greg said still hanging on to her, "I would never miss my favorite niece's birthday party" he whispered in her ear. "Especially her sixteenth!" He joked.

"Funny, Uncle Greg," she sighed.

"Where are Aunt Mary and my cousins?" Maria asked.

"I think Aunt Mary snuck in the back door with some goodies and the kids are around here somewhere. I'm guessing they went to the tree house."

"I'm guessing you're right!" Maria quipped and ran off in that direction.

The yard looked as beautiful as ever. Greg remembered the first time he saw it. Lush green lawn, tree lined back yard and an enormous Weeping Willow along the side where two long picnic tables are set up for lunch. That day was special. His friend from the department of social services had brought Maria from the hospital in a newborn car seat that looked like a basket. John and Sara had no idea any of this was happening.

Greg walked to meet his friend at the car. As they made their way to the huge front porch where Sara and John were waiting, Greg made the introductions. They still had absolutely no inkling of what was about to be. When his friend unveiled the basket and picked up the baby, Greg said, "I know it's a lot to think about, but she's yours if you want her."

There was never any question. Sara and John held and looked at that baby with awe and with tear-filled eyes for hours, until it was time to return her to the hospital. Sara stayed with Maria at the hospital nearly around the clock until they were awarded foster care. Maria stayed with them until the adoption was finalized.

Greg walked up the steps to the expansive front porch. The white wicker furniture was adorned with several pitchers of homemade iced tea and lemonade. Fresh fruit platters were intertwined with vases of cut flowers and plated cheese and crackers. It all reminded him of a Better Homes and Gardens cover.

He opened the screen door and shouted, "Is anybody home?"

"Come on in Greg" Sara said with excitement in her voice. "We're all in the kitchen."

The kitchen was at the back of the house and Greg made his way down the long, center hallway. John, Sara, and Mary were all busy putting last minute touches on lunch. In the center of the counter sat a large birthday cake. Gone were the days of the character cakes that appealed to young children. Today, they were celebrating a young woman, whether they liked it or not.

A two tier, rectangular cake with white icing, pastel colored piping, and fresh cut flowers with cherry nut filling dominated the table and was just what the fourteen-year- old ordered. John and Sara decided early on that they would try a parenting technique that allowed Maria's input into decisions. They had veto power of course. Maria would state her choice in a matter and was encouraged to justify her thinking. They felt this approach built confidence, fairness, and deductive reasoning. Greg Webster had some influence in the Shand's thinking.

"So how many are you expecting?" Greg asked no one in particular.

"About thirty, I guess" Sara responded, "but we have enough food for twice that."

The kitchen island and the dining room table were both filled with sandwiches, appetizers, pizzas, and chicken wings. There were also a few healthier options for the adults.

"I guess it's time to get this started" Sara said, "John, would you and Greg round up the kids while Mary and I take the food out to the tables?"

"Sure, Sara." "We have our orders, Greg," John joked.

Greg and John went out the back door toward the tree house. This was not a typical tree house. John and Greg decided to build it for the kids after Greg and his family relocated from Clifton Park. Greg and Mary's kids, though young, were still disappointed about the move. Greg thought it would be a good project for all of them. The kids could get to know each other, and it would take their minds off the move.

The tree house was more in line with a two bedroom raised ranch. In this case, it was raised about fifteen feet above the ground. They had selected an area with several large trees that were spaced about eight to ten feet apart. Instead of a ladder going straight up, they built a three tiered, wide staircase that they thought would not only be safer for the younger kids but would also facilitate the transport of furnishings.

There was a living room, a small kitchen with a fridge and microwave and two bedrooms. The only thing missing was a bathroom. The kids loved it here. When they were younger, it was a playhouse. As they grew, it became their hangout. There were countless numbers of sleepovers throughout the years. John and Sara even visited the treehouse on occasion when Maria was staying over at the Webster's place.

"Hey kids," John shouted, "it's time to party!" About twenty-five teenagers came marching down the ramps from the treehouse.

Chapter 3

It was late when the Webster clan arrived home from Maria's party. Even the kids were exhausted. Jillian and Jocelyn gave their parents goodnight kisses and headed right upstairs. Jack was ready to follow, but Greg asked him to stay behind.

"Jack, I was hoping to talk with you for just a minute."

"Sure Dad, what's up?"

"Jack, I've been invited to speak at your school this semester. I wanted to get your take on that."

"That's great Dad! Congratulations!"

"Thanks, son. Are you sure you don't mind?"

"Of course, I don't mind. I'm proud of you Dad, and I think it's cool that you will be there. Do you know the date?"

"Yes, two weeks from Tuesday. I believe it's at 11 am in the main lecture hall. Will you be there?"

"I wouldn't miss it, Dad."
"Thank you, Jack."

"I love you, Dad. Goodnight."

"Goodnight, son, I love you too."

Jack hustled up the stairs. He seemed energized by the talk. Greg was as well. He decided to watch a little news before going to bed.

"Mar," he called up the stairs, "I'm just going to catch the late news before coming up."

"Okay, hon," she replied, "I love you. Goodnight."

"Goodnight, babe, I'll be up soon."

Greg grabbed the remote and powered the TV. He flipped through three or four channels before finding a headline that grabbed his attention. A cable affiliate station out of Albany was showing a LIVE remote story from Plattsburgh, NY. In the background, the cameraman was focused on heavy smoke rising behind some similar looking buildings.

The correspondent was well into her story, but Greg was able to pull the pieces together. The timeline appeared to be early afternoon. According to the reporter, there was an explosion on the campus of S.U.N.Y Plattsburgh, a school located just west of Lake Champlain, near the Canadian border. There were no fatalities, but several were injured, and at least three were listed as critical.

An interview with a New York State Police spokesperson didn't reveal any information about the nature of the explosion. He stated that interviews were being conducted and police were examining footage from security cameras on the campus. He was able to confirm that the explosion occurred in the science building. He credited the small number of casualties to the lunch hour.

"Most of the students were at meal break at the time of the event. If it were twenty minutes sooner, the building would have been packed with student and faculty, many of which retuned to campus just today. If anyone has any information about this event, you are encouraged to call the New York State Police on our hotline. Thank you."

Greg watched the hotline number scroll across the bottom of the screen as the on-site reporter returned the viewers back to the studio. The host in Albany tuned into their local reporter who was ready to interview the Provost from Albany State University. Greg muted the volume and tried to digest what he had just heard.

"It could have been Jack's school" he thought to himself. His son stayed at home an extra day to celebrate Maria's birthday, but tomorrow he would head back to Syracuse. Greg believed they would find an accidental cause for the explosion, "first week back, lots of explosive stuff in a science building" he assured himself. His gut wasn't buying it. Greg turned off the television and the lights, double checked the door locks and headed upstairs to do something he hadn't done in quite a while. He cracked open the doors to the kid's bedrooms and watched them sleep.

Morning came quickly for Greg. He couldn't sleep well after the news and wished he hadn't known about it until this morning. It was Sunday, the girls would sleep in a bit, including Mary, but Greg knew Jack would be up soon. He fed the coffee maker, dumped some water in and turned it on. He pulled a package of bacon out of the fridge along with the eggs, butter, and bread. He wondered when a pound of bacon became twelve ounces.

The aroma of brewing coffee began filling the air as Greg cracked the eggs into a bowl to be scrambled. He opened the sliding door to the back patio and breathed in the fresh, early morning country air. He loved it out here. Moving to High Falls was the best thing that could have happened for him, and his entire family.

He missed his friends at the health department, but he stayed connected with some of them. Frequently at first, then more sporadically as time passed. His boss, Tom, retired shortly after Greg left for his new job at the hospital. He missed Tom's sense of humor. On second thought, he missed Tom's never ending attempts at being funny.

He also missed the harmless sexual banter he had with Christine, and he wondered, just for a moment, if anything more would have happened had he stayed. He and Mary were not doing so well at the time, but he had other opportunities and passed on all of them. Besides, he loved Mary, and Christine was a good friend.

The smell of coffee and bacon must have made its way up the stairs. Greg knew this because he heard footsteps coming. Thunderous, more than one pair. In just moments, everyone except Mary was in the kitchen, fighting each other for cups, stealing strips of bacon and making fun of each other's hair. It was a happy, memorable moment for Greg, made more poignant by the news of last evening.

"How about if we sit as humans do, and have a nice breakfast together?" Greg suggested. They all got quiet and just looked at each other, then they erupted in laughter. That was enough to bring Mary down as well. They all grabbed what they wanted to eat and sat around the kitchen table and counter. The conversation covered a wide array of subjects including the birthday party and revisiting Maria's birth story.

Over the years, that story brought tears of sorrow and joy to all of them, but it also bound them to each other. They grew up realizing how fragile life can be and it made them better people. All of the children had become caring, sensitive, and giving adults.

Greg and Mary realized growth in their own lives and their relationship as well.

When there was a break in the conversation, Greg asked for everyone's attention. It took a moment or two, but now they were all looking at their father.

"I just want to address something I saw on the news last night. I don't want to alarm you, and I'm sure this is an isolated incident, but it's at times like this that being aware can save lives," Greg began.

"Okay, I'm alarmed," Jocelyn said.

"That makes two of us" Jillian chimed in.

"Alright, I get it." Greg shut it down. "Maybe I should have just come out with the story."

"You think?" Mary added her two cents.

Greg re-arranged his thoughts.

"There was an explosion at a state university yesterday. There are no fatalities as yet, but several were injured." He had their undivided attention now.

"They have just begun the investigation so there isn't a lot of information available. I'm telling you because I want you to always be aware of your surroundings. If you see something, say something. Pay attention to your instincts."

"Which school, Dad?" Jack asked.

"Plattsburgh." He answered. "It happened in the science building, right around lunch time."

"That's good, right? I mean most of the students were likely at lunch."

"That's correct Jillian, that along with it being a Saturday probably saved a lot of people from harm."

"What do you think happened, Dad?" Jack again.

"If I had to make a guess, and I really hate to speculate, I would say either an accidental chemical combustion or a mechanical failure of some sort, maybe gas. But at this early stage, you cannot rule out an intentional exercise."

"You mean like terrorists?" Mary asked.

"Perhaps. Or maybe someone just didn't want to be back at school."

"Still terrorism." Jack said.

"Yes, it is. Anyway, until they know more, I want you all to be more diligent about your surroundings. Okay?"

They all nodded agreement. Greg looked at all his children and then at Mary. She knew Greg well enough that if he was worried, there was probably a good reason. She loved that he was able to talk so honestly and openly with the kids.

"Jack, I especially want you to be extra careful when you head back to Syracuse today. Look around, notice things. Check under your bed."

There was laughter. "Check under my bed?" Jack asked.

"Could be a spider or something. You've been gone a long time."

"Yeah, thanks for that vision, Dad. I'm sure I'll sleep well tonight."

"Can I help you pack your car?' Greg asked Jack.

"In a hurry to get rid of me?" he responded.

"Well, your mom and I have some personal things to do and…"

The kids all started humming and got up to leave the room.

"TMI," they said in chorus, as they scattered.

Chapter 4

The black BMW pulled into the end of the driveway which was no more than a dirt road. The entrance was surrounded by tall, thick weeds, which secluded it well this time of year. The winding path continued through the woods for nearly a quarter of a mile. At the end, the low, sprawling house awaited.

It was built in the late nineteen eighties and was still in the original configuration and décor. The house was a split level design with the basement completely underground, allowing for not even a hint of natural light with the exception of what poured in when the front door was opened. The staircase going up from the front door led to a beautiful open layout of kitchen, living room and dining room.

There were plenty of windows on this level, all containing privacy glass that allowed sunlight in but no reflected light out. Even with every light on inside, the house would look deserted from the outside.

Off the living area, a wide corridor went off from the right to a group of three bedrooms, all with ensuite bathrooms. To the left of the living/dining area, another shorter corridor led to a single bathroom and closet. Everything on this level was oversized and encompassed nearly three thousand square feet. The basement below had the same footprint but was set up quite differently. A small entry sitting area was open to the staircase. To the right and straight ahead were solid walls with heavy doors.

He parked in one bay of the three car garage which was located to the right of the front entrance and set forward of the house by about fifteen feet. At the back of the bay, a door giving access to the basement opened underneath the stairs to the main level. With the garage door fully closed and locked, he entered the house.

The lights were programmed to come on automatically as he made his way toward the stairs. As he climbed the five steps to the main level, another sensor triggered the main floor lighting. He felt at peace being back. It was a long ride from the Canadian border but a nice one. He enjoyed driving Interstate 87 for about forty-five minutes, knowing no one would be pursuing him. When he reached Keeseville, he exited I-87 and headed west toward Au Sable Forks and on to Lake Placid, passing Whiteface Mountain on the way.

A perfect summer ride through the Adirondacks. Nothing felt better after an exhausting day of setting off bombs. When he reached Saranac Lake, he turned on to Rt. 3 which turned into Rt. 30 just above Tupper Lake. He could have chosen to head toward Rt. 12 which would lead him toward Utica but decided to stay on Rt. 30 to enjoy the view of the many lakes he would pass along the way. Once he reached Fonda on Rt. 30A, he could take Rt. 5W for the final stretch.

He decided to stop at the Gerardi's Ice Cream Shop in Fonda for a sandwich and ice cream. Although he didn't partake often, he did enjoy an occasional Gerardi's ice cream. It had been a long day and he hadn't had his customary, daily meal yet. He took his meal and drove to the lock 13 parking area of the Erie Canal. The ice cream cone was about gone when he reached the lot. He got out of his car and carried the sandwich to the unoccupied bench along the river. As he watched the water spill over the gateway, he thought about his family.

When the sandwich was gone, he climbed back in the car and drove west. He drove through the village of High Falls then headed south toward home. Now, standing in the cool living room, he decided he could wait for morning to prepare for his next event. Building a bomb when you're tired is probably not a great idea. But first, he would say goodnight to his mother.

Chapter 5

Greg was on his way to work. The hospital was an easy fifteen minute drive from home, so he decided to give his son a wakeup call. "Good morning, Jack! Did you sleep okay?"

"Yeah" he said as he yawned, "I was doing great until the phone rang."

"Sorry about that Jack but I wanted to touch base with you before you went off to class."

"It's alright, Dad, I knew you would call. You're pretty predictable that way."

"I think you mean reliable, Jack."

"Yeah, okay Dad. Whatever you say."

"Well, you needed to get up anyway, right?"

"Right, I wouldn't want to miss my first class which is at one o'clock," Jack said with more than a hint of sarcasm.

"Oops. I get it. I just wanted to make sure you were safe and settled in."

"You mean more than I was at nine o'clock last night?"

"Go back to sleep son, I'll call you in an hour," Greg joked.

"Thanks for the call Dad, I love you."

"You too Jack." Greg hung up just in time to pull into the parking garage. He wouldn't accept a "Reserved for CEO" space as offered, but he did concede to a devoted area for all management. Truth be told, on nice days he preferred to park outside. He locked the car, a two year old Toyota Highlander and headed for the stairs, bypassing the elevator.

"Good morning, Kathy" he said as he entered the administrative suite. "Hold all my calls and don't let anyone near my office today Kathy. I'm going to play video games all day."

"As you wish," she answered. "Your first appointment will be here in five minutes."

"How much do we pay you?" he said snidely.

"Not enough, Mr. Webster. The work I can take but putting up with your humor is additional."

"Hey, don't forget you once tried to seduce me right there in that conference room."

"As hard as I try, Mr. Webster, you won't seem to let me." She said with a smile.

It took a while for Greg and Kathy to have a normal work relationship after the incident. Greg moved past it right away, but Kathy had a challenging time and not with just the job, but with the loss of a friend and the embarrassment of his actions. Now, fourteen years later, they could joke about it.

"Who is my first appointment, Kathy?"

"Dr. Ingraham," she said and gave Greg a grin.

"Really? Awesome!" Greg said. Sometimes he acted like such a kid.

Richard Ingraham had become a good friend. He and John Shand were instrumental in helping Greg solve and expose the mystery around the hospital killings of 2001. Richard had since retired from his job as house physician, but he and Greg stayed in touch. About every two months, Richard would call Kathy and ask to be placed on Greg's schedule without him knowing about it. Greg was always pleasantly surprised to see him.

"Speak of the devil," Kathy announced.

"Good morning, Kathy," Richard greeted her. "My, you're looking lovely today. "And good morning to you Greg although you don't look so hot" he joked.

"Thank you, Dr. Ingraham," Kathy replied.

"Thanks for nothing, Richard. I hope you brought the donuts," said Greg.

Richard followed Greg into the office. He did bring donuts, as usual.

"How have you been, Richard? Family okay?"

"All good, Greg, thanks. I think I'm driving Marilyn crazy being around most of the time, but she tries to keep herself busy. She volunteers a lot."

"Yes, I see her around here every now and then," Greg replied.

"Yeah, here at the hospital, the library, the elementary school. Basically, anywhere I am not." They both chuckled a bit.

"And how about you? What are you doing to keep busy, Richard?"

"Oh, you know, this and that." Greg waited for the rest of the answer. "I smoke cigars and swear a lot. It seems to work for me."

"Maybe you should volunteer here as well," Greg stated with excitement.

"I don't think so. I wouldn't look good in one of those pink jackets." Richard said.

"Still a smartass I see," quipped Greg.

"Hey, Greg, what do you make of this explosion at SUNY Plattsburgh?"

"Funny you should mention that, Richard. I saw it on the news Saturday night, and I haven't been able to get it out my head since. Anything new as of this morning?" Greg asked.

"They found the cause of the explosion. It was indeed in the science building, and get this, it was a cadaver." Greg thought about that for a minute.

"A cadaver? What do you mean?"

"A bomb was planted inside a cadaver in the medical science lab.."

"How do they know that, Richard?"

"I guess it had something to do with the million little pieces of human tissue they found scattered throughout that section of the building."

Greg said, "Do they know how it got there or who was responsible?"

"They don't know who, but they have a couple theories on how. Either somebody walked into the lab and planted it, or the cadaver came from the supply company ready to blow." Richard answered. "They're looking into the supply company now."

"Have any of the victims succumbed to their injuries, Richard?"

"Not yet. Three of the ten injured are still listed as critical. It could have been a whole lot worse."

"I agree," Greg responded, "I felt compelled to give the kids a serious talk before sending them all back to school. I don't worry about the local kids so much but with Jack away at S.U. I really took it to heart."

"I can imagine. I'm glad mine are all done with college. It's a different world out there today."

"Yes it is," Greg agreed. "Let's have one of those donuts!"

Chapter 6

Ben cruised along the winding road, taking in the scenery, and carefully obeying the speed limit. It was only a twenty minute ride from his house in the wilderness to the hardware store on the outskirts of Herkimer. He had been working at Smitty's Farm and Home for nearly six months now. It was vastly different from the city life he was used to, but things change.

Sometimes he was assigned the opening shift which started at 7am, but he preferred the closing shift which ended at 8pm. Today was a closing shift. That meant that Ben would be pretty much on his own just before the place closed. It was a perfect setup really. Not only did he have the privacy and access to the materials he needed, but he also received a twenty percent discount.

He wasn't always interested in explosives. That was something new. In fact, his life had changed demonstrably in the last year. If someone had told him he would one day be working in a hardware store, he would have laughed in his face. He was raised to be well above that. It was supposed to be Ivy League all the way.

Life in Boston was swell. He enjoyed his studies and he liked Harvard in general. The ease of getting around the city suited him and his hobbies well. Of course, there were times he needed to use his own vehicle, but the MBTA was his preferred mode of getting around. One pass could get him on the subway, bus, ferry, and rail, also known as the T.

From his extremely comfortable, private apartment just off Boylston Street, he could catch the T just a dozen blocks or so to the Harvard Medical School. From there, Fenway Park was a fifteen minute walk. He wouldn't call himself a baseball fan necessarily, but he was a fan of Fenway. He was extremely interested in people watching and Fenway was as good a place as any to do it. Ticket prices were expensive, but thanks to dear old dad, money wasn't an issue.

Being a medical student required a good deal of his time, although not as much required by the majority of the other students. Most of it came pretty naturally to Ben. In fact, one could say he grew up around it. Dad didn't believe Ben knew the value of a dollar and he was probably right. When Ben was young, he wasn't spoiled or lavished with toys or gifts. His father was very frugal and tried to instill his behaviors on Ben.

It worked while he was young because Ben truly had little choice, but as he grew and became more aware of who his father was, Ben learned how to leverage some control over him. At some point, he learned to like material things. He always had at least one safe ride and a good roof over his head.

All through his early education, Ben was tightly controlled. Small private schools in remote locations mostly. His high school years were spent at an expensive prep school in the Catskill Mountains. He went home about once a month to visit with mom and dad which became more strained as he got older. It wasn't that they were not likeable, but more that they really didn't know how to relate to a teenager.

His dad worked a lot, and his mom was more akin to hired help than a mother. She was expected to raise the child as dad instructed and if he found fault, there was a price to be paid. She seemed very afraid to make any decisions without consulting him first. The fact that he was hardly ever around didn't help matters. Ben actually liked being away at school. He felt it was better for everyone. In spite of everything, he loved his parents.

He pulled into the lot at Smitty's and parked the car toward the very back near the employee entrance. It was just before 1pm and the place looked busy. By 7 o'clock, it would slow down. The farmers were getting their livestock in for the night, and the construction crews had finished for the day. For the last hour, it would be just some local homeowners dropping by to shop.

He would have time between customers to pull his own list together. Once everyone went home, he would lock the doors and ring himself out. He was careful to always pay for his purchases. He would never want to be accused of stealing.

He would work late tonight to get ready for his morning drive north. It seems like he just got back, but things must keep moving forward. Most of the components were in place when he left this morning, but he needed a few things from the store which he would have by the time he left. He is trying to be care not to stockpile supplies at home. "Can't be too careful," he told himself. Perhaps mother would keep him company while he worked.

Chapter 7

The University of Vermont, located in Burlington, is nestled between the shore of Lake Champlain and the Green Mountains. The medical college is the fifth oldest in New England and the seventh oldest in the country. It boasts an admission rate of roughly 1.4 percent.

Burlington is the largest city in Vermont with a population of 210,000. It has been voted the best college town in America more than once and is considered a jewel of New England. The shop keepers in the city are busy gearing up for the onslaught of students, parents and visitors making their annual fall return.

At the medical college, things are at a fever pitch. The classrooms have been prepared, the students are enrolled and housed, and the faculty is ready to go. In the anatomy lab, twenty-four cadavers lay in wait on twenty-four tables spaced four feet apart. Second year medical student will begin the gradual examination and dissection soon.

The volunteer corpses had all been embalmed and arrived in the last few days from a company that specializes in medical school supplies. The temperature in the lab is maintained at a cool sixty degrees during the day and just fifty at night to help preserve the bodies. Keeping the room cool is no trouble at all from November to March when the outside norms hover around 20 degrees, but the warmer months require quite a bit of mechanical cooling.

The outdoor temperature on this late summer day is a wonderfully comfortable seventy-two degrees. It's a few degrees below the normal for this time of year, most likely attributed to the winds crossing the lake from the northwest. Still, there are plenty of people filling up the green spaces around the campus.

Ben had scoped out the property before he pulled the job at Plattsburgh, which is just across the lake. It's only thirty miles but it takes over an hour to drive it if you take the bridge. Otherwise, it can be closer to an hour and a half with traffic to go up and around. He thought about doing both jobs at the same time but decided against it. He couldn't risk getting caught in traffic getting from one place to another. He was much less likely to draw attention escaping through the Adirondacks from Plattsburgh. From Burlington, he would head south through Vermont and cross into New York near Lake George.

The bomb was already in place. He just needed to be within five hundred feet to activate it. Once activated, he would have twenty minutes to vacate the area. He decided to do it just after lunch. The last job was effective, but he knew a death or two would heighten the excitement a bit. By one-fifteen, students and faculty should be back in the lab.

This size bomb wouldn't bring the building down but would certainly take out a few walls and several windows. With the lab on the second floor, he anticipated "at least a partial ceiling collapse on the floor below. Not enough to take out lives, just create one hell of a mess. It was now just before noon. He would need to park far enough away to make a quick escape, but not more than a ten minute walk from where he needed to be to trigger the timer on the detonator.

He drove around until he found the right spot. It was just a minute from the highway with no traffic lights in between. He wanted to avoid any security cameras that might be mounted to the light posts. There was one camera on the back, left corner of the building nearest his car. He would disable this at the very last minute to avoid signaling security of a potential problem. At 12:45, he climbed out of the BMW. Show time.

Chapter 8

"Kathy," Greg said as she walked back in after her lunch break. "Is my schedule clear for the next ninety minutes?"

"Nap time?" She questioned.

"Ha, funny!" he said. "I was thinking about having lunch outside the building today."

"Let me check," she said as she walked around her desk to face her computer monitor. "It looks good to me. You next appointment is at 3:30, you have plenty of time."

"Great! Would you ask John Shand if he could join me please?"

"Of course, Mr. Webster."

Greg walked back into his office. He flopped down in the guest chair in front of his desk. He was immediately taken back to the first time he visited City Hospital. So much of his life had changed because of that day and the few days that followed. Looking back, he was astounded by how much had happened in that small stretch of time. Was it luck? Hard work? Diligence? He didn't know. Perhaps all three. He thought about the friends he had made and about the souls that were lost.

"Mr. Webster, Dr. Shand said he would be happy to join you if you're buying."

"Tell him no deal, Kathy!" Kathy just stood in his doorway, waiting for his next words.

"Just kidding. Please tell him to stop here on his way out," Greg said.

"I already did," Kathy replied.

"Am I that predictable?" Greg whined.

"I would think of it as reliable," she answered.

"We've been working together too long, haven't we?" Greg asked.

"Why do you ask?" she returned.

"Smartass," he said under his breath. Maybe not quite under his breath.

"Hey, are we going or what?" John Shand said, popping his in from the hallway.

"I'm ready," Greg answered, and followed him down the hall.

"Thanks for joining me, John. Where would you like to go?"

"Hey, I'm just your date, I thought you had this all figured out. If I knew I was going to have to think, I would have stayed at work."

"My God! It's contagious!" Greg exclaimed. "She put you up to this, didn't she?"

"She said she had been toying around with you." John answered.

"So, you had to join in. And if she told you to jump off a bridge?"

"Easy, Dad, it's all good." John laughed.

Greg drove.

"Where are we going, Greg?"

"Don't you worry about it, John. I wouldn't want you to have to think. You'll know when we get there."

Ten minutes later, they were at the IHOP.

"Really?" John said.

"Don't start buddy, I like IHOP. Besides, this is one of the first places I dined when I first came to town."

"Well yeah, back then you didn't know any better!"

"Out of the car, John."

It wasn't always like this...well, yes, it was always like this. Good friends who could kid around. It was about 1:30 when they arrived at the restaurant. There was still a good crowd and they had to wait for a table to open up. As they stood by the counter, Greg noticed a television mounted near the ceiling. He could hear it, but the scrolling banner said "BREAKING NEWS...EXPLOSION rocks another university...

Greg was looking for a waitress to turn up the volume. He grabbed John's arm,

"Come with me!" He said excitedly. John followed. They got in the car and turned on the radio. Greg tuned it to a new station.

"Vermont State Police have verified that an explosion occurred at around 1:20 this afternoon at the University of Vermont. Authorities on the scene have not released any information regarding casualties or reason for the explosion. They did, however, confirm that it took place in the medical school lab just as students were returning from lunch. Leslie Mangrove from our NPR affiliate in Burlington has this."

"Witnesses on the scene are reporting chaos on the university campus. They will not let our crew anywhere close to the campus for fear of interfering with emergency vehicles. We are stationed downtown where the atmosphere is very somber. A student who ran from the area of the explosion to downtown told us this."

"I was on the first floor of the building when the explosions happened. The building shook a little and the ceiling began to crumble. Someone yelled "get out" and we all headed for the doors. When we got outside, it was raining glass and there was smoke and an acrid smell in the air," said a young girl who was still very shaken.

"Did you see anyone with injuries?" asked the reporter.

"Yes, there were some people coming down from the second floor who had cuts and scrapes, some looked like they had something in their eyes. Several people were laying on the grass in the common outside the building and emergency workers were starting to arrive."

"Did anyone see what happened?"

"I didn't hear anyone say what happened. I didn't stay around; I just ran with the crowd."

"That was a report from our Burlington affiliate. It seems clear that it will be a while before any verifiable details will emerge from this calamity. It does appear to be terribly similar to the attack just days ago at the SUNY Plattsburgh campus just across Lake Champlain. The latest information we have on that situation tells us that three people are still listed as critical but the other seven have been released from the hospital. The survivors concur that the explosion originated in the Anatomy Lab and was somehow related to a cadaver. We will be back shortly."

"Greg, are you alright?"

"No, John. I'm scared. Would you mind if we reschedule lunch? I've lost my appetite."

"That's fine, Greg, let's go back to the hospital. You can call Jack on the way."

Chapter 9

Kathy was surprised to see Greg and John return so soon. "Is everything okay?" she asked.

"No, Kathy, I'm afraid not. There was another university bombing today. Can you ask Richard Ingraham to return as soon as possible please? And see if Bill Dillon can come in for a chat. And Kathy, please keep my schedule free until my 3:30."

"Your 3:30 rescheduled, Greg, you have the rest of the day open. I'll have the kitchen send over some food and beverages for the group."

"Thank you, Kathy." She picked up the phone and got the wheels turning. Greg and John stepped into the small conference room and closed the door.

"What did Jack have to say, Greg?" John had heard Greg's end of the call as they drove back from the restaurant. Greg's concern was quite apparent. John understood perfectly.

"He was certainly upset and felt sympathetic toward everyone involved, but he feels safe where he is and doesn't see how Syracuse University would fit in. He's probably right, but until we know more of the details, I would rather believe that every college is a target. No one should be making assumptions."

"I like the way you think, Greg, and I trust your instincts. I'll help any way I can."

"I know you will, John, and I appreciate that. There may not be much we can do. The FBI will be in charge now that the attacks have crossed state lines. Probably the ATF and Homeland Security as well. I've never had much interaction with those agencies. What I can do, is find out what, if anything, the Department of Health has to do with controlling or monitoring medical school cadavers. John, do you have any connections at either Plattsburgh or UVM?"

"No one comes to mind immediately but let me think about it. I can also look through the curriculum vitae for our current medical staff to see if any of them have a history with either of those schools."

"Great idea, John, I wouldn't have thought of that."

There was a knock on the door. Kathy opened it a crack and said, "Richard and Bill can be here in thirty minutes."

"Thank you, Kathy." She closed the door behind her.

"John, should we reconvene in thirty? I think I'll call Albany to see if anyone I know still works there."

"Sounds good, Greg, I'll begin looking through our physician roster." John stood and left the room.

Greg leaned back in his chair. He pulled the phone toward him from the middle of the conference table and dialed his old office.

"Department of Health Investigative Division, this is Christine."

"Good afternoon, Christine, it's nice to hear your voice."

"Greg, my old friend, how is the fishing out there?"
"Stepped right into Tom's shoes, didn't you, Christine?"

"Someone had to, and you bailed on us!"

"Touché!" Greg replied.

"How can I help you today, Mr. Webster?"

"What do you know about cadavers, Christine?"

"You mean other than the one I'm married to?"

Chapter 10

The bomb went off at 1:15pm as planned. Ben had been off the campus for almost ten minutes by then. He thought about heading east toward I-89 but that went toward the airport. He was well aware that airports drew a lot of attention immediately after something like this. He opted instead to jump right on Rt. 7 south. He was out of Burlington in less than three minutes.

He would have ample options for exiting Rt. 7, heading back into New York. Again, it was a pleasant late summer day, and he would enjoy the opportunity to unwind while taking in the majestic scenery that surrounded him.

He left home early this morning, around 8am. He was usually up well before that, but he and mother stayed up late last night. He was putting the final touches on his work and talking a blue streak while mother just watched and listened. She could be a real partier at times.

He did all this type of work in the seclusion of the rear end of the basement. Originally built as a bomb shelter, the thick concrete and leaded walls provided enough silence that the only audible sound was one's own breathing. It was a very comfortable space, large enough to hold all his tools and some his father had left behind, and still provide ample space to move around.

Mother's room was nearby which made it quite convenient. She wasn't able to do the stairs anymore and she was just too heavy for him to carry. If she grew tired before he did, he could help her back to her own room. He wondered why Dad didn't have an elevator installed, though mother never complained about it.

She was still sleeping when he left this morning. He checked on her, gave her a kiss and promised he be back before dinner. She didn't have much of an appetite lately, but he tried to encourage her to eat a little something once each day. Most of the time, she would just keep him company while he ate. She always wanted to hear about his day. She would be delighted about today's accomplishments.

The car radio was tuned to WUVM, the universities' student managed station. On the way up, the DJ was playing a lot of contemporary music that catered to students. "Crap," his father would call it. If it wasn't Mozart, Stravinsky, or Schubert, it was crap. This mornings' "crap" had given way to non-stop news. Dad would have liked it.

He wasn't hanging on every word because he didn't need to. He was the only one who knew exactly what happened. He listened for key words like explosion, bomb, anatomy lab, cadaver, confirmed dead, wounded, police and no clue. The numbers they were tossing at this early phase included four dead and as many as seventy inured. UVM Medical Center was having a busy day.

He adjusted his seat to include a more reclined angle, changed the station back to "crap" and turned the volume down low. He opened his window and breathed in the clean and cool mountain air. Immediately he knew he wasn't in Boston anymore.

He missed it though. "The country is nice, but the city is so alive," he thought.

He hadn't had a date in over six months. He thought about that often. He was a little bashful, but the girls seemed to be attracted to him. He thought he looked okay, not movie star quality but not bad either. He dressed nice and his manners were good. He had a nice car but that didn't seem to make a difference in Boston. In fact, most girls never saw his car. He relied on public transportation most of the time.

He particularly liked girls who hung out at Fenway. There was something different about them. He had met girls at other places as well. Sometimes at bars, some were at school, even one where he worked part-time. He didn't need the money as much as he needed the social aspect of working.

He met Amanda at Fenway. It was just last summer. The Sox were at home for a double header against the Yankees. This was the matchup that brought out the most loyal, die-hard Red Sox fans. She was seated in the row in front of him so most of what he saw was her copper colored hair tucked into a pink Baseball cap with a red "B" stitched on the front. She was also wearing a Red Sox jersey with the number 34 and the name Ortiz on the back.

Underneath the jersey, she wore cutoff jean shorts and open leather sandals. Her bra was pink. He could tell because the jersey was unbuttoned enough that he could look right down her cleavage from his seat above her. She appeared to be there by herself. There was another young lady seated to her left but after several minutes of observing her, he noticed there was no communication between them. On her right, the seat was open.

By the top of the second inning, he made his move. He first went up the stairs to the landing to use the bathroom. When he came back, he went straight to the seat next to her and sat down like the seat belonged to him.

"What's happened so far?" he asked.

"Nothing so far, six up, six outs," she said.

Her face was as pretty as the rest of her. He checked her fingers, one ring on the right index. Her nails were painted the same color pink as her hat and her bra. She was all girl except for the uniform.

"You look like a serious fan," he stated, "are you here often?"

"Whenever I can be," she replied without taking her eyes off the field.

"Me too," he said, "this is my favorite place in Boston."

She turned to look at him. Their eyes met. Hers were blue, just like his, but much prettier. "How often are you here? she asked, still looking.

"As often as I can be. School usually interferes with the early games but today, my classes were over early."

"Where do you go to school?" she asked.

"Harvard Med," he replied. Are you in school too?"

"Not right now. I finished my undergrad at BC in May and now I'm taking a break before grad school."

"That's cool, what will you study?" he quizzed.

"If I knew that, I would be there now," she responded.

"Undecided, I hear you. I wish I could take a semester or two off. It doesn't work like that for med students. Even if they don't give your spot away, you miss a semester and you will never catch up."

They continued the banter for the rest of the game, pausing only for the exciting plays. When the seventh inning stretch came around, he asked her if she would like to walk up to the concession stand and get a beer. She accepted with a smile. They returned to their seats, beer in hand and finished watching the Sox lose 3-2 in nine.

"Amanda, are you staying for the second game?"

"I'm not sure, are you?"

"I could if you wanted to but if I had a choice, I would rather take you to dinner."

"Wow, it's been a while since I've been on a dinner date. Will there be sex after dinner?" she asked. If Ben had false teeth, he would have spit them out. His face blushed and his tongue felt frozen for a minute. She just looked at him, feeling his embarrassment. "Just a thought," she said, "no pressure."

"After, before, or both, your choice," he said, feeling like he recovered nicely.

"Do you live nearby?" she asked.

"I do," he replied.

"Then I say we start there. Is there a Chinese take-out on the way?" she raised her eyebrows.

"There can be!"

Amanda grabbed his hand, and they joined the slow but steady march toward the exit.

It was time for a bathroom break. He was coming up on Middlebury where his direction would change. He would get Vermont Rt. 7 and head west to Vermont Rt. 30. Middlebury was also a college town so he would have a choice of facilities. It was either now or wait until he crossed into NY near Glens Falls. He chose now.

The first place he came upon was a Gerardi's shop. It was too early to eat, although ice cream sounded good, but he was disciplined enough to avoid the temptation. He parked the car around the back. He stretched a little as he exited the car, then walked toward the entrance. He didn't notice it while he was sitting, but as soon as he stood up, he knew he was a little wet down there.

It had been a while since that happened and he knew it started when he was thinking about his first date will Amanda. When he entered the store, he walked straight to the back toward the rest room. The men's room was occupied so he just folded his arms and waited. He hadn't looked down, but he hoped there wasn't a wet spot showing through his pants.

The ladies' room was also occupied and there was a young lady waiting her turn. She was dressed in a tiny pair of shorts that almost disappeared inside her and a sleeveless halter top. Her hair was wet with the heat of the day and the coolness of the air conditioning made it obvious that she was braless. She looked a little slutty, but he liked it. Mother wouldn't approve.

Ben could feel himself becoming engorged. She was looking right at his crotch, and she was offering a flirty little smile.

He looked down now and not only had he soaked through his pants, but his erection was also obvious. He was hoping the door would open soon. It did. Both the men's and women's doors opened. She gave him a wink as she moved toward the door. He smiled back.

It was a private restroom, so he locked the door, unzipped his pants, and took it out. His underwear was soaked in front, and he was hard. He finished urinating, wiped everything off with some tissue, zipped up, flushed the toilet, and washed his hands.

When he walked out of the restroom, she was not there. He felt both disappointment and relief. He took a deep breath and headed for the door. He turned the corner, heading toward his car at the back of the lot. When his car came into full view, he saw her. She was resting her mostly naked ass against the car next to his.

"Follow me," she said, and climbed into her car. She started it and waited for him to do the same. When she held Ben's car start, she put hers in drive and pulled away. When she reached the road, she turned right. At the first intersection, she turned right again. They stayed on this road for about five minutes. They were clearly leaving the confines of the highway.

They were heading south on Creek Road. The traffic was thinning quickly. To his right, he could see the creek. It was another three minutes before she turned and made a small divergent to the right, onto a dirt road.

About five hundred yards in, they came to a small clearing. She pulled up and turned off her car. He pulled up next to her and did the same. She came over to his door and waited for him to get out. She took him by the hand and led him down a path. They were only on the path for maybe thirty feet before they reached the creek's edge. There was a small grassy area just before the thin, sandy edge of the water.

The air was cooler here and she led him to a spot that was shaded by a large tree. She faced him, took both of his hands, and placed them on her breasts. His heart was racing, he felt faint but euphoric. She left his hands there and moved hers to his crotch. She squeezed tightly, but not enough to hurt. This was not her first rodeo.

With one quick move, she reached up and pulled off her top. If there was any doubt before, there wasn't any now. She was naked from the waist up. Another quick move and her shorts joined her top on the ground. She reached for his belt and gently unbuckled it. She pulled the belt out of the belt loops on his pants and held it like a weapon. She stared at him, waiting for him to drop his pants. He was staring at her naked body, and it was clear she wanted the same opportunity.

He unbuttoned his pants and removed them, his underwear, and his shoes in one motion. He quickly removed his socks. She took his hand and took a few steps further into the shade. She selected a soft spot on the grass and sat down but not before kneeling and showing him her back side.

She was now laying on her back with her legs spread slightly. He couldn't be absolutely sure but from what he could see, she was shaved clean. He knelt down between her legs and that's when she spoke her first words since they left the store.

"Not so fast, cowboy. On your back." He lay down beside her on his back. She then sat up and sat on his chest. "You have a little work to do first." She worked her way up his chest until her smooth pussy was right in his face. "Try this, I think you'll like it."

He started softly and slowly, but she didn't want any part of that. He could see just a glimpse of her arm moving above her thigh and then he felt the sting of the belt on the side of his leg. It wasn't enough to hurt. It made him hotter. She gave it to him once again.

"Harder," she said and brought the strap down again. "Harder, deeper, faster!" she said softly at first but with every swing of the belt her volume increased. He raised his hands and grabbed her breasts. He squeezed.

"My nipples," she cried as she swung the belt once more. He was pinching her nipples and bucking his hips. His cock was just barely rubbing against her ass.

"Harder, pinch, more, more, more," she brought the belt down again, each swing had a little more force. It hurt, but in a good way. She was moving her hips wildly now, grinding against his face, his tongue stiff, trying to penetrate her.

"Pinch, pinch, pinch, harder!" With every command, every swing of the belt, she moved her hips faster and harder. She wasn't working the belt anymore, both her hands were on his chest, bracing her so she could move her hips harder. She reached for his nipple with one hand and pinched hard.

"Come on," she said, "give it to me, give it to me, give it to me. She was thrusting harder, pinching harder until finally her legs started to quiver. She let go of his nipple and her hips slowed down. Her legs were still shaking, her voice changing from a high pitch whining to a deep, satisfied moan. He just laid there, not licking any more, just still. He let her set the pace of her recovery.

He was still rock hard, but it was well worth the wait. He could feel more than a little soreness at the top of his thigh where the belt landed time after time. He didn't care.

When her breathing slowed back to normal, she dismounted from his chest and sat next to him. Nothing was said. They just sat quietly. After a few minutes, she handed him the belt and got on all fours. "Your turn, cowboy," she said with a happy but tired smile.

He didn't use the belt much, just a gentle tap now and again. If she was disappointed in that, she didn't show it. She was a powerhouse though, controlling the motion from her end. He just went along for the ride. When she had finished a second time and her hips were quivering once again, he took the lead and made himself happy. They both collapsed onto the cool grass.

After a few silent minutes passed, she stood up, put on her clothes, kissed him lightly and walked away. No words, and he was fine with that. He was pulling on his pants when she reached her car. She looked back and said "see ya, cowboy."

Chapter 11

John had already joined Greg in his office when Bill Dillon and Richard Ingraham arrived. Kathy had arranged for food and drink as she promised. A tray with a variety of small sandwiches rested in the center of the conference room table. Around it, there were individual serving size bags of chips, napkins, paper plates, silverware, and cutlery. There was also a small silver tub loaded with beverages and ice.

The door opened and Kathy introduced Bill and Richard. Greg and John stood to greet their guests.

"Gentlemen, thank you for coming," Greg started. "Bill, it is great to see you again. Richard, thanks for coming back. Please have a seat and help yourselves to whatever you would like." There was light, casual conversation while everyone loaded their plates. When everyone was seated, Greg began again.

"Let me just say how much I appreciate all of you being here. You didn't have much notice, but you managed to drop whatever you were doing and that means a lot to me."

"This doesn't sound good," said Richard.

"Sounds like work to me," Bill chimed in.

John followed, "Hey, I'm on the clock, take your time."

They all turned to look at John. "Keep it up and you won't be," returned Greg.

They all had a good laugh.

Greg turned more solemn. "I'm sure you are all aware of the recent university bombings that have been dominating the news. I've asked you here because I know you are all great thinkers and experience tells me that together, we are far greater than the sum of our individual parts. I know it's not our problem to solve as we really have no authority, but it's apparent to me that somehow, medicine is a factor."

"I'm not sure how I can help, Greg, since medicine isn't really in my wheelhouse," Bill said.

"No, but security is, and I think you can be a great conduit for the flow of security and surveillance information. John and Richard can coordinate the medical component and I'll deal with the various government agencies."

"What makes you think any agency would want us, or allow us to be involved?" Richard asked.

"Good question, Richard. I don't think they *will* want us involved, but I do think I can put some pressure on the Governor to open some doors. Do you remember the fuss he made over us the last time? We made the health department look really good, and he's the head of the health department and every other state agency."

"That was a long time ago, Greg. Do you think anybody still remembers, or cares for that matter?" Bill asked.

"I think what Greg is saying is, we need to make them care. This may be the beginning of a long, threatening situation. They need as much help as they can get. I agree with Greg that somehow, whoever is behind this is pissed about something that has it's beginning in healthcare."

"I think you're right, John," Richard said. "It could be a medical student that was expelled or couldn't make the grade. Maybe a faculty member who was let go, or even a disgruntled patient or family member that had a lousy outcome," Richard added. "The fact that both attacks were perpetuated in the anatomy lab leads me to believe that not only are they related, but that the labs were targeted for a reason."

"I'm going to throw out an idea and you tell me if any of it sticks," Greg said. "I'm going to call the Governor and I'll also talk to the health department about who controls science supply companies, particularly those that furnish cadavers. Richard, once I get the Governor's buy in, would you and Bill be willing to take a ride to Plattsburgh and nose around a little? John, I know you didn't have much time, but were you able to identify anyone on our medical staff who came out of UVM?"

"Barbara was running the database when I left to come here. I can see if she has produced anyone."

"Don't bother," Richard interrupted. "He's right here."

John and Greg were both surprised by this. "You graduated from UVM, Richard?"

"I did. It was obviously a long time ago."

John said, "Would you know anyone who is still there?"

"I doubt it," Richard answered, "but I may still have an in. I've given some money to the school over the last several years, good size checks in fact. I think the Dean may take a meeting with me."

"Wow!' said Greg, "why didn't I know that?"

"Don't feel bad Greg, I don't know where you went to school either. The truth is, I never really cared much." There was laughter again.

"Okay, so that's our way into Vermont. How soon can you and Bill get up that way, Richard?"

"I don't know, I'm pretty busy with all the swearing and cigar smoking right now, but I guess I could shake loose just about any time."

"And you, Bill? How is your schedule?" Bill took out his phone and opened his calendar. He looked at the screen for a moment then replied,

"I have a dental cleaning in November."

"We're just at the end of August!" Richard exclaimed.

'I guess I'm good then." Bill said.

"I feel like I'm working with Harpo and Chico here!" Greg joked"

"John, try to contact the Dean of Admissions at both schools to see if you can grease the skids a little. We will need a contact to get on to both campuses. Richard and Bill, see if you can agree on a schedule for the next couple of days. Book a room up there, live it up, talk to the people in town as well as at the schools. I'll pick up the tab. I'm going to get on the phone to see if we can make some friends at the State Police, FBI, and Homeland. Can we reconvene in the morning?"

They all agreed and departed the conference room to get started on their specific projects. Greg stopped at Kathy's desk.

"Thank you, Kathy, the accommodations were perfect. We're all set in there for now. I'm going to lock myself in the office to make calls. Could you arrange for coffee and pastries for 9am tomorrow please?"

"Yes, Mr. Webster, and I'll hold your calls the rest of the afternoon."

"Excellent! Oh, you will need to let John, Bill and Richard know we'll be meeting at nine."

"Of course, sir."

Greg closed the door behind him and picked up the phone.

Chapter 12

The girl left the grassy are near the stream first. Ben stayed behind for few minutes, trying to make sense of what had just happened. He leaned on the hood of his car, looking out at the water. He was sweating a little, his legs were shaky and he could feel the soreness on his thigh and his knees where he had been kneeling during the final ten or twelve minutes of their lovemaking.

He got back in the car, turned the AC on and backed out onto the dirt road. He didn't see which she went but he guessed she went back the way they came. He figured if he went the other way and followed the creek, he would connect with Rt. 30 again before catching Rt. 4 west of Rutland. Creek Road was very much like most of Vermont, deserted.

As he made his way south on the winding road, he replayed the last hour over again in his head. He could still taste her on his face. He could smell her natural perfume everywhere. He liked it. It reminded him of the first few dates with Amanda. She was also a take charge kind of girl. More talkative and she didn't wield a belt, but there were similarities. She enjoyed sex and she was good at it. She liked trying new things and she was very much a girl underneath the sports clothing.

It turned out that she was a fan of clothing, period. She owned different style clothing for every occasion, including sex. She would always surprise him with her outfits. She could look perfectly normal on the surface but then as the night went on, and the layers came off, she was anything but conventional underneath. Ben didn't even know what the things were called. He knew what stockings were and he had seen the little thong underpants before but the lacey things she wore on top, he had no clue what they were.

It didn't really matter because they never stayed on for very long. It was usually take-out at his place and sex either before or after. The few times they went to her place, it usually involved toys. She had quite the arsenal. He wasn't familiar with them, but she was patient and instructional. He didn't mind because it seemed to make her happy.

Life was good then in Boston. He attended classes and completed his assignments and he attended Red Sox games with Amanda. Then, he took a job. It wasn't much, just a few hours, three days a week after school. It was a short hop on the T from school but in the opposite direction from his apartment. He usually arrived by 4pm and was finished around 8pm.

He had found the job listing on the bulletin board in the lobby of the anatomy lab at school. It was for a company called ReadiMed and they were looking for a first or second year medical student. The job wasn't extremely well defined but included receiving inventory and filling orders. More information would be available at the time of interview. He tore off the phone number from the strip at the bottom at the advertisement and stuffed in his pocket. The next morning before class, he called.

An interview slot was open later that day. He was supposed to meet up with Amanda around six. The plan was to eat something on the way to Fenway and then catch the game at eight o'clock. After he agreed to the interview, he called her with a change of plans. He told her about the interview and said he might be late, so he would just meet her at the ball field by the start of the game. She was fine with that.

He jumped on the T right after his last class and headed east toward ReadiMed which was located on Wilmington Street. It was a three block walk from the T station which took about seven minutes at a quick pace. The building was just three stories above ground. Other businesses shared the building with ReadiMed but it appeared they occupied most of the space. He walked to the entrance on Wilmington Street and entered.

He walked into a pleasant but small waiting area. There were only four chairs and two end tables in the room. On the far wall was a reception desk. He approached to find no one there. He looked around the small area behind the glass and could see a door that opened to the rear. He didn't see any movement. Finally, way off to the side of the reception window, he located a button. Next to it in small print was a sign that said, "Ring for Service."

He pressed the button and immediately heard a loud buzzer that sounded like it was coming from the back of the building. After a half minute, a young man came through the door at the back of the reception room. His name tag identified him as Jeremy.

"Can I help you?" he asked.

"My name is Ben Kovak, I'm here for a job interview."

"Hi, Ben, I'm Jeremy, have a seat for a minute, I'll let Mr. Willett know you're here.

"Thanks," Ben replied and took a seat. On the table in front of him, were several catalogs with the heading "ReadiMed

Scientific Supply Co.." He picked one up and began leafing through it. It was filled with full color pictures of everything you have ever seen in a hospital or doctor's office. There was a separate catalog for every specialty.

They sold everything from mouthwash to plastic kidneys, stretchers, urinals, combs, vaginal speculums, tongue depressors and even cadavers. You name it, they sold it. He always wondered where all this shit came from.

His dad had a bunch of this stuff laying around the house. Now, he knew where he got it. Maybe not this particular distributor, but one just like it. His peripheral vision picked up on motion inside the reception area. Jeremy was with another guy. Ben assumed it was Mr. Willett.

"Mr. Kovak, go to that side door and I'll buzz you in."

Ben walked to the door and as soon as he got there, he heard the buzz and the electronic door latch release. He was familiar with that sound. He pulled on the handle and it opened.

"Hello, Ben, I'm Gerry Willett. My friends call me Willi but you can call me Mr. Willett."

"Nice to meet you Mr. Willett."

"I'm just kidding about that Ben, call me Willi."

"Okay, Willi." Ben replied.

"Damn kids don't have any respect for your elders!" Willi exclaimed.

"Gee, I'm sorry, Mr. Willett."

"Just kidding again son. Okay, let's move beyond that, shall we?"

"Ben, ReadiMed is one of the top three scientific supply houses in New England. We stock about two hundred thousand different products for the healthcare and scientific industries. Our customers consist of schools, laboratories, hospitals, and funeral homes. Our motto is "From Cradle to Grave, We've Got You Covered." Catchy, don't you think?"

"Extremely," Ben replied.

"I like you already, Ben Kovak!"

"Thank you, sir, I like you too."

"Ass kisser, that's a quality I admire in a young recruit. Ben, there are reasons that I prefer to hire medical students. Do you know what they are?"

"We're usually broke?" Ben joked.

"That's in the top five Ben, but there are better reasons. Number one, you can pronounce most of the words we use. If you can't say prosthesis correctly, you're probably not going to sell any either. Number two, you're probably not afraid of most of this crap. Do you know how many non-medical students have lasted less than a day here?"

"Twelve?" Ben guessed.

"It's a figure of speech son. I don't know the exact number, but twelve will work, I guess. You're a bit of a wiseass aren't you Ben Kovak? I like that in a new recruit. The third reason is that you have at least two more years of school left which means you're going to be hungry for a while longer. The fourth reason is...I forgot what the fourth reason is and who gives a shit? You, Ben Kovak?"

"No sir, not me, sir," Ben snapped as if asked by a military superior.

"Alright then, let me show you around. By the way, you work four hours a day, three days each week and maybe a half day Saturday here and there. I pay ten USD for each and every hour that you work. You get the major holidays off with pay, prorated of course, and if I like you, I may just give you a little bonus around Christmas time. You want the job or not son?"

Ben didn't even think about it. He liked this guy and he wanted to work for him.

"Yes sir, Mr. Willi, I want the job!"

"Then shake my hand son, we have a deal. Come on, let's have a look at this crazy stuff."

Ben hadn't had this much fun in a long time. Willi showed him the entire, huge warehouse. He described what his job entailed and promised he wouldn't be working alone for at least a few weeks. The phones were turned off at 4pm so the evening people didn't have to be disturbed by that. The main goal was to get the orders ready to ship out the next morning. Willi warned him that it was a steady pace and could be quite physical at times.

When the tour was over, Willi had him complete some paperwork, made a copy of his license, and handed him a twenty dollar bill.

"Most employers won't pay you to interview, Ben. I'm not most employers. Now you get on out of here, Ben. You're too ugly to have a date but I'm sure you'll find something to do." Willi shook his hand again and buzzed the door open. "See you tomorrow at 4pm sharp!"

Ben walked out onto Wilmington Street and headed toward the T station. He pulled the phone out of his pocket and checked the time. It was almost 7:30 and he was going to be late. He sent Amanda a text explaining the situation. A minute later she texted back. "Don't rush. Grab two beers on your way to the seats!"

He found it hard to believe that nearly six months had passed since then. He missed her. This afternoon with the mystery date was fun but he still missed Amanda. "Not my fault," he told himself. He was nearing the turn on to Vermont RT. 4. He would soon be crossing back into NY. From there, it would be another ninety minutes to home.

He was getting hungry. He may just stop at another Gerardi's. They were all over the place in that area and besides, it worked out pretty well the last time.

Chapter 13

"You forgot?" Mary said, as Greg walked in the door.

"I'm sorry honey, it was a really ragged day. I was either in meetings or on the phone the entire day. John will understand, he was in my meetings too."

"John didn't remind you?"

"He was busy as well, Mary. Maybe he forgot."

"Alright," Mary said. "Just hurry and get ready."

Greg was tired. It was nearly seven o'clock and he had been going non-stop since early morning. At least he had something to show for it. He was trying to multi-task now, changing his clothes, brushing his teeth, applying deodorant, and planning the next steps.

His contacts in Albany had been supportive of his involvement. The Governor would open the doors for them with the State Police and the Health Department. He was also going to call Governor Tallin in Vermont. No promises, but Tallin was a friend and it looked promising.

"Greg!" Mary called, "I'll be waiting outside." Greg grabbed a light jacket from the closet and headed down the stairs. It sounded like Mary had downgraded to passive aggressive. She hated to be late.

"Coming right now, darling." Mary was on the porch. "You look very pretty tonight, dear." Greg tried. It wasn't working. They walked to the car and he opened Mary's door for her.

"Over-reaching, aren't we?" Mary said with just a touch of snarky.

"Ok! I forgot, I am late, I am human, mea culpa!" Can we just get past it now and try to enjoy ourselves? Please!"

"Okay," she pouted, "but no business talk tonight."

"I'll try to avoid it," he said.

It was less than a five minute drive to John and Sara's house but the area was pretty dark at night. They could have walked at this hour but returning home at the end of the evening would have been difficult. Jocelyn and Jillian were already there. They went over for a cookout earlier and were planning to stay overnight in the treehouse.

They pulled into the driveway and could see the lights from the treehouse casting shadows of the branches across the back lawn. The wrap-around front porch was aglow from the small lamps placed on the wicker tables and the few tiki torches placed theatrically around the perimeter. Sara really knew how to decorate. Greg knew it made Mary a little jealous at times.

John and Sara opened the front door as Greg and Mary approached. "Come on in guys," Sara said enthusiastically, "it's going to be a bit buggy out here for a while. I think we should start indoors."

"That sounds fine, Sara," replied Mary. Greg and Mary followed their hosts inside to the sitting room near the back patio. The room was softly lit and there was a very small fire in the fireplace. It didn't throw any heat, just a few embers for show. There were some snacks in crystal dishes scattered around the room and two bottles of wine rested in iced tubs next to a small table holding stemware.

"Please help yourselves," John said, "you're all family here." And they were. The first few minutes of these gatherings were always a tad formal, but then it was no different than being home. Shoes off, feet on the couch, and self-service. Greg poured a glass of Chablis for Mary and a rich red for himself. He passed a tray of mixed nuts to everyone. The girls each took a handful while Greg and John passed. The boys were not about to share the fact that they had lunch just a few hours before.

"Are the kids out for the night?" Mary inquired.

"I doubt it, they haven't had dessert yet." Sara said.

"Good point," Greg chimed in. "They'll be coming around for sure."

John turned on the stereo, which was tuned to a Utica station that played soft, classic rock. It featured songs they were all familiar with. John Denver was filling up their senses with 'Annie's Song.' Mary and Sara were singing along. It was a perfect setting and everyone was settling in and settling down.

Greg wanted to talk to John about the progress he made today but that would definitely stir the pot with Mary. He would rather swallow glass. Now, if Sara brought it up, he would be off the hook. He would need to wait and see.

Just then, the DJ faded out the Denver tune and dedicated the next song to the souls lost and those injured in the college blasts. Greg couldn't believe it. He waited for someone to respond. Anyone.

"Isn't that terrible?" Sara finally spoke out. "I can't believe another school was targeted!"

"I know," said Greg, "what is the world coming to?" He was trying to edge the group toward a full blown conversation. John looked at Greg and very gently shook his head from side to side as if saying "don't go there Greg, nothing good can come from it." No one else spoke. He waited. After a what seemed like an hour, Mary said "I worry about Jack being away at school."

There it was, Mary of all people just gave him the green light. "It worries me too, dear. Colleges can be so vulnerable to these kinds of attacks. You know, I was speaking to some old friends in Albany today about it. They still don't have any real clues about who may be behind it or how they are getting the bombs on campus. In fact, they were wondering if I could lend some assistance."

"How could you be any help to the state, Greg, you run a hospital now." Mary said.

"Well, they believe that the attacks may be driven by someone with a link to healthcare. They still remember what we were able to do here with a small, dedicated team and suggested joining forces."

"What would that look like? asked Sara.

"For starters, it would mean pulling our team back together. Then, we would need to be allowed to share the evidence they have gathered so far. We would have access to a contact at the FBI and Homeland security in addition to the Governor's offices in New York and Vermont."

"Isn't most of your team retired?" Mary asked."

"Retired, but still available. I spoke with them today."

"That is exciting, Greg," Sara said. "John, did you know about this?"

Greg jumped in, "John and I have had some conversations about the issue, but what you're hearing now is the first time he is hearing it as well. So, John, it looks like we have been asked to assist our government. What do you say?"

"I'm all in Greg, I will be happy to do anything I can to help out. We all have children in school, how could we just stand by?"

"Something smells fishy here." Mary said.

"I'm sure that's just the Mohawk, honey." Greg responded.

That broke the ice a little and they all smiled.

"You guys were amazing the last time. But it was dangerous!" Mary's tone changed.

"That was when things were happening right under our noses. There's no way we would ever be in the same county with the people behind this, let alone the same building." I assure you; we will not be in any danger." Greg said.

"It is our children you're looking out for, and I mean that collectively. Whether we know them or not, they are all our children." Sara said. "I think it's a very noble gesture, Greg."

"Thank you, Sara."

Mary didn't say any more. Greg was pretty sure he would hear more about it later. It wouldn't matter, he would do what he needed to do.

"Hey, what's for dessert?" Maria asked as she burst through the back door with Jillian and Jocelyn in tow.

"It's in the fridge but wash your hands first!" Sara said.

Greg caught John's attention and winked.

Chapter 14

Mary had a good time at the Shand's house the night before. She was cranky before they left but she was better by the time they got back home. Greg coming home late bothered her more than it should have. She had flashbacks to when she was stuck in Clifton Park with her three young children and Greg was out late several night a week. She knew it was his job that kept him away, but it didn't make her any less alone.

When the hospital ordeal was over, thing began to settle down. When Greg took the CEO position and they moved to High Falls, everything got better and it has stayed that way. Greg was home more, the kids were very independent, she loved her house and money wasn't tight anymore. So, she really had no reason to be upset. She passed it off as just a moody moment. She apologized to Greg on the way home.

He understood and he apologized for being late. They held hands on the ride home. Between the wine, the making up and an empty house, Greg and Mary found themselves trying to remover each other's clothing on the way up the stairs. They made love a few times a month but it had become a bit rote. This night was different and they couldn't keep their hands off each other. If anyone walked in tonight, they could just follow the line of clothing to their bedroom.

The morning sun was breaking through the trees, splashing the bedroom walls with prisms of different shapes. Greg rolled over and looked at the clock. "Oh crap!" He exclaimed. Mary shot up in bed.

"What's wrong?" she asked.

"I'm going to be late for work." He rolled toward her and kissed her. Then he kissed her again more deeply and slowly. Mary pulled down the covers to expose her breasts.

"Oh babe, I really need to get going, I'm sorry." She quickly rolled over and wiggled her naked butt.

"Just a quickie," she said. "Two minutes and you can be in the shower."

Greg threw the covers off the bed exposing her entire backside. He climbed on her back. She was still wet from the night before and he slid in easily. She gave a lustful cry as he entered her. She overestimated, as Greg was done in less than a minute. He remained that way, not moving for several seconds.

"I love you" he whispered as he kissed her neck and shoulders. "Thank you!"

"I love you more," She spoke.

Greg hopped off and went to the shower. He wet and shampooed his hair, then the curtain opened and Mary climbed in. "Need your back washed?" she asked.

He looked down at her hands. "That's not my back."

They finished their shower, dressed, and went downstairs to make coffee. While Mary poured the coffee, Greg grabbed the toast from the toaster, spread a little peanut butter on it and put one piece on each plate. They stood at the counter and ate.

"What's on your agenda, my dear?" Greg asked.

"Sara and I are going to Herkimer to do some shopping. Is there anything you need?"

"I think I'm fine but thank you!"

"Okay, if you think of anything, call me."

"I will hon. Thanks again for last night. And this morning, and the back wash."

"My pleasure, Mister, come again soon. Be sure to call first, I wouldn't want my husband to walk in on us."

"I sure will, Ma'am." Greg winked at her and walked out the door.

Mary had thirty minutes to do her makeup, get dressed and be at Sara's house. She placed the dishes in the dishwasher, refilled her coffee cup and took it upstairs with her. She couldn't believe how fulfilled she felt. She had married a great man and while there were some rough times early on, she realized that she couldn't be happier, right now.

She looked at herself in the mirror. She had aged, there was no denying it, but she still looked good. She believed she looked better now than she did ten years ago, proof that her life had changed for the better. She promised herself that she would pay more attention to her husband. She would begin my making herself even more appealing to him. Shopping today was going to be fun.

She was still on schedule when she closed the front door behind her. A five minute drive to Sara's and off they would go. They did this about once a month. Shopping, lunch, and a lot of chit-chat. They found that they had so much in common now that their children were older. Mary considered Sara her best friend and she was certain Sara felt the same. They were both so lucky.

She pulled into the driveway and Sara was waiting on the front porch. She skipped toward the car. "Good morning Sara," Mary offered.

"It certainly is!" Sara answered. I am on top of the world today!" she continued.

"Isn't it wonderful?" Mary asked, "I feel the same way."

"Do we need to compare notes?" Sara asked.

"How much detail do you want?" Mary asked.

"Only the good parts!" Said Sara. "I can't wait! First though, remind me to stop at a hardware store on the way home. John needs something for the bathroom. Okay, you first!"

Chapter 15

Ben backed the car out of the first garage bay, closed the door remotely and headed off to work. He was still tired. The drive home last night seemed to take forever. The first part of the day was exciting and seemed to go by quickly. The second segment was even better but that final hour and a half drive was grueling. He went to bed early enough but he couldn't get to sleep. His mind was all over the place. He should have showered before bed but he didn't want to lose her scent. It drove him craze all the way home.

He tried talking to mother about her but she didn't want to hear it. "You continue to set yourself up for hurt," she said. "Girls will do that to you. You're better off alone, believe me." He wasn't in the mood for her nonsense so he took her back to her room. She was talking of course about his experience with Amanda.

He tried to make preparations for his next event but he couldn't focus. He knew mother wouldn't approve of him masturbating in her house but he really didn't have a choice. It was the only way he was going to get any sleep.

Now that she was in her room, she wouldn't be any the wiser. So, he got comfortable on his bed, turned on the TV and pushed the play button on the VCR. He liked this one. It reminded him of the last time he made love with Amanda.

She enjoyed being tied up. Last summer when he brought her home to meet mother, she wanted to be tied up. She found the upright table in my dad's workshop. It had straps at the ankles, waist, and chest to keep her from falling forward. That would hurt. He tried to talk her out of it, he thought doing it in bed would be just fine but she insisted. Of course, she brought some of her pretty things along with her on the trip and she wanted to wear a particular one.

After she was dressed, she stood at the foot of the table and asked him "front or back?"

He told her to choose, either way was fine with him.

He heard a horn blowing. Again, how annoying. Three quick blasts of the horn now. Ben looked up and realized he was stopped at a stop sign. He must have dozed off for a moment. He took his foot off the brake and proceeded forward. He was just a few minutes away from Smitty's.

Ben parked in his usual space and entered through the back door. The smell of fertilizer was like a shot of adrenalin. He suddenly felt wide awake. He worked his way around the counter at the back office where they stocked specialty items and made keys. He signed on to the computer and punched in. He was on time.

He picked up his to do list and read it while he walked into the store. It was only noon and as expected, it was busy. In no time he was being paged through his headset. 'Ben, customer needs assistance in electrical.' Ben straightened his green vest with his name tag pinned to the left breast pocket and headed toward electrical. He turned down aisle eight and froze. It was Amanda.

He was looking at her back, but the shape, size, and hair color were all hers. He swallowed hard and took a deep breath. Approaching he said, "how may I help you?" He watched her turn as if in slow motion. The coppery hair swinging slowly around her shoulder. He stared as her face came around and then stopped. It was not her. He began breathing again.

"My dad sent me in to get a replacement for this but I can't seem to find it." She handed him a square black item. He looked at it for just a second.

"That's a fifty amp breaker. Let me guess, farm equipment?"

"How did you know?"

"You are in farm country," Ben said.

"Yes, but there must be at least a hundred motors and gadgets that require a fifty amp breaker!" she spoke.

"The truth?"

"Yes, the truth," she insisted.

"When you were turned away from me, I notice some straw on your backside. I guessed it was from the seat of your truck. How am I doing so far?" Ben asked.

"Aside from the fact you were staring at my ass, I'd say you did pretty good!"

"Noticing and staring are two very different things, you know," Ben returned.

"Really? Explain please."

"Okay," Ben replied, "I quickly noticed as I approached you in the aisle, that there was some straw stuck to your pants."

"How does that differ from staring at my ass?"

"If I were staring at your ass, I would never have noticed the straw."

"You're pretty quick, cowboy!" she exclaimed.

Ben thought for a second. "Cowboy?" what were the chances.

"I can tell you something else, if you want to hear it," he said.

"Okay, tell me something else," she requested.

He was staring at her chest when he said this. "It's for a milking machine, the breaker I mean."

"And why would you say that?"

"I figure you work on a dairy farm," Ben continued.

"And why would you 'figure' that, Ben?" She was staring at his name tag.

"Because I also noticed that you had Iodine stain on the back of your a...pants."

"You are pretty amazing, Ben. Tell me one more thing," she said as she moved closer.

"Pink."

"What?"

"Pink, your underwear is pink."

She paused for a long spell then she unbuttoned her jeans, and looking at his eyes the whole time, turned her side to him and pulled the waist of her pants down several inches. She dropped her head to look. His head followed.

"Sorry, Ben, I'm not wearing any."

As she turned to walk away, she said, "thanks for your help, cowboy."

Ben said, "Hey!" she stopped and turned toward him. He pointed to his own breasts with both hands.
"Not there either." She smiled, turned, and walked to the register.

"Ben, customer needs assistance in aisle eleven," rang through his headset.

Chapter 16

Greg should be tired, but instead he felt invigorated. The afternoon was just beginning and he already felt like he has accomplished an entire day's work. Nothing like three orgasms in eight hours to get the day stared. He tried to remember if that had ever happened before. The short answer was no.

Bill, Richard, and John were in his office with coffee and Danish in hand at 9am sharp. They all seemed as excited to be involved as he was. By 10:30, they had a plan in place. Bill and Richard were hitting the road tonight. They would visit SUNY Plattsburgh first, allowing time for things to calm down a little before heading over to Burlington.

They had two rooms booked at a decent hotel near the campus. Finding rooms was not as easy as one would think following an explosion. Worried parents and news crews occupied a good percentage of the available rooms. One week earlier, they may have been shut out.

They would stay two nights in Plattsburgh and then two nights in Burlington where they were able to secure two rooms at a bed and breakfast in the downtown area. It wasn't cheap but Greg didn't mind. The downtown location would give them easy access to the campus and allow them to interact with city residents. Greg knew from experience that often times, the word on the street was worth more than the reported news.

John was able to secure meetings for Bill and Richard with the Provost at both schools. He told them that the guys were collaborating closely with the authorities investigating the case and that their specialties were medicine and security. It was easier than Greg imagined. John was also scouring hospital and state licensing databases looking for anything that might illuminate a health professional with a gripe. A needle in a haystack came to Greg's mind but he also knew the value of incidental findings.

He approached it like a jigsaw puzzle. One piece tells absolutely nothing. Two or three connected pieces can give a clue. Completing the border forces your attention to the center and that narrows the process down by about eighty percent. From that point on, the puzzle comes together quickly. They didn't need everything right now, just the border and a little luck. Greg was aware that if the bombings stopped now, lives would be spared. He also knew that each subsequent bombing would provide more clues and a greater chance of identifying the person or people behind it.

Greg would function as the command center. He could fulfill his duties as hospital administrator and coordinate the flow of information up and down the chain. The work he had done over the past fourteen years acquiring good people, training them, and trusting them made his job easier. Evaluate, encourage, and empower was his mantra. So far, so good.

In addition to his own crew, there were several key people he needed to interface with regularly: Governors Ryder of New York and Tallin of Vermont; Special Agent Summers, FBI; Major Anderson, Homeland Security; Dr. Blumenthal, DOH; Christine, DOH and Russ Lang, DOH, Forensics Lab. Based on his initial phone call to each, he was expecting any pertinent information to begin arriving any time.

All he knew for sure was that the explosions did originate in the anatomy labs and that they were either in, close to or under a cadaver. They were still tracking down where the cadavers came from. In order for them to do that, they needed to know which cadaver blew up. To determine that, they needed DNA. They had plenty of pieces of human flesh but it would take time to identify each piece. Estimates ranged from weeks to months. He thought it was best to look for alternate ways to solve the mystery.

Just for kicks, Greg browsed the internet for medical supply sources. There were hundreds of listings. He narrowed the search by adding northeast US. That was better, but still a lot. He added the word cadaver. He found some interesting results. Apparently, cadavers can come from many sources. Individuals may will their body to science, next of kin can make the decision to give a loved one to a medical college, and some are unknowns with no identification and/or no next of kin.

The one common factor is that nearly all bodies are embalmed before going anywhere. A company from Connecticut can recruit a body from California. That body would be embalmed by a private undertaker in that state and then shipped to a supply company who would then deliver or ship it to a medical college. "That is a ton of variables," Greg said to himself. Once again, he was unsure where to begin.

It was after 1:00pm by the time Sara and Mary finished lunch. They had a fun filled morning of shopping and storytelling. They behaved like adolescent girls, watching each other trying on clothes. For every ten articles they tried, they ended up purchasing just one. It was usually more about the chase than the capture.

Mary accomplished her goal of finding a few undergarments that Greg might enjoy. She was excited just thinking about the possibilities. According to Sara, she and John enjoyed a similar evening. With the possibility of the children coming inside, they were more discreet. There was no trail of clothing leading up the stairs and everything was done in the dark. With the windows open, they also needed to keep their lustful voices in check.

After shopping, they dined at Altomar's, a local, family run Italian eatery that had been there for generations. Herkimer wasn't very large but they did have several good stores and restaurants. The ease of getting on and off Interstate 90 helped. If they really wanted to do high end shopping, they would go further west to Syracuse or east to Albany where large Malls hosted hundreds of shops.

They were headed back on Rt. 5 East when Mary said, "we forgot the hardware store!"

"That's okay," Sara assured her, I think there's one up ahead a ways. If not, I'm sure John can wait a day. It's just a toilet that keeps running. It's not like my hair dryer died or anything!" They both got a laugh out of that.

"Are we lucky or what?" Mary said with some humility. "We have more than I ever expected."

"That, we are, Mary." We have good men, great children, nice homes, and free time. What else could we want?"

"I want our children to have hope for a happy life." Mary replied. "I don't like the changes taking place in the world. Too much violence and too little respect for life and for each other. It saddens me."

"I know, I feel the same way," Sara said softly. I look at the way Maria came into this world and it blows me away. We are so fortunate that our husbands are the men they are. Not everyone would do what they did."

They remained quiet for a moment, their eyes wet with gratitude and love. Mary reached over and touched Sara's arm. "I love that we are friends, and I love you, Sara.

"I love you too, Mary,' she replied. "Friends forever!"

"Amen to that, Sara. Amen to that."

A few minutes later, almost out of nowhere, they noticed the sign. 'Smitty's Farm and Home.' "There it is Sara, take the next right."

There it was, sitting at the crossroads of nowhere. This little intersection between High Falls and Herkimer showed no promise at all yet here was a fairly large hardware store. It sat just far enough off the main road that you wouldn't find it if you weren't looking for it. Sara found a parking space right up front and pulled in.

There was a roof that extended ten to twelve feet toward the parking lot that covered the sidewalk and a variety of outdoor equipment and supplies. There were several push mowers, a few riding mowers and several pallets of grass seed, fertilizer, and pest control on one side of the entrance.

On the other side were plastic Adirondack chairs in a variety of colors and some live plants. It looked like they were gearing up for fall because the spring and summer plants were gone and the tables were loaded with Mums.

The girls browsed around the plants for just a moment before entering the store.

"It's pretty nice in here," Mary said. "I can't believe I never knew about this place."

"No need, I guess, we have a couple in High Falls," Sara replied.

"I suppose so," said Mary," but I feel like I should be observant of my surroundings."

"Greg would agree with that," she replied, "he's always after the kids to be more aware of what's around them. I guess that's a good thing."

"Here we are, Mary said, "the plumbing section."

"Can't you feel the excitement?" Sara quipped.

"Not quite like the lingerie department earlier," Mary said.

"But they do carry a lot of phallic looking tools and parts!"

Sara laughed. "We know where your mind is."
"Look!" said Mary, "a stopcock!"

"That's terrible, Mary. Besides, wouldn't you rather have a go-cock?"

"Can I help you, Ladies?" said the tall, young man behind them.

The girls looked at each other and smiled. "How long have you been there?" Mary asked.

"Oh, just five or six minutes," the young man answered. "Are you in the market for a fill valve today?" he asked.

"I beg your pardon," said Sara.

"That thing in your hand, it looks like an old fill valve. Are you having trouble with your toilet?"

"Oh," Sara replied, suddenly embarrassed. "Yes, I'm sorry. You caught me off guard."

"I do apologize, ma'am. I think what you need it right over here." He led them to the other end of the aisle. "The part you brought in is just one part of the fill system. I can sell you the replacement for just that part but I wouldn't recommend it."

"Why is that, Ben?" Sara asked, looking at his name tag.

"Because it may not work with the current chain, handle or flapper."

"Wow, I never knew there was so much to know about flushing a toilet," Mary added.

"All you need to know to flush, ma'am, is how to pull the handle. Repairing a toilet requires a little more knowledge. That is why I recommend this complete fill valve assembly. If this part is worn out, you can bet the other parts aren't far behind. It really costs just a few dollars more and it will save your husband an extra trip back to the store."

"Now Ben, why would you assume my husband is going to repair the toilet? Maybe I'm going to make the repairs." Sara challenged him.

"I didn't mean to offend you ma'am; it was just a guess. Here's the thing, you came in with the part in hand. If you had done this before, you would have known what you were looking for. Secondly, you're wearing a wedding ring and third, your hands are too soft and pretty. My guess is you have never taken the cover off a toilet, let alone fix one, no offense. And there is one other indicator, if you don't mind me saying so."

"Well, you've gone this far, you may as well finish," Sara suggested.

"You don't know a stopcock from a go-cock," he said, smiling.

The girls looked at each other with a look of surprise. They couldn't tell if he was shaming them or flirting with them. Mary took a chance. "Do you know the difference, Ben?"

"I believe I do," he said confidently. "Can I demonstrate for you?"

Sara jumped in. "Not today, Ben, I think we have all we need, thank you. You have been very informative." She grabbed Mary's arm and pushed her toward the cashier.

They could hear Ben behind them saying "come back soon, ladies."

Mary and Sara jumped in the car and quickly became overcome with hysterical laughter.

Chapter 17

It was after 1:00pm by the time Sara and Mary finished lunch. They had a fun filled morning of shopping and storytelling. They behaved like adolescent girls watching each other trying on clothes. For every ten articles they tried, they ended up purchasing just one. It was usually more about the chase than the capture.

Mary accomplished her goal of finding a few undergarments that Greg might enjoy. She was excited just thinking about the possibilities. According to Sara, she and john enjoyed a similar evening. With the possibility of the children coming inside, they were very discreet.

There were no trails of clothing leading up the stairs and everything was done in the dark. With the windows open, they also needed to keep their lustful voices in check.

After shopping, they dines at Altomar's, a local, family run Italian eatery that had been there for generations. Herkimer wasn't very large but they did have several good stores and restaurants. The ease of getting on and off Interstate 90 helped. If they really wanted to do high end shopping, they would go further west to Syracuse or east to Albany where the large malls hosted hundreds of shops.

They were headed back on Route 5 east when Mary said, "we forgot the hardware store!"

"That's okay'" Sara assured her, I think there is one up ahead a ways. If not, I'm sure John can wait another day. It's just a toilet that keeps running. It's not like my hair dryer died or anything!" They both got a laugh out of that.

"Are we lucky or what?" Mary said with some humility, "we have more than I ever expected."

"That we are, Mary, we have good men, great children, nice homes and free time. What else could we want?"

"I want our children to have hope for a happy life," Mary replied. "I don't like the changes taking place in the world. There is too much violence and too little respect for life and for each other. It saddens me."

"I know, I feel the same way," Sara said softly. I look at the way Maria came into this world and it blows me away. We are so fortunate that our husbands are the men they are. Nit everyone would do what they did."

They remained quiet for a moment, their eyes wet with gratitude and love. Mary reached over and touched Sara's arm. "I love that we are friends, and I love you, Sara."

"I love you too, Mary," she replied, "friends forever!"

"Amen to that, Sara. Amen to that."

A few minutes later, almost out of nowhere, they noticed the sign. 'Smitty's Farm and Home.' "There it is, Sara, take the next right."

There it was, sitting at the crossroads on nowhere. This little intersection between High Falls and Herkimer showed no promise at all yet here was a fairly large hardware store. It sat just far enough off the main road that you wouldn't find it if you weren't looking for it. Sara found a parking space right up front and pulled in.

There was a roof that extended ten to twelve feet toward the parking lot that covered the sidewalk and a variety of outdoor equipment and supplies. There were several push mowers, a few riders and several pallets of grass seed, fertilizer and pest control on one side of the entrance.

On the other side were plastic Adirondack chairs in a variety of colors and some live plants. It looked like they were gearing up for fall because the spring and summer plants were gone and the tables were loaded with Mums.

The girls browsed around the plants for a moment before entering the store.

"It's pretty nice in here," Mary said, "I can't believe I never knew about this place."

"No need, I guess, we have a couple in High Falls," Sara replied.

"I suppose so," said Mary, "but I feel like I should be more observant of my surroundings."

"Greg would agree with that," she replied, "he's always after the kids to be more aware of what's around them. I guess that's a good thing. "Here we are, the plumbing section."

"Can't you feel the excitement?" Sara quipped.

"Not quite like the lingerie department earlier," Mary replied, "but they do carry a lot of phallic looking tools and parts!"

Sara laughed. "We know where your mind is."

"Look!" said Mary, "a stopcock!"

"That's terrible, Mary, besides, wouldn't you rather have a go cock?"

"Can I help you ladies?" said the tall, young man behind them.

The girls looked at each other and smiled. "How long have you been there?" Mary asked.

"Oh just five or six minutes," the young man answered. "are you in the market for a fill valve today?" he asked.

"I beg your pardon," said Sara.

"That thing in your hand, it looks like an old fill valve. Are you having trouble with your toilet?"

"Oh," Sara replied, suddenly embarrassed. "Yes, I'm sorry. You caught me off guard."

"I do apologize, ma'am, I think what you need is right over here." He led them to the other end of the aisle.

"The part you brought in is just one part of the fill system. I can sell you the replacement for just that part but I wouldn't recommend it."

"Why is that, Ben?" Sara asked, looking at his name tag.

"Because it may not work with the current chain, handle or flapper."

"Wow, I never knew there was so much to know about flushing a toilet," Mary added.

"All you need to know to flush, ma'am, is how to pull the handle. Repairing a toilet requires a little more knowledge. That is why I recommend this complete fill valve assembly. If this part is worn, you can be the other parts aren't far behind. It really costs just a few dollars more and it will save your husband an extra trip back to the store."

"Now Ben, why would you assume my husband is going to repair the toilet? Maybe I'm going to make the repairs," Sara challenged him.

"I didn't mean to offend you ma'am, it was just a guess. Here's the thing, you came in with the part in hand. If you had done this before, you would have known what you were looking for. Secondly, you're wearing a wedding ring and third, you're hands are too soft and pretty. My guess is you have never taken the cover off a toilet let alone fix one, no offense. And there is one other indicator if you don't mind me saying so."

"Well, you've gone this far, you may as well finish," Sara suggested.

"You don't know a stopcock from a go cock," he said smiling.

The girls looked at each other with a look of surprise. They couldn't tell if he was shaming them or flirting with them. Mary took a chance. "Do you know the difference, Ben?"

"I believe I do," he said confidently. "Can I demonstrate for you?"

Sara jumped in. "not today, Ben, I think we have all we need, thank you. You have been very informative." She grabbed Mary's arm and pushed her toward the cashier. They could hear Ben behind them.

"Come back soon, ladies."

Sara and Mary jumped in the car and quickly became overcome with hysterical laughter.

Chapter 18

Ben stopped at the grocery store on his way home from Smitty's. He bought a microwavable burrito, a bag of chips and a sports drink. After locking the garage door, he went straight up to the kitchen to prepare his meal. He placed the burrito in the microwave and placed the drink in the fridge, He pulled out another bottle identical to it. It was the only other thing in the fridge.

Having food in the house made it more difficult to adhere to his one meal a day discipline. That's how he grew up. Dad made sure that mom followed his rules about it. After all, he had grown up that way and it suited him well. Mom did what she was told. She never spoke back and never challenged his authority.

It wasn't easy for her. She came to this country at his request. A mail order bride, they used to call them. She was much younger than he was, probably thirty years or more. She was pretty but stern looking. Even with all the time Dad spent away from home, she would adhere to his every rule. She spoke little English when she arrived according to Dad, so he grew up understanding Russian and English although he never was able to speak Russian with any proficiency.

When Dad was away, Mom was talkative and friendly toward Ben but when he was home, she needed to pretend she ruled as he would so she became an extension of him. He wasn't sure that she was ever really happy. He always felt like he was raised by an indentured servant as opposed to a mother. Except she was his mother. She was the one who made sure he got on the bus in the morning and off in the afternoon. She was the one to talk to the school officials and took him shopping.

They didn't leave the house often. He never went to see a doctor or a dentist, his dad took care of all that at home. They made Ben as invisible as he could possibly be while still making him a part of society. He would hear them talk at times about the necessity of Ben's anonymity. It wasn't until just before Dad went away that he learned the truth about everything.

Ben finished his meal, threw the paper plate and napkin in the trash, and placed the uncompleted drink back in the fridge. He pulled his wallet from his back pocket and removed the copy of the credit card slip that he had taken on the way out of the store after he closed.

His name was Charles T. Chalmers. The card didn't include his address but Ben looked it up in the system. He also had his telephone number. "That's why you don't sign up for the rewards program," he thought aloud.

It would be easy enough for Ben to find his daughter, though he didn't even know her name. He could just ride by the farm and scope it out. Dairy farms start operating pretty early in the morning so he could swing by before opening the store on his next day shift. He had a few days before that happened and he needed to focus his time on his next attack.

The electronics were all set and the explosive was already on site. He just needed to finalize his approach plans, change all the batteries, and study the map of the area and campus. This time he would need to leave the day before and perform the surveillance. It was a longer drive so staying over the night before would allow him to execute the plan earlier in the day meaning he could be back home by mid evening.

He had already scheduled the days off from work. Now, he needed to call Mr. Willett and schedule himself for a weekend shift. After he left school, he had a heart to heart with Willi. He told him his mother was ill in upstate NY and he would need to take some time off from school. Willi was worried about him because he knew the chances of returning to complete medical school were against him. Ben assured him that he was in good standing with the school and that they would hold his place for the next year.

Willi trusted Ben. He was a great employee. Always on time, never in a hurry to leave and always accepted additional shifts without question or argument. Ben's orders were accurate and out on time. He even offered suggestions for improvements in the operation which Willi accepted and in almost all cases, implemented. Ben and Willi reached a deal that while Ben's mother needed him home, he could work weekends as often as he was able. It was a perfect solution for everyone.

Ben was tired. It was actually a fun day at work. He accomplished what he needed to personally and he made some new friends. The young Amanda look-alike was a sure thing. She was hot and ready and she was fun to boot. The older girls might be possibilities, especially Mary. He only knew her name because the other one called her that. He hadn't run the personal information from that purchase yet but there wasn't any real hurry. He had other things to take care of first.

It was time to say goodnight to mother and hit the bed. He sure missed Amanda. Perhaps he would visit her while he was in Boston. He made a mental note to call Willi in the morning.

Chapter 19

"Good morning, everyone!" Greg almost shouted as he entered the kitchen." Good morning, Dad"

"Hi, Dad,"

"Good morning, darling!"

"So, one enthusiastic, thank you Jocelyn, one still asleep, thank you Jillian and one very satisfied and appreciative, thank you, Mary."

"Oh, come on you guys, do you have to talk about that when we're around?" Jillian complained.

"Talk about what?" Greg said.

"You know, Dad, S.E.X." Jocelyn spelled it out.

"If you can spell it, you can say it. All together now…S E X!" Greg was the only respondent. "Oh guys, it is not a dirty word! It's only bad if either of you try it before you're 25! Right Mary?"

"You're on your own here, darling." Mary responded.

"Okay, I appreciate your support, Dear, don't expect much tonight!" Greg threatened.

"Oh, now I see," Jillian chirped in, "S E X can be used as currency, you can purchase with compliments or withhold when someone disagrees with you or doesn't support your position."

"Alright," Greg said, "you're going to be late for school."

"The bus isn't even here yet," Jocelyn stated.

"Well, you don't want to make the bus driver wait."

"Speaking of that, Dad, when am I going to get a car?"

"A car, you can't even SAY SEX! What good is a car going to do?"

The girls got up and shook their heads. "I feel sorry for you, Mom."

"Thank you, dear, have a good day at school."

"That didn't go exactly as I planned," Greg said.

"You think?" said Mary.

"You could have helped me out! There is strength in numbers," he said.

"Maybe, but it would have to be a bigger number than two. Greg, did you want to know when your parents were having sex? Or even if they were having sex? Most kids find that a little creepy."

"That's because we don't talk about it. We try to protect them from it and it is not an ugly thing. You know, in some countries sex is not taboo at all."

"Name one." Mary challenged.

"Holland, in Amsterdam, it's on display in storefronts!"

"That may be but I wouldn't want to see my mother or father in the window. I did have an uncle once who I thought was pretty hot, but I was like eleven."

"Okay, Mary, I give up. Anyway, I really appreciate what you did last night. You were beautiful and very exciting. Thank you."

He went to her and gave her a big kiss. "I have others," she whispered.

"I'll be home early," he growled.

"So will the girls," she answered.

"We can use John and Mary's treehouse!"

"Do you know what mosquitos would do with an outfit like that?" Mary asked.

"Do they make outfits like that for mosquitos?"

"Go to work, Greg."

Greg grabbed his keys and walked out the front door. He had much to do today and almost all day to do it. He instructed Kathy to keep his schedule as light as possible. His first stop was to see Harold Mease.

He called the office.

"Good morning, Kathy, how are things looking for today?"

"Very light, Mr. Webster, just as you requested."

"Excellent. I'm going to stop by Mease Mortuary on my way in. I should be back by 9:30 or so. If you need me sooner, just call."

"Sounds good, Mr. Webster. See you then."

Greg rolled the window down halfway. The early morning air was getting a little cooler now but it was fresh and invigorating. He turned on the radio to NPR. News occupied a good eighty percent of the morning airtime and that gave him a good ten minutes of headline before arriving at work. He used to watch the morning news while having breakfast but he realized that time was better spent talking with the family. That didn't play out this morning.

The host was in the middle of the five minute segment on politics. He hated this part. His job required that he keep up on political news considering that sixty percent of his revenue came from the federal government. But his personal opinion was that you couldn't elect anyone whose first priority wasn't themself. Even those with good intentions quickly became part of the machine.

"Next up, local and regional news, when we come back." This is what he wanted. After a two minute request for donations, the local news came on.

"Around the nation and particularly In the northeast, colleges and universities are adding security and reviewing procedures and policies designed to protect students. The State University of New York system announce that it was looking to add bomb sniffing dogs to the security team. Officials indicated it would take up to six months to acquire enough trained canines to have one dog at each campus. In the meantime, local Sheriff's offices and the State Police would work to coordinate interim measures utilizing their own canine teams."

"The FBI and Homeland Security authorities say they do not have any new information to report and are still asking eyewitnesses to come forward if they have anything to report. Our sources tell us that DNA results from the human tissue left at the scene from medical cadavers could take months to process. We will have more after these announcements."

Greg switched the radio off. He continued on Rt. 5 toward the edge of town. He had a flashback to the first time he visited Mease Mortuary. It was here that he realized what the killer's M.O. was. From there, breaking the case went quickly. He could see it coming into view. He hadn't seen Harold Mease since he retired from the Board of Directors at the hospital six or seven years ago. Harold was partially responsible for Greg being offered and accepting the CEO post at City.

He was slowing the car now, ready to turn into the parking lot. It hadn't changed much. It was still a beautiful house/funeral home. A large, welcoming front porch with a nicely manicured lawn and landscaping. Something did look different but he couldn't put his finger on it. Maybe it was the color. He remembered it as being grey but it seemed lighter now. Greg thought that perhaps it was he who had changed.

There weren't any other cars parked out front but he decided to take a chance. He pulled up right in front of the entry stairs. As he climbed, the door opened. "Good morning," the gentleman said, "my name is Maury. How may I be of assistance?"

"Good morning Maury, I'm Greg Webster, the CEO of City Hospital. I was wondering if I could see Harold Mease." There was a long pause. Maury looked like he had swallowed a bumble bee.

"Maury?" he said.

"Oh, so sorry sir, won't you please come in."

Maury opened the door wide for Greg.

"Thank you. I've been here once or twice over the last fourteen years; you know viewings mostly. "

"Of course, I hope you found our services worthy. Our goal is to exceed expectations."

"Yes, I thought they were very nice, you know, considering the circumstances."

"Of course, we're never going to be in the running for top entertainment venue."

"Exactly!" That's very funny."

"A sense of humor in an undertaker. Who knew?" Maury smiled.

"So, Mr. Mease, is he around?"

"Of course, I'm sorry to say Harold has moved to a retirement home in South Carolina."

"I'm sorry to hear that. Is he alright?"

"Yes, quite well in fact. He was no longer a fan of the long winters; it exaggerated his arthritis and his emphysema. But he's doing much better down there."

"And you're the new owner?"

"Yes, my wife and I are co-owners. Harold still holds a small percentage of the business, enough to help with his rent. Hilton Head Island is beautiful but not inexpensive."

"Doesn't the summer heat bother him?"

"One would think so, but he rather enjoys it. I'm sure on the warmest days, he remains inside where it's cool."

"Maury, I'm just thinking back here a little, did you work for City Hospital at one time?"

"Yes, I did. In fact, my wife and I both worked there. It was when you first took over as CEO. Right at the end of that horrible mess. My wife was a nurse on the second floor at the time, perhaps you remember her, Linette Jansen."

"Yes, I do remember that name. She worked there for a while after I came on board. Two or three years maybe?"

"A little more than two. Good memory!"

"I remember because she cared for a very dear friend of mine who was in the hospital for quite a while. She was well liked and very compassionate."

"That's my Linette." Maury smiled proudly.

"Maury, let me tell you why I'm here." Maury looked nervous again.

"I'm doing a little background work for New York State and the FBI."

Maury thought he might shit himself.

"I was wondering if you could explain to me how scientific donations of cadavers work. I understand that there are various ways one can donate but what I need to know is how that actually happens. How for example would a body get from your funeral home to a medical or other scientific laboratory."

Maury calmed down.

"Of course,"

Greg thought to himself, "man, if he begins one more sentence with the words 'of course,' I'm going to shove him in a casket."

Maury continued, "you see, the body needs to be embalmed before it can be transported. A local funeral home usually provides that service. From there, it could go to a school or lab directly if that client so specified, or it could be sent to a supply company. The supply company would then sell the cadaver to a customer."

"Good. What chain of custody is put in place to make sure everything is carried out accurately."

"Of course."

"Didn't I warn you about that?" Greg thought to himself.

"The local funeral director would complete and file the death certificate with the county. Disposition would be listed as either the final location if it's a lab or school or, the supplier."

Greg was afraid to ask another question. "Is there anywhere else besides the county office of records that one could search on a broader basis?"

"It may be worthwhile to check the records of the recipient."

"Whoa, that was a close one,"

"But of course, that depends on what you're looking for.

"There must be an empty casket around here somewhere!" Greg was biting his tongue. "For example, the recent bombing at the universities, if it were me, I would first ask to see the records

from the recipients, then one could determine where the cadaver came from."

"Thank you for your time Maury, you have been a big help. Please say hello to your lovely wife for me."

"I will, thank you. Let me show you out."

He opened the door for Greg. "Thanks again,' Greg said.

"Of course! My pleasure."

Greg could feel the hair stand up on the back of his neck.

Chapter 20

Greg was back in the office well before 9:30 and that included a stop for coffee. He always had a cup at home in the morning and it was readily available at work, but every now and then he wanted a decaf from Gerardi's. They had the best coffee on the planet and any local would tell you so. Since he had never really left the area, he had been a fan forever.

After he checked in with Kathy, Greg locked himself in his office and started making phone calls. The first was to Richard. He wanted to make sure Richard and Bill got checked in alright in Plattsburgh.

"What are you calling so early for?" Richard greeted him.

"And a good morning to you to! Did you wake up on the wrong side of the lake?"

"I think you mean bed, and when you sleep alone, there is no wrong side." Richard gave it back to him.

"So, you're just grumpy in the morning? Greg inquired.

"No," replied Richard, "I'm usually grumpy until about 9pm, then I mellow out just before bed."

"Great, poor Bill." Richard said.

"He'll be alright, he's tough, unlike you."

"So, are you going to accomplish anything today or are you just taking advantage of my good will?" Greg asked.

"What I'm taking advantage of is your credit card. You should have seen the breakfast we had this morning! For just two people, the food covered the entire table."

"You must be tired now, perhaps you should lay by the pool today, or maybe get a massage!" Greg suggested sarcastically.

"That's a great idea! Do they do that here?"

No one could keep up with Richard and Greg knew it.

"I surrender!" Greg said.

"Good, now we can talk business. We hit the streets early this morning, walking around and chatting with people. I smoked a couple cigars as we walked and I refrained from swearing at anyone."

"How human of you, Richard. What have you found out so far?"

"Well, for starters, Cindy has a suspicious looking mole on her left shoulder."

"Who is Cindy and how do you know that, Richard?"

"Cindy is the waitress at the restaurant where we had breakfast, and she showed me."

"Do I need to ask why?" Greg said.

"You don't need to but I'm not going to tell if you don't ask." Silence. More silence. "Okay, I'll tell you. I told her I was a doctor and she wanted to show me."

"Did you tell her you were a gynecologist?" Greg said anxiously.

"No! Think about what she would have wanted to show me then!"

"Good point, Richard."

"Did you gather any useful information? Anything that might pertain to this case?"

"Not yet but we have a meeting with the provost at 11:00 this morning."

"Great, in the meantime, see if you can extract some useful information from the city people. And Richard, the next time your phone rings and it's me, don't answer. I'm calling Bill from now on."

Greg was on a roll. First Maury, 'OF COURSE' and now, Richard. He should leave this up to the FBI. So what if a few hundred more innocent people died, at the rate he was going, he might kill a couple himself.

"Kathy," he said when she answered the phone, "can you come in here for a moment please." She hung up and two seconds later was standing in his office.

"Kathy, could you just shoot me now?" Greg begged.

"And ruin a nice suit? Forget it!" She walked back out and closed the door.

Greg took a breath and dialed his next number.

"Department of Health Investigative Unit, this is Christine."

"Finally, a sane person to talk to!" Greg said in despair.

"I'm sorry sir, you have reached the wrong department. Hold on and I will reconnect you to the operator."

"Christine, DO NOT hang up on me!"

"Bad day, Mr. Webster?"

"You have no idea, Christine."

"You're not thinking of coming back, are you Greg?"

"Wow, the entire world is out to get me and I'm trying to do something good." Greg sounded defeated.

"I'm sorry Greg, what can I do for you?"

"I don't suppose Russ Lang would be in today, would he?"

"He would be if he weren't on a trip around the world."

"Payback is Hell, Christine."

"So I've heard. Hold on and I'll connect you."

Greg heard a click and then ringing again.

"Forensics, Russ Lang."

"Russell, it's Greg Webster. How are you?"

"Hey, Spider, I'm good, it's nice to hear your voice. What kind of trouble are you in this time?"

"Nice opener, Russ. Believe or not, I'm working with the FBI and Homeland on these college bombing cases. I was wondering if you had any thoughts yet."

"Gee, that's great, Spider, but why you?"

"It's a long story, Russ, let's just say I volunteered and they didn't say no."

"That works for me. We have received several large, plastic tubs of body parts and we're trying to make some sense of them. And that's just Plattsburgh. The state of Vermont will be handling the other explosion, at least coordinating it. I'm sure at some point, we will each be involved in both. We have isolated a few remnants of the bomb itself."

"Anything that will help us?" Greg asked excitedly.

"It looks like the outer casing was made of polyvinylchloride and we also found small pieces of what is probably a rudimentary timer."

"It sounds like a professional job," Greg stated.

"I'm not so sure," Russ responded, "I've seen more professional bombs in my time, even if homemade."

"What makes them different, Russ?" Greg dug.

"It's not typical to see PVC used to encase the explosives. If the intent is to cause as many life-threatening injuries as possible, a metal casing is the popular choice. We would typically see galvanized pipe. PVC shatters into tiny pieces or just melts from the extreme heat. The next thing is the timer components. If I had to guess, the attacker used a cheap digital kitchen timer. Don't get me wrong, it obviously worked but bomb makers who don't want to blow themselves up would use something more reliable, a little heavier duty. Having a bomb go off in your car on the way to the job site could ruin your day."

"It sounds like you're saying the components you have identified thus far could be purchased at any hardware store. Is that a fair statement?"

"I would say that's very fair. And if I had to guess again, so could the explosive. We haven't identified all the materials but I do know that nitrogen and phosphorus are among the ingredients. That's two of the three main components of fertilizer."

"Russ, you have been a great help, as always. Can I call again in a few days?"

"You can call anytime, Spider, I hope I'll have some new information for you."

"Thanks, Russ."

Greg hung up the phone and walked to his office door. He opened it and asked Kathy to see if John Shand had a few minutes.

Chapter 21

"Mother, I need to go to work today. I have a lot going on right now so you will just have to forgive me. What's that? Yes, I will be gone this weekend as well. I already told you that remember, I need to go to Boston to work and take care of a few things. That's right, I'll be back on Monday. By the way, I'll be taking a road trip tomorrow as well. I won't be home tomorrow night. I know Mother, I'll make sure you have everything you need.

Ben kissed his mother goodbye and headed toward the garage. He could hear his mother crying in her room and he felt terrible.

"You screwed up, Dad! You should be here caring for your family!" He screamed inside his own head. "I can't believe you left this all up to me and yet, here I am trying to avenge you. I must be crazy. "

He pulled out of the garage and used the remote to close and lock the door. He turned on the radio, attempting to quiet his brain. He was more easily agitated lately. He thought it was because he missed Amanda. He also couldn't stop thinking about river girl. He didn't know how else to refer to her, so he chose the river girl.

He wondered if he would ever run into her again. He even thought about riding back up there and just spending the entire day sitting in the Gerardi's parking lot if he had to. It seemed too risky and he realized she might never show up. He did have another option though and that's where he was going right now.

The news was just starting. School budgets, teacher shortages, blah, blah, blah. "Enough already!" he screamed at the radio. "Talk about me now! I am the news." A few days and he was already off the front page. It won't be long before he makes the headlines again. Tomorrow he would pack up the car and head south. It looked like a good day for traveling, although he wasn't fond of the traffic.

He was accustomed to the east-west bound traffic driving to Boston but driving south was different. An hour south of Albany, the New York City traffic would start kicking in. He liked to drive at the posted speed limit but down there, you could get trampled if you didn't try to keep up with the flow of traffic. He would survive. He knew full well how to do that. His dad deserted him before he was ten years old and his mother, well Mother was Mother.

He turned onto Lepper Hill Road which was the corner where Smitty's was located. It was only 6:30 in the morning and he didn't need to be at work for another five and a half hours. He was leaving plenty of time in case the farmer's daughter wanted a roll in the hay. He wasn't really a fan of hay but he never knew he a fan of grass either. Sometimes you just had to play the cards you were dealt. He was surprised when he thought of that expression. He was familiar with it because he had heard it before but ironically, he never played a game of cards in his life.

He thought it funny that he had never been on this road before. His place of employment sat right on the corner of this road yet he had never attempted to explore it. He was excited, everything was new. It was pretty, green, and open. The hills climbed slowly until the road disappeared and then back down he went. He imagined a roller coaster felt that way.

There were twists and turns with a farm here and there. He slowed at every farm to see if he could spot a name or number. He figured he couldn't go much further before leaving the county so it had to be coming up soon. He was correct. Off to the right, before he could see an entrance, he spotted a truck with the name C.T. Chalmers' Dairy. It looked like he still delivered dairy products to homes.

The barn and some pasture were fairly close to the road with the farmhouse set back a ways. He didn't see many cows out so he assumed they were in for the morning milking.

He pulled into the driveway. He had his excuse all prepared in case he ran into old man Chalmers instead of his lovely daughter. He drove slowly and quietly up to the barn. There were lights on inside the barn as well as the milkhouse. He parked twenty yards away and turned off the car. He didn't see anyone and all he could hear was the steady clicking of the milking machines.

He approached the barn carefully. Looking in all directions as he made his way closer. The large barn doors were open affording him a wide angle view of the inside. Not seeing anyone, he stepped inside. The barn was long and wide with two rows of stanchions on each side of the middle. He guessed there were at least one hundred-twenty heads. On the wall where he entered, he could see the light switches and the breaker panels for the machinery.

He was just standing there when she stepped into the center opening. She stopped and looked for a long moment. He could tell she was suspicious. She didn't recognize him.

"Good morning miss, I'm sorry to bother you, It's Ben from Smitty's."

She started walking toward him.

"Where is your green vest, Ben?" she asked.

"I leave that at the store, besides, I'm not on the clock yet." Ben answered.

"So, what brings you here cowboy?"

"I brought you a spare fifty amp breaker. We had some complaints about them failing now and then and I didn't want you to have a breakdown."

"Had a lot of complaints in the last two days, Ben?" she quizzed him.

"Well, I guess it's been going on for a little while but I wasn't aware. Otherwise, I wouldn't have sold it to you," he lied.

They were only a few feet apart now. She was just as pretty this time of day as she was before.

"Ben, are you sure you aren't here just to see if I'm wearing a bra and undies?"

"N..no," he stuttered. She just smiled at him.

"It's okay Ben, I knew you'd be coming around sooner or later. I didn't think it would be this soon but I'm not disappointed."

"You're not?" She walked right up to him, leaned into him, and gave him a big kiss.

Ben was a bit stunned and she could tell.

"Don't get your knickers in a twist, Ben, I don't bite...hard." She gave him a little wink.

"So, what do we do now?" Ben asked.

"The way I see it, Ben, you have two choices. You can either stay here and milk cows or you can stop by after work and pick me up for a real date. Have you ever milked a cow?"

"No ma'am."

"The you have one choice. What time can you be here?"

"I close up at eight, I could be here by eight-ten."

"On second thought, I'll meet you at the store a few minutes after eight. Will everyone be gone by then?"

"Make it eight-fifteen to be on the safe side," Ben countered.

"You like playing it on the safe side, cowboy?"

Ben didn't know what to say.

"No worry Ben, you have time to think about it. Now get out of here before someone puts a shot gun upside your head. Besides, I still have a hundred teats to wash."

Ben smiled, turned, and ran out of the barn. He still didn't know her name.

Chapter 22

The State University at Plattsburgh sat primarily between Broad and Rugar Streets right at the bend of the Saranac River. The science building that housed the Anatomy Lab was an easy entrance off Broad. Bill and Richard arrived early to spend some time driving around the campus. They found the science building as well as the provost's office. It wasn't a huge, sprawling campus and the two buildings were easily walkable from a central location.

"Richard, before we park, can you drive from the science building to Broad Street please?" Richard didn't question him, he just started driving. Without traffic, it took less than a minute to get there.

"If I'm not mistaken, a left here will take you to I-87 and a right will take you Rt. 9. Assuming that the bomber was not a current student, getting out of here after the explosion would have taken no time at all."

"What makes you think it wasn't a student or faculty?" Richard asked.

"The second bombing," Bill replied, "gaining access to one lab as a student makes sense, but not two. "

"Do you think UVM was chosen because of proximity?"

"I'm not sure," Bill said, "without any other clues, that seems feasible."

Richard had turned the car around and was heading back toward the provost's office.

"Hold on, Richard." Bill was staring across Broad Street at a storage facility. It was one of those U-Rent type places with steel corrugated walls and doors.

"What is it, Bill?'

"The security camera on the corner of that building, it's facing directly at this intersection. Okay, you can continue driving now." Bill pulled out a little pocket notebook and jotted down the name of the storage place.

Richard found a place to park in a visitor lot, between the Anatomy lab and the Administration building. They climbed out of the car and Richard pulled a cigar out of his pocket.

"Richard, I'm going to take a lap around the lab while you enjoy your stogie. I'll meet you back here in ten minutes and we'll still have time to make it for our meeting."

"Sure, take your time, Bill."

Richard found a bench on the grass at the edge of the parking lot. Bill walked off toward the lab. The building was cordoned off with yellow caution tape that read 'Police Do Not

Cross' every three feet for the entire length of the tape. Bill stayed well outside of the tape as he walked the perimeter of the building.

There was still debris scattered across the grass. He felt sure they had picked up most of it and anything that might be evidence was long gone. The front approach to the building had two security cameras mounted up high at each corner. Both were facing the entrance. He walked to his right and rounded the corner of the building. There were no cameras on this side so he continued around the back. Here, he found two more cameras, similar in placement to the front and again, both were angle toward the entrance/exit.

He advanced around the left side of the building and again found no cameras. As he walked back toward Richard, he noticed the student distress phone. It was a small box mounted on a post with a weather shelter built around it. In the top section, above the phone box was a light. With the sun shining, it was hard to see but he thought the light was purple in color. He moved closer to the booth and that's when he saw it, the small black dome of a hidden security camera. He took out his notepad.

Richard was sitting back on the bench, head tilted back and looking like he was asleep.

Bill stood a couple feet in front of home and waited.

"You know, you're acting kind of freaky just staring at me like that!" Richard said without even opening his eyes.

"I think it's freaky that you knew I was here," Bill replied.

"I can hear, gumshoe. Are you ready to go?"

"Just waiting on you, smiley."

They walked to the admin building, approached the reception desk, and announced themselves.

"Good morning, I'm Doctor Richard Ingraham and this is my assistant, Bill. We have an appointment with the provost.

"Your assistant?" Bill asked.

"Please have a seat gentlemen, I'll let her know you're here."

"Your assistant?" Bill asked again.

"I thought it would be easier that way. She doesn't care who you are, I was just cutting a corner." Richard answered.

"Dr. Ingraham, Dr. Waring will see you now. This way please."

The boys followed the receptionist down the hall.

"You better let me do the talking in there." Richard said.

"I do know how to talk, you know." Bill replied.

"Here we are gentlemen. Right through this door. Have a wonderful day!"

She was gone. Richard and Bill were standing in front of a frosted glass door. To the left of the door was a square placard that read 'Helen Waring, EdD.'

"What is a provost?" Richard asked.

"And you want ME to be quiet?" Bill said as he opened the door.

The office was much larger than they anticipated. There was a desk straight ahead, an office with two desks to the right and another office with a closed frosted glass door to the left.

There were four young ladies involved in various activities milling about. The girl at the desk ahead of them was on the phone.

"I feel like I'm in the principal's office in grade school," Richard said.

"I have a feeling that was a familiar place for you," Bill quipped.

"I was a fairly frequent visitor; I wasn't well understood as a child."

"And now?" Bill asked.

"What? Now I'm fine."

"Would you like a second opinion, Doctor?" Bill asked.

The young lady completed her call and walked around her desk to the men.

"I'm sorry to keep you waiting, gentlemen, you must be Doctors Dillon and Ingraham. I'm Shelly, let me escort you in."

Shelly moved in front of the men and opened the door. Dr. Waring, this Dr. Dillon and Dr. Ingraham."

Shelly moved aside, out of the way of the hand shaking, and left the office, closing the door behind her.

"Please, have a seat." Dr. Waring waved at the chairs at the front of her desk.

"I understand you are working with the Governor's task force investigating the attack."

"That's correct, Dr. Waring, Mr. Dillon and I are here under the direction of Greg Webster who is working directly with the Governor, the FBI and Homeland Security."

"And what is your role, if I may ask."

"I'm here because of the possible link to the medical profession and Bill is a security and surveillance expert."

"And what is your background, Dr. Ingraham?" Bill was smiling inside because he knew what was coming.
"I'm a retired gynecologist," he answered.

Helen just stared at him, silently.

"Hard to connect the dots, isn't it?" Richard said.

"I'm having a little trouble, yes," she replied.

"Dr. Waring, my name is Bill Dillon, not Dr. Dillon. I'm afraid you received some wrong information. I'm not sure this news traveled all the way up here but we were part of the team that resolved the killing spree at City Hospital several years ago."

She thought for a moment. "Yes, I do remember that. I was at Syracuse at the time." She pointed at one of the certificates on the wall behind her. "Wasn't that a nasty situation?"

"Indeed, it was. Anyway, Greg Webster was a department of health investigator at the time and we were asked to help him solve that case and ultimately, we subdued the killer. The Governor was quite impressed with our work and has asked us to join the team. We are here to ask some questions and gather some information from a different angle than is customary with police agencies," Bill added.

"I see, and what is your background, Mr. Dillon?"

I was the head of maintenance and security at the hospital until I retired a few years ago." He could see where this was going.

"And before that?" she asked.

"Before I joined City Hospital, I was a civilian surveillance expert for the Federal Government. Before that, I attended M.I.T. where I received a master's degree in mechanical engineering and information technology. Prior to that, I was in the United States Navy."

Helen was quiet. Richard had his head turned to Bill but didn't say a word.

"So, where do we begin, gentlemen?" Helen asked quietly.

Ingraham spoke first, "I would like to review all purchase orders and delivery receipts related to the Anatomy Lab from May of this year through, and including, last week."

"I would like to meet with campus security to review video footage from the day prior to the explosion up to and including the day after the incident," Bill stated.

Helen sat with her hands folded while they made their requests.

"Shelly will coordinate your requests but it may take a little time."
"No hurry," Richard exclaimed, "we have all afternoon." Just in case she was thinking she could drag them back in there tomorrow.

"I would like to look around campus while we're waiting if that's alright," Bill said, "Will we need some sort of pass?"

"Shelly can take care of that on your way out. I appreciate your involvement fellas; I hope you find something useful."

Helen opened the door for her guests and gave Shelly her instructions. Helen returned to her office.

"I underestimated you, Bill," Richard said. I wasn't aware of your credentials, I apologize."

"No big deal, Richard, but thanks."

"Sure, but you're still MY assistant."

"Whatever you say, Richard."

Shelly handed them each a Distinguished Visitors Pass.

"This should get you where you need to go. Please let me know if you need anything else."

Chapter 23

Ben had just finished his conversation with Mr. Willett. It was all set; Ben would work Saturday and Sunday this week. Willi didn't care what time Ben came or left, he trusted him to get the work done and he had his own key. Jeremy was also scheduled to work so Ben would have company at least part of the time.

Ben sat in his car near the back door of Smitty's. After leaving the barn this morning, he drove back home to take care of a few things just in case it was a late night. He was planning to get an early start in the morning now that his evening departure plan had changed. He had a few hours to kill before starting his shift so he decided to go to the flower shop and pick something up for the farmer's daughter.

He thought about bringing take out but he guessed she would have had dinner by then. If he were wrong, he could take her out somewhere. He even thought about offering to go back to his place but it felt too soon. Mother didn't approve of Amanda so he doubted she would like this one either. He told her repeatedly that he was fine and that the breakup didn't bother him. She wouldn't believe him.

The radio in Ben's car was on and the news was about to begin. He turned the volume up.

"This is WCDN news in Albany, I'm Roselyn Smith, Thanks for joining us. Our top story this hour is an update of the recent college bombings. The New York State Police in Albany are investigating a lead in the case and are saying it looks promising. An eyewitness in the case told officers that she observed a late model black sedan leaving the UVM campus just moments before the explosion.

She believed the vehicle was a Saab or perhaps a BMW but couldn't be sure. She is certain that it had New York plates. She was pretty far from the car as it exited a parking lot at the rear of the campus but as far as she could tell, it looked like it had one male occupant. More to come."

Ben turned off the radio. "Big deal," he thought, "there are probably a million black, imported cars in New York." He pulled the key from the ignition and climbed out. As he walked in the back door, the smell of the fertilizer hit him right in the throat. He thought he would be used to it by now with all the close up work he has been doing with it. It smelled different at home but he didn't know why.

He woke up the computer screen and signed in. He was officially on the clock now. He was hoping for a busy day so that the time would go by faster. He was excited about his date. He couldn't remember ever making a first date. They were always impromptu, hook up deals. He wasn't troubled by this approach but the waiting was harder.

"Ben, customer needs assistance in aisle twelve." The call in the headset startled him.

"I'm on it," he responded. Aisle twelve was just a few steps from where he was. He left his area and into the store. He just about ran into her.

"Excuse me," he said, as they bumped lightly.

"Oh, I'm sorry, I didn't see you coming," said the lady.

"Hey, I know you, you were in here yesterday with a friend."

"Yes, I was. It's Ben, right?"

"That's me," he said as he pointed to his name tag.

"Yes, well, I asked the young girl up front and she sent me back here."

"I'm glad she did, how can I help you?"

Mary thought he was a handsome young man. He caught her attention the last time, but she was looking a little harder now that Sara wasn't there to observe. There was something about him that threw her off balance. He was young and handsome but there was something else. He was a little cocky, a touch over-confident maybe. His banter had sexual overtones that both frightened her and excited her as well.

"My husband sent me in to have some keys made. I understand you're the guy who can do that."

"Yes ma'am, that and a whole lot more."

"There it is. He's doing it now," she thought. She let this one go.

"Good then, I need four reproductions of this particular key." She held the key out to him.

He reached for the key and made sure that his hand contacted her skin. He smiled as he pulled the key away.

"This will take a few minutes," he said. "Would you like to shop around or stay and watch me work?"

"There it is again. This guy is full of himself," she said to herself. She thought it would be best if she let him do his work without distraction.

"I'll have a look around. I'll be back in ten minutes; will that be enough time?"

"Ten minutes in kind of quick, don't you think? I usually like to take my time." Ben said.

She knew exactly what he was talking about this time. "I don't know what he sees in a woman my age.." she stopped herself. Just yesterday she was admiring her looks. She turned her husband on more in the last few days than she had in the past ten years. She was worthy of his attention, but why did she want it? Did she want it? She was confused, she was happier in her marriage now than almost ever. She even acknowledged that verbally to Sara just yesterday.

This was just a foolish woman headed toward middle age having a flirty moment with a young man. She didn't want him, she was just feeling good about herself and accepting a little attention.

"But that is why you came here, to this store," she heard her inner voice say. "Maybe, she answered herself, "but I didn't really want anything to happen, this kid is closer to Jack's age than mine!"

She didn't even know where in the store she was. She had been looking at things but could not remember a single one of them.

"What's the matter with a man Jack's age?" that inner voice asked again.

She couldn't answer that. She looped around the store and headed back toward the key department. He was still working at it; she could hear that little cutting machine grinding away. She stepped up to the desk slowly trying not to alarm him. He turned off the grinder, removed his goggles and looked at her.

"Good timing," he said, "did you find anything else you would like today?"

Mary could feel herself blush.

"I think I have everything I need for this trip."

"Very well, how would you like to pay for that?"

He stared straight into her eyes. He seemed to be waiting for her to say,

"Can we take it out in trade?"

She hoped she was just thinking that and didn't actually say it. He was still staring.

She turned her eyes to her purse and pulled out a credit card. She handed it to him and again, he made sure their skin touched.

He swiped the card, made two copies of the receipt, and asked her to sign.

"Thank you, Mary." He handed her the card, her copy of the receipt and a small bag containing the keys.

"If you have any trouble with those, just let me know, I'll make it right."

"You have been very kind, Ben. Thank you."

Mary turned and almost ran for the door.

Ben folded his copy of the receipt and placed the fifth copy of the key inside. He placed a piece of clear tape over the edge to seal it and placed it in his pocket. All in all, a pretty good start of his shift.

He looked at the receipt again. Mary Webster, that name seemed familiar.

"Ben, customer needs help in bed," he heard in his headset.

Chapter 24

Bill's phone was ringing. It wasn't the best time but he noticed it was Greg calling.

"Excuse me guys, I'm sorry but I need to take this call." Bill excused himself from the table.

"Hello, Greg."

"HI Bill, how is going up there?"

"I think we're making progress, it's hard to see the forest from the trees, but I feel like we're finally getting close to something."

"That's great. Have you been paying attention to the news at all?"

"I haven't had much chance today, what's up?"

"Vermont State Police have verified an eyewitness report of a vehicle leaving the scene just before the explosion. A small black import, late model with a single male occupant."

"Did they see the plate?" Bill asked.

"Only enough to know they were from New York."

"That's a start," Bill said.

"So, tell me what happening on your end." Greg requested.

"I'm reviewing security cam video footage as we speak. There are a few mounted cameras near and around the science lab but so far, we haven't found anything. I have some other ideas though; I just need time to check them out."

"What is Richard up to?"

"I think he's out in the quad telling all the young girls he's a gynecologist and showing them his cigar."

"That sounds about right."

"He is actually, going through all the orders and deliveries from and to the science building. "I haven't spoken to him since around 11:30 this morning," Bill answered.

"Well, keep up the good work. Make sure you look for a small black car when you're reviewing footage."

"Will do, chief."

"Oh, one more thing, Albany forensics has some fragments of the bomb. The housing was made of PVC."

"PVC?" That seems a little odd."

"That's what Russ Lane said as well."

"Ok Bill, I'll check in again later." Greg said and hung up.

Bill returned to the security guys and told them about the small black import. They continued to roll the tape.

In the admin building, Richard was sitting in front of a computer, scrolling through digital orders and receipts. He required a little help learning his way around the screen and the keyboard. He was glad the hospital had forced the physicians to use a computer, otherwise, he wouldn't know shit about them.

He was returning to his search of the cadavers. There were six different suppliers for the twenty four corpses they received. His first review could account for twenty-three of them. He was sure he made a mistake so he went on to look at other purchases and deliveries for the same time period looking for anything that would have been near the cadavers. He came up empty.

On his second review, he still came up one cadaver short. The lab listed twenty four bodies on the tables but Richard could only find twenty-three deliveries that matched up with orders. He was going to have to find someone who could help him. He walked back to the purchasing office but they had already left for the day. The only other place he knew was the provost office.

He found his way back there and discovered Shelly still working at her desk. He explained the situation to her and she seemed very willing to help him. Her shift ended in twenty minutes, after which she would be happy to meet him in the space where he was working.

Richard went for a walk outside while he waited. He moved away from the building before lighting up his cigar. The sun was just about at its peak for this time of year. It got cooler earlier this far north and the air felt a bit thinner. Summer was his favorite time of the year. It wasn't always that way.

Summers in the Bronx were not only hot, but they were also dirty. He was never meant for city life; it didn't suit him. Even as a child he dreamed of getting out of there. There was a noticeable absence of breathable air and what air there was, smelled different. That much concrete, brick and asphalt seemed to create an atmosphere of its own. The small amounts of green areas were difficult to get to and usually packed with people who each seemed to own at least five dogs.

From a young age, he knew what he had to do and he knew it wouldn't be easy. As hard as the public schools were trying to offer a good education, the growing failure of keeping economic balance was making it impossible. The longer families stayed, the poorer they became.

Falling in with the wrong crowd was easy in a place like this. He didn't want any part of it but sometimes if it wanted you, that was enough. He was a good student and that would be his ticket out. Humor was his ticket to survival. He learned early that being funny could keep him from getting his ass kicked. The trick was using that tool appropriately, never in class and never around the people that could grease the skids for him down the road.

It served him well over the years, although as an adult it was harder to control and truthfully, he didn't care. He paid his dues. He brushed the ashes off the half smoked cigar and headed back inside. He made sure to take a few deep breaths of that fresh, cool mountain air that most folks around here probably took for granted.

Shelly was just getting ready to turn off the lights when Richard returned. "I'm ready, Dr. Ingraham." Richard backed into the hall and waited for Shelly to lock the door.

"So, what office are you working out of?" she asked.

"I've never been very good at remembering directions or following them for that matter but I can find my way back there," he assured her. "How long have you been working here, Shelly?"

"I'm just starting my third year," she responded.

"And do you enjoy the work?"

"I do, most days'" she followed.

"I can tell you from many years of experience that every job has its bad days. The key is to let them slip by and don't go back looking for them. It's water under the bridge," he offered.

"It's never about the work," she said, "it's the attitudes of some people that ruins the day. I like being here for the students and I can handle most of the faculty but there a couple of 'pains in the ass' that I find hard to tolerate. Pardon my French."

"Gee," Richard said, "I have been able to speak French all these years and never even knew it. I'm guessing it's Helen."

"How would you know that?" she stated with amazement.

"I guess I've learned how to read people over the years. When I come across one, I either ignore them, avoid them, or kill them."

Shelly stopped walking and stared at him.

"Alright, I exaggerate sometimes. If it's bad enough, maybe you should look into a transfer. Is that possible?"

"It is, and I've thought about but I feel like I would be quitting. I should be able to handle it." She sounded a bit defeated.

"You're young and you may not realize it yet, but life is short. If someone isn't treating you right, you need to move on. Just dust off your shoes and move on. Sometimes making a hard decision, even when it doesn't feel right, can wind up being the best move you'll ever make. My advice is don't spend any more time around assholes than is absolutely necessary."

"I like you Richard, you remind me of my father."

"He must be a great man!"

"He is," she said proudly.

They made their way back to the makeshift office that Richard was assigned. Shelly re-traced Richards steps and came to the same conclusion, twenty-four bodies and twenty-three receipts.

"There is obviously some problem here," she stated, "let me work on this for a while this evening. Is there a number where I can reach you once I figure it out?"

"I appreciate that, Shelly. I will be staying in town tonight so let me give you my mobile number."

Chapter 25

It was almost 6 pm when Bill and Richard met back at the car. They were both tired.

"You ever feel like you're getting too old for this stuff?" Richard asked.

"Most days, I feel like I'm too old to get out of bed, but I still do," Bill responded. "I just wish I had someone to get up for. Since Sadie passed a few years back, the drive just isn't there like it used to be."

Richard sat quietly. He was thinking about Marilyn and what a wonderful life they have. He couldn't imagine being without her even though they spent a good portion of their days going in different directions.

"I'm sorry, Bill, that must be hard."

"Most days, I keep myself busy enough to not notice much. It's at the end of the day, the quiet before bed, and in the morning that I really miss her. I can't get used to waking up and not seeing her beside me or hearing her stirring in the kitchen. She was my anchor. I couldn't always see her but I knew she was there, keeping me from drifting away."

"Isn't it ironic," Richard began, "when we're young, guys refer to their spouse as an anchor, the old ball and chain, but later in life, those terms take on a whole new meaning. They are the constant in a rapidly changing world."

"I know one thing," Bill said. "If I could do it over, I would retire a whole lot earlier, travel more, walk hand in hand more, make love more."

"You mean while most of your parts still worked?" Richard joked.

"That too, my friend. Now before we have dinner, you make sure to give Marilyn a call."

"I'm going to do just that, Bill. Let's go back to the hotel. Richard started the car and they left the campus. When they reached the intersection of Broad Street, Bill noticed the camera mounted on the storage facility across the street once again. He took out his notepad.

Chapter 26

Greg, Mary, and the girls had just sat down to dinner. Mary had made chicken parmesan and pasta, one of the kid's favorites. She needed to do something to bury the shame she felt from her encounter at the hardware store. She told herself nothing happened, it was just innocent fun, but she didn't believe herself. Pounding chicken breasts into cutlets seemed to be a good way to vent.

"So, how was everyone's day?" This was always Greg's way of breaking the ice.

Nobody said a word. Par for the course. He tried again.

"Come on, someone go first. I'm sure something interesting happened to one of you."

"My day was pretty ordinary, Dad, typical stuff like class, homework, dismissal," Jocelyn opened it up.

"Jillian, how about you?"

"Let's see, I got married in first period, had sex in second period and delivered a baby on the bus on the way home."

"There, you see, that wasn't so tough. Was this your own baby or someone else's? I get that you girls think talking about your day is boring, but we are interested in what you're doing. I mean school just started for the year, surely some things have changed. Any new teachers, new students, hunky transfers from other schools?"

Mary was barely paying attention. She couldn't shake the feeling that she had somehow been unfaithful.

"How about you're day, Mary? Anything fun happen?"

"My day was typical too dear, nothing real exciting. Oh, I did have the four new keys made as you suggested."

"Great, I'm sure that was exciting!" he joked.

"About as exciting as a trip to the hardware store can be. A true statement," she thought.

"I just want to say that I think it's important for a family to talk to each other. I remember being your age and thinking how awkward it was to talk to my parents, but it doesn't need to be that way. We need you to trust that you can talk to us about anything without fear of judgement or retribution." Greg said.

"Can this really just be coincidental?" Mary thought. "It's as if he's talking directly to me."

"That's all I'll say for now. If anyone wants to talk, I'm listening. Otherwise, I'm going to tell you about my day."

No one spoke up.

"There may be a little progress in the school bombings. I spoke with the Albany office today and it appears they have a couple leads. Not necessarily case crackers but leads none the less. I should also be getting a report from Dr. Ingraham and Bill Dillon later this evening."

"Do you think it's all over now, Dad?" Jocelyn asked.

"I hope so honey. If the attacker is local to that area, it could well be over. I guess time will tell."

Just then, the phone rang. Mary answered.

"Yes, he's right here, John, hold on."

Mary passed the phone to Greg. "John Shand," she said.

"I think I'll take it in the den, Mary."

Greg left the table.

"Hello, John, what's going on?"

"Hi Greg, I hope I didn't interrupt your dinner."

"We were just finishing up, John, your timing is perfect."

"Greg, this may be nothing more than trivia for the future but I thought I would run it by you."

"Sure, shoot, John."

"The medical staff database we have been checking turned up one doctor in City's history who went to both Plattsburgh and the University of Vermont. Do you want to make a guess?"

Greg thought about it. It was there somewhere but he just couldn't pull it out.

"I'm going to give up, John."

"Kyle Seike."

Greg was silent, just the mention of that name sent a chill up his spine.

"Wow! There is a name I didn't expect."

"Nor did I, Greg. Didn't I just read that he died?"

"Yes, it was in the paper about two, maybe three weeks ago. He died in prison, I think."

"Then I guess it's just coincidence," John added.

"I can't see any immediate connection but I also know not to ignore any facts. I'll think about that for a while." Greg said.

"Have you heard anything from the 'odd couple'," John asked.

"Not since this afternoon. I expect they'll call before the night is over unless they stay out late, tying one on at my expense."

"Seriously," John responded, "I don't see these guys being able to stay awake much past nine."

"You're probably right. If I hear anything, I'll let you know."

Greg ended the call with John. He couldn't stop thinking about the Kyle Seike connection to Plattsburgh and UVM. He remembered asking Dr. Seike about his education the first time he interviewed him in the morgue. He remembered because he sensed that Seike's demeanor changed when Greg asked that question, like "how dare you question my credentials?" He knew there was no way he could be involved with this. He was in prison for one thing and he was now dead, for another.

As long as Greg was in the den, he decided to do some research on SUNY Plattsburgh. He jumped on the computer and searched the university. He found pages of results but clicked on the main website for the school. He was primarily interested in the medical programs. He was somewhat surprised at what he found.

While the school offered no doctorate programs in medicine, it did provide pathways to a variety of medical fields, including everything from research to physical therapy. It was a self-proclaimed leader in preparatory B.S. degrees that would enhance an applicant's attractiveness to schools of medicine, pharmacy, laboratory, physical therapy, physician extender and countless others.

Greg found it interesting that an anatomy lab on a campus without a medical school would have twenty-four cadavers at one time. He didn't believe that most medical schools had access to that many. He would make a mental note to call the school and make some inquiries. Suddenly, Greg was more confused about a possible connection between the first and second bombing. One medical school and one pre-med program. It was beginning to look like proximity was the common factor.

Greg returned to the kitchen but everyone was gone. Judging by the lights that were on outdoors, the girls had gone to the tree house. He stood at the foot of the stairs and listened. No music or other sound coming from the second floor. He started back toward the kitchen and heard the faint sound of water running inside the pipes and inside the walls. He walked back to the stairs and climbed them.

It wasn't coming from the kid's bathroom off the hall so it had to be in the master bathroom. He walked around the foot of the bed and to the bathroom door. Mary was in the shower. He was a little surprised by this, Mary was a morning shower person. They were exceptions of course, like after gardening on a hot day. The shower was glass enclosed on two sides offering a great view of the occupant.

The walls were just steamy enough for Greg to get close without being noticed. He stood quietly and admired his wife. He thought she was more beautiful now than when they met. He didn't want to frighten her and he felt a little creepy just watching so he backed out of the bath and called her name.

"I'm in the shower," she answered.

Greg re-entered the room.

"I can see that," he said. "Is there room for two?" he asked.

"Actually, I'm ready to get out," she said as she turned off the water.

"Story of my life," he said, "a day late and a dollar short."

"Actually, you're only a few seconds late and a couple hundred dollars short," she said seductively.

"Oh really," Greg said, "is that what we've come to? What do I get for two hundred," he asked?

"The same thing you get for free but I'm two hundred ahead."

"Oh, the iniquity!" Greg replied.

Mary stepped out the shower with a towel wrapped around her.

"I'll give you twenty to drop the towel."

"I don't know," Mary said, "I already turned the mailman down at fifty."

"Fifty!" Greg exclaimed. "No wonder postage keeps going up!"

Mary approached Greg who was now sitting on the edge of the bed.

"How about if I let you have it for free?" She dropped the towel. He put his arms around her and kissed her breasts which were level with his lips.

"It sounds good to me," he mumbled.

"It's not polite to speak with your mouth full," she scolded.

Just then, they both heard the back door close. Mary ran to the closet to get her robe. Greg sat nonchalantly at the edge of the bed.

"Hi Dad, where's Mom?" Jillian asked.

"She's in the closet," Greg answered.

"Why?" Jocelyn asked.

"I put her in time out."

"Why?" Jocelyn asked again.

"She threw her wet towel on the floor," Greg said parentally.

"I don't understand adults," Jocelyn said as she walked out of the bedroom.

"You shouldn't even bother to try," Jillian said as she followed her sister out.

"Why are you still in there, Mary?"

"Because my robe is over by the shower. Can you hand it to me?"

"Do I have to?" asked Greg.

"Only if you ever want to see this body again," she answered.

"Jillian was right, sex is currency."

The phone rang just once. "Dad, it's for you!" Jillian shouted.

"Okay honey, I'll take it downstairs." Greg grabbed the robe and handed it to Mary.

Chapter 27

"Hello!" Greg answered.

"Greg, it's Richard, did I catch you in the middle of sex?"

"What? No!" Greg objected.

"See Bill, I told you he wasn't getting any. Did you want to talk to him about something else?"

Bill grabbed the phone from Richard. "Hey, for an assistant, you're getting pretty ballsy!" Richard added.

"Greg, sorry about that, I guess it's past this four year old's bedtime. The next time, I'm charging you a babysitting rate on top of expenses. Let me put the phone on speaker so we can both hear you. Are you still there?"

"Yes, Bill, I'm here," Greg responded.

"Here is what we have so far. Richard worked all day looking at orders and receipts for cadavers. He discovered a discrepancy. Their records indicate they had twenty-four bodies but only have receipts for twenty-three."

"That's right, Greg," Richard interrupted, "I checked several times myself and I also had Shelly take a look. We are one body over."

"Who is Shelly?" Greg asked.

"Shelly is the nice girl we met from the provost's office," Richard replied.

"Does she have any suspicious moles?" Greg joked.

"Not that she showed me." Richard responded.

"Okay, so we're missing a delivery record for one body. It could be a clue. What else do you have?"

"I reviewed all the video from the campus security cameras," Bill answered this time, "there was no evidence of the black car anywhere but we did find one camera that was not recording."

"Let me guess," Greg said, "it was the one watching the exit."

"That would be correct. We checked the camera and it had clearly been tampered with. I have one more lead I'm following up on in the morning. I do have some good news to report," Bill said happily, "one of the emergency telephone locations may have caught a glimpse of our guy. Usually, these stations just have a light and a phone box but the ones on this campus have cameras as well."

"That's ingenious!" Greg stated, "are you able to make a photo of it?"

"The camera only captured a portion of his face but I think we have enough to approximate his height, build and hair color," Bill replied.

"That's great! Bill, if you can send that to me, I'll forward it on to the agencies."

"So, let's talk about next steps. Bill, you keep working the image angle and Richard, we need to find out where that twenty fourth body came from. Also, John made a connection from our medical staff to Plattsburgh and UVM. Kyle Seike attended both schools. I know it doesn't mean much but it's worth checking it out. Richard, do you think Shelly can help you dig around in that sandbox?"

"I'm not sure how much access she has but I know she would be willing to help. I'll be checking in with her in the morning, Greg."

"Greg, it's Bill again, we need to be at UVM by noon tomorrow so we will be wrapping up here by ten and then heading over. We'll contact you when we're done with our meetings there. I'll get that image out to you right away."

"Sounds good, thanks guys, we'll talk soon."

Greg was gone. Bill and Richard looked at each other. "Nightcap?" Bill suggested.

Chapter 28

The shoppers had cleared out by 7:45 and the other two associates had counted and closed their registers before 8:00. It was now 8:08 and the farmer's daughter would be arriving any minute. Ben was nervous. He had felt a degree of anxiousness all evening but now, he was full blown nervous. He was amazed at how much more comfortable he felt when the meetings were spontaneous.

He didn't have any real plan, except to wait and see what she suggested. He did manage to have the flowers ready for her. It was almost dark when Ben saw the headlights wash the inside of the store with light. He watched the car pull toward the back door and moved in that direction.

He waited for her to knock and then unlocked the door. When the door swung open, she was standing a few feet back and the halogen lamp mounted above the door painted her in an angelic wash of light that softly blurred her outline. Her mid-length strawberry blonde hair appeared to be tied back. She was wearing khaki colored shorts that were snug but not extremely short, brown sandals and a white top that was mostly sleeveless and was long enough to cover the top of her shorts.

"Please come in," Ben said, You're right on time."

"Hey cowboy," she smiled. She had a bag in her hand. "I brought a few things just in case you haven't had dinner." "That's very thoughtful, thank you!"

"My pleasure, Ben. Was it a difficult shift?"

"I'm not sure I can say that I have ever had a difficult shift, some are just busier than others. Tonight, was a lighter one."

"Before we continue," Ben said, "I would like to know your name. I can't bear to think of you as just the farmer's daughter any longer. I know your last name is Chalmers and I've been playing this game in my mind all day to guess what first name would seem like a natural fit. You know, how you hear names and they just fit?"

"So, let's continue the game for a while. Tell what you came up with?"

"Would you like to sit down?" he offered. They were still in the back office section by the key machine. There were three chairs in that area. They chose the two closest together.

"Alright, these aren't in any order, I'll just throw them out as I think of them. The first is Candi, probably short for Candice. I like the double 'C' of the first and last name. Next would be Charlotte, again the double 'C' and it's close to your father's first name of Charles. Maybe they even call you 'Charlie.' Miranda comes to mind next, not sure why except that the three syllable first name balances the two syllable last name. Laura came to mind as well, it just sounds like a farmer's daughter name, I guess. Let me know if I'm getting close."

"I will but if you're getting tired of this game, I'll just tell you."

"Another minute, did I have any of the reasoning right?" he asked.

"Yes, it is three syllables."

"Okay, good clue. It's not Tabitha, Emily, or Bethany, I don't think."
I'll give you one more clue," she offered, "it begins with 'P'."

Ben thought long and hard this time. Pamela, Petula,.." His brain froze, he couldn't think of anymore three syllable 'P' names. He was ready to concede...

"Priscilla! He shouted out. There was silence.

"You are pretty amazing, Ben, you got it!"

"Priscilla," he thought, "seems a little feminine for a farmer," he joked. "That's a beautiful name for a beautiful girl. Actually, it sounds like a movie star's name, Priscilla Chalmers."

"It sounds like an old movie star's name," she replied.

"I like the old movie stars; they were built differently then. Today they choose women who are too thin, they look gaunt. Back then they looked normal, healthy, they had full thighs, they were voluptuous!" Ben exclaimed.

"So which category do I belong in, Ben?"

"You are definitely in the latter. Actually, I'll create a new category just for you, perfect!"

"You are very kind, thank you. The full figure look is a result of hard work on the farm. I wasn't supposed to be a farmer, it just turned out that way."

"What are you supposed to be?" Ben inquired.

"When I was younger, I had dreams of being an artist. I'm not sure which modality I would have fit into, but I felt I belonged somewhere in the art world."

"So, what happened that stole your dream, Priscilla?"

"My mom died. I was fourteen and I had two older sisters. They were close enough to finishing school that they were able to move on but being the last one home, I felt like I needed to stay. I couldn't leave my father all alone to run the farm and care for himself. He's a good man and he deserved better."

"I'm sorry, Priscilla," Ben said empathetically.

"Thanks. I'm not complaining really, it's not what I expected but it's honest, important work and I enjoy it. I have only nature's clock controlling me and I believe that's more liberating than working for some stranger."

"I am sure you're right," Ben said. "Alright, now that I know what to call you, what's in the bag, Priscilla?"

"Just some homemade biscuits with honey butter, sharp cheese from our dairy and some chocolate milk. A meal fit for a king!" She giggled.

"I couldn't come up with a more perfect menu if I tried," Ben said.

"I have an idea," he said, I think we should have a picnic right here in the store. I have some moving blankets we can throw down on the floor, I have camping pillows and battery operated lanterns and I even have a radio! What do you say?"

"I love it," she replied.

Ben went off to get the supplies while Priscilla unpacked the bag. When he had gathered things together, he created a secluded little spot in the camping isle. When it was all set, he went back for Priscilla.

She had found a couple trays in the back office space and used them to set up the food. She had remembered to bring a tablecloth, cutlery and napkins and the trays looked country formal.

"All set on my end," Ben said when he arrived. "Wow! This looks great!"

He was looking at the spread she had created. He went to the back of the space and turned off all the interior lights. He turned on his flashlight and said, "follow me." As he grabbed one of the trays, Priscilla picked up the other tray and followed him. Ben kept winding through the aisles, taking the longest way back possible to make it feel like they were moving deeper into the wilderness.

When they arrived at the site, Priscilla was amazed at what he had done. With just the glow of the camping lamps, she would no longer know that she was inside the building. The radio was turned very low and tuned to a station that played country classics. George Jones was singing "He stopped loving her today."

"This is unbelievable, Ben, you are so creative."

"I've had a lot of practice, I used to set up forts and camps in my room all the time."

"Did you have brothers to play with?" Pricilla asked.

"No, I'm an only child."

"That must have been lonely at times," she said.

"I've spent a fair amount of my life alone but I'm not complaining either. You make the best of what you have, right?"

"That's right," she said as she poured the milk into the glasses. Ben had set up a small round wire mesh table and two matching chairs near the blanket. Priscilla couldn't tell in the low light but Ben had inflated an air mattress and covered it with the blanket.

"I thought it might be more comfortable to sit at the table to eat. Then we can lay down and look up at the stars if you wish," he suggested.

Priscilla looked up toward the ceiling to find that Ben had opened a package of stick on, glow in the dark stars and placed them above the campsite. She was blown away. Ben held her chair as she sat. When he had taken his own chair, she handed him a glass of chocolate milk.

"A toast," she said. "To two lonely kids who will not be alone tonight. Cheers!"

They clicked glasses and Ben felt something he never had before.

"Cheers," he repeated.

Chapter 29

Greg had just received the email from Bill that contained the image. It showed most of the height of the suspect except for the top part of his head. His face was only half visible and a good portion of that was out of focus due to motion. He was obviously walking quickly as he passed the camera. The text from Bill that accompanied the photo explained that considering the angle of the shot and the height of the camera location, Bill guessed the male was between five-eleven and six-one. He was thin but not skinny maybe around one-hundred and sixty-five pounds. His hair looked dark brown to black.

He sent the image from the computer to the wireless printer. In a few seconds, the printer came to life and pushed out a full size copy. The enlargement blurred the features even more so he decided to just send the file to the various agencies and let them try to enhance it. He created a new email to his contacts at each agency, embedded the image and hit the send button. It was now out of his hands.

He put the computer in sleep mode and turned off the lights. He left the printed copy on the desk and made his way upstairs. It looked like Mary was asleep already so without turning on the lights, he made his way to the bathroom and closed the door. He washed up and brushed his teeth. He emptied his bladder one last time, washed his hands, turned off the light and opened the door.

The was a dull light on somewhere in the bedroom and he could hear music but ever so faintly. Looking toward the bed, it appeared that Mary had gotten up. Maybe she went to use the other bathroom, he thought. Then he looked toward the closet.

He could only make out Mary's silhouette standing in front of it. As his eyes adjusted to the darkness, she became more visible. She was now moving slowly toward him. He stepped forward toward the bed. She came closer and he could detect a hint of perfume. When she was three feet away, he could see that she had on a shimmery garment. He could see the moonlight reflecting off of it. He watched the curves of her torso and she continued to move slowly toward him.

She was almost close enough to touch now but she stopped, allowing him to take in the entire view. He couldn't say what color it was for sure but he could see her cleavage extend the full length of her chest. It was lacey at the edges and the legs were cut high on the sides revealing the smooth beauty of her thighs.

She reached out a hand to him and pulled him closer. When they were just a foot apart, she took both of his hand and placed them on her breasts. He felt the silkiness of the material under his fingers but in his palms, he felt her naked warmth..

Her bare nipples protruded proudly through the open fabric. He moved his hands slowly across her chest to get a sense of what she was wearing. As he moved his hand outward, he could fell her naked nipples under his thumbs.

He brought his finger and thumb together on each side and pinched gently. She let out a sigh and tipped her head back. He seized the opportunity and kissed the front of her neck, his hands still in place, squeezing just a little harder.

He was still working his way around her neck when he slowly removed one hand from her breast. Working his way down the side of her abdomen, he could feel the softness of the material. When he reached the bottom he expected to feel the cool texture of her thigh but it was still a silky material.

He kept going, moving his one hand lower down her leg while keeping a firm grip on her breast with the other.

He realized what he was feeling now. She had panty hose on underneath the other garment. This was something new. His other hand left her breast and made its way south.

For the first time, he was aware of his own state of excitement. He turned slightly to her side so that he could press himself against her thigh without blocking the work of his hands.

He brought his hand back up her leg moving to the inside of her thigh. As he got higher, she separated her legs just enough to allow him passage. He arrived at his destination expecting to find a nylon blockade. He couldn't have been more wrong, or more pleased. His hand found her soft wet opening and he entered slowly.

She pushed against him, letting him know that she wanted more. He let her set the pace which she was happy to do. She quickly reached her first orgasm. When she regained her composure, she moved Greg to the bed. Sitting him down at the end of the bed, she pushed him back and began to undress him. As if performing an exotic dance, she slowly and gracefully undressed him.

With her husband totally naked and still lying at the foot of the bed, she climbed up and straddled him. Without a word, she slid down the length of him.

"You are so beautiful tonight, Greg whispered, "what did I do to deserve this?" he asked.

"Everything," she replied. "

When they were finished and were facing each other, exhausted from their lovemaking, Greg said, "it looks like you went shopping again."

"This old thing?" she joked. "I've had this for a few days now. I picked it up earlier in the week when I went shopping with Sara."

"I really like it!" Greg exclaimed. "And I really love you."

"I love you too, Greg, and I'm sorry if I ever let you forget that."

"I always know I am loved, darling, I just wish that I could do these special things for you. It always seems to be about the women dressing seductively to please her man. I hope you know that I would do anything for you," he said sincerely.

"I know," said Mary, and I'm glad you feel that way."

"Really?"

"Yes, because the next time, you get to wear this outfit! It's not the most comfortable thing in the world. But I did enjoy doing it for you."

"Does that mean this is the end for that garment?" he asked.

"No, it just means that we have to try all the others first."

"Others?" Greg said excitedly. "How many others?"

"You will see my dear. You will see."

Mary and Greg held each other tight and fell asleep.

Chapter 30

Ben and Priscilla had been talking for almost three hours. After their light picnic style dinner, they moved the table and relaxed onto the air mattress. The conversation just moved from one topic to another with ease. They shared some laughs. Priscilla shed a few tears but the highs and lows were all experienced in a state of total comfort. Neither had ever felt this comfortable before.

There was a pause and Priscilla looked at her watch.

"Wow, it's eleven o'clock already," she said. "I can't believe it! Where did the time go?"

"I don't know," Ben agreed, "it seems like you just got here. Do you need to go?"

"I'm afraid I do, Ben. I don't want to, I'm having a wonderful time but I need to be up before five in the morning to start my chores."

"I understand. Can we do this again?" Ben asked.

"I would love to, perhaps we can begin earlier the next time." Priscilla suggested.

"Yes, of course, I usually work just two or three late shifts a week. How about next week? I think I have the early shift on Tuesday."

"That would be fine. You wouldn't have any time this weekend, would you?" she asked.

"I'm sorry, Priscilla, I work one or two weekends a month in Boston and unfortunately, this is my weekend to work."

"Of course, the supply place you told me about, Willi's place," she said, excited to remember his name.

"You're a good listener. And a great speaker and you're not too hard to look at either."

"You didn't even get a chance to guess the color of my underwear!" she said, disappointedly.

"I don't even want to think about that as you're about to walk out the door. Can I get a raincheck?"

"Absolutely, we can start with that the next time," she offered.

"Tuesday then," he confirmed. "Would three o'clock work?"

"Yes, I'll ask my dad for a couple hours off, he won't mind."

"Excellent, let me walk you out to your car," Ben offered.

"Let me help you pick up a little bit first," Priscilla responded.

"Thank you but no, you need to get home and get some sleep. It will take me five minutes to clean up."

Ben helped her up. She packed up her picnic supplies and walked with Ben to the back door. He walked her to her car, helped her pack the things away and opened her door.

"Ben, I can't remember when I have had a better time. A girl could fall for a guy like you, cowboy!"

"One can hope," he said and leaned toward her to kiss her. Her lips were soft, full, and seemed happy to meet his. It was long and tender.

"Until Tuesday," she said softly.

"Tuesday," he smiled. "Be careful driving home."

Ben closed her door and she drove off. He needed to get going as well. He decided to leave tonight and drive until he became sleepy. He changed his mind about the route. He would head west to Ilion on NY Rt. 5s. From there he could pick up Rt. 28 south to I-88 which turns into I-81 near Binghamton. He could follow that to just south of Scranton, Pa. and grab I-476 directly into Philadelphia.

The traffic at this time of night would be negligible. If he slept for just an hour or two, he could be there before the sun was up. That would give him time to canvas the area first and make any adjustments. A little after 10am, he would be back on the road and back home by late afternoon. That would still give him a day to get ready for Boston.

Chapter 31

Richard was awake, showered, dressed, and packed before 8am. He looked around the room one last time, grabbed his wheelable suitcase and walked out. He took the elevator down to the lobby and walked toward the restaurant to meet Bill.

Bill saw him walk in and waved. "Good morning," Bill said as Richard approached. "How did you sleep?"

"Good morning, Bill, I slept like a rock. I think it was that Manhattan I had before bed."

"Which one, the first, second or third?" Bill asked.

"You know, they came so fast, I count it all as the first," Richard responded.

"How about you, Bill? Sleep well?"

"I had a little trouble falling asleep but that's nothing new. After that, I slept fine. I am ready to face the day."

"Listen Richard, I would like to run by that storage place on Broad before we go back to the school. We should be able to have breakfast and get over there in plenty of time."

"Would you mind dropping me off first at the Administration building?" Shelly agreed to meet me at 9:00."

The waitress came by to take their order. They both started with black coffee. Bill ordered two eggs over easy and dry toast. Richard asked for the special which was two eggs, 2 pancakes, two strips of bacon and two sausages.

"You forgot the gravy, Richard." he said as he looked around the room.

"What are you looking for? The restrooms are over there." Richard pointed over his shoulder.

"I was trying to find the resuscitation equipment in case you keel over before you finish breakfast."

"Very funny, Bill, maybe you can get a regular gig here as a standup. I'm a doctor, I know what I'm doing. Besides, I'm not sure how much longer I want to stick around. This world is screwed up in case you haven't noticed."

"Oh, I've noticed. You're right. I apologize. You should get all the enjoyment you can out of life."

"Thank you, that means a lot coming from a firecracker like you."

The breakfast came and they ate quickly. One of the few things guys this age can still do quickly. They paid the check, checked out and walked to the parking lot. Bill dropped Richard off as requested then drove across Broad Street and pulled up to the office of the storage facility. The neon OPEN sign was blinking.

He stepped up to the desk. There was no one there but behind the desk, the entire wall was covered with TV screens showing scenes from the security cameras. Every five seconds, the images changed. His eyes were darting back and forth trying to catch a captured image that was facing Broad. He couldn't keep up with them.

The door behind the counter opened and a young man in a uniform came through.

"Can I help you," he asked.

"I hope so, my name is Bill Dillon and I'm a consultant working with the FBI, State Police, Homeland Security and the University, investigating the recent bombing."

"Do you have any identification, Mr. Dillon?"

Bill pulled out his license, military ID, and the pass he was given at the school. The kid behind the desk looked it all over then said, "How can I help?"

"I was wondering if any of your security cameras face Broad Street. I have been looking at your images here but they're moving so quickly I can't keep up."

"No problem, Mr. Dillon, come on back in the office and we'll see what we can do."

"Thanks, Luke," that was the name on his shirt. "You can call me Bill." The men disappeared behind the same door Luke walked out of just a few minutes ago.

Richard and Shelly were in his makeshift office. Shelly was working on the computer, looking for any records for Kyle Seike. While she was busy looking, Richard was watching Shelly work. "You really know your way around a keyboard," he said. "Kids today have it made. At three, I was playing with rattles and maybe a few building blocks. Today by three, you guys have your first Cisco certification. I'm really impressed."

"Thank you, Dr. Ingraham. The problem is that there are like a hundred million of us that can do this."

"That may be true, but no one seems to be having trouble finding a job in the field. And please, call me Richard."

"I will try, Richard but it feels like me calling my dad by his first name."

"You're a good daughter, Shelly."

"Hey, while you're doing that and I'm pretty much doing nothing, let me ask you something. Were you able to find anything more on the twenty-fourth cadaver?"

"I'm afraid not, but I did make an itemized list of the others." She pulled a sheet of paper out of her backpack.

"Across the top, you will see the six sources of the bodies. Down the left side is the donor's name and age and inside the grid, you will find what date the body arrived and who delivered them. Behind the top page you will find a copy of the individual delivery slip with specific information such as supplier or funeral home phone number and the contact information for all the delivery services."

"Shelly, this is superb work, how long were you here last night?"

"Don't you worry about that, Richard; it has been interesting and a pleasure to assist you."

"That's very nice of you, Shelly." Richard felt emotionally vulnerable. "I want to adopt you," he said.

"Oh, that's sweet," she replied "but having two fathers to keep track of my whereabouts is probably more than I can handle. However, you can never have enough friends, right?"

"You are absolutely right. You have a friend for life."

Shelly stopped typing. "That's it, I'm at the end."

"The end of what?" Richard asked.

"The end of the search. I have scoured these pages looking for anything regarding Kyle Seike but aside from him being a student here and graduating from here, there is little mention of him. It seems as though he kept a low profile."

"Okay, one more thing. I was talking to my boss last night and he mentioned that twenty-four cadavers for a school that doesn't offer a graduate degree in medicine seems unusual. What do you think?"

"Well, we do offer a number of undergrad degrees in medical fields. We have a very high rate of transfer to post graduate programs. Part of the reason for that is our ability to offer things other schools may not."

The anatomy lab is one of those things?" Richard asked.

"Yes, and what allows us to do that is money."

"Endowments?" Richard followed.

"Exactly, somewhere along the line someone or several someone's gave a lot of money to fund that lab."

"Is there any way to find out where the money is coming from?" Richard asked.

"Absolutely!" Shelly exclaimed. "Give me just a few minutes and I'll have it for you."

"That's wonderful." If you don't mind, Shelly, I'm going to find the men's room and then take a quick walk outside."

"Not at all, Doc, I'll be here when you're ready."

Bill was reviewing video and still shots from the day of the bombing. Luke had helped him locate the camera facing Broad Street and that's where Bill was focusing his attention. He began the tape at 11:30 am, about forty-five minutes before the explosion, and ended it at 12:45 pm, or thirty minutes after the bomb was detonated.

There was one clip that he kept going over. He would run the tape back and forth until he narrowed it down to the one minute interval that he wanted. There it was. It was 12:08 pm. Two cars approached the intersection. The first was a white chevy which was trying to make a left turn, across the flow of traffic which was heavy. It took about 30 seconds before a break in the west bound lane occurred. With that car out of the way, Bill could see the small black sedan stopped at the intersection. The license plate was too far away to be legible plus the cars passing by didn't leave enough of an opening to see very well.

At 12:09:13, the black car turned right, moving with the eastbound lane. The plate was unobstructed for just a second or two but was still too far away. He knew the FBI could use enhancement techniques to visualize the plate but he wasn't going to get any further here. Bill went out to find Luke.

"Luke, I found what I was looking for. Is there a way to make a copy of thirty seconds from camera 14?"

"Sure, I just need a USB drive."

"I don't have one on me. I can run to a store and get one and come back," Bill offered.

"No worries, I'm a part-time I.T. student. I'm sure I have a spare in my bag."

Bill followed Luke back into the video room. Luke searched his bag for a moment and came out with one.

"Here you go!" Luke handed him the drive.

"Can you copy 12:08 to 12:11 for me?"

Luke placed the flash drive into the USB port on the playback unit. He rewound the display to 12:08:00 and pressed record. When the three minutes were up, he pressed stop, removed the flash from the device and handed it to Bill.

"Here you are, my friend."

"Luke, what you just did will probably save lives. How much do I owe you?"

"I'm happy to help but, if you want to kick in two dollars for a replacement USB, I'd be cool with that."

Bill pulled out his wallet and handed him a twenty.
"Let me get you some change," Luke said.

"Keep the change, Luke, You're a hero! It was nice meeting you."

Bill reached out his hand and Luke shook it.

Richard had had enough of the cigar. He brushed the hot ember off on the bottom of his shoe and walked across the grass to make sure his shoe wasn't on fire. Then he continued on into the building. Shelly was checking her phone messages when he came back in.

"Boyfriend?" he asked.

"No, 'Dad,' just friends."

"I take it you get that a lot," Richard said.

"Dad's just joking about it but it does happen frequently. Here's the funny thing, if I came home one day and said, 'Dad, I'm engaged,' he would be devastated."

"That's a big moment for any dad." Richard said. "A father's number one priority is to protect his little girl, even when she is no longer little. Being males ourselves, we know what creeps we can be."

"I have something for you," Shelly said.

She handed him a few sheets she had printed, then turned back to the computer screen.

"You can follow along, and those are yours to keep."

"Thank you." Richard said and looked down at the top sheet.

"These are all of the sources of donations to the anatomy lab over the last forty years. You can see there are large ones and small as well as one time donations, trusts, and endowments. This program started with the Naum and Elisheva Weinfeld Endowment. It was started in 1986 with a corpus of $500,000, which was a lot of money then.

"It still sounds like a lot of money!" Richard added. "Is the endowment restricted?"

"Yes, the interest from the investment of the endowment can only be used for the procurement, maintenance and disposal of human anatomical subjects for the undergraduate study human anatomy."

"Do we know who these people are?"

"The gift was from Sigmund and Allis Weinfeld in memory of their parents."

"Shelly, you are the best." He took a piece of scrap paper from the trash and wrote his home and mobile number next to his name. "If you ever need anything, this is the first number you call. Aside from your father of course."

"Bill is waiting for me outside, our work here is done. You don't know it yet, but your time and effort has probably saved lives. Thank you for everything. It has been a distinct pleasure and an honor to meet you."

Shelly stood to hug him. While they embraced, Richard whispered, "Don't take shit from anybody! You are better than them."

Richard broke the embrace and walked out. He was choked up and didn't want her to see.

Chapter 32

The drive to Philadelphia was smooth and easy. He stopped to use the bathroom and decided to rest for a while. There were very few people on the road at night, mostly truckers. Ben parked between tow rigs in the truck section of the rest area. It was secluded and he thought the hum of the motors running the air conditioning and lights of the cabs would help him sleep. He was right.

He awoke two hours later feeling refreshed although a little stiff from sleeping in a sitting position. He hit the road and reached his destination just as the day was dawning. The traffic in and around Philadelphia was just starting to pick up. He took I-476 to I-76 to US 1 to reach Old York Road. The Albert Einstein Medical Center was just off Old York.

There was a one way loop that encircled the U shaped building. He knew that the package containing the bomb would still be in the receiving area which was located on the west side lower level. He wouldn't even need to leave his car this time. Once he reached the south edge of the west wall of the building, he would be well within five hundred feet.

With his reconnaissance complete, he would just need to kill a few hours before it was time to detonate. He could do it earlier, but the effect would not be as profound. Few people would be around now. He could move it up an hour and still be very effective but the traffic at 9 am would make getting back to the highway more difficult.

He noticed a barber shop on Wagner Avenue as he was riding around. They opened at 8 am and walk-ins were welcome, according to the sign. It had been a while since he had a real haircut and with a date coming up in a few days, he liked the idea of being productive while he waited.

He drove around that part of the city for another twenty minutes and then found a place to park not too far from the barber shop. He climbed out of the BMW and began walking the half block to the shop. He never noticed the parking kiosk just behind the car.

Chapter 33

Greg had slept in a little longer than usual and Mary was already out of bed. "Too bad," he thought, "we could have had a little refresher of the night before." He wasn't sure why Mary was suddenly becoming his real life sexual fantasy, but he wasn't about to ask questions. He was happy to just accept the gift without knowing where it came from, for once.

He turned on the shower to let it warm up while he emptied his bladder. He was reminded that he had sex last night, instead of one stream of urine, there were three. Luckily, all three remained inside the bowl. He took his shower, dressed, and headed downstairs. The kids had already left for school and the kitchen was empty except for some dirty dishes.

Greg poured himself some coffee and placed bread into the toaster. He picked up the morning paper and glanced over the headlines. On the front page of the second section was the picture he sent to the FBI. Above it, the headline read, "Do You Recognize This Man?"

He skimmed the article. The police and FBI would like to question this man. If you know him or his whereabouts, please contact local authorities. He may be driving a black foreign sedan. "Okay, brief but effective," Greg thought. He looked around the first floor of the house but couldn't find Mary. He went to open the refrigerator and that's when he saw it.

"Good morning darling, TFLN, I went to Sara's for coffee. Didn't want to wake you, have a great day!" Mary had written.

TFLN, he got it. Thanks For Last Night. "Typical woman," he thought, "off to brag about her night." Greg finished his coffee and breakfast, checked to be sure he had his wallet, car keys and phone, and left the house. He was hoping for some good news from Bill and Richard.

"What do you mean, you may know this guy?" Sara said.

"I'm saying, we may know this guy. Look at the picture!" Mary pleaded. She had taken the image that Greg had printed from the den.

"Mary, you can't even see his head! How can you tell it's him? From what you told me, I think you're just a little infatuated with this kid. Maybe you should just let it go for now."

"I know, Sara, it doesn't make any sense. Why would a store clerk from High Falls be involved in blowing up a school? It's just something about my encounter with him. There is something not quite right about him."

"You mean other than he tickles your fancy?"

"He didn't tickle anything, I was just confused for a minute. That doesn't discount the odd feeling I have."

"So then tell Greg about it. Let him have him checked out."

"How can I do that without telling him the whole story?"

"I don't know, just say you ran into him in the store and he gave you the creeps. Then, when you saw this picture, you made the connection."

"I don't know," Mary said," maybe I'll just let it go for now."

"I wish I had said that," Sara kidded.

Chapter 34

John was in Greg's office when Kathy came in.

"I'm sorry to interrupt," she said, "Bill Dillon is on the line."

"Put him through, Kathy. John, stay for this."

The phone rang.

"Good morning, Bill, I'm going to put you on speaker. Are you there?"

"I'm here, Greg, good morning. Richard is here as well."

"Good morning, John," Bill said, "You are also on speaker because I don't want to place my head that close to Richard's."

"Understood. What's going on guys?" Greg prompted.

"We have some worthwhile news, fellas, I think we found a connection to Kyle Seike and we have video of the black BMW."

"That's great! John and Greg both said, "tell us about it."

"Richard has been working closely with a young lady at the school while I was looking for security cameras in the area. His girl, Shelly, found out that the reason SUNY Plattsburgh can afford an anatomy lab that rivals most medical schools is because of an endowment that was set up many years ago in memory of Allis and Sigmund Weinfeld. Do those names ring any bells?"

"Yes," Greg said, Alex Winfield and his brother Kyle Seike."

"That's right. They gave a half million dollars in 1986 with the stipulation that the money can only be used to buy, store, and dispose of bodies."

"That sounds like 'The Godfather' endowment," Greg joked.

"Right? Anyway, there is no trail to who is involved now that Seike is gone."

"I'm not sure there needs to be, guys. The beauty of an endowment is that it becomes its own entity. The money invested just sits in an account and the interest is used to fund the program. It goes on in perpetuity. Besides, if I remember correctly, Kyle didn't have any next of kin other than Alex."

"So, this could be a dead end," Richard said.

"No, I think it makes the connection between the schools and Kyle. We just don't know how that plays out in the bombings. What will be interesting, is if you find something similar at UVM. Now, how about the cameras?"

"Right, I made a visit to the storage facility across Broad Street from the main entrance. After reviewing hours of tape, I found a camera that was pointed right at the exit. To make a long story short, I have thirty seconds of video that shows the car, the driver, and the license plate.

It will need to be enhanced to be able to see enough detail but I think it going to be definitive. I also know that the car turned east toward RT.9 and not west toward the Northway."

"Great work guys! We need to get that video to the police. I'll call the FBI and tell them you have it in your possession. Expect a call or a visit. At that time, you can also tell them the driver's direction after he left. Maybe they can check locations along Rt.9 for witnesses. What time are you due in Burlington?"

"We're going to head over there now. Our meeting is at noon. We will check in with you tonight."

"Thanks guys." Greg ended the call.

"What do you think, John?"

John didn't have a chance to answer. Kathy walked in and said, "Greg, turn on the news!"

Chapter 35

Emily stopped at the café on the way in. She wasn't used to working the early shift and felt like she needed several cups of coffee to wake up. Steve had asked her to switch shifts with him a couple weeks ago. She didn't mind helping out but it did break up her routine.

Her daughter Ruby was in afternoon kindergarten so mornings were usually relaxed. Making breakfast for the family and getting her husband out the door for work was her daily push. After that, she could take her time getting ready for her noon arrival at the hospital.

Today, she would be the first one to arrive in the receiving department. She would need to unlock the doors, get the equipment and computers turned on and print the list of expected deliveries for the day. When she came in at her usual time, all of that was already done and she could just hit the ground running. It was now 7:30 am and she was at her assigned post.

The lights clicked on with a hum. She walked around the main room turning on computer and printers. She then went to the break room and prepared the Mr. Coffee for its long day of work. The next two people would arrive at 8 am followed by six more at nine.

By noon, a dozen employees would be staffing the receiving department. It wasn't an accurate name because distribution was a large part of their workload. Of the twelve people working the staggered day shift, three could be out of the department at any time making deliveries to the various units.

The 8 am team had arrived so Emily took a moment to check in with her mother-in-law who had offered to help to get Ruby to school. Ruby adored her grandmother so no issues were expected but Emily wanted to be sure, more for her own satisfaction than anyone else's. When she returned to the department, she began pulling the packages earmarked for delivery today.

Most routine items that arrived were inventoried and placed on shelves until they were requested by a department. Every now and then, an item arrived that was needed at a specific date and time. Emily was working on those items.

Sometimes they arrived weeks ahead of schedule, as was the case with three items that were scheduled to go out today. She set the three packages on the work counter and opened them one at a time. The first was a special order part for a C.T. unit in Medical Imaging. Nothing unusual, often times the part would arrive before the installation was scheduled. The second package was a pacemaker that was going to the cardiology department and the third was an anatomical replica of a human pelvis.

This was slated to go to the Ultrasound Training Program. She unpacked the packages and checked the packing slip against what was actually in the box. Everything looked fine. She found the pelvis interesting. She had wanted to go to school for medical imaging several years ago and had actually been accepted to the program, but then she found out she was pregnant with Ruby. She took the job in Receiving because of the hours. She could drop

Ruby off at school and her husband picked her up. If there was ever a problem, Mom would fill in the gaps.

She unpacked the Pelvis. It was much heavier than she imagined. It was the size of an adult human and contained the pelvis, a portion of the lower lumbar spine and a portion of the femurs. It also was filled with all the organs that are usually found in a human pelvis so that ultrasound students could practice locating and differentiating them.

The top was rounded like a real abdomen and had a soft touch. The back was a three inch thick piece of black non-transparent plexiglass. The front was clear. After checking it out, she placed it back in the box and moved it to the cart for delivery. She did the same with the other two packages. The cart would stay in the department until early afternoon at which time they would be delivered.

Chapter 36

It didn't take out any exterior walls. From outside no one would know that a bomb just exploded. That was until hundreds of workers and visitors started running out into the streets. He had set the timer for fifteen minute so he was already joining the northbound traffic on I-476 by the time it went off.

He had the radio tuned to a local news station. The normally scheduled program was interrupted. The announcer was ill prepared to handle this sort of breaking news and it showed. His delivery was fragmented and he was obviously nervous. All he could make out was a bomb, casualties, stay away from that area, and the police are not commenting.

He switched channels to NPR. This guy was much more professional. He didn't have any more information than the last guy but he was calmer. He talked about police and ambulances on the scene but was reluctant to speculate about casualties. No one at the medical center had issue a statement and the few witnesses they interviewed were so upset that they weren't making any sense. He turned the radio off.

It was just short of three hundred miles to High Falls and he would need to stop once for fuel. He was fairly certain no one would be looking for him and he definitely was not worried about using a credit card. Ben Novak didn't exist, his mother and father made sure of that. He had no identity other than to himself.

He had shared a lot of his superficial secrets with Amanda and even with Priscilla in just the few hours they had spent together, but what they knew just scratched the surface. The darker, deeper secrets had never been shared, they couldn't be. He knew that no one would ever understand, how could they unless they lived a similar life. He took what comfort he could from each new acquaintance, knowing it couldn't last.

Ben was alone for almost as long as he could remember. A few minutes here and there with his father and mother of course, but mother was mother. He was more the parent to her than the reverse, especially in recent years.

He did have a few other care takers over the years, someone to watch over him when he was younger. None of them lasted very long and their lives were just as lonely as his. Matilda was blind and lived by herself. She was never married and had no real family. Now that he thought about it, the same was true of all the caretakers. Loners and handicapped. Each one lasted only a year or so, until they voiced some concern over his welfare. Once that happened, they would disappear. It was his father who always made those decisions.

Ben often wondered if he had other family around. He was never told of aunts, uncles, grandparents, or cousins. Whenever he asked about that, father would say, "it's just us and that's all we need. We have each other." Except they didn't. Maybe his parents felt that way but he sure didn't.

The ride was going well. The sky was overcast but it wasn't raining, at least not yet. He would drive another hour before needing to stop for gas. He reclined his seat a little and thought about girls. He liked them a lot, in spite of mother's warnings. He thought less about Amanda lately, probably because of river girl, Priscilla, and Mary. River girl was exciting, Priscilla was special, and Mary was intriguing.

He hadn't had much experience with older women. He would flirt with them occasionally but none of them seemed interested. Mary was different. He knew the minute she walked back in the store that she liked him. She seemed very open to his attention, almost like she craved it. She was also afraid to let herself go there. It seemed to him that most people were too concerned with maintaining proper balance. They worry too much about hurting others. That never really bothered Ben.

He tried the news one more time. Nothing new.

Chapter 37

Greg, Kathy, and John were glued to the TV in the small conference room. There was live footage of smoke billowing out of the windows of the lower floor of the building. Fire trucks, ambulances and police cars surrounded the building. The news crew was set up in a small park across the street from the hospital. A reporter was interviewing everyone he could, trying to find someone with firsthand information.

"I am speaking now with Peter Smith who was working on the ground floor when the explosion occurred. Mr. Smith, please tell us what you saw."

"I was in the corridor outside the receiving department when I heard what sounded like a loud fireworks, you know, the ones that flash and then a few seconds later make a deep boom. The floor was shaking and the walls instantly cracked, sending clouds of dust everywhere."

"Is it your belief that the explosion occurred in the receiving department?"

"I can't be sure," he said, "I know it was close by."

"Did you see any injured people?"

"Yes, after the explosion, I started running toward an exit. On the way, people were coming out of doorways into the corridor, some of them had scrapes and burns. They were all walking, so I grabbed a couple of them by the arms and hurried them to the exit."

"Thank you, Mr. Smith. We are taking you back to our studio for more information."

"Thank you, Jim. That's Jim Drake Live from Albert Einstein Medical Center where less than an hour ago an explosion took place in what appears to be the ground level of the west wing. We will be heading back there shortly. Right now, we have Special Agent Taylor Summers of the FBI on the line. 'Special Agent Summers,' thank you for joining us."

"Good to speak with you," he replied.

"Agent Summers, is this explosion connected in any way to the university bombings in New York and Vermont?"

"I'm afraid it's way too soon to know. In fact, we still don't have any concrete evidence that the New York and Vermont bombings are connected. There are similarities but nothing conclusive. We also don't currently know what caused the explosion in Philadelphia or whether it was intentional."

"You believe the other two were intentional?"

"Yes, we have evidence that explosives were planted in both of those situations."

"Do you have any new information in those investigations, Agent Summers?"

"We have some new leads that we are following up on now, but it's too soon to comment."

"Thank you, Agent Summers. We are now going back to the scene at the hospital."

Greg turned off the TV. "What do you think, John?"

"The only thing we know for sure is that it is healthcare related," John replied.

"And all three were teaching facilities," Kathy added.

"That's correct," said Greg. He walked to his office and the others followed. He sat behind his desk and activated his computer. Neither Kathy nor John interrupted him. They knew he was following a path.

"Albert Einstein Medical Center," he said as he typed. He looked at the list of residencies.

"They do not have an anatomy lab," Greg said, "at least not one with dissection of cadavers. The doctors in these residency programs finished their dissection years ago."

"That seems to separate this from the others," John said.

"If this was a bombing at all," Greg added. "I guess we will just have to wait and see. I wonder if Bill and Richard have heard about this. Let's give them a call."

Greg dialed Richard's phone. On about the fifth ring, Richard answered.

"I thought you weren't going to call me anymore?" Richard opened.

"I thought you weren't supposed to answer anymore?" Greg countered.

"Do you really want to do this dance?" Richard said.

"Not really, my feet are still sore from the last time!" Greg said. "Have you seen the news?"

"We just heard," Richard said. "We are in the car, on our way to UVM. Is there anything to indicate it's the same attacker?"

"Nothing yet. If it was a bomb, it didn't have anything to do with a cadaver." Greg said.

"How do you know?"

"They don't have cadavers at that school," Greg replied. "I guess we just stick to our game plan for now."

"Alright, Greg, we will give you a call at the end of the day."

"That sounds good. Good luck!"

Greg thought about what to do next. He picked up the phone again.

"Jack, how are you?"

"I'm good, Dad, I knew you would be calling."

"Now how did you know that? Greg asked.

"I've been watching the news," Jack replied.

"Well, it really has nothing to do with that, I'm calling because I confirmed my presentation at SU."

"That's great, Dad, when it is?"

"Next Tuesday at 11:00 am. in Dineen Hall. Are you familiar with it?"

"I sure am, which room?" Jack asked.

"Which room?" Greg replied.

"Yes, Dineen Hall has several lecture rooms."

"I wasn't aware of that. In that case, I don't know. I'll get there early and find out."

"I'm sure they'll have it posted somewhere, I'll try to find it for you."

"Thanks, son, that would be great!"

"Dad, are they related?"

"The explosions?"

"Yes."

"It's not the same M.O., but we don't know much about the Philly explosion yet. I don't have a guess at this point," Greg said. "Are you doing alright?"

"Yes, I'm fine. Everyone okay at home?"

"Other than the estrogen/testosterone imbalance, I would say all is well."

"Hang in there, Dad. I look forward to seeing you next week!"

"Will you have time for a late lunch or dinner afterward? You can pick the place?"

"I think I can work that out, it sounds good."

"I'll talk to soon, son, I love you."

"I love you too, Dad. Goodbye."

Chapter 38

Ben made it to just north of Binghamton before stopping for gas. The restrooms were located before the gas pumps so he stopped there first. He made his way to the restroom and used a urinal. When he was finished, he flushed and moved to the sink to wash his hands. He looked in the mirror and admired his new haircut. He thought it looked good. Mother would think it was still too long. Priscilla would probably approve.

He left the men's room and headed for the exit. As he passed the entrance to the store, his eye caught the news stand. "Do You Recognize This Man" was on the front page. Below the caption was a photograph of a young man. The top of his head was missing in the picture and the image was blurry. The clothes looked familiar. He knew it was him but he wasn't worried. "Grasping at straws," he thought as he left the building. He pulled the car up to the pump, turned it off and filled the tank.

He got back in the car, started it, and drove off. Just a few miles up the road, he thought he noticed a police vehicle coming up quickly. There was still at least a half mile gap between the two but it was closing fast. He could make out the silhouette of the vehicle with the trademark search light profile on the driver's side. When it was perhaps fifteen car lengths back, it turned on the flashing lights and siren.

Ben was alarmed but not frightened. He knew how to stay cool in these situations. He let up slowly on the gas pedal until his speed was just a few MPH under the limit. He knew he wasn't speeding but he didn't want it to be close enough to cause concern. He could now make out the colors and insignia of the vehicle, it belonged to the New York State Police.

He thought about an alibi, where would he be coming from? He could say he was coming from Corning, yes, the Corning Glass Factory. He thought that would work. The car was close now so he turned on his right signal and started to decelerate and pull to the right.

Just then, the police car pulled left and sped around him. He looked in his review mirror then pulled his car back onto the highway and picked up speed. He hadn't even broken a sweat. He was cool and collected. His father would have been proud.

About a mile up the road, the trooper had pulled over another car. "Probably picked him up at a speed trap," Ben thought. It was a black car, similar to his. He decided to get off at the next exit and take back roads for a while. He wouldn't stop again until he was home.

Chapter 39

Bill and Richard had taken the short ferry ride across Lake Champlain from Rocky Point, NY to South Hero Island. From there, they took Rt. 2 across the easter part of the lake to I-89, then south to Burlington. The entire trip was a little over an hour. When they were just outside of Burlington, Richard's phone rang. It was a number he didn't recognize but he answered anyway.

"Hello," he answered.

"This is Special Agent Summers, FBI, are you Dr. Ingraham?"

"The one and only," Richard replied.

"Dr. Ingraham, Greg Webster said you have some video footage for me, is that correct?"

"My assistant, Bill Dillon has it."

"Do you know where he can be reached?" said Agent Summers.

"Yes, he is in the seat next to me."

"And where are you gentlemen now?" Summers asked.

"Just pulling into Burlington, Vermont."

"I'll be there in thirty minutes, where can I meet you?"

"We are on our way to a meeting at the university, can you meet us there?"

"Yes, inside the main gate is a small park to the left. Wait for me there."

"Will do, Agent Summers, thirty minutes."

Summers hung up.

"Who was that?" Bill asked.
"Your buddy Summers from the FBI, he wants the video."

"How much is he willing to pay for it?" Bill asked.

"I'll tell you what," Richard said, "after I get out of the car, you can ask him."

"How about if I let you out here and you can walk the rest of the way?" Bill replied.

"That's better than going to jail, let me out," Richard said.

They drove on. The front gate of UVM had stone pillars on both sides of the driveway with a wrought iron arch across the top that said Universitas Viridis Montis, Latin for university of the green mountains. Inside the gate and to the left was a small park with about a dozen parking places.

They parked and got out of the car. They walked on to the grass from the pavement and Richard pulled out a half smoked

cigar. He was ready to light it when Bill nudged him.
"What?" Richard asked.

Bill pointed to a sign that read 'Smoking in Designated Areas Only' there was also a picture of a cigarette with a red circle and a line drawn through it.

"What's your point?" Richard said.

Just then, a black sedan pulled up next to their car.

"You think this is him?" Richard asked.

"Do you think a student is driving that?" Bill responded.

He was walking toward them.

"Bill Dillon?" he asked.

"I'm Dillon," Bill responded.

"Special Agent Taylor Summers, FBI," he held out his hand. Bill took his hand. "Nice to meet you, Agent Summers, this is Richard Ingraham."

"Dr. Ingraham, nice to meet you. It sounds like you guys have been busy up here."

"Just trying to help out," Richard said.

"We appreciate it," Summers responded, "Do you have the file?"

Bill pulled the USB drive from his pocket and handed it to Summers.

"It's going to need some enhancement but I think you'll find some interesting information there."

"I will get it off to the lab ASAP,' Summers said. With that he turned around and headed back to his car. When he reached it, he turned and said, "You boys be careful and stay out of trouble. Thanks again."

"You forgot to ask about the money." Richard said.

Chapter 40

"Emily…Emily…Emily…" the doctor kept calling. "Emily, squeeze my hand if you can hear me." The doctor waited for a response. "It's going to require a little more time Mr. Lasher. She's had quite a traumatic experience and her brain is in protection mode. She will come out of it soon, I assure you."

"Thank you, doctor. How long do you think she will need to stay in the hospital?"

"Once she wakes up, and if we don't find any other injuries, I think she could be discharged within a week. She will require lots of follow up appointments as an outpatient and possibly additional surgeries for the broken bones. She is a lucky woman Mr. Lasher and you are certainly a lucky man. I'll check back a little later."

Emily could hear voices far off in the distance. They were friendly and familiar but the overlay of continuous ringing made it difficult to make out the words. She couldn't tell where she was, it was dark and it smelled like the night air after a fireworks display. Periodically, she felt a jolt of pain in her back and right thigh. The back of her left hand had a burning sensation. She remembered going to work and making coffee. She didn't remember dropping

Ruby off at school. She was sorting packages. Yes, there were three of them, she remembered.

One package was going to x-ray, some sort of part. She was reaching, pushing herself to remember. Something for cardiology…it wasn't a heart, it was…a pacemaker! She tried a little harder now, almost straining to…straining, "don't strain Ruby, just sit, and relax, think of something else. Don't strain, you will hurt yourself!"

Now she was in the bathroom, Ruby wasn't there. She was straining but not to go potty, she was pushing with her arms. The air was hot and she couldn't see, it like sand was in her eyes. She was lying down, and it felt like cool grass on a hot summer day, but it wasn't soft. It was very hard and cold and wet.

She tried to stand up, she was straining to stand up but her foot wouldn't come under her. She forced herself to open her eyes but they burned and she had to close them again.

She was tired and decided to lay back down and take just a little nap. She knew Ruby always felt better after a nap. She would feel better and be able to get up and see once she was rested. If only the ringing would go away, it was really annoying. She could hear sirens now too, a parade maybe, fireworks, sirens, the smell of phosphor, the cool grass and hot air, it was the fourth of July! Just a little sleep and I will be much better.

She could feel pressure down below, like she had to pee but her bladder didn't feel full, just pressure. There were other feelings around that same area, deep pain, like center of the bone pain. She didn't like that, how could she rest with that pain going on. Where is everyone else? Why am I alone here on this cold, wet floor? It's the floor, not grass. It's tile, like the bathroom tile at home. Why would she be on the floor? Frustration was setting in. She tried to move her legs. The left one moved but the right one wouldn't cooperate. She tried harder but the pain in her pelvis worsened. Pelvis, she thought, why does that sound familiar? She tried rocking back and forth. She was moving, it was working, "Emily, wake up," Em, I'm right here, wake up honey."

Why would Brian be calling me, why must I wake up? Did I oversleep? Oh no, I overslept and Brian is going to be late for work, I need to get up, get up, get up, she moved to get out of bed but the bathroom door flew off its hinges and was coming at her, she ducked but there was no place to go. She crouched down behind the toilet. The toilet? Wait a minute, the toilet, the hard, cold floor, the boxes, the pelvis, the pelvis blew up! HELP, HELP, HELP!

"Emily, it's alright honey, I'm right here."

"Brian, is that you?" She could hear his voice but she couldn't see him. Brian, where are you?"

"I'm right here, Emily. Take my hand, I'm right here."

"Brian, I can't see you!"

"I know hon, there are patches over your eyes. You're going to be ok, it just temporary. Take my hand."

He placed his hand over her right hand. Emily grabbed it hard.
"Brian, what's happening?"

"There was an accident, Em, you were hurt but you're going to be okay. Everything will be okay." Brian pressed the call button by the bed.

"It was the pelvis, Brian, the pelvis blew up."

"Okay honey, I know, you're going to be okay. Try to relax, you are alright now. You're in the hospital and the nice people here are taking care of you."

A nurse came in the room.

"Mrs. Lasher, I'm one of your nurses, my name is Tricia. I'm going to give you something for the pain. You were in an accident but you're safe now. You are in Jefferson Hospital, do you know where that is?"

Emily nodded her head yes. "I know where that is, but why am I not at AEMC?"

"Because that's where the accident happened, Emily. They needed to evacuate that hospital. We can talk about that later, for now, try to relax and let that medicine work. I'll page the doctor and let him know that you're awake."

The nurse looked at Brian and whispered "that medicine should kick in soon. She will be drowsy but awake. Do what you can to comfort her but it's best not to provide too many details this soon. The doctor should be here soon. If you need me, press the call button."

Brian held her hand and rubbed her head until she settled.

Chapter 41

It was just after 3:30 in the afternoon when Ben arrived home. Except for the near traffic stop on I-81 it was an uneventful ride. He stopped to get the mail and newspaper out of the boxes then drove down the long driveway but didn't pull up to the garage. He left room to pull the truck out of the third bay. He entered the house through the first bay and went upstairs to get the key.

When he returned, he backed the truck out into the driveway and pulled the BMW in. He then pulled the truck into the first bay. This would be his main ride for now.

He set the mail and news down on the kitchen counter and went back downstairs to say hello to Mother. The door to her room was closed but he could hear the television from the hallway. Mother was laying on her side watching Benny Hill reruns. She did like British humor. Hello, Mother, Ben said, "I'm back in one piece."

"Yes, it was a successful trip, thank you. If you don't mind, I would like to change the channel to a news station. They might be talking about me. What did you do with the remote? Never mind, I found it."

Ben scanned the channels until he landed on a 24 hour news station. It looked like he would have to suffer through the global and national news first. "It smells a little musty in here Mother. It's probably time we freshen you up." Ben turned the ventilation system to high and sprayed some deodorizer around the room. "That should do it, don't you think? What do you know Mother, I made the national news! That's a pretty big deal, right?"

The anchor was briefing the audience about the bombing. After a few seconds, a Philadelphia reporter was broadcasting from the scene.

"Police are saying that the explosion that rocked the ground floor of The Albert Einstein Medical Center was indeed the result of a bomb. Experts from the Philadelphia Police Bomb Squad found residue and fragments in the Receiving department. The explosion damaged a large portion of that space as well as adjoining rooms. The total number of injuries is still unknown but authorities speculate that it could be as high as thirty. The death toll now stands at six with three others in critical condition. Area hospitals are reporting a large number of walking wounded visiting their emergency rooms. Police state that it is too early in the investigation to provide any more details."

"What do you think of that, Mother? Your boy is becoming famous! I think Dad would be proud. What do you mean, I'm just like him? I am not anything like him or you for that matter. That's not true Mother, I do have respect for death, I'm just not as respectful of life. I guess Dad did rub off on me a little bit, but when you grow up around it, it's bound to happen. Wouldn't you agree?"

Ben got up and walked to the door. "You have a lot of nerve talking about Dad and me that way. He has provided everything we need. Sure, he couldn't be around much but look at this nice house, nice cars. For crying out loud, Mother, you haven't had to lift a finger around here for years. He rescued you from that awful existence in that communist country and brought you here, where you could be free. Don't you feel free, Mother?"

He slammed the door and went to his work room. He didn't like raising his voice but sometimes, he just couldn't help it. Like that time with Amanda. He didn't mean for it to happen but when he walked in and caught her with that other girl, what was he supposed to do? He may not have been so angry if it was another guy, or maybe he would have, it's hard to know what would happen if the situation was different. Either way, Amanda was *his* girl.

Sure he was working more frequently, but he liked his job and he couldn't spend all his time watching baseball and screwing. That's all she wanted after a while, and it wasn't just him. She wanted videos, sex toys and fancy clothing. Some of the things she wore to the stadium were just outrageous. The guys would look her up and down. That's probably where she met her girlfriend. Mother was right about her, she was not good for him.

That night he went to her house, he knew something was going on. She hadn't answered her phone or text messages. He knew she continued going to baseball games without him because he followed her a few times. That night was one of them. He watched the two of them flirting with each other, their hands touching, Amanda leaning in so close it looked they were kissing. He followed them to his apartment. What kind of nerve does it take to bring a date to your boyfriend's apartment?

He had a rag soak with chloroform in a plastic bag inside his pocket. He also had a vial of propofol that his dad kept around the house in his backpack along with a syringe. His dad had plenty of experience with the drug and talked to him about it when he was young. Years later, when he found the vial in the work room, he researched it online.

He knew his own apartment very well. Plus, he had his key. He would wait a few minutes and let them get comfortable in the place. Amanda was sure he was working that night so he was the last one she expected to see. It was a nicer than average apartment. It had a foyer entry that led to a rather long hallway. About halfway down, there was another hall that went left and right. The first door off the left was a bathroom while the first door off the right was the bedroom. The bedroom then expanded back along the hallway so a person in the hall couldn't be seen by someone in the bedroom or the bath.

He would wait until one of them needed to use the restroom. If they were planning to have sex, and he thought they were, it would happen sooner rather than later. Amanda had turned the stereo on in the living room which Ben found to be very thoughtful of her. He had made his way down the darkened hallway to the other side of the bathroom where there was an alcove. He waited for someone to come.

As he predicted, the bedroom door opened and Amanda's friend came out. She was pretty, about five-four and maybe one-hundred twenty pounds with dark shoulder length hair. She, or someone else had already removed her pants and top leaving her to make the trek to the bathroom in her underwear. He let her go into the bathroom. He could hear her tinkle and flush. It sounded like she was brushing her teeth, probably with his toothbrush.

When he heard the water stop, he prepared himself. She walked out of the bathroom and headed straight toward the bedroom. She had taken only two steps when he reached around her face with the rag. He held it tight to prevent her from making noise. She was kicking backward at his legs but that only lasted for fifteen seconds. He held the rag in place for another minute or two to be sure she was out.

He moved her body to the other side of the bathroom door and waited. He could enter the bedroom and take Amanda but he knew she would put up a fuss. It would be easier to wait for her to come looking for her friend.

He could hear Amanda's feet hit the bedroom floor. He waited behind the opened bathroom door. "Tori," she called. "Where are you?" The light was off in the bathroom so she turned toward the kitchen. In a moment she was back again. "Tori, did you leave?" When she didn't answer, Amanda walked to the bathroom. She turned on the light but not finding anyone, she turned it back off and swung the door closed. That's when Ben pounced on her.

He put the rag to her face and turned her body away from him so that she couldn't knee him in the crotch. Her legs were thick and muscular and when she landed a blow on his shin, it hurt. He held the rag tightly until her legs stopped and her eyes started to close.

"It's your own fault, Amanda, I'm not owning this one. I liked you a lot, probably more than I have ever liked anyone. I didn't deserve to be cheated on but you do deserve this. He dragged Amanda's limp body to the bedroom and lifted her up onto the far side of the bed. He went back for Tori who was starting to move so he placed the rag back over her face until she went back to sleep.

"Not to worry dear, you will be very sleepy, very soon." He dragged her flaccid body back to the bedroom and laid her next to Amanda. He had to work quickly now. He gave Amanda another dose of the chloroform while he fumbled around in his backpack for the vial and syringe. He needed both hands now.

He attached the needle to the syringe and pushed some air into the bottle. It was harder than he imagined and required all his strength to pressurize the vial. He withdrew about twenty ml. He took a shoelace from Amanda's sneaker and used it as a tourniquet. He slapped her arm a few times until a vein popped up. He slowly pierced the skin until he could feel the vein give way. He pulled back gently just enough to see blood return. Then slowly and with even pressure he pushed the plunger. Amanda flinched her arm just once before the propofol took effect. He was in the clear.

When the syringe was empty, he refilled it. Pressurizing the vial was easier this time because almost half the volume was gone, creating more room for air. He filled the syringe, tied the shoestring around Tori's upper arm, found a vein and carefully pierced the vein with the needle. He loosened the shoelace and pushed the plunger slowly. Tori's eyes flew open and stared directly into Ben's. He looked at her and said, "He who laughs last laughs best, Mother always said."

He closed her eye lids with his hand. Both girls were sound asleep and would be for the next several minutes until their hearts stopped beating. Their breathing had already ceased. Ben checked Amanda's pulse, it was faint but still there. He did the same to Tori. Still pretty strong but it wouldn't be for long.

"What to do now," Ben thought. Two beautiful girls in one bed. He began to undress Tori first. He knew what to expect from Amanda and there seemed to be some poetic justice in Amanda watching him make it with her girlfriend.

He left his memory in the past and returned to the now. "How quickly the tide can turn. Isn't that right Mother? Mother? I said isn't that right?" She didn't answer. She knew how to dodge the tough questions.

Ben turned his focus to the task at hand. He pulled a two inch diameter piece of PVC off the shelf. He cut it to ten inches in length and glued a PVC endcap to one end. While that was drying, he started to mix the ingredients for the next two bombs.

Chapter 42

The meeting with the provost at UVM went much smoother. It didn't hurt that Richard was an alumni. Bill gave his credentials willingly at the beginning of the conversation to speed things along. The administrative assistant at UVM was a young man named Patrick Dunham. He was very efficient and helpful. The boss had given him the green light to establish any and all connections Bill and Richard needed.

Bill asked for a session with the head of security and Richard asked for someone to help his with reviewing documents for the procurement of medical cadavers and the anatomy lab donor list. Patrick asked the gentlemen to give him thirty minutes to process their requests. Bill and Richard walked outside to wait.

The early September sun was bright but was losing some of its summer strength. The temperatures this far north were beginning to dip overnight making for cooler mornings. Richard was content to smoke a cigar and call home while he waited. Fortunately, there was a designated smoking area nearby.

"I'm going to take the car and drive around campus a bit," Bill said. I'll meet you back here in about twenty."

"Sure thing, Bill," Richard responded.

Bill pulled away and Richard dialed the phone. "Good morning dear, I had a quick break so I thought I would call and hear your lovely voice."

"Good morning Richard, is everything alright?"

"Sure, everything is fine, I guess I'm just missing you."

"That's sweet," Marilyn replied, "I miss you too. How is the investigation going?"

"We wrapped up at Plattsburgh this morning then made our way over to Burlington. We're just waiting for our appointments to be coordinated, it shouldn't be more than twenty minutes."

"How does the old place look?" she asked.

"It looks young, but then again, I'm looking at it through older eyes. I guess I've been feeling my age more these days."

"It's happening to all of us, dear. I don't think there's anything to worry about, just try to enjoy yourself."

"I am really, I guess I look at these young adults and wonder what kind of world they're inheriting. It seems to get worse by the day. College students shouldn't be worrying about bombs blowing up their schools. They should be worry free, at least for a few more years."

"Every generation felt the same way. Our parents were worried about World War Two and Korea. We were worried about Vietnam. I don't know if there is a generation alive in this country that doesn't believe their generation was better off than their children's. For all the conveniences and technology they have at their fingertips, I wouldn't trade places with them for anything." Marilyn said.

"I would like to be able to chase you around the house like I did when we were young," Richard replied.

"I could just make it easier for you to catch me," she said seductively.

Marilyn still possessed her youthful beauty while Richard felt he had aged immensely.

"What will I do once I catch you?" He joked.

"Anything you want," she replied.

"I really do love you, Mar," he said.

"I know you do, Richard and that is the most important thing of all. Let's plan a date night when you get home. How about it?"

"I'm in," he said. "Gotta go babe, I'll talk to you soon."

"Have a great day, Richard."

He ended the call and realized how lucky he was to have her. Maybe he could still chase her around now and then. Richard put what was left of his cigar out on the bottom of his shoe. He walked across the grass to a waste receptacle and threw the butt away. He reached into his pocket, pulled out two new ones and threw those out as well. "It starts today," he told himself.

Bill was just pulling into the parking lot. Richard met him on the sidewalk and they moved together toward the provost's office. Patrick was waiting for them.

"Thank you for waiting gentlemen, here are each of your schedules." He handed them a printout that included who they were meeting with, at what time and the location with directions. "Mr. Dillon, your meeting will be taking place in the security office which is in the Information Technology building just across the courtyard. It will be in the basement level, just follow the signs. Dr. Ingraham, your meeting will be right here with yours truly. There is an office down the hall we can use that offers computer and printer access."

"That's great Patrick, I appreciate your help," Richard said.

"Richard, call me when you're finished and we will catch up," Bill said.

Bill walked out the door. "Are you ready, Richard?" Patrick asked.

"Lead the way, Patrick."

They walked past several offices, a lavatory and what looked like a breakroom. The office was near the end of the hall. It had two desks that were butted up against each other, face to face. The computers had large, flat panel monitors and the lighting in the room was dimmed. There was also a small table with two chairs across from each other.

"Richard, why don't we start at the table and map out what we want to accomplish here today. Once we have a plan, we can move to the computer stations. Will that be alright with you?"

"Yes, Patrick, thank you."

"The information I was given states that you are interested in how, when and from whom we received the cadavers. The second item is where does the money come from to support the anatomy lab. Does that sound accurate?"

"It does. You are well prepared."

"Thank you, Dr. Ingraham. Do you mind if I ask what your specialty is?"

"Not at all. I was board certified Obstetrics and

Gynecology. The last few years of my career were spent as a hospitalist."

"I see," Patrick replied, "and how do find yourself involved in this investigation?"

"I'm glad you asked," Patrick.

He wasn't really but the man had a right to know. So, he told him the whole story behind the assault at City Hospital and his role in solving the case. Of course, he did embellish a little making his role sound more important than it was.

Patrick listened with what appeared to be genuine interest. When Richard was finished, Patrick thanked him and motioned for them to move to the computers.

"I'm going to pull the information related to the procurement of the cadavers for this semester. Let's pull a chair around so you can watch what I'm doing." Richard grabbed a chair and moved it to the other side of the desk.

"Here we go!" Patrick exclaimed.

Bill was meeting with Devon Winston, Chief of Security. Bill took some time explaining the situation for Devon. Then he asked to see video footage from all of the security cameras from 12:30 pm to 2:30 pm on the day of the explosion.

"That's a lot of footage," Devon announced, "we have a total of forty-five cameras around the campus. It could take you the better part of a week to review all that."

"I think we can narrow it down. Do you have a map containing camera placement for the entire campus?" Bill asked.

Devon stood up and moved to a metal cabinet with shallow drawers. It was designed specifically to hold blueprints and schematics. He pulled out several sheets that measured about twenty-four by thirty-six inches. He carried them to an angled display counter where they could be laid out in full. Bill followed him.

"Here is the security building where we are currently. Here is the anatomy lab over here. Each of these small, numbered circles is a security camera. The numbers correspond to a channel on our recorders.

If you select the cameras you're interested in, we can dial up the time for each camera. But remember, it's two hours of footage for each camera. We can play back up to six at a time."

"So what if we identify the cameras I want to see and begin five minute before to five minutes after the explosion and go from there? We can keep moving the time out each way in five minute increments. With any luck at all, we can narrow that ninety hours down to just a few. These numbers that are along the walkways, are they pedestrian call box cameras?" Bill inquired.

"They are. There are twelve scattered around the campus."

"Alright, let's work from the anatomy building and spread out slowly. Can we tell which way the cameras are aiming from this diagram?" Bill asked again.

"Yes sir, the little arrow at the edge of the circle will tell you which way the camera is pointing. In addition, a red circle denotes an emergency call box camera while blue indicates a wall mounted camera," Devon clarified.

Bill looked at the schematic for a few minutes. He took out his notepad and pen and began writing numbers.

"Alright, let's start with 10, 11, 13, 15, 18 and 21. Start rolling at 13:15 and end at 13:25. We are looking for either a young white gentleman about six feet tall with a slender to medium build or, a small black BMW. How many eyes do we have?" Bill called out.

"We can put one man on each playback monitor," replied Devon.

"Great, let's get started."

Chapter 44

"Sara, I promise, just go out there with me to take a look. If you still don't think it can be him, I'll drop it." Mary said.

"And if you're still not sure?"

"I'll tell Greg about it."

"I don't know, Mary, there is something weird about it."

"Is it any weirder than our husbands pretending they're detectives?" Mary asked.

"I guess not, but I still don't like it."

"Then just do it for me?" Mary begged.

"Alright, but we better get going so we can be back before the kids get home from school."

"Thank you, Sara! I'll drive."

They climbed into Mary's car and headed west toward Smitty's.

"How is Jack adjusting to school?" Sara asked.

"He seems to be doing fine. Greg talks to him more than I do but according to him, he's great. Greg is going out there next Wednesday to see him."

"What's the occasion?"

"Oh, nothing special. Greg is giving a talk at Syracuse University so Jack is going to sit in and then they are going to dinner."

"Just a father and son day?"

"I think so, I want them to have the time together. Greg really misses him, I mean he really loves the girls too but Jack was a little special. I think Greg feels outnumbered sometimes."

"It sounds like Jack being away is working in your favor as far as Greg and you are concerned."

"It has been great lately and I think our last shopping spree has a lot to do with it."

"The new outfits make me feel sexy again and Greg is responding in a big way."

Sara started laughing.
"What," Mary asked.

"He is responding in a BIG way?" Sara repeated.

"What are we, twelve?" Mary said.

"Sorry, couldn't help it. It's HARD to control." Sara continued.

"Okay, make fun if you want to, I think you're just jealous."

"John and I have great sex when we want to."

"Do you want to borrow my outfits?" Mary smiled.

"No! We're fine, thank you, but I would like to go shopping again soon."

They were pulling into the parking lot. Mary pulled up near the front entrance.

They entered the store and looked around. There were two cashiers up front but they didn't see Ben. The store was pretty busy but they made their way to the back. Still no sign of Ben. Mary noticed another associate helping a customer in aisle ten. When the customer had what they needed, Mary approached him.

"Excuse me."

"Yes ma'am, how can I help you?"

"I was in the other day and a young man named Ben was assisting me. Would you know if he is here today?

"I'm sorry ma'am, Ben is off today. Is there something I can help you with?"

"No, I was sure he said he would be here today. That's alright, I'll stop back another time."

"Would you like to leave him a message? I'll get a pad and pen for you, follow me."

Mary and Sara looked at each other, then followed.

They were at the key making station. The gentleman handed Mary the pen and paper just as he received a call in his headset.

"If you'll excuse me, another customer needs assistance. You can leave your note on the desk here and I'll make sure Ben gets it tomorrow."

"Thank you," Mary said but he was gone.

"Mary, look at this."

"What is it?" Mary asked.

"It's the calendar for August and September. It's their work schedule. We can write down the days Ben was off and compare them to the bombing dates, if he was at work, your question is answered."

"Great idea," Mary said and began writing down the dates. When she was finished, she put the pad and pen on the desk but took her notes with her.

Chapter 45

Emily was awake but drowsy. The patches still covered her eyes and that made her feel claustrophobic. She called out for Brian and he was right there. He took her hand.
"I'm here Emily, you're doing fine. Are you feeling better Em?"

"I would feel better if I could see," she answered.

"Someone needs to tell me what happened. Where is Ruby?"

"Ruby is with Mom. I talked to her just a little while ago and everything is fine. She wanted me to give you a kiss." He leaned in and kissed her. Tears welled up in his eyes and he held his lips against her forehead for a long time. She tried to reach up with her hand and realized she had in IV in it. She lowered it back down.

"What happened, Brian? Please tell me."

"All we know right now is that there was an explosion at the hospital. I'm sure we will find out more soon. In fact, the police came by a while ago, hoping to talk to you. The nurse wouldn't let them wake you up. She said she would call them when you were awake. Should I let her know?"

"Yes, please."

"I'll be right back," he said.

"No!" she yelled, "use the call button, I'm afraid to be alone."

"Sure Em." He pressed the little red button. A minute passed then Tricia came in the room.

"I see you're awake. How do you feel?" she asked.

"I feel frustrated and afraid," Emily answered.

"I can imagine. How is the pain?"

"I'm sore mostly. My bottom hurts."

"No doubt. You have an IV line in your right hand that is giving you pain medication on a regular basis but I can give you more by mouth if you need it."

"I think I'm okay for now." Emily said.

"Brian said the police were looking for me. I can talk to them now."

"Are you sure, I can hold them off a bit longer."

"I'm sure. I need to know what happened."

"Okay then, I'll give the detective a call. Excuse me."

Tricia left the room. Brian didn't know how to fill the silence. He knew she couldn't handle the truth right now. She wasn't even aware of the extent of her injuries.

"Would you like a sip of water?" he asked.

"Yes, please, my mouth is really dry." He held the cup and placed the straw to her lips. She opened and closed her lips around the straw and gave deep pull. She swallowed and then stopped. The straw stuck to her bottom lip so he tugged it gently away.

"It hurts to swallow," she said.

"Emily, when you arrived here, you were covered wish ash and small particles of who knows what. They rinsed your eyes and your mouth several times but it will be a while before it all dissipates."

Tricia came back in but not with the police. It was Dr. Bennett, one of her many doctors but the one who seemed in charge.

"Good afternoon, Emily, I'm Dr. Bennett and I'm coordinating your care. How are feeling?"

"I'm alright, I guess. I'm sure you know more than I do," she replied.

"Well, then let's bring you up to speed, shall we? At roughly 9:30 this morning, there was an explosion in your department at AEMC. I can't really speak to what caused it but the police will no doubt tell us soon. You were found on the floor of the bathroom. Does that sound familiar?"

"Yes, vaguely."

"It appears that the bathroom door blew off its hinges and knocked you to the floor. It was the door covering you that may have saved you from further injury. Now, let's talk about your injuries. When the door hit you, it pushed you into the toilet and then to the floor. We think the toilet is responsible for most if the injury.

There is a good chance that your pelvis hit first, before you fell to the floor. Toilets are hard and they don't give much, usually. Not true in your case. You hit with such force that the toilet tank split in two. Unfortunately, so did your pelvis."

Brian couldn't read Emily's expression because of the bandages over her eyes. She seemed very stoic so far.

"When the pelvis breaks, it rarely breaks in just one place. Think of a hard three ring pretzel, if you crack one side of a ring, the other side will crack as well. In your case, it broke in three places. One or three, the treatment is the same, bedrest. The more serious issues have to do with your femur and your lower spine."

"Spine?" she repeated.

"Yes, you have a compression fracture of the fourth lumbar vertebrae with some posterior displacement of the L4-L5 disc. These issues are all fixable but will take some time, and that's not all bad.

You see, usually when someone has a displaced fracture of the femur, there is a good deal of pain associated with it. Because of the pressure from the protruding disc on the spinal cord, you are not sensing all the pain you should be. The downside is we can't leave the disc that way for long.

"Dr. Samuelson is one of our orthopedic specialists and he will talk to you about his recommendations for repair of all these issues, when he stops by later today. Emily, do you have questions for me? I know that was a lot of information all at once."

"Yes," she answered. When can I get the bandages off my eyes? I can handle the rest but I must be able to see."

"We usually wait forty-eight hours before removing the bandages but we can take a peek tomorrow and see how you're healing. Does that sound fair?"

"I guess fair would be not getting blown up in the first place but since that ship has sailed, it sounds fair enough."

"You are a very strong woman, Emily, and you have a sense of humor to boot. I will stop back later this afternoon but if you need anything, the nurses here will take good care of you."

"Thank you, Dr. Bennett."

After he left the room, Emily asked for Brian.

"Right here, Em."

"What are we going to do?"

"WE, are going to get you better. I have already been approved for time off and my mom is fine with helping however she can. One day at a time, sweetheart."

Tricia came back into the room. "Feel up to more company? The police are here."

"Yes, thank you."

Tricia walked out as the two men came in. They were dressed in plain clothes.

"Mrs. Lasher, I'm detective Mangrove and this is detective Olivera, we're with the Philadelphia Police Department. We would like to ask you some questions if you feel up to it."

"Of course," she replied, "I think you already met my husband."

"Yes, we did. Mrs. Lasher, can you tell us what happened this morning?"

"I'll try. I arrived at work around 7:30am which is an unusual time for me. I usually work from noon until 8:00pm."

"Why the change?" Mangrove asked.

"A coworker asked me to switch with him just for the one day."

"Did he ask you this recently?"

"It was two weeks ago, he had a personal obligation this morning."

"Do you know what that obligation was?"

"No, I didn't ask. We have done this before. We have a pretty cooperative group in the Receiving Department."

Brian was waving his hands, warning the offices not to tell her.

"I see, can you give me the name of the person you changed shifts with?"

"Steven Mowrey."

"Thank you, sorry to interrupt. Continue please."

"I was the first one in so I turned on all the lights and equipment, put the coffee on and then grabbed my list of items that were designated special delivery."

"What makes them special?"

"They were special order items that don't get stocked like daily supplies. Some times that are delivered weeks before they are needed and we hold them until the release date. Today, there were three such items."

"Do you remember what they were?"

"Yes, a pacemaker, a part for a C.T. scanner and a pelvis."

"A pelvis, ma'am?"

"Yes, it was an anatomical replica used for teaching ultrasound techs. It was soft on top like a real abdomen and black plastic on the bottom. The space in between held the replicated internal organs."

"How big would you say it was?"

"I would say about sixteen inches square by twelve inches deep and it was very heavy."

"And that was scheduled for delivery today?"

"Yes, the order said do not deliver prior to today's date."

"Do you remember where any of the boxes came from?"

"No, I'm sorry."

"What were you doing at the moment of the explosion?"

"I had checked the items and then moved them to the cart for delivery. That cart was just waiting until afternoon to be delivered."

"Why wait until afternoon?"

"Because morning is the busiest time for those departments."

"Okay, then what did you do?"

"I went to use the bathroom. I was washing my hands when the door blew in on me."

"Thank you, Mrs. Lasher. May we contact you again if we think of any more questions?"

"Please do. Detective?"

"Yes."

"Was it really an intentional bombing?"

"It sure looks that way, we found traces of explosives and fragments from what appears to be a pipe."

"Thank you, officers."

Chapter 46

Greg picked up the phone. "Mr. Webster, Dr. Shand is here to see you."

"Thank you, Kathy, send him in."

"Hi, John, what did you find out?"

"This can't be a coincidence anymore, Greg, Kyle Seike did his residency at Albert Einstein in Philly."

"But it still doesn't add up, John, they don't have an anatomy lab there."

"They don't anymore but they did when Kyle was there," John responded. "They must have. How can you offer a residency in pathology and not have cadavers?"

"That's a good point, John but where is the connection? He's no longer alive, who would want to get revenge or whatever this is for him? What gripe could they have?"

"Perhaps he made a friend in prison. Or, maybe he paid someone on the outside to do it. What if he knew he was dying and he wanted to get back at the world for locking him up?" John said.

"We need to talk to Agent Summers and our guys up north. See if you can get Bill or Richard on the phone and I'll reach out to Summers. You can use the phone in the conference room next door."

"Sure, Greg, what should I ask them?"

"Just find out what they know."

John left Greg's office to go next door. Greg racked his brain trying to find a connection. He dialed the number for Taylor Summers.

"Agent Summers," he answered.

"Taylor, it's Greg Webster, how are you?"

"I'm Fine, Greg, I was just going to call you. You can go first."

"Okay, we just confirmed that Dr. Kyle Seike attended school at all three of the bombing locations but were having trouble with who or why someone would be acting on his behalf."

"Did he have a wife or children?" Summers asked.

"Not that we're aware of, Taylor. With all that went down here, there was never any discussion about any family. He lived alone in a house in town here before he went to prison. He did have a brother, Alex who was CEO here at the time of the murders."

"Yes, I'm familiar with that. I'm going to make some calls to find out where his brother is and who he had contact with while he was in the joint. Maybe he had visitors or received letters from someone."

"That's great. What did you have for me, Taylor?"

"It was definitely a bomb in Philly. The bomb squad found similar explosive residue as well as fragments of the pipe."

"Same pipe material?" Greg asked.

"Yes, PVC."

"But it couldn't have been in a cadaver this time, I checked and they don't have an anatomy lab."

"You're correct. Philly police interviewed a survivor who worked in the Receiving Department. She checked in three packages this morning and remembered them all. They believe the bomb was encased in a study aid. It was a replica of a human pelvis. They found pieces of it in the room and it all tested positive for residue."

"So that makes me think a medical supply firm may be involved. Is someone looking at the purchase orders?"

"Yes, we have people on it now. It may take a while though, that entire area was destroyed in the explosion along with the staff."

"How did the witness survive?" Greg asked.

"She was in the restroom, the bathroom door blew in and covered her up. She's badly beaten up but alive."

"That's amazing!" Greg said.

"She's a lucky girl. Greg. I need to run, I'll catch up with you soon."

"Thanks, Taylor."

Greg hung up and walked next door, John was still on the phone with Bill and Richard. He sat down and just listened. Bill was talking.

"They had over ninety hours of video during a two hour window but we were lucky. We narrowed the window to ten minutes centering on the reported time of the explosion and reduced the number of cameras by identifying the ones on the perimeter parking and exits. In less than an hour, we had what we came for."

"Hey, Bill, It's Greg, sorry I'm late. I've been in the room for the last minute or two so I think I'm up to speed. Was it the same car?"

"It was the same car and it looks like the same guy. One of the building mounted cameras got him as he walked back to the car. We zoomed as much as we could here but we still can't make out his features or the plate. Which reminds me, did the FBI have any luck with the other images?"

"I just got off the phone with Summers and he didn't mention it, so I'm going to say no. He did say that the fragments and the residue are a match to the other bombs.. They also have an eyewitness."

"Someone saw him?" Richard asked."

"No not him but she did see the bomb."

"And she's alive to talk about?" Bill asked.

"She is, in fact, she handled it before it exploded. At the time it detonated, she was in the bathroom and the inward exploding door covered her up."

"Amazing," Richard said, how long between when she handled it and when it exploded?"

"About two hours," Greg answered. "Bill, when did the bomb explode at UVM in relationship to when you caught the guy leaving the campus?"

"Let me check my notes," Bill replied. There was a moment of silence. "It appears to be a little less than ten minutes."

"Ten minutes," Greg repeated. "That must mean that he used a device to trigger a timer. How far of a walk was it from the anatomy lab to his car?"

Bill again, "A young guy like that, not more than four minutes."

"Okay," Greg said, "now we know something we didn't before. He has some sort of handheld unit that triggers a timer that requires him to be within a certain distance. He gets back to his car in time to be off the campus before it blows. He doesn't care about watching it, and he doesn't place it. He gets within the range of the bomb just long enough to trigger the timer."

"That means he was in Philadelphia this morning," John said, "we need to let the FBI know."

"John," Greg said, "go to my office and call Summers again. Bring him up to date and ask him about the previous photo of the tag. As soon as we finish here, I'll be in. Thanks"

John left the room and Greg continued with Bill and Richard.

"Good work, Bill. I'm sure Summers will be giving you a call about the video. Richard, how was your day?" Greg asked.

"I quit smoking!"

"Gee," Greg responded," not what I was looking for but that's great! Any particular reason?"

"Yes, I want to be able to catch Marilyn."

"Catch her doing what?" Greg continued.

"You know, just keep up with her. I've been slowing down and she hasn't so I figured I would get myself in a little better shape."

"I'm proud of you, Richard," Greg added.

"Maybe a couple hip and knee replacements would help as well," Bill joked.

"It's not the knees or hips I'm worried about, if you know what I mean."

"Do they make a replacement for that?" Greg asked.

"Just hope you never have to find out," Richard answered.

"Okay, I guess we digressed there a bit, did you find anything out today."

"I thought you would never ask!" Richard said, "I have interesting news as well. This young guy Patrick is a whiz with computers. Anyway, he traced the receipts for the cadavers and just as in the Plattsburgh case, the numbers didn't add up. They had one more body than receipts.

But this Patrick kept digging, he was not going to let this go. After about two hours, he found an invoice that was not logged in the receiving department because the body came from a supply house that was new to UVM.

"Typically," Richard continued, "a system number is generated when an order is placed. If it's the first time they're doing business with the company, they set up a company profile including this number. Apparently, that requires an additional step. In this case, the cadaver arrived before that was completed and it was never logged in as received."

"Was Patrick able to locate the information for the company?" Greg asked.

"Yes, he was. it was from a funeral home in Boston. Weng Li Mortuary on Tremont Street in Chinatown."

Greg wrote the information down "Anything else, Richard?"

"As a matter of fact, there is. Patrick couldn't track any money given to the school on behalf of Kyle Seike or Alex Winfield. I also called Shelly at Plattsburgh to see if a similar situation may have occurred within the receiving sequence there. She researched the invoices and found one that had not been set up. It looks like nobody was calling for their money so it didn't trigger any red flags."

"Let me guess," Greg said, Weng Li Mortuary."

"Correct!" Richard said, "give the man a cigar!"

"Funny, Richard. Can I just say what a great pair of detectives you are? And what a great picker of detectives I am?"

"Thank you, Greg," Bill replied. If it's alright with you, Greg, Richard, and I are going take a slow ride down Rt. 7 on our way back. There may be some cameras along the way that snapped a picture of our guy."

"I think that's a great idea. Summers will be contacting you for that footage from UVM. Just have him meet you if you're already on the road."

"Will do. If you need us to do anything else, just give a call," Richard offered.

Chapter 47

Ben was still upset with Mother's attitude and equally upset with his response. He would apologize later but right now he needed to focus on the task at hand. He didn't know where the next event would occur, or when for that matter, but it wouldn't be too long. He seemed to have misplaced the forceps he used to pack the pipe. It wasn't like him to misplace anything but none the less, they were missing.

He knew there would be more around somewhere since Dad had enough tools to start his own hardware store. Where to look? There were so many cabinets in this room. This very big room with cement grey walls and grey steel cabinets. It all blended together. "May as well start at one end," he thought.

He checked the first drawer on the wall to his left, just right of the door. It was mostly cutting instruments, scissors, knives, scalpels, and all sizes of saws. The second drawer contained syringes, needles, ligatures, and tubing. Ben knew what some of them were for but not all.

The largest drawer on the bottom was filled with papers. He moved the papers around thinking there might have been other items buried below but it was just more paper. There were some old newspapers among them. Local and regional newspapers mostly from August of 2001. He pulled them out and sat at the desk to peruse them. The First was an edition of the Herkimer Times. He didn't see anything noteworthy on the front page, so he leafed through it quickly.

On the first page of the second section there was an ad for a local funeral home. There were six names of recent departures, all were circled in red ink.

He set that one aside and pulled out the next. Again, there was nothing of interest on the front page, or the first section for that matter. His attention was drawn to the first page of the second section, the obituaries. This time there was a listing with five recent deaths, all residing at Mease Mortuary, the same parlor that was in the previous paper. All of the names circled in red. He wondered why his dad would keep junk like that around.

He dug a little deeper and found a stack of newspaper clippings, all about the same size, paperclipped together. There must have been fifty or more obituary sections in the pile. They were dated and some of the names were circled in red. Not all of them were from Mease Mortuary and some went back a few years. He had no idea what it meant but he placed them aside and kept going.

He pulled out a newspaper from late August 2001, this time on the front page was a picture of his dad. The headline read 'Local Pathologist Arrested in New York Airport.'

He remembered the day before that vividly. He was nine years old and he was at a different NY airport. He and dad had taken a limousine from home to New York in the very early hours of the day. The limo went to JFK first. Before Dad got out, he told me that I would be going to LaGuardia to catch a different flight but we would end up at the same airport in Vienna. He promised Ben would be there waiting for him when I arrived just a couple hours later.

Just before he was to get out of the limo, the driver said, "change of plans, Ben, we're going back home."

"But what about dad? Ben asked.

"We can talk about that on the way," the driver said.

Ben had learned not to ask questions, both parents usually dismissed them anyway. On the way home, the driver told him that his father had been taken into custody by the police in New York. He didn't know when he would be coming home. A caretaker had been arranged for and the driver would stay with him until she arrived. He guessed the driver knew that his mother wasn't able to care for him.

The story was continued on page two. Ben turned the page. The story started about halfway down the page 'Dr. Death Trying to Flee from page 1.' There was a lot more text but what caught Ben's attention was a small picture of another man. The caption read, NYSDOH inspector solves case of mysterious murders at local hospital.'

Ben read the article from the beginning. He had since learned what his father had been up to but he never heard about this guy. 'Greg Webster visited the hospital for the first time just days before the apprehension. Along with some hospital employees, Webster was able to discover the players involved and set up a sting operation in coordination with the state and local police. He and his new friends are being hailed as heroes in a crime that no one knew was being committed.'

Ben had seen that name just recently but he couldn't place it. He continued reading through the stack of papers until he tired of them. He knew what they thought his father had done but he wasn't bothered by it. He was about to even the score now and he would continue until he thought it was enough.

Then it hit him, Greg Webster, Mrs. Greg Webster, the credit card from Smitty's. Ben knew when he touched her skin that they would meet again. He also knew that her second visit was just to see him.

How fortuitous that she gave him a key to her house. He could extract revenge on her husband in more ways than one. He didn't know what it was yet but somehow he just found his next event. Ben's attitude suddenly leaped upwards. He would tell Mother when he apologized later. The bombs could wait a while, but right now he would get ready for his trip to Boston.

Chapter 48

Taylor Summers was on his way to meet the geriatric 'Hardy Boys' in Vergennes when his phone rang. "Agent Summers," he answered.

"Agent Summers, it's Greg Webster."

"So soon?" He responded sarcastically.

"I have some new information for you. Have you met with Bill and Richard yet?"

"On my way to meet them now."

"Good," Greg said, "I can rain on their parade. Our boy was in Philadelphia this morning."

"How do you know that?"

"Too many similarities. If you take just the fragments and residue, you can draw the conclusion that it the same guy, but I think I know how he is detonating the devices and if I'm right, he had to be in Philly this morning."

"I'm listening," Summers said.

"In both the New York and Vermont bombings we have footage of the guy and the car. In each case, he is seen leaving the campus seven to ten minutes before the explosion. Why would he risk being there if he didn't have to be?"

"He's whacked, maybe he just likes the fireworks," Summers replied.

"Then why leave early? If he went to all that trouble, why wouldn't he stay to watch it? That wouldn't make any sense. My guess is he carries a device that triggers the timer that you found pieces of in Plattsburgh. When he builds the bombs, he sets the timer for fifteen or twenty minutes, which leaves plenty of time to be in close enough proximity to trigger the timer and get off campus well before it goes off. He's four or five miles down the road before the people know what hit them."

"It's an interesting theory, Greg. I'll have our guys in PA check it out. Is that it?"

"No, there's more but you're going to want to write this down. Can you pull over?"

"I'm FBI, I can pull over anywhere I want."

"Then pull over," Greg said.

"I'm not stupid, Webster, I'll find a safe spot, hold on."

Greg was holding for maybe a minute.

"Alright, I'm over."

"We found the missing paperwork for the cadavers, one at Plattsburgh and the other at UVM. There was a snafu in the invoicing system and the bodies arrived before they had set up the accounts for the vendor. Both cadavers came from the same supplier, which in this case is a funeral home in Boston."

"Boston?" Summers questioned.

"Boston," Greg confirmed. These bodies can come from anywhere. It's like any other commodity, there is a seller and a buyer."

"I thought people donated their bodies," Summers replied.

"They usually do but there still needs to be records finalized, embalming and shipping, sometimes it's more like a broker than a seller I guess. Anyway, bodies go all over the country."

"Do you have a name of this funeral home?"

"What do you think?" Greg boasted.

"Let's have it," Summers said.

"Meng Li Mortuary in China Town."

"That's where these bodies came from." Summers wanted confirmation.

"That's what the invoices said," Greg responded.

"Is there more?" Summers inquired.

"Nothing meaningful, at least not yet. All three of these schools were attended by Kyle Seike. We found out that he and his brother Alex Winfield donated a boatload of money to Plattsburgh as an endowment to keep the anatomy lab operational. The same is not true of UVM and we don't know about Einstein."

"What would the money connection be?" Summers asked.

"It doesn't look like there is any but you may want to ask Alex."

"Do you know where he is, Greg?"

"Not a clue but I'm sure you can find out. If you need my guys down in Philly, let me know."

"I think we can handle it, Webster."

"I'm sure you can. Check the security cameras around the perimeter of AEMC. I'm almost certain you will find the black BMW."

"Will do. I better get moving. I don't want to keep your boys waiting. They're not getting any younger."

"Neither are we Summers, neither are we."

Summers called his office.

Chapter 49

Mary and Sara were sitting on the front porch at the Shand's house. The girls were home from school and were hanging out in the tree mansion. The day was cooler than normal, especially up on the hill overlooking the Mohawk.

"What are you going to do Mary?" Sara asked.

"I don't know, I really don't want to bother Greg, I know he has a lot on his mind right now."

"What would he *want* you to do, Mary? What does he always tell the kids?"

"I know, if you see something, say something." Mary responded.

"So what's the harm in saying something? Is it because you don't want Greg to find out you went there?"

"That's some of it but I also don't want to accuse someone without any proof," Mary said.

"First of all," Sara said, "Greg only needs to know we stopped there to get the plumbing part for John while were out shopping. Secondly, you wouldn't really be accusing him of anything just by telling Greg."

"I suppose that's true," Mary conceded. "Alright, I'll tell him when the time is right. Hey, maybe we should find out what kind of car he drives. If it's a black sedan, that will make it that much more convincing!"

"How do you suppose we do that?" Sara asked.

"We drive out there tomorrow!" Mary exclaimed.

"And if he's not working?"

"The other guy said he would be there tomorrow." It's only fifteen minutes away," she added.

"I have a counteroffer. We go shopping in the morning and swing by Smitty's on the way home," Sara proposed.

"You're going to buy some sexy outfits, aren't you Sara?"

"I'm not telling."

"You know I'll know, I'll be right with you! I can help you pick them out. After all, I do have a proven track record," Mary said.

"I guess you'll find out tomorrow," Sara said.

With that resolved, the girls went on to other topics.

Chapter 50

Bill and Richard left Rt. 7 and made a shallow right turn onto Rt. 22A just north of Vergennes. Richard had been through this area many times since his years at UVM. He was particularly fond of a café that looked out at the falls on Otter Creek. They asked Agent Summers to meet them there.

They had been waiting fifteen minutes before Summers showed up and Bill was amazed that Richard hadn't said one word about a cigar. He seemed truly determined to give them up. They were seated at a small table on the terrace of the café when Summers pulled up.

"Agent Summers," Bill said, "how was the drive?"

"I was enjoying it until your boss called me."

"We know the feeling," Richard said. "Did he have anything good to say about us?"

"You, no. He does like to brag on himself though."

"Agent Summers, we know Greg way too well to buy that lie."

"You got me," Summers said, "I should know better than to try to fool you guys."

"You got that right, we're too old to be fooled!" Richard said.

"So, I hear you have some footage for me."

"Yes, I do," Bill said as he handed him the USB drive. "We have about a minute of him coming in and a little less than that going out. Have you been able to get a plate number off the first video we gave you?"

"Not yet. They must be having a little trouble with the enhancement." Summers seemed a bit embarrassed.

"This one is much better, they shouldn't have any problem." Bill added.

"We are looking at tape from the area around AEMC now. Your boy Greg is sure he was there too."

"You don't seem so certain, Agent Summers."

"I've been at this a pretty long time and quite honestly, you guys make it seem way too easy. It's not that I don't believe you, I just don't understand how you do it." Summers said.

"Maybe you think too much," Richard said, "when I was an intern, I thought I knew everything. They could throw any question at me and I would rattle off the textbook answer. I thought I was hot shit. Then I made a few mistakes. I knew the right answers but I hadn't developed that sixth sense, the one the really great surgeons have. You have to trust your gut and you have to know how to listen. The patient will tell you the answer to their problem if you listen close enough and long enough. Every doctor in my day didn't care what the patient said, what the fuck did they know? We were the doctors and listening to them made us look weak, at least that's what we thought."

"Are you saying we don't know how to listen?" Summers said defensively.

"All I'm saying is that sometimes we think we know so much more than the average person that we get in our own way, create our own obstacles. Sit in a courtroom and watch a plaintiff's lawyer tear apart a reputable physician.

'Dr. Jones, did Mrs. Smith tell you she was having back pain?'

'Well, yes but…'

'And Dr Jones, did Mrs. Smith tell you at every office visit for three months that she was having back pain?'

'Well, yes but…'

'No further questions, your honor.'

It's 'get out your checkbook' time. Professionals are not inherently good listeners. Greg Webster is an exceptional listener and an insightful questioner. And Bill and I don't do too badly ourselves. Some of that comes with age but most of it comes from knowing when to get your ego out of the way."

Summers didn't say a word. "There endith the lesson," Bill said quoting Elliott Ness. They finished their drinks and Summers thanked them for their efforts and he sounded just a little more humble this time. After he left, Bill looked at Richard and said, "It looked like you were having fun there."

"I was probably too hard on him. I don't know anything about how he does his job."

I don't think it's his job you were addressing and neither do you. I'm proud to know you Richard Ingraham. You can be thorny, but you can be trusted."

"Thank you, Bill, that means a lot coming from my assistant."

They smiled at each other, paid the check, and hit the road. They backtracked a little to get back on VT. RT. 7 south. They progressed a little more slowly now, looking for any place that might have a security camera. The area was pretty rural so there weren't many opportunities for them. They stopped at a gas station and a couple food places but no luck. If they found two cameras out there it would have equaled the total population.

They drove on until they came to Middlebury. "This is a great little town, Bill. This is where all the good looking girls hung out back when," Richard said.

"How do you know it's not still true? Do you want to check it out?" Bill offered.

"No, it will just make me feel old."

"You're only as old as you feel, Richard."

"Yeah, most days I feel like I'm a hundred. Especially when it comes to my bladder. Pull over at the next stop, will you?"

Bill looked up ahead and saw a Gerardi's Shop. "Will this do?"

"Perfect, it must be all the coffee I drank today," Richard said.

"You didn't have any coffee today," Richard joked.

"Smartass!" Richard said as he got out of the car. "I'll be right back."

Bill got out to stretch and decided to walk around the building. He observed a security   camera on every corner of the building. He walked inside and found a few more. It was a long shot but what did he have to lose? He went up to the register and introduced himself. "How would one get a look at your security footage?"

The young lady replied, "wait here a second." A moment later Bill was talking to the manager who led him to a table. "Have a seat, Mr. Dillon. My name is Larry, how can I help you?"

"Nice to meet you, Larry, you can call me Bill. Are you aware of the recent bombings in Plattsburgh and Burlington?"

"Yes, of course," Larry answered.

"I am part of the investigative team as is my partner here." Richard just joined them from the restroom. "We have just completed our reviews at both campuses and are looking for security footage that may have filmed the suspect. We know it's a long shot but with your store being located on one of the major roads leading from that area we thought it may be worth a try."

"I'm happy to assist anyway I can but we don't make those decisions at the store level. You would need to go through corporate for that. I can give you a contact number and the address if that will help."

"We understand and yes, that information would be very helpful. Where is corporate, Larry?" Richard asked.

"Our headquarters is in Ballston Spa, New York. It's less than two hours south of here."

"You have been a big help, Larry, you take care now."

"Anytime, gentlemen."

Bill and Richard left the store. "It's not too far out of our way," Richard said.

"It's getting late now, I'm not sure anyone would be around by the time we got there." Bill returned.

"You drive and I'll give them a call," Bill said.

Chapter 51

Special Agent Charis Andrews had just completed her walkthrough of the blast site at AEMC. She was assigned this case out of the Washington bureau following a phone call from Special Agent Taylor Summers from the Albany office. He claimed his team of investigators had found a probable link to the upstate New York and Vermont bombings.

The FBI was coordinating the investigation from the time it crossed the border between the two states. Now that a third was involved, teams from across the country were either involved or on alert. Her team on the ground consisted of Capt. Mac McGraw of the Philly P.D. and Maj. Thomas Anderson representing Homeland Security.

The three of them had met before the walkthrough and compared notes. McGraw had a team looking at video from the hospital and the four blocks surrounding it in each direction. The chaos at the site was making it difficult to review the onsite footage as most employees evacuated the building. Even after the 'all clear' was called, many were either told to stay away or just took it upon themselves to not return.

Philadelphia foot patrol was canvassing the neighborhood looking for witnesses. Homeland was ruling out terrorist groups and Agent Andrews was working the three state connection. There was another FBI team from Boston getting involved based on the interstate shipping of cadavers that originated in Boston and delivered to SUNY Plattsburgh and UVM.

"Captain McGraw, what do we have from the street cams in the area?"

"Nothing yet but our best bet is the views from the hospital system and we haven't been able to access them," he replied.

"This guy had to scope the place out beforehand, maybe the day before or earlier this morning. What about parking meters and parking lot passes? My guess is he got out of the car at some point," Charis said,

"I'll give a call to headquarters to get an update," McGraw replied.

"What's your take on this, Major?"

"Nothing about this looks like an outside terrorist attack. The bomb was too small and the body count is less than what they look for. We've also never seen PVC pipe used as a carrier. The M.O. doesn't fit," Anderson replied.

"You're probably right but we never saw pressure cookers before Boston either."

"Roger that, Agent Anderson." McGraw was walking back.

"We have something, a meter cop handed out a ticket early this morning over on Wagner, about two blocks from here. It was a black BMW with New York plates."

"Did they run the plate?" Andrews asked.

"They're doing it now," McGraw answered.

"What time was the ticket issued?" she followed up.

"Shortly after 08:00," he replied.

"Is it faster to walk or ride?" she asked.

"Walk," he responded.

"Lead the way."

The two block walk took about six minutes. McGraw pointed out the parking spot where the BMW was ticketed. Andrews looked up and down both sides of the street. "Where would I go if I had an hour to kill?" she thought to herself. Then the irony of her thought offended her. "Choose your words and your thoughts carefully," she warned herself.

Across the street she noticed an Italian restaurant, a tattoo parlor, and a laundry. Looking up her side of the street were another restaurant, a barber, and a gym. She thought for a moment, "The Italian place wouldn't be open for breakfast. He wouldn't be able to count on the timing of getting a tattoo, he might be late and he would leave blood and skin cells behind. He's probably not going to do laundry in less than an hour so that takes care of that side."

She couldn't tell from her position what type of restaurant was up the street, she would have McGraw check it out. "A workout and a bombing in one morning would be a little too much excitement for me but Mac could check that out as well." The barber shop made sense to her. The sign outside claimed they were open at 8:00am and it would be low risk, one or two people in there at best.

"Mac," she called, "check out that restaurant up there and the gym. First, see if they were open at 8:00 this morning and if so, ask them a few questions. Major Anderson, come with me." Mac went off in one direction and Charis and Tom headed toward the Barber shop.

This wasn't your old fashioned shop with executioner style leather chairs and a red and white pole out front. This was for young people, she guessed, men primarily. The Barber was a young man, maybe thirty years old, good looking and worked out, perhaps at the gym next door. There was just one customer in the shop and he was in the chair.

"What can I do for you officers?" he said as they approached. They were both in casual clothes so this guy was either pretty astute or in trouble a lot. He didn't look like the latter.

"I'm Special Agent Andrews, FBI and this is Major Anderson, Homeland Security. Are you the owner?"

"Yes, Michael Gerard," he replied, as he sanitized his hands and then held one out to shake. "How can I help you?"

"Was there a young man in here this morning, about six feet tall, slender with dark hair?"

"I had three of four that would fit that description this morning. What time would it have been?" Gerard asked.

"Between 8:00 and 8:30," Andrews replied.

"He was my first customer."

"What can you tell me about him?"

"He seemed like a nice guy, he didn't have a lot to say but he answered questions if I asked. He was a good looking kid maybe twenty-three to twenty-five."

"Do you remember what he was wearing?"

"I sure do. He wasn't a Philadelphia kid, that I know. His pants weren't baggy enough and his shoes, they were, I don't know how to describe them, they were old."

"Do you mean old as is worn out?"

"No, I mean old as in 'grandpa' old. Something that went out of style a while ago."

"Color?"

"The shoes were dark brown, the slacks were medium grey and he wore a short sleeve shirt that was a lighter sage green with an insignia on the sleeve."

"Do you remember what it said?"

"I had an apron over him so I just caught a glimpse as he was getting into the chair. I think it began with an 'S' maybe 'SM' but that's all I caught."

"Did he mention anything strange?"

"When he looked in the mirror just before he left I thought I heard him say 'Mother will approve."

"How did he pay, Mr. Gerard?"

"He paid with cash and he was fair tipper."

"One last question, Mr. Gerard, what do you do with your hair clippings?"

"I sweep them up place them in that container with the lid on it over there, and then dispose of them at the end of the day."

"Would his hair be in there?" asked Andrews.

"His and about eight others."

"We'll need to take that container."

"Can you settle for just the bag inside?"

"That would be fine. You have been a great help Mr. Gerard, thank you. And by the way, I like your shop!"

Andrews and Anderson went outside where McGraw was waiting for them. "There is nothing here Agent Andrews," he said.

"That's ok, we have what we were looking for. Gentlemen, I'm going to get this back to the lab at Quantico, let's keep in touch today via phone. I'm particularly interested in video, but at least we have the plate number now."

Chapter 52

"Goodnight, Mr. Webster," Kathy had popped her head in Greg's office to say she was leaving.

"Goodnight, Kathy, have a great evening!"

"Don't stay all night. Whatever it is, it will still be here tomorrow."

"That's a definite, Kathy. I'm not far behind you."

Greg's phone rang. "Should I get that before I go?" Kathy asked.

"I've got it but thank you!"

"Greg Webster," he answered cheerfully.

"Mr. Webster, my name is Charis Andrews with the FBI, Taylor Summers gave me your number. I hope I didn't catch you at a bad time."

"Not at all Ms. Andrews, it a pleasure to meet you."

Charis already had a good feeling about this guy and it had nothing to do with this phone call. "Thank you, Mr. Webster. I must admit that I feel like I already know you."

"Really, Greg said, "and how would that be?"

"I studied your case in college. It was a number of years ago in a criminology course."

"That must have been a great college!" he said jokingly.

"It was, and I think you're familiar with it. Does Union College ring a bell?"

"Wow! A loud one," he said. "That was a long time ago."

"It probably hasn't changed much," she replied,. It's landlocked so it really can't expand."

"That is true," Greg responded.

"Anyway," Charis continued, "I'm a big fan and I wanted you to know that. I'm also calling because we identified the owner of the car used in the bombings."

Greg stopped breathing for a second. Somehow he knew bad news was coming.

"It was registered in Herkimer County, New York, Mr. Webster. It feels to me like someone is digging up bones," Charis said.

"Do you know who it's registered to?" Greg asked now that he had found his breath.

"Yes, Sigmund Weinfeld."

"That's interesting, Charis. I'm sorry, may I call you Charis?"

"Of course. Would you like me to call you Greg?"

"Please do, it makes it so much more comfortable."

"Even when the topic is uncomfortable?" she asked.

"Especially then. I'd rather get bad news from a friend than a stranger. I'm sure you know that Sigmund Weinfeld is aka Kyle Seike and I'm sure you are also aware that he died in prison a few months ago."

"Yes, I know all of that and it alarms me," Charis replied.

"Tell me why, Charis."

"Because for now, we are at a dead end, pardon the expression. We checked the system for Kyle Seike, old addresses etc. but the only thing on file under either name is the home he had in High Falls up until the time he was captured."

"How about his brother Alex, could he be involved? He would certainly have an axe to grind," Greg offered.

"That's the first place my mind went as well. Alex is alive but not so well. After he was released from jail, he relocated to Mexico where he has been living a few blocks from the ocean. He had a little money that the prosecution couldn't get to and he has been living off that and keeping a low profile. According to his parole officer, he was recently diagnosed with cancer and the prognosis is not good."

"I'm sorry to hear that," Greg said honestly. "He may have been a little naïve but he wasn't a killer nor did he seem aware that his brother was. What about prison contacts? Has anyone been released lately that Kyle may have made friends with?"

"We're looking into that now," Charis replied. "I have also asked for a full financial auditing for both Kyle and Alex, under both names."

"That's smart. What should I be doing now Charis, besides watching my back?" Greg asked.

"I seem to remember you have some pretty sound ideas about that, the most important of which is 'be aware of your surroundings'."

"I was that memorable?" Greg joked again.

"You were to me but I'm young. I would like you to be around in thirty years to ask me again!" she exclaimed.

"You have my number, Charis, don't be afraid to use it."

"And you have mine now, so, ditto."

"Thank you, Agent Andrews."

"My pleasure, Mr. Webster."

After they hung up, Charis called an old acquaintance.

Chapter 53

Ben said goodbye to Mother and left the basement. He opened the first bay of the garage, started his truck, and backed it out. He rode much higher than he did in the BMW. He was heading to work for the last time before leaving for Boston. He was debating whether to leave in the evening or wait until sunrise tomorrow. It depended on how his day went.

He apologized to Mother last night before bed. Ben wasn't sure she understood or if she truly forgave him but he did it and he felt better as a result. Mother would have to deal with her own feelings about it. Ben was tired when he turned in having stayed up late preparing the basement for visitors. It was a good thing he was covering the late shift at the store.

He tried to remember the last time visitors came to his home. The most recent ones he could bring to mind were Amanda and Tori. They didn't care for the three hour ride from Boston but who could blame them, they had to be a little cramped back there. He got them inside and settled although they were a little stiff from the journey. He assured them that the stiffness would pass after a day or so and sure enough, it did.

Ben wasn't one hundred percent sure he was operating the equipment correctly but his dad left good notes and the results seemed pretty fair. He was certain he would do an even better job this time. 'Practice makes perfect' Mother always said. It was much easier for the girls on the return to Boston. They were dressed much more appropriately and felt flexible enough to sit up in the seats. Amanda had lost her front seat privileges after what she had pulled and Ben had grown to like Tori a little better.

That night at the apartment had become a little crazy. After they all made love for a while, Amanda tried to make a comeback, the tough girl that she was. It appeared that twenty ml. of propofol wasn't quite enough for everyone. He only brought one vial of fifty mi. so he gave the remaining ten to Amanda, not that she deserved it. He could have chosen a much harsher demise but he didn't like things to get messy. It did the trick and he was free to go about his business.

When they returned to Boston, Ben drove them over to the warehouse. It was after hours and no one was around. He brought then in through the loading ramp and over to the huge cooler. They weren't alone, two other guests were there as well. One was scheduled to go to SUNY Plattsburgh and the other to the University of Vermont but Ben had other plans. He thought Tori deserved to go to UVM and poor Amanda would have to settle for Plattsburgh.

That night, Ben prepared the shipments and notified the trucking company. The purchase orders and the packing slips were the easy part. Dad had all kinds of books and articles at home that included instructions on how to forge legal documents. Dad was a pro at that. He had been doing it his entire life. It was because of his father's cleverness and carefulness that Ben would never be found.

It was just before noon, Ben was so deep in thought that he didn't even remember the ride from home to the store. It was a satisfying memory once he got over the hurt. He parked the red Toyota Tacoma four by four in his usual space at the rear entrance. Ben climbed out of the truck, locked it, and went inside. The smell of fertilizer hit him like a brick. He kept walking to toward the back room.

After punching in, he pulled the green vest on over the sage tee shirt, strapped on his headset, and went to work. If the day went well, he believed he would leave right after his shift ended.

Chapter 54

Mary and Sara left for the mall in Syracuse as soon as the kids were on the bus. The drive took a little over an hour and they arrived just as most of the stores were opening. They started by getting a coffee and walking through the halls window shopping. The serious stuff would begin when the coffee was gone.

"I think we should call to see if he's working today," Sara said.

"Is that really necessary?" Mary asked.

"Yes, how else will we know?" Sara followed.

"We drive around the parking lot, no black car, no foul."

"Are you serious, Mary? We need to know if he's there. If he's not working today, his car wouldn't be there. The black car only helps if he's working today."

"You're right, Mary said, I'm not thinking straight."

Mary pulled out her phone and search the web for Smitty's. She found the website and pushed the icon for call. She put it on speaker so Sara could hear too.

"Good morning, thank you for calling Smitty's this is Roxie," said the girl who obviously started the day with a lot more coffee than they had.

"Yes, can you tell me if Ben is scheduled to work today please?" Mary asked.

"He's here until closing. Can I put you through to him?" Roxie offered.

"No, thank you, I'll be stopping by later. Have a good day!"

"Happy now?"

"Don't be snippy with me, you know I was right," Sara said.

"So, where do we begin?" Mary asked.

"Let's see," Sara said, "Victoria's Secret or Frederick's of Hollywood?"

"Well, are you going for the sexy wife or the cheap hooker look?"

"Is there a difference? You're the supposed expert on the subject," Sara answered.

"Then I say Victoria's. If that doesn't have the desired effect, you can go cheap the next time."

"If I put any of this stuff on and it doesn't have the desired effect, I'm filing for divorce!" Sara exclaimed.

"Not to worry," Mary said, "we will find just the right thing."

And they did. Mary even picked up a few new things for herself and Greg. They had an early lunch and were back on the road by noon. As they climbed the ramp onto I-90 East Mary could see the roof of the Carrier Dome of Syracuse University in the distance off to her right. She thought about Greg and Jack and what a good time they would have next week.

They left the interstate at the Herkimer exit and changed their route to NY 5s heading east. In a short time they would be coming up on Smitty's.

"Mary," Sara said, "what if this guy Ben is really involved in this?"

"What are the odds, Sara?" Mary responded, "why would a guy from High Falls be involved in bombings that far away? It doesn't make sense to me. I think I was just caught up in a hormone swing and that picture sitting on the desk in the den startled me."

"I agree with you," Sara said, "and I don't think we're going to find the black car today."

They pulled off Rt. 5s into the parking lot. There were seven cars in front and four around the side. One was black but couldn't be mistaken for an import. Mary felt a sense of relief deep inside of her.

"Can we put an end to this now?" Sara asked.

"Absolutely!" she replied.

Chapter 55

Bill, Richard, Greg, and John were meeting at the hospital to share information. Kathy had lunch brought in for them. They shook hands, wrapped up the informal welcomes and took their seats.

"Help yourselves guys, I'll begin while you eat and then we will go around the room. I had a very interesting call yesterday from an FBI agent in the Washington bureau. Her name is Charis Andrews and she seems like a very sharp girl. She was assigned to the Philadelphia case and was on the scene. Our guy's car was illegally parked a couple blocks from the bombing before detonation. It appears he got himself a haircut while he was waiting for the right time. A meter maid issued a ticket."

"That means they have a plate number, right?" Bill said.

"Yes, Bill, that's correct, Greg said, "And guess where the car was registered?"

Silence.

"Would you believe, Herkimer County?" Greg answered his own question.

"You must be kidding," John said.

"I wish I were. Here is another tasty morsel of information. It is registered to Sigmund Weinfeld."

"How can that be?" Richard asked, "he's dead. Besides, he changed that name decades ago!"

"Yes, he did," Greg agreed. "It seems to me that Kyle was keeping both identities going for some reason and I think if we can figure out what that reason is, the rest of the story will come together."

"Greg, are any of us at risk?"

"I don't see how but Agent Andrews suggested we be careful. Let's come back to this. I would like to hear what everyone else has found out. Who's next?"

"I'll go," Bill offered. "Richard and I stopped at a Gerardi's Shop just north of Middlebury, Vermont on the way back yesterday. While Richard was relieving himself, I walked the perimeter of the building and found lots of security cameras. We spoke with the store manager who couldn't help us directly but did give us contact information for corporate headquarters."

"They're in Saratoga Springs, right?" John asked.

"Close, but no cigar. Oh, sorry Richard. Anyway, they are in Ballston Spa. They agreed to have security wait until we were able to get there. We told him our story and shared our credentials and he agreed to share the video from that store.

We looked at tape from the thirty minutes after the bombing at UVM until two hours afterwards. The drive from Burlington to Middlebury is about an hour. We hit paydirt at T+57 minutes."

"That's great!" Greg exclaimed. "Did you see the car?"

"We saw a lot more than that," Richard piped in.

"We did," Bill continued. He parked the car in the back of the store where we were able to get an excellent view of the plate, HKR 7101. He went into the store and came out six minutes later. We also watched the video of when he was in the store. He stood in line for the men's room while he checked out a girl waiting for the lady's room."

"She was worth checking out," Richard interrupted again.

"She was pretty and about ninety years younger than Richard," Bill joked. "Anyway, she went in first and when she came out, our boy was inside the restroom. She walked out to her car, which was right next to his and waited. When he came out a minute later, she was resting on the hood of her car. Not even ten seconds went by before they both got in their cars. She led and he followed."

"Are the working together?" John asked.

"We have no way of knowing that but it sure seemed like they knew each other."

"Could you see the plate number of the girl's car?" Greg asked.

"It was a small red Hyundai, Vermont vanity plate MIRIDE26," Bill replied.

"That's a great find gentlemen!" Greg said, "we need to get that to the authorities."

"You know, Greg, we're not all that impressed with Agent Summers, so maybe you should hand this information off to Andrews," Richard suggested.

"That is exactly what I plan to do. Richard, anything new from you?" Greg asked.

"No, I've just been supervising my assistant. We gave Summers everything else we had, yesterday."

"Greg," Bill said, "in light of the information regarding the Herkimer plate, I would like to contact our friend at Gerardi's again to check security feed closer to home. Maybe they can help us figure out where this guy lives."

"Good idea, Bill. John, anything to add?"

"Nothing right now but I think I'm going to try to dig into Kyle's past a little more. There must be something other than what we know about him."

"That's good, John. You check out his medical past while the FBI looks into his prison life. You never know what kind of new friends you might find in the big house. In the meantime, be aware of your surroundings, you can't be too careful."

Chapter 56

"Agent Andrews," the voice answered.

"Charis, it's Greg Webster. Do you have a minute?"

"Of course, what can I do for you?"

"It's something I can do for you."

"I'm all ears, Greg."

"It must be hard for you to get a uniform on!" He joked.

"I manage," she responded. "I'm sure you have more for me than that."

"Do you remember anything about my team from the hospital murders?"

She thought hard for a moment. "I remember that you pulled together some hospital employees to help you and if I'm not mistaken, you even included a couple actual law enforcement people."

"We needed the guns," Greg quipped. "Well, my guys are helping me again on this case and they, as usual have done an amazing job so far. They tracked our boy down at a convenience store the day of the Vermont bombing. They have video of the car, the guy, and the license plate. They may even have an accomplice."

"I can't find guys out of the academy that take that kind of initiative. How did they do it?"

"They asked nicely. You may remember from your days at Union that we have a family run business up here called Gerardi's Shops. Great coffee and they make their own ice cream. Anyway, my guys stopped at one of their shops in Middlebury Vermont on their way home yesterday. They noticed the store had security cameras mounted outside and they asked the manager about them. They were directed to company headquarters and the rest is history."

"Nice work, would they like to come work for me?"

"I'll ask them but you would probably need to agree to take the entire team. I can send you a copy of the footage. I think it will be self-explanatory. What's the best way to get it to you?"

"How big is the file?" Charis inquired.

"It's only 5 megabytes."

"I'll send a secure link to your email, just respond and insert the file."

"You'll have it in two minutes. Let me know that you received it please."

"I will. Thank your guys for me. I hope to meet them someday."

"What about me?" he whined.

"You're a little needy, aren't you? Yes, I hope to meet you too."

"That's better. Enjoy the movie!"

Greg hung up and dialed Jack's number. He didn't feel as though he needed to worry the rest of the family, but with Jack away, he seemed more vulnerable.

"Hi Dad," Jack answered.

"You saw the news?" Greg asked.

"I did. You know young people watch and listen to the news too. It's an unspoken requirement."

"I just wanted to be sure you knew and I wanted to hear your voice."

"You can call anytime just to talk, Dad, you never need a reason." Greg was amazed at how his son had matured. He felt enormously proud.

"Thanks, Jack. I'll let you go. Be aware of your surroundings son."

"I will Dad, and I know 'if I see something, I'll say something.'

"Right, I will talk to you next week. I love you."

Greg waited for Jack to hang up. For some reason, he couldn't hang up first.

Chapter 57

Ben was having a good day. The traffic at work was steady and the day seemed to be going by quickly. He was just finishing loading two fifty pound bags of dog food into a customer's car when he noticed the car just sitting in the parking lot. He knew right away that it was Mary. She didn't see him around the side because he was mostly in the trunk of the car. She was with her friend again. He though she was pretty too but she wasn't interested in him like Mary was.

They only stuck around for a minute. Mary was probably trying to get up enough courage to come in. Her friend talked her out of it, he concluded. "Soon enough Mary," he thought, "we will have our time together." He hadn't worked out the entire plan yet but he had formulated a good outline. It couldn't be a long relationship because he would be leaving the country with Pricilla soon. He would make it fun while it lasted.

He thought about what he would like to do with her. Since Amanda had lured him into a menage a trois, he thought it may be fun to take her friend as well. He hadn't decided yet. He had time to consider it. No rush. Sometimes, he liked being spontaneous. "Ben, you have a customer in aisle eight please."

Ben looked at his watch, just a few more hours. He made his way to aisle eight and was surprised to see Priscilla standing there with a basket in her hand. His heart quickened and he could feel his attitude elevate. "Hi, Ben," she said, I'm not here to bother you. I just wanted to see you and say hello."

"I'm glad you did, I've missed you."

"I have missed you too," she replied. "I brought some dinner for you. I wasn't sure if you usually take a dinner break when you work the late shift but if not, you can take it home with you."

"That's very kind of you, Priscilla. I'll be driving to Boston tonight, I'll just take it with me. That will be perfect!"

"Oh good," she said. "Have a safe and productive trip. I look forward to seeing you Tuesday." Priscilla turned to walk away.

"Hey, Priscilla?" she looked back, "do you have a passport?"

She stopped to think. Not about whether she had a passport or not, but the oddity of the question.

"No, why do you ask?"

"Oh, I was just thinking that Canada is not that far away and it's supposed to be really nice this time of year," Ben lied.

"It sounds nice, Ben. I really haven't traveled very much. I guess when the cows take a vacation, I will too." She knew that sounded cold and pessimistic but it was the truth. She wouldn't be able to leave her dad with all that work. "I'm sorry, Ben, that sounded like I was unappreciative and I'm not. The thought of getting away sounds lovely, thank you. It just doesn't sound very realistic right now."

"I understand," he said. He didn't understand at all. When he needed to do something, he just did it. If someone gets hurt along the way, that's just the way it goes. "We can talk about it another time. I should get back to work but thank you for the dinner."

"You're welcome. See you Tuesday?" she asked.

"Yes. See you Tuesday." Ben hustled down the aisle to the back room. He set the basket down and walked back out. He was thinking of a way to get her on a plane to Austria. The passport and fake names wouldn't be an issue, he could make all that in a matter of a few hours but he wasn't sure how he could get her on the plane. That would take some deep thought.

"Ben, customer needs a carry out up front."

"OKAY!" Ben shouted. He quickly coughed a few times very loudly to cover it up.

Chapter 58

Charis was back home in Greenbelt, Maryland in less than two hours. She had put in the request to track the new plate number before she left Philadelphia. She was hoping the answers were waiting in her inbox by the time she signed in at home. She unlocked the door to her apartment, performed a quick sweep of the space and then locked the three deadbolts from inside. She triggered the alarm before removing her holster.

She loaded her glass with crushed ice and slowly poured a Diet Coke so that it wouldn't create a head. She hated the foam. She left her drink to chill on the desk and went to her room to change into something more comfortable. She emerged moments later in a pair of Quantico shorts, a pink FBI sleeveless T-shirt and fluffy slippers. Ass kicking time was over.

She powered up the computer and signed into the FBI personnel website. She had twenty-two unread messages. She took the oldest first and worked her way up to the most current. It was mostly unimportant stuff. Nothing life or death about it. She would still address all of it but she always prioritized first. About halfway through the list she found it.

She opened it up. Vermont plate MIRIDE26 belonged to Veronica Sweet, age 27, resides at 1121 Foote Street, Apt. 3, Middlebury, Vt. 05753. Her driver's license picture showed a pretty girl with blonde hair and blue eyes. Five feet-two inches tall and weight one-hundred-eighteen. No arrests, no warrants, one ticket for a bald tire. The registered vehicle is a Red, 2013 Hyundai Elantra four door.

Not what Charis was expecting. Going from a bald tire to multiple bombings was like going from kindergarten to medical school. It had to be checked out. She forwarded the information with a request to interrogate to her counterpart in Albany. She had met Taylor Summers a couple times at conferences but her gut reaction suggested he was not top shelf FBI and most likely a bit of a slimeball. She requested that he contact her immediately after the interview.

She specifically said she was to be contacted even though tomorrow was a Saturday. She even suggested that he wait until morning to ring Veronica's doorbell because Saturday was always a better bet than Friday night to find someone at home, especially a young someone. She read the rest of her email, responded to the ones that required attention and then jumped over to the FBI main site.

She wanted to enter a request for a cell phone search. She didn't have a phone number or a name. She had no account information at all. She knew it wouldn't be easy nor quick but it was worth a shot.

She filled out the request asking for a cell phone tracking using GPS that would have been in the vicinity of Plattsburgh, NY, Burlington, VT, and Philadelphia, PA within thirty minutes of the bombing at each location. She wasn't absolutely sure but she was hopeful that the cell providers would be able to run a data search based on her criteria. Succeed or fail, the companies had forty-eight hours to comply. She realized she was changing the weekend plans of several individuals.

With that completed, she moved to the sofa, drink in hand, and turned on the TV using the remote control. She scanned the program guide to see what was on. It was mostly junk as usual. She narrowed it down to The FBI Files and a rerun of Bewitched. She thought Bewitched would be more realistic. She made it through most of the introduction before falling asleep.

She had made it off the couch and into bed before midnight. At 2:17am her phone rang. She answered on the first ring. "Andrews," she said with a dry throat. "Who? Summers? "Hold on a minute." She sat up in bed and turned the lamp on. She grabbed the note pad that was always on the bedside table and flipped to a clean page. "Go ahead."

"I don't think the girl was involved," Summers said.

"First of all, why are there tonight? I suggested waiting until morning."

"I had nothing better to do."

"Did you take back-up?" she asked.

"For what? She's a marshmallow for Christ's sake, I didn't need back up," Summers replied.

"How about a witness for starters? And how could you be so sure she was alone?"

"I watched her for a while. Nobody went in, nobody came out. The lights went out, I waited a while and then I went in."

"And what if she cries foul, Summers? Do you know any of the rules?" She realized this wasn't going to get her anywhere so she talked herself down. "What did you get?"

"That was a first time meeting, she hooked up with the guy right there at the store. Never saw him before and hasn't seen him sense."

"What do you mean, hooked-up?" Andrews pushed.

"He follower her to a spot by the stream and they hooked up."

"What did they talk about?"

"It appears that she is not the talking type. According to her, she gave a few instructions and he followed them. He never said a word."

"And you believe her?"

"Oh yeah," Summers replied as if he had first-hand knowledge. She didn't want to know.

"You have a written statement?" she asked.

"Yes I do," he answered.

"How long were they together?"

"About twenty minutes. She had to get to work," he said.

"Did you follow up on that?" she quizzed him.

"It was a little late," he said, "but I'll check it out when they open in a few hours."

"Let me know," Andrews said and hung up. She really didn't like that guy.

On the other end, Summers waited for the call to end and walked back into the bedroom. "Where were we, grass girl?"

Chapter 59

The kids and Mary had gone up to bed. Greg assured Mary he wouldn't be up late. He turned off the house lights and went into the den. He turned on the small desk lamp and woke the computer up. He wasn't sure where to start so he opted for the beginning. He pulled up the website for the local newspaper and went back to August of 2001.

He typed in 'Seike, Kyle' and waited for the responses. It was only seconds before a long list appeared. He leafed in and out of the stories looking for anything that mentioned family. Aside from the discovery during the investigation that Alex and Kyle were actually brothers, Greg didn't find a thing.

The state seized his house in High Falls as well as any liquid assets he had accumulated. He opened the story regarding the disposition of assets that ran several months after the trial was over. The house was sold at fair market value and the liquid assets were valued at one hundred twelve thousand dollars. That seemed like an extraordinarily low amount for a single guy who had been making nearly twice that every year for decades. Maybe he kept a stash of cash somewhere or perhaps it was in someone else's name.

"Of course," he thought, "if I were doing something illegal I wouldn't put the money in the bank." If it were left in his old house chances are it would have been discovered by now. He had to have sheltered it under a different name.

He didn't have the first clue about how to trace something like that down. He got out the newspaper portal and typed in his name in the web browser. He harvested about a hundred hits, many of which were links to the articles he just saw.

There was one entry that looked different. It was dated May 1980. The internet would have been in its infancy then. He clicked it open. It took a while before he knew what he was looking at. It was a copy of an immigration form that someone took a picture of and uploaded. Greg wasn't clear about the connection to Seike. Nowhere on the document was his name listed but somewhere behind the scenes, it attached to Kyle.

The document was written in what Greg believed to be Russian. There was one name that appeared repeatedly,

Kovatikova. He hit the print button and waited until he heard it come to life, then he opened his email browser and entered Charis Andrews' name. He typed in the subject line 'Help.' He clicked on 'attach file' and loaded the PDF of the document into the message. He then added, 'I don't know any Russian. Do you?'

Greg sent the email off, put the computer to sleep and turned off the lights. He made his way through the dark to the stairs and headed for bed. He moved stealthily to the bathroom, closed the door quietly, brushed his teeth and used the toilet. After he washed up, he turned out the bathroom light and carefully opened the door.

His eyes hadn't adjusted to the dark so he felt his way around the bed, pulled the corner of the covers back and got in gently. He turned toward Mary to give her a goodnight kiss. He turned on his side away from her. Less than a minute later, he felt her arm around him.

"I went shopping today," she whispered.

Chapter 60

Ben arrived at his apartment before midnight. There was very little traffic once he cleared Albany. Even for a Friday night, the Boston traffic was mild. He parked in his usual place and started to get out when he realized he hadn't transferred his parking permit from the BMW to the truck. He would call the office in the morning and ask for a new one.

He grabbed his duffle bag, the basket Priscilla had given him and the miscellaneous bag from the bench behind his seat. He entered his building from the underground garage and took the stairs. He never used the elevator. He opened the door at the third floor and stepped into the carpeted hallway. The apartments here were large so there were only six units on each floor. He hardly ever saw any of his neighbors coming or going.

Unit 304 was the closest to the stairwell. He put his key in and turned the handle. Just as he left it, tidy and clean. The air was a little stale so he turned the AC down a couple degrees and set the fan to high. He moved his bags to the bedroom and set the dinner bag on the kitchen counter.

He opened the fridge and pulled out a bottle of water. The bag contained fried chicken, biscuits, gravy, and mashed potato. He made himself a plate and put it in the microwave.

He hadn't had a meal yet today and he was hungry. The food smelled great. When the timer went off, he took the plate from the microwave and his beverage and went to sit in the living room. He placed his food on the coffee table, picked up the remote and turned on the TV. He took a biscuit from the plate and dipped it into the gravy. As he chewed, he surfed the channels for an all-night cable news channel. He settled in on one and then sat back with his dinner in hand.

He wasn't sure he ever tasted fried chicken before. He liked it. He was so hungry that the food only lasted a few minutes. He brought his plate and bottle to the kitchen and cleaned everything up. Mother would be proud, she hated a mess. He wondered how she was doing back at home, alone. He returned to the living room just in time for the national news.

The introduction included a fire in Colorado, severe storms expected across the south and an update on the Philadelphia Bombing. The announcer encouraged him to stay tuned. He sat patiently through the four useless commercials.

"Police are saying they have new information regarding the Thursday morning bombing at Albert Einstein Medical Center in Philadelphia. In addition to video footage from security cameras, authorities say they have possible DNA evidence and eyewitnesses who saw the bomber."

"We're not ready to release any names at this point but we are getting closer. I can tell you that we are working closely with the FBI in New York and Vermont and that we feel strongly that an arrest will be made soon."

"I doubt it," Ben thought. He knew they couldn't have positive information about his identity. He didn't exist. They could have a picture of him though so he would need to be careful for a few more days. He had no idea about what DNA they may have. It was probably just hype to make him nervous or make everyone else less nervous.

He turned the TV off and got out his laptop. He looked for the reservation number for Lufthansa Airlines. He could have purchased online but he didn't want to leave a digital trail. It was almost 1:00am, so he shouldn't have to wait long. The call was picked up almost immediately. Within ten minutes, he had two one-way tickets to Vienna. The first was for Korben Kovak and the other for Martina Kovatikova. One quick picture change in the passport and Priscilla becomes Martina.

Ben was ready for bed. It had been a long day and he had a heck of a week coming up, starting with getting to the warehouse early the following morning. What he needed to do wouldn't take very long but he needed to be uninterrupted. He didn't think Willi would come in on a Saturday. It was almost certain Jeremy would come in at some point, but definitely not 9:00am.

While he was getting ready for bed, Ben thought about the difficult time he had with Amanda and Tori. It was easy getting them in to the warehouse but getting them prepared for shipping was tough. Lifting them into the reinforced cardboard box without breaking it took all the strength he could muster. An embalmed person weighed about the same as any other stiff, unless of course they were gutted at autopsy.

He could have done that at home before he embalmed them but he wasn't up to cleaning the mess and Mother would have a fit if he left the basement messy. Plus, he needed to sit them up for the car ride back to Boston and he didn't want them to seep. Adding the extra weight from the bombs stuffed in their uteruses didn't help.

He managed it okay. They were all packaged and ready to ship by morning. He had two other cadavers to ship as well so he used the same return address on the shipping form and label, Meng Li Mortuary, Boston. It would take weeks if not longer to unravel that one. Everyone would be happy except Mr. Li.

"More good times," he thought. He was going to miss Boston and his job just like he missed medical school. He was very used to missing things.

Chapter 61

Charis couldn't get back to sleep so she decided to check her email once more. She noticed a message from Greg Webster that came in around 10:45pm. She clicked to open it. It was a very short message but she knew where he was going with it right away. "Good thinking, Greg," she said to herself.

She started a new email to a friend in the bureau who was a Russian translator. "I would appreciate any help you can provide, TY, Charis." That's all it would take. Most of the agents she worked with were bright and intuitive. Then, there were the others, like Summers. She wondered how they all graduated from the same training program or even how some of them got in. Most likely, a friend in Washington made it happen.

There was another email that she missed. It came in just after Greg's and it was from the genetics lab. She summarized it in her head. "Seven hair types, four were dark color, we will have the preliminary DNA on those sometime tomorrow." That was a lot quicker than she thought. She wasn't sure what she would do with the information other than run it against everyone else in the world who has ever had a DNA test performed. She was too tired to think about it now. Maybe in the morning. She did her best thinking in the shower.

Chapter 62

Greg was going to tell her what he knew. That was before she surprised him in bed. He was torn. He heard his own voice saying, "if you see something, say something," but he did not want to worry her unnecessarily. There was nothing to indicate that he was a target. The recent bombings were far away disconnected from him. "But not disconnected to Kyle Seike and Kyle Seike would forever be connected to him." Deep down he acknowledged it, so why was he having trouble saying something?

Mary had drifted off to sleep already, exhausted and content, but Greg was wide awake. Not that he wasn't content, he was blown away by Mary's passion and generosity. He just couldn't get his mind to take a break. When he considered the likelihood of any direct risk to him or his family, the only one who fit in to the killer's current M.O. was Jack. While nothing pointed to Syracuse University playing a role in Seike's past, it was a college and therefore a potential target.

Greg tried to discount that fact by rationalizing that Albert Einstein Medical Center was primarily a hospital, "but one where Kyle did his residency," the other voice said. He bargained with himself. He would talk to Jack about it but leave Mary and the girls out of it for now. That seemed to satisfy him. He turned on to his side and took a few deep breaths. He closed his eyes and tried willing himself to sleep. It didn't help.

Greg smoothly and quietly slid out of bed. He found his robe in the dark and pulled it around him then edged toward the door. He turned the handle fully before pulling, attempting a soundless exit. The door opened about six inches then squeaked.

Mary moved but didn't wake up. He made it out the door and closed it gently behind him, lifting it slightly to eliminate the noise. It worked and he was on his way downstairs.

He pulled a bottle of water from the fridge and walked to the den. He sat at his desk and woke the computer up. "If I'm awake, you're awake," he said softly. He didn't have a plan but he was hoping one would come to him.

He started by checking his mail. There were no new messages that he was interested in. He thought about calling Jack then realized getting at call in the middle of the night from Dad would scare the crap out of him. That would wait until morning. There was one thing he could do.

He signed into his hospital email and began composing a new message. Peter Forester replaced Bill Dillon as the head of security several years ago. Greg had asked Bill to select his successor and he did a great job. Greg started typing his name and the box automatically filled.

"Good morning, Pete, I would like you to implement a new procedure first thing this morning. We need to scan all packages we receive before they enter the main hospital building. I'm not sure how we go about setting this up but perhaps the detached garage can be cleared out for a few days to allow all packages to be delivered there. I am open to other ideas if you have them.

You will also need some scanning equipment that will detect possible explosives. Your first call should be to the local police to see if they can either assist or advise. I will sign off on any budget requests for the project. This project will only last a week or less and I'm sure you already know that we need to keep this absolutely quiet. You, me, and the purchasing manager are the only ones inhouse that should know about it. I'll talk with the police chief in the morning as well. Thanks, Pete."

Greg already knew that Pete was not going to have a good day. He also knew he could and would handle it. "Evaluate, Educate, and Empower," that was Greg's mantra. It had worked so far. Greg signed out of the City Hospital system and open his web browser. It pulled up his last search and the Russian document opened back up. "Talk to me!" he demanded. It didn't.

Chapter 63

Ben arrived just before 7:00am. He was awake earlier but didn't want to draw any attention from the night police surveillance. He entered through the front door and silenced the alarm. He thought about his first visit here and how excited he was to take the job. Now, as he stood in the small reception room, he realized tomorrow would be his last day.

He didn't know what the future held for him but he didn't have time to worry about it now. He unlocked the door to the warehouse and stepped in. He walked down the long corridor to his left toward the shipping station which was located just inside and along the left wall of the bay doors. He set his miscellaneous bag on the counter then walked up and down the aisles looking for the perfect box. Something large enough but ordinary and labeled in such a way that everyone could ignore it.

He walked quickly, eyes scanning left and right, and up and down. The aisles were three feet wide and the shelves were stacked to eight feet high. He was in the medical section when he decided he needed something from the scientific area. He skipped three aisles including the one where the formalin was kept. He had helped himself many times to the boxes that held three two-quart bags each. He wouldn't require them this time as he wasn't planning on embalming anyone.

Ben made a left tuned and stepped into aisle twelve. "Ben, customer needs assistance in aisle twelve," he could hear his memory call through his headset. He pushed that away and focused on the boxes. Halfway down the aisle and at eye level on the right, he found what he was looking for. It was an overhead projector. The size was perfect, there was a lot of hollow space inside the metal frame and it wouldn't seem at all out of place.

He slid it onto his shoulder and headed back to the packaging counter. He set the box down, carefully opened with a sharp box cutter and pulled the unit out. "A piece of cake," he said to himself.

He turned the unit upside down and removed six screws that held the bottom cover on. He set the cover and screws aside and opened his bag. He carefully withdrew the white PVC pipe from the bag and set it on the counter.

He needed something to wrap it in. At the other end of the counter was a box of plastic bubble wrap. He unwound about three yards of it and set it on the counter. He placed the pipe on top of one end of the plastic and began to roll it slowly and carefully.

The package looked like a roll of wrap that was a foot long and six inches in diameter. He placed it in the cabinet and secured it with tape to make sure it wouldn't shift. Ben replaced the bottom cover and screwed it on tight. He placed the housing back in the box, placed a little extra bubble wrap around the sides and sealed the box where he had cut it.

He weighed the box and measured it then completed the information for the label. The box would be on a FedEx truck this morning for delivery Monday afternoon. He was very careful with the label. "Syracuse University, Dineen Hall, L.R. 201, 950 Irving Ave, Syracuse, NY 13210. Attn: Greg Webster. Requested for 10:00am Tuesday." He was sure that would get it there.

"The internet is a wonderful thing," Ben thought. All he had to do was type in Webster's name and up it came. It seemed as though Mr. Webster was making a second career out of speaking about the case.

That part was over and it wasn't even 7:45 yet. Ben decided to take a break and think about how he might get Priscilla aboard the aircraft against her will. It wasn't going to be easy but he had plenty of time. FedEx wouldn't be here until 9:00am and there wasn't a lot more to do at the warehouse.

Chapter 64

Greg was up and dressed by 7:30 even though he hadn't slept much. He told Mary he was going out to get donuts and stop by the hospital. Neither of the girls was awake yet and Mary was still resting in bed. He stopped by the den first to check his email.

The first thing he noticed was a response from Charis. "Greg, I received your request. A friend at the bureau is translating it for us. I hope to have something later today. I also expect to have a decent headshot of the bomber later this morning. It will hit the airwaves this afternoon. The suspected accomplice turned out to be nothing. I'll be back in touch today."

The second message was from Peter Forester. "That's a big ask, Chief, especially on a Saturday. Fear not, it will happen. The garage is a good idea. Thanks!" Seeing nothing else, he put the computer to sleep and walked briskly to the front door. On the way out, he locked the door behind him, something he rarely did.

He started the car but before putting it in gear, he dialed Jack's number.

"It's pretty early, Dad. It is Saturday there too, right?"

"Yes, it is and what a pretty one!," Greg exclaimed.

"I wouldn't know," Jack replied, it's still dark out here. The sun rises in the east, remember?"

"Is that still true?" Greg joked. "I know it's early and I apologize. I just got some news and I wanted to talk to you right away. It stays between you and me for now, ok?"

"Of course, Dad, are you alright?"

"Oh sure, nothing like that, just a little news about the bomber. It looks like he has ties to the City Hospital killings or at least to Dr. Seike."

"How do you know that, Dad?"

"Seike attended all three of the attack sites and they found who owns the car. It is registered to Seike as well."

"Does that mean the guy is in High Falls?"

"I don't think so Jack, it just means that the car was registered in Herkimer County. My guess is someone Seike was in prison with is out and seeking some sort of revenge. He could be anywhere."

"What do you need me to do, Dad?"

"Just the usual, Jack, be aware of your surroundings. That's all you can really do."

"What about you guys? Are you taking precautions?" Jack asked.

"It's not his M.O. to come after individuals, his game is facilities and that's why another school bombing seems more likely. As far as anyone can tell, he has never had anything to do with S.U. so it doesn't seem likely he would come out there. By the way, the FBI should be releasing his picture to the media today so that should keep him in check. That's in addition to knowing what kind of car he drives and his plate number. It's going to be hard for him to hide."

"Alright, Dad, I will be as careful as I can, I promise."

"I know you will son. Hey, I'm really proud of you. I just wanted you to know that."

"Thank you, Dad, I'm proud of you too. Hey, that reminds me, I know which lecture hall you're assigned to on Tuesday. You're still planning on coming, right?"

"Oh yes, I wouldn't miss it!" Greg replied.

"Great. Ok, do you have a pen?" Jack asked.

"I'm driving at the moment but I'll remember it. And if I don't, I'll call you the same time tomorrow!"

"That's what I'm afraid of, Dad."

"I'll remember," Greg promised.

"Alright, it's LR 201. Take the center stairs up and turn left. It will be the first door on your right. I plan on being there early to get a good seat so I'll meet you by the stage."

"What stage?" Greg asked.

"All the lecture rooms have stages, Dad. Don't worry, it's only about a three foot fall."

"Thanks, Jack, I appreciate the encouragement."

"You'll be fine, I'll see you there Tuesday morning."

"Alright, I love you, Jack."

"Ditto, Daddio, have a good day!"

Greg listened for the click. For some reason he felt like he had to hold on to every moment. That was true with Jack and everyone at home. He was noticing that he held on longer to hugs and kept eye contact long after the other person looked away.

He stopped at the bakery and picked up a dozen donuts for home and a dozen for the hospital. Pete and his people deserved at least that.

Chapter 65

By 11:00am Charis had the image of the killer. It was approved for release and would hit the press in time for news at noon. It was a decent picture of a fairly handsome guy. He didn't look the type but sometimes they don't. She called Summers.

"Agent Andrews, how can I help you?" he answered.

She really did not like this guy. "I want you to show the photo to Veronica Sweet and confirm this was her guy."

"I already did, she confirmed."

"The photo came out just a few minutes ago, how did you.." she stopped herself. "Never mind," she said. "Please place an update in the system so that everyone else knows." She hung up. "That bastard slept with her last night!" She was furious but her anger wouldn't help her. She would find a way to prove it then have his ass discharged.

She placed a call to Greg Webster.

"Hello," Greg answered.

"Good morning, Greg, it's Charis Andrews."

"Hi Charis, it's nice to hear from you. Tell me you have good news," he said as he closed the door to the den.

"I do have some, Greg, and I'm waiting on more," she replied. "The picture of our suspect will be hitting the news at noon. With any luck, someone will recognize him right away."

"That is good news, Charis. I assume you will be adding a hotline banner to the story, will that be a local number or FBI?"

"It will be a tollfree number that will ring at FBI headquarters. They will then dispatch local authorities as needed.

"Perfect. Any other news?" Greg prodded.

"Nothing yet. I haven't heard back from the interpreter nor have we made any headway on Seike's finances but rest assured, people are working on it as we speak."

"I'm sure they are Charis. I thought about what you said about being careful and I implemented a security measure at the hospital. I really don't think he would have reason to attack here but I guess you can't be too careful."

"I agree. May I ask what you did?"

"I would be happy to share that with you. We moved all of our receiving to a detached garage, hundreds of feet from the main building. We will screen it all there before it is sent to the hospital. We have asked the local police for help with the screening and they agreed. The hard part is keeping it quiet. If word got out, every patient in the place would be pushing their own wheelchair and stretcher down the road."

Charis laughed. "Like one of the old Three Stooges episodes!"

"You remember those? You seem a bit young for that."

"I didn't see the originals and I doubt you did either," she replied, "The reruns were popular when I was at Union. A bunch of us used to get together and watch."

"Mostly guys, I'll bet," Greg added.

"You're right, that was a bonus. The girls just couldn't find the humor in it. My dad used to talk about the show all the time. He would try to re-enact the episodes all by himself. Nobody found it funny but the way he would laugh while doing it made me laugh as well."

"Was your dad in law enforcement too?"

"No, he was old school, marry young and get a job kind of guy. He was a laborer and carpentry for a while then went back to school to become a teacher. He wanted better for me."

"Every parent does. Was he proud of your choice?" he asked.

"He was and he still is, he just worries about me all the time," she said.

"I have two daughters and I know just how he feels. I also have a son and I don't worry about him any less. In fact, I called him early this morning. He's away at college and I spent the night worrying about him so I decided to call and tell him what was going on."

"He's away at college and you called him early on a Saturday morning?"

"I know, he let me have it too but I needed to do it. I have been careful not to tell the girls too much. Not because they're girls but because I didn't want to create unnecessary fear. My son being away at college seemed more relevant."

"Where does he go to school?" she asked.

"Syracuse," he answered.

"Go Orange!" she said. "That's a great school."

"It must be, they invited me to speak to a mixed session of criminal justice, psychology, and sociology. I'm scheduled there next Tuesday in fact."

"That's great! Will your son be in the audience?"

"He said he would and he's usually good at his word."

"What time is the event?" she asked.

"Begins at 11:00am, Dineen Hall, LR 201. Are you planning on making it?" he kidded her.

"If we catch the bad guy before then," she replied.

"Then I really hope I see you there," he said.

"So do I Greg, so do I."

They chatted a little more. Greg asked Charis to call when she had more information and she promised she would.

Greg opened the den door and entered the kitchen. There was note on the fridge from Mary saying she walked over to Sara's house and to call if he needed her. He took a donut from the box and went to the TV. It was well before noon but the local channel went with the story as soon as they received the picture. There on the screen was a young man who didn't look much older than Jack.

"Authorities are looking for this Herkimer County man for questioning in the University Bombings. If you have any information as to his identity or whereabouts please call the number listed below."

Greg didn't recognize the young man but there was something about him that did look familiar. Greg grabbed the car keys and went out the door. A few minutes later, he was walking through the Shand's back door. John, Sara, and Mary were sitting at the kitchen table.

"Turn on the news," Greg said. "John, call Bill and Richard to see if they can come over."

Chapter 66

The FedEx driver was right on schedule and never checked the return address. Jeremy arrived around 9:30 and they worked together to fill the rest of the orders. By 11:00, they were all done. Jeremy asked Ben if he wanted to go for an early lunch but Ben declined. He said he had a few things he needed to take care of.

Jeremy said goodbye and left the warehouse. Ben watched his car drive away then turned on the news. The small TV took a moment to warm up and when it did, Ben was staring at himself with an 800 number scrolling across the bottom. He turned the TV off and gathered his things. On his way out, he walked down the mortuary supply aisle looking for makeup. He stuffed four or five items in his bag and left the building, locking the door behind him.

He moved calmly to his truck, got in and buckled his seat belt. He needed to think for a minute but first he had to get away from this building. He drove back toward his apartment but he wouldn't park in the garage. A place on the street would be better if he could find one. He didn't think anyone at the apartment would be looking for him. He never met his landlord nor any of his neighbors. His rent was paid in advance for the year.

It required driving around the block several times but a parking spot finally opened up very near the garage entrance. He took his bag from the back seat, locked the truck, and ducked into the garage. He went to the stairs, opened the door, and began the ascent. He was just reaching the second floor when he heard the door above him open. He heard two voices speaking while he opened the door to the second floor and stepped through, out of the stairwell.

With his back to the exit, he listened as the voices got closer. Thirty seconds later, they were gone. He opened the door and re-entered the stairway. He took the steps two at a time until he reached level three. He was into the hall and then into his room in just seconds. He locked the door behind him and moved to the sofa.

He turned on the TV. He scanned through channel after channel and found the same breaking news story time after time. Some were showing footage from the bombings while other were speculating about who the man was.

On one of the channels, the reporter was conducting a phone interview with an FBI Agent. "We're putting all the pieces together as we speak with more information becoming available every minute. We think we will have a name to go with the picture very soon."

This was going to make Ben's last few tasks more difficult but not impossible. He didn't think he would be made this soon but he did have a contingency plan. Ben closed his eyes and counted his breaths until his pulse slowed down. His father taught him how to do this before he left. He said Ben would need it at times when he was scared or uncertain. Over the years, Ben mastered the technique.

He spent the last fifteen years scared and uncertain. Setting the alarm clock to wake up for school. He didn't dare miss a day or someone might come looking for him. Receiving grocery deliveries without being seen and making sure the recording was always set to play. "Just leave them by the door please," he heard his mother's voice. A few seconds pause and then, "thank you." After ten seconds, the recording would repeat itself just in case the delivery person had a follow-up question. Every now and then when one of the hired help was there, they would actually answer the door to create a smoke screen.

Not many people came to the door. Just the fact that it was a quarter mile down a dirt road kept most folks away. When someone did come, the door was never answered. Every once in a while he would find a flyer stuck in a groove somewhere. They were usually from a religious group who thought that even souls that far off the grid needed salvation. He knew scared, he knew loneliness and he definitely knew uncertainty.

His pulse was down to fifty-eight beats per minutes. That was a far cry from the eighty plus where he started. Time to relax and think of a plan.

Chapter 67

They all followed John into the living room where he was turning on the TV. John had already called Richard and Bill who were on their way. It didn't matter which channel John tuned to, they had all interrupted their regular schedules for the breaking news.

When they posted the picture of Ben, Mary grabbed Sara's hand. "Oh my God!" she said softly. "We know this guy, Greg." Greg wasn't sure he heard her above the noise of the TV.

"I'm sorry honey, I didn't hear you."

"Sara and I have met this man. He works at the hardware store where we bought the plumbing stuff for John on the way home from shopping."

Greg didn't know what to do or what to say. "Why didn't you say something?" he asked.

"We didn't know until just now. When I saw that printed copy in the den a few days ago, I told Sara I thought he looked familiar. We didn't want to point a finger without being sure. That picture didn't show his entire face even. We stopped again yesterday to see if there was a black car in the parking lot that matched the description the police gave."

"Did you see him again?" Greg asked.

"No," Mary responded, we called ahead to see if he was scheduled to work and he was. We just drove through the parking lot."

"Did you see the car?" John asked.

"No," Sara replied, there was only one black car but it wasn't the one."

Greg was dialing his phone.

"Are you calling the police?" John asked.

"FBI," Greg responded, they will coordinate the police."

"Hello, Charis," Greg said before she had a chance to say hello. "I have something for you. We know where the kid works!"

"Are you sure?" Charis questioned.

"Yes, both my wife and her friend identified his picture on the news."

"Where is it," Charis asked.

"It called Smitty's Farm and Family and it's on NY Rt. 5 south about three miles west of High Falls."

"Hold on the line, Greg, I'll be right back." She didn't wait for a response. Greg heard the phone click. They continued to watch the news.

"Are the kids all here?" Greg asked.

"Yes, they're in the tree house," Sara responded.

"I think we should bring them in just in case," John said as he walked toward the back door.

"I think 5 south is about to be blocked off for a few miles," Greg said.

Charis returned to the line.

"Greg, local and state police have been notified and are on the way."

"Thanks Charis, that was a lot more efficient than me calling the locals."

"I agree, good move. Hey, I have some more news, we have a name to go with the face."

"I can tell you that his first name is Ben," Greg offered.

"And you would be partially correct. His full name is Korben Kovak and we have an address for him. He is or was a medical student at Harvard. That's how we found his name. We cross-referenced his face with all college IDs in the northeast."

"Wow, that's pretty impressive. Charis, is there any link to me, City Hospital or Kyle Seike?" Greg asked.

"Not yet, but it's only a matter of time," she replied.

"And you said you have an address. Is it local?"

"Yes, does 402 Bayard Street ring a bell?"

Greg thought about it then looked at around the room. "Does 402 Bayard Street mean anything to you?" he asked the group. No one had heard of it.

"No, Charis, it does not ring any bells here," Greg replied.

"We have a team on their way, so we will know soon. I also have information regarding Boston and the document you found online. The Boston funeral home that supposedly sent the cadavers is thus far a bust. They denied having anything to do with it and at first glance, it seems believable, but we're going to dig a little deeper.

There were some communication difficulties that will require follow up with a translator. The document, however, may hold promise. Martina Kovatikova appears to be a mail order bride. It was a popular thing for a while. Anyway, we're trying to track down her history and whereabouts as well."

"So if the cadavers didn't come from the funeral home, then where did they come from?" Greg asked.

"We don't have an answer for that yet. We're looking into the transportation logs of companies working out of the Boston area."

There was something tickling Greg's brain but he wasn't sure what it was.

"Charis, will you check back with me when you have anything new please?"

"I will stay in touch throughout the day Greg."

They hung up. This kids were all in the house and Bill and Richard had arrived.

Chapter 68

"Let's have a seat everyone," Greg suggested. "I want to bring everyone up to speed on what's happening with the university bomber. Jillian, Jocelyn. and Maria, I want you to hear this as well. I know it may sound scary and I apologize. I didn't think that you would need to know about this at all because it wasn't happening anywhere near us but there is now good reason to believe that the perpetrator has ties to our area."

"Ties like how, Dad?" Jillian asked.

"We don't know the full extent yet, honey but we believe he lives around here and perhaps even works close by. The FBI is following up on leads as we speak and I'm hoping we will have more information before the end of the day. I just want you to be super aware of your surroundings until this is over. There is no reason to believe that he has interest in any of us but we can't be too careful."

"What have you learned recently, Greg? Richard asked.

"Well, the work that you and Bill did is the reason the FBI even has a picture and a name for this guy. Sara and Mary also had a role in identifying him and where he works. We know his name is Ben Kovak and he has been working at Smitty's Farm and Family on 5s just outside of town. The police are probably there right now. They have a home address that they obtained from records from Harvard where he has been a medical student."

"So where does he live, Dad?" Jocelyn asked.

"On the other side of the river, Joc, but let me clear, anything said here today cannot be repeated outside this room. Is that clear?" They all agreed. "This is an active investigation that involves our local police, the state police, and the FBI. We need to let them do their jobs. There are still many unanswered questions and we don't want to alarm the public or let the suspect know that we are on to him."

"I think that ship has sailed, don't you Dad? I mean the guy's face is all over the news." Jillian stated.

"That's a good point, Jillian and yes, he is on the news but you will notice that the police on the news won't give specific information unless they are certain that what they say is accurate. They also need to maintain the element of surprise to be able to capture him without the threat of injury to innocent people. The best way we can help right now is to not speculate or spread rumors and to be aware and report anything strange."

"What can we do to help, Greg?" John asked.

"For starters, the girls can remain in the house when they are not in school. Let's not use the tree house until further notice. As for the adults, we can discuss that once the girls have gone upstairs." Greg looked at the girls until they grasped what he was implying. They all pushed away from the table and moved toward the staircase as instructed. When Greg was sure they were out of hearing distance, he began again.

"Let's go around the table and share not only what we know, but what ideas each of us may have. Let's start with Mary and Sara."

The ladies looked at each other to see who would speak first. Sara spoke up.

"Early in the week, Mary and I went shopping in Herkimer. John needed a part for one of our toilets and I said we would pick it up for him while we were out. Well, we got distracted and drove right out of Herkimer without stopping at the hardware store.

We seemed to remember a store on the way home that may carry the part. We found Smitty's Farm and Family just a few miles up the road. Neither Mary nor I had ever been there. We went in and it was a pretty nice store.

Anyway, it was just a moment or two when this young man asked if he could help us. I showed him the old part and he walked us right to the replacement. He seemed very knowledgeable and nice. We looked around a little and then left."

"When you asked me to have the keys made, Greg, I returned there and Ben helped me again. He took the old key and made copies while I shopped around. When I returned to the key making station, he had them ready for me."

"What can you tell us about him, girls?" Greg asked.

"He seemed normal for the most part. I did have an uncomfortable feeling though, especially the second time. He seemed to over-extend his reach when he took the key and again when he handed the new ones back, kind of like he was trying to make contact with my skin. I guess it felt like he was trying to flirt with me," Mary explained.

"How did you pay for the purchase, girls?" Richard asked.

"I paid with a credit card," Mary said.

"Me too," Sara added.

"Greg, he may have your address. You too, John," Richard said.

"I suppose that's true," Greg said.

"Mary," Richard said, "you didn't watch him make the keys, right?"

"No, I went looking around the store," she replied.

"He may have made an extra key, Greg," Richard hypothesized.

"Good point, Richard," Greg said, "we need to change the locks. Mary, see if you can reach the locksmith and ask him to come over today to re-key the locks. Tell him it's an emergency. If he gives you a hard time, bring the phone to me please. Tell him we will meet him at home in an hour."

"Bill and Richard, do you have anything new?" Greg asked.

"I don't have anything," Richard replied.

"I'm waiting for the security guy at Gerardi's to call me back. He is checking the video from the days of the bombings. Our hope is that the suspect shows up along his path so that we can pinpoint his location," Bill added.

"Greg," John said, "What should I be doing? I feel helpless right now."

"I know," Greg acknowledged, "it looks like we need to see what the FBI comes up with. I'm not sure there's much we can do besides be careful. Let's talk about what we can do to set up our own safety net. We know our house may be compromised so we are changing the locks. What else should we be doing?"

"We should think about driving the kids to and from school if this goes on past the weekend," Sara suggested. "Mary and I can alternate drop offs and pickups."

Mary nodded her head in agreement.

"That makes sense," Greg said, "be sure to let the school know Monday morning."

"I can be around to keep an eye on things," Richard offered, "especially while you're at work, Greg."

"Thank you Richard, that would be great. I do have some important meetings this week and I will be in Syracuse for several hours on Tuesday. I will be leaving here around 8:15am and should be back by late afternoon."

"I'll make myself available all day Monday and Tuesday. You don't mind me hanging around, do you, Mary?"

"I welcome the company, Richard. Thank you!" Mary exclaimed.

"I think I'll come over too, Mary," Sara said, "if you're going to have this handsome personal security hanging around, I want to be a part of it."

"Easy ladies," Richard said, "I need to stay focused. It's been a few weeks since I had to take care of two women at one time."

"We're not talking about holding the door at Walmart here stud," Bill added.

"Hey, Abbott and Costello, that's an image I can really do without!" Greg shouted. "Besides, we're trying to be a little serious here. I'm dealing with the FBI on one hand and the Keystone Cops on the other."

Once everyone stopped laughing, the room grew quiet.

"Is there anything else?" Greg asked. No one spoke up.

"Okay then, Mary, we should get going. If I hear anything else today, I'll pass it along. Otherwise, let's meet tomorrow at our house for dessert around seven o'clock. We can go over details for the week then."

Greg and Mary gathered the girls and walked to the car. On the way, Greg leaned toward Mary and whispered, "anything new in the closet?"

"Yes, but I was thinking I might keep it for Richard," she replied.

"Anything old in the closet?" he countered.

Chapter 69

Charis had been to the gym for a quick workout and was on her way home when her phone rang. "Andrews," she answered. "Alright, I'll be home in ten and I'll check it out. Thanks for the call." It was one of the calls she was waiting for.

"Another typical Saturday night," she thought. Her life had become her work or maybe her work had become her life. Either way, she was spending the weekend alone. She had her routine, check on dad, get in a good workout, do more work than she was expected to, and then fall asleep to a good movie. All while slimy agents like Summers were sleeping with witnesses. She would never cross that line.

She had requested a cell tower report for Summers' phone, which she needed her supervisor's permission to do. She explained the circumstances and the request was approved. Once she could prove that his phone hadn't changed location for many more hours than it would take to interview a witness, she would interview the girl to determine if it was consensual. If it was, he would be off the hook but if she were to state that he in any way applied pressure, he was done.

She arrived home, went through her usual security screening, locked herself in and turned on the shower. She turned on her computer and started to undress. The sign on screen appeared and she entered her user ID and password. The most recent email was the one she was looking for. "Re: Kovatikova, Martina" She left the page open and moved to the shower.

She was trying to put the pieces together in her mind. The hot water usually helped with this process. She mentally reviewed her list. She had the information on Martina although she didn't yet know what it was.

She was waiting for several requests to be fulfilled most importantly, the DNA from the suspect's hair recovered from the barber shop. She was also waiting on DNA from the Plattsburgh and UVM cadavers. The identities of the unregistered cadavers could provide a clue to the suspect's history which then may lead to his whereabouts.

She was hoping to have news today regarding the results of the listed address of the suspect and the investigation of the funeral home in Boston and the shipping carriers in that area. She would be happy if she could check even two or three things off her list by the end of the day.

Charis cut her shower short because she was anxious to read her mail. She turned off the water, stepped out of the shower and dried herself off in front the mirror. She looked at her reflection and thought "this is too good to be staying home every weekend."

She threw on some old, comfortable clothes and put the tea kettle on. While that was heating she returned to the computer. She clicked on the top email and there was a copy of the document she had asked her friend to review and translate. The fields contained black type for the original data and red for the translations.

Martina was born in 1960 in Verbilki, Soviet Union during the Krushchev era. She was left at an orphanage when she was three days old. At age eleven, she was sent to a school for orphaned children which was also a work camp. When she was seventeen, she was working in a bakery and sharing a two bedroom apartment with three other young women. Shortly after, she completed the forms for immigration to the United States.

Charis was looking for the sponsor. She continued reading through the document and finally came across the name, Sigmund Weinfeld. She recognized the address, 402 Bayard St., High Falls, NY, the same address listed for Korben Kovak. It was no longer a coincident, Kovatikova was shortened to Kovak. Ben had to be a relative. A brother maybe? That didn't make sense, the age is too far apart. "A son!" she thought, that made perfect sense.

Charis picked up the phone and dialed her contact at the New York State Police.

"Detective Lawrence, how may I help you?"

"Good evening, detective, Agent Andrews, FBI. I hope I'm not troubling you?"

"No trouble, Andrews, what else would I be doing on a Saturday night?"

"I just had that same conversation with myself," Charis replied. "I need a favor, the local P.D. in High Falls was supposed to be checking out an address today but I haven't heard back. I was hoping you may have some information."

"They have been keeping busy at that hardware store outside town. They may not have gotten around to it yet, it's a pretty small force. We had a guy over there too, let me give him a shout and I'll call you right back."

"Thanks." Charis hung up and turned back to her computer. A new email came though while she was on the phone. This one was from the genetics lab and it was what she was waiting for, the hair analysis from Philadelphia.

There were three samples that seemed to fit the physical description of the suspect. She needed more specific information. She started a new email to her boss and forwarded the lab data.

"I need these three samples cross-referenced with the DNA from Kyle Seike, aka Sigmund Weinfeld, the City Hospital conspirator. You should be able to retrieve his data from prison records. NEED RESULTS ASAP!" She hit the enter key. "Let's see who else is working tonight," she said to herself. Her phone rang.

"Andrews."

"Lawrence, here is what I found out. The kid wasn't at the store. They confirmed he is an employee but his last shift was yesterday which he finished at 8:00pm. Our guys are sweeping the place for prints and DNA. I have a name for you, it's a girl who came to the store looking for him. She said she just met him and they are supposed to have their first date Tuesday."

"What's the name?" Chairs asked.

"Priscilla Chalmers, I'll text you the address and her phone number."

"Great, thanks. Did you get the suspects address from the employer?"

"Yes, it's the same as the one from the kid's college info, 402 Bayard."

"That all ties together then, that's good news!" Charis exclaimed.

"Not all that good," Lawrence replied.

"What do you mean?" Charis asked.

"That address is a cemetery," he replied.

"I don't suppose there is a house in the middle of it," she quizzed.

"There are a few actually," he replied, "all one bedroom, concrete walls and locked iron gates."

"Mausoleums," she said.

"Afraid so," Lawrence replied.

"Have a good night, Lawrence." Andrews said.

"I will if you do," Lawrence said.

Charis hung up. She thought about her next moves. Somewhere there needs to be a real address for these people. Motor Vehicle Department, banks, schools, doctors, drug stores are all places that require addresses. She wouldn't get far tonight or the rest of the weekend for that matter. She checked her mail one more time. There was one new email form genetics. It could be a response already. She opened it.

The primary victims from the explosions at the New York and Vermont universities have been identified. They weren't really victims, they were already cadavers but in each case they found human tissue attached to the PVC pieces of the bomb housing. It seems the unique PVC pipe leaves larger fragments than metal pipe bombs.

Once they had the DNA from the bombs, they ran it through several police and military databases for comparison. The two hits came from the missing persons list in Massachusetts. The tissue from Plattsburgh matched a girl named Amanda Reynolds and the one from UVM was Tori Linngard. They were reported missing within two days of each other. The reports were filed with the Boston Police Department.

The connection was beginning to be clear. Kovak went to medical school in Boston and the cadavers came from Boston so he had a hand in getting them there, but how? He couldn't have sent cadavers from Harvard, they would have missed them but it was worth checking it out. It didn't appear that the Chinatown funeral director was involved but that should be looked at again. The other possibility would be other suppliers. Other mortuaries? Hospitals? Scientific suppliers? What would the link be? She needed to find out what the suspect did in Boston besides going to school.

She opened a new email to her boss. *"LEAD IN BOSTON, CATCHING FIRST FLIGHT OUT"* Before shutting down her computer, she browsed available flights. There was an early one leaving DCA at 6:00 in the morning and arriving in Boston at 7:30am. There were no late night flights. That gave her the evening to keep searching for clues. She could also call Greg Webster with an update.

Greg answered the phone on the fifth ring. Charis was just about to hang up.

"Hello," Greg said with very little breath.

"Greg, is that you?" Charis asked, "you sound winded."

"I was exercising, just finishing up, I'm a little out of breath."

"I can tell. It's kind of late to be exercising, how do you sleep after you exercise so late?" she asked.

"Like a baby," Greg replied, obviously having trouble catching his breath.

"Were you jogging?" she asked.

"Pushups mostly," he replied.

"You should try a little cool down after a work-out, you know, a little walking."

"I was just about to start my cool down, which is passing out on the bed for ten minutes then walking to the bathroom," Greg replied.

"Oh!" Charis exclaimed, "oh my, I'm sorry Greg, oh boy." She was really embarrassed.

"Some detective you are!" Greg joked.

"Yeah well, why don't call me back in a few minutes. Or more! Yes, take all the time you need."

"Honey, Greg said, say hello to Charis," he put the phone next to her ear.

"Hello Charis," it's nice to meet you, how are you this fine evening?" Mary asked.

"I'm really sorry to bother you, Mrs. Webster, I had no idea."

"Mrs. Webster?" Mary replied, "I'm just the babysitter."

"Could you please put Greg back on the phone?" Charis pleaded.

"So, how is your night going, Charis?" Greg joked.

"Not nearly as well as yours," she replied. "You know I have to call the police if that's really your babysitter."

"It really is. Oh and tell them not to worry about handcuffs, she's already wearing them." Greg was laughing now. Charis could hear Mary laughing in the background as well.

"Give me five minutes to...well, I'll just call you back in five." Greg offered.

Charis hung up and took a walk of her own, inside her apartment.

Chapter 70

Ben had put a plan in motion. His first step was a call to Jeremy. He told Jeremy that he was not the bomber, that it was a case of mistaken identity. He wanted to call the police to let them know but he was afraid to do it alone. He convinced Jeremy to come to his apartment where they would wait for the police together.

When Jeremy arrived, Ben offered him a beer which he readily accepted. They sat on the sofa and Ben told him how he had nothing to do with any of what was going on. The police were right about him living in Herkimer County but that was it. He assured Jeremy that the truth would all come out eventually.

Jeremy downed his beer quickly and Ben got him another. Jeremy told him that he believed him and that he really enjoyed working with him. He thought he was a cool guy and a good worker and he told him that Willi thought so too. When Jeremy was halfway through the second beer, he began to slur his speech a little. Ben knew he had little time to finish his preparations.

The suicide note had already been written and placed in the refrigerator. One of the two spare bombs he kept in the apartment was under the bed and the other was safely stored in his truck.

When Jeremy could no longer keep his head up, Ben helped him move to the bed. When he fell asleep, Ben tucked him tightly into the covers. He put the beer bottles in a bag along with the vial of sleeping pills. He took the keys to the truck and the bag, walked out the door and didn't bother to lock it behind him.

He got into his truck, triggered the timer, and drove away. He was several blocks away when he heard the percussion of the explosion. He could hear the sirens in the distance as he approached the warehouse. There weren't any cars present and he knew Jeremy wouldn't be stopping by. He parked down the street a ways and grabbed his miscellaneous bag from the back seat.

He let himself in the front with his key and left the second note in the office. This one thanked Mr. Willett and said he couldn't live with the guilt. He was sorry. He placed the bomb in the farthest part of the warehouse so that the least amount of damage would be done. In all likelihood, it would just blow out the overhead door.

He went out the way he came and returned to the truck. He triggered the timer for fifteen minutes and headed toward Rt. 9. He would take that west to I-90 west for just a few exits. Then he would get on to Rt. 20 west until he was back in NY. He was close to the entrance of I-90 when the second bomb detonated.

Ben was re-thinking the plan to take Priscilla with him to Austria. He didn't know how to make the date on Tuesday work now that they were looking for him. It was probably best to go alone anyway. Two people are easier to spot than one.

His disguise was all ready and pretty failproof. He wouldn't have any issue clearing security on the US end nor entering Austria. Perhaps in time, Priscilla would agree to come to him. His own survival and escape were his priorities.

He would be home in a little over three hours where he could relax for a while. He would prepare the house for demolition and spend some final quality time with Mother. Nothing to do now but sit back and listen to the news.

Chapter 71

"Greg, I am really sorry," Charis started, I should not have called so late."

"It wasn't that late Charis and don't be sorry, there is a lot going on right now and we need to be in contact."

"There seems to be more going on at your house than at mine," she stated.

"I take it you're not married," Greg said.

"I am not, and that's okay, in this line of work it's hard to have a good marriage. I can't begin to tell you how many people I work with that are divorced."

"I'm sure it would be difficult to find the right partner but it shouldn't be impossible," Greg offered, "I think most professions can be hard on a marriage. How many women do you know that are married to men who work long or unpredictable hours, or travel out of town frequently? The secret is choosing the right partner for the job."

"I see your point," she replied, "perhaps I need to try harder, or at all for that matter."

"Unless you have food delivered regularly, you're probably reducing your chances by sitting home on the weekends," Greg joked.

"Enough about my problems, let's talk about yours," Charis suggested.

"Do I have problems?" Greg asked.

"I'm not sure. The address we had for Ben Kovak turned out to be a local cemetery."

"That's the address the employer had too?" He asked.

"Yes. On a positive note, a young girl was asking about Ben at the store but we haven't had a chance to interview her yet."

"Can I do it for you?" Greg offered.

"It wouldn't be official but I guess it wouldn't hurt. Her address is not far from the store where he worked. I'll email you the address and her name and number."

"I'll try tomorrow," Greg said, Sunday may be a good day to find people home. What else do you have?"

"We received DNA confirmation for the source cadavers at Plattsburgh and UVM. We are still looking into how they got there but we know who they were. The bodies belonged to two young girls from the Boston area. The DNA was a match from a missing persons list."

"That's terrible," Greg said. "When were they reported missing?"

"In July of this year, less than two months before the bombings."

"So this whole thing was planned well in advance," Greg speculated.

"It's beginning to look that way, but we still don't have a motive. We may be getting closer to a connection to relatives. That form you had me look into regarding Martina Kovatikova may provide some answers. It looks like she was a mail order bride from the Soviet Union. We are trying to find out who she belonged to and where she might be now."

"Charis, can you send me an official request to look in our hospital records for Ben and Martina? It's a long shot but if they lived around here, there is a chance they had services done at the hospital." Greg realized what has been at the back of his mind for a while. "I wonder if Kovatikova became Kovak once she was in this country. Could she possibly be Ben's mother?"

"That's a great question. The age seems about right and shortening last names was a popular thing for immigrants at the time. I'll search under both names going forward."

"Once I receive your request, I'll check the medical records for all the names," Greg replied. "What else do you know?"

An internal communique flashed across Charis's screen. "Hold on Greg."

Greg remained silent until she returned.

"I just received a notice from HQ that two bombings have been reported in Boston. One was in an apartment building and the other at a warehouse several blocks away."

"Do you think they have anything to do with us?" Greg asked.

"Too early to tell. Let me see what I can find out. Let's touch base tomorrow, Greg. Is there any time that I shouldn't call?" she said jokingly.

"First thing in the morning, around noon and after the sun goes down," Greg replied.

"You wish! I'll talk to you tomorrow."

"Goodnight, Charis."

Chapter 72

Greg had called and spoken to Miss Chalmers earlier that morning. She said she would have time to talk after the morning milking. It was now approaching 9:45 am. Greg had just made the turn onto Lepper Hill Road. He passed Smitty's on the left as he turned the corner. They opened at 10:00 on Sunday and so far there weren't any cars in the lot.

Greg wasn't sure if he had ever been on this road but he liked it. The long grass in the meadows was still deep green and the trees were still full. It wouldn't be long until they began their change before falling to the ground. The road was hilly and curvy making it fun to drive. He hugged the line turning left and the shoulder when he turned right. It made him think back to when he first got his driver's license.

He wondered what separated kids like him and kids like Ben Kovak. He thought about the kids he grew up with and how they turned out. As far as he knew, none of them had any trouble with the law. His own kids ran in similar circles, average families, some living through divorce but none of them seemed troubled. Maybe he just wasn't aware of what was going on under the surface. He didn't believe a young boy from a normal family could commit the type of crimes young Ben was accused of.

He had been on Lepper Hill Road for quite a while and was worried that he may have missed his turn. Just then, he noticed a big red barn and a truck parked in the driveway that read Chalmers' Dairy. He turned right into the drive and pulled up behind the truck. The barn was to his left and the house was straight ahead but way up the driveway.

A young lady stepped out of the barn. "Mr. Webster, I'm Priscilla."

Greg walked toward her with his hand extended, "it's a pleasure to meet you, Priscilla, I'm Greg. Thank you for meeting me."

"It's no trouble at all Greg, shall we walk to the house?"

She led the way and Greg followed. When he caught up to her he said, "I expected to find you in coveralls with mud up to your elbows."

"You haven't spent much time on a farm, have you? We have running water now and electricity," she said jokingly.

"I apologize, I didn't mean any disrespect. I thought when you said you would be finishing your milking I just assumed you could get kind of dirty doing it."

"Oh I do, but I left time enough to get a shower in, it's my usual Sunday routine." Dad gets off to church and I get showered. Then I make Sunday dinner for us both."

"It's just you and your dad here?" Greg asked.

"Mom died several years back and my siblings have all gone off. It's the price that comes with being the youngest. I'm not complaining though, it's honest work and I like it. I couldn't leave dad alone."

Greg found himself feeling sorry for her but he didn't know why. "I'm sorry to hear about your mom. You seem like a great daughter."

"Thank you, Greg. Now that's not why you came all the way out here, so let's talk turkey. But first, may I offer you a beverage? I have iced tea, coffee, apple juice and the best tasting milk in the county! All of the above come with fresh biscuits."

"Well, how could I turn down the opportunity to try the best tasting milk in the county?"

"Excellent choice, have seat anywhere you like and I'll be right back."

She was only gone two minutes but it was long enough for Greg to know that he liked this girl. She returned with two glasses of cold milk, a plate full of biscuits and a small tray with butter, jam, and silverware. Greg had a feeling that this wasn't their everyday China and stemware.

"Please help yourself, Greg," she said as she handed him a cloth napkin.

"You really didn't have to go to all this trouble, Priscilla but I'm glad you did."

"We don't have too many visitors here so I am thrilled to be able to do it."

She passed the plate of biscuits and Greg took one. She then placed the tray of condiments and he took some butter and jam and placed them on his plate. The biscuits were still warm.

"These look and smell delicious!" Greg commented. "Let me guess, the butter and the jam are homemade as well."

"You are quite intuitive, Greg. Enjoy!"

Greg spread a little butter and jam on his biscuit and took a bite. He thought he had died and gone to heaven. "If my wife could have cooked like this, I would have kept her! Kidding of course, my wife is an excellent cook but these are amazing." He followed the biscuit with a sip of milk. "You are right, I haven't tasted milk like this since I was a child."

"Thank you. To be honest, this is the milk of your childhood. It is fresh from the cow, not homogenized nor pasteurized. The way God intended."

"Isn't that dangerous?" Greg asked.

"Only if you're trying to keep it around for days or weeks like they do at the grocery store. We ship our whole milk to a regional seller along with several other farms. When they receive it, they take care of the homogenization and pasteurization. Here, we drink it the old fashioned way."

"Well, it's by far the best I've ever had."

"I told you so. Greg, why are you here?"

"As I said on the phone, I wanted to ask you some questions about Ben Kovak. You don't have to answer them and if you tell me to go away, I will. I have been working with the FBI on this case and they have given me permission to contact you."

"I will answer whatever I can, I'm afraid I won't be of much help. I really only met him three times and the first time was for only a minute."

"That's fine, Priscilla, there is no pressure here. Tell me about your first meeting."

"It was less than a week ago. My dad asked me to go to the hardware store to get a replacement breaker. Ben showed up in my aisle to assist me. He was funny, kind, and helpful. We didn't even talk much, just a little flirting I guess. I don't get out much."

"I understand, I get out all the time, I'm married and I still flirt now and then. All innocent of course. I just like people and I enjoy having fun. Life can find a way to be all serious if you let it."

"Exactly, Ben was a breath of fresh air. Anyway, I got the part and left the store thinking that was the end of it. The next morning, he showed up in our driveway. It was early, before seven, I think and he came with this lame excuse that he sold me a defective breaker and brought me a replacement. I knew right away he was just making up an excuse to see me again. I was tickled."

"Of course, how romantic is that?" Greg said.

"Right! So, I asked if he had ever milked a cow and he said no. I told him I had no use for him at that moment but that he could come by another time and take me on a real date. We settled on that Thursday evening. I would meet him at the shop at closing time. I did, and it was amazing. I brought a picnic dinner because it was late and I get up pretty early every morning. I figured he probably hadn't eaten yet and we wouldn't have time to drive somewhere to get a meal."

"Were you right?" Greg asked.

"I was, but it was the way he responded that blew me away. He told me to stay put for a few minutes. I waited as instructed and pulled the food from the basket and set up a tray. By the time I was finished, he had one aisle of the store set up as a picnic site. There was an inflatable bed on the floor, a small table and chairs, a camping lantern and anything else he needed to make it feel like we were really outdoors.

He walked back to the office for a minute and turned out the lights. It was magic, he had even hung glow in the dark stars above us! He had music playing quietly on the radio and we just talked for about two hours. We seemed so in tune with each other. How could I have been so wrong?"

She became teary all of a sudden. Greg put his plate down and reached for her hands. She began sobbing. He let her cry until she started to let up on her own. He then tried to comfort her.

"Priscilla, there are many things we don't know yet about this investigation and about Ben. Maybe he is involved and maybe not. We all want to trust our hearts and to follow them. I can't think of a single woman I know who wouldn't have the same impression you had at a time like that. It doesn't make you a bad judge of character."

"I just can't imagine he could be a killer. I can't imagine it. How can someone be so kind and so evil at the same time?"

"That's a good question and one that I am not qualified to answer. I can only say from my own experience that I trusted people who turned out to be anyone but the people I thought they were. It happens."

"Do you think he's the one? Do you believe he did all those horrible things?"

"I don't want to believe it. I don't want to believe that any child is capable of evil things. The problem here is that the evidence against him is adding up quickly. But, I also believe that everyone should have their day in court so I am not passing judgement. Tell me what the two of you talked about." Greg said.

"It seemed like everything and nothing. It just flowed so easily, it was like we had known each other since birth. I talked about coming from a big family and he talked about being an only child. I told him about my mom passing and he talked about his dad passing." He seemed very lonely at home and how he was the only caregiver for his mom."

"Did he ever mention his parent's names?" Greg asked.

"I don't believe so." Priscilla answered.

"Did he say where he lived?" Greg continued questioning her.

"Only that it was in High Falls. He called it a beautiful place, set back off the road, and he said it was a safe place," she replied.

"And he was an only child?"

"Yes, I'm sure that's what he said. I remember because I had just finished telling him about Timmy and he responded by saying he was an only child."

"Who is Timmy, Priscilla?"

"Oh, I'm sorry, Timmy was the youngest until I came along. I don't really remember him because I was so young when he disappeared. It was right here on this farm. I was just a baby and

Timmy was a little over two. Mom had several little ones to chase after and life on a farm is not the same as in the city, especially for children. We were always encouraged to go off and play while our parents did the chores.

It must have been a school day because some of the older siblings were gone. Mama had me in the bassinette and Timmy was running around while she was hanging laundry out to dry."

"How many siblings did you have?"

"There were six of us then, three boys and three girls. Timmy ran around the front of the house without Mama noticing. Only a few minutes had gone by and she went looking for him. She checked the barn and inside the trucks but she couldn't find him. Dad was out making a dairy run and the morning help had already gone for the day.

Anyway, Mom phoned the sheriff and told him what was going on. When dad arrived home, there were several police cars here, as well as some volunteers. They were all searching the grounds and the woods for little Timmy."

Greg was afraid to find out how this story ended but he didn't interrupt.

"As I said, I was a baby so none of this is firsthand. Mom and dad didn't talk about it much and I was probably four or five before I heard about it for the first time. I can only imagine how difficult it was for my parents and for my older siblings. I was the lucky one, Greg, I didn't remember any of it. I didn't know enough to ever miss Timmy."

"Priscilla, was Timmy ever found?"

"No, they looked everywhere for him. It took a couple years before they gave up looking. I do remember that our home was pretty somber for a long time. My mother blamed herself and was never really the same. Dad just became a quiet, serious man. He always loved us and he became very protective of us but he was forever changed too. I'm not sure how we got here Mr. Webster, I apologize for getting off course."

"You have nothing to apologize for, Priscilla, I am so sorry for your loss. Priscilla, may I ask how old you are?"

"I'll be twenty-two in December."

"So that would mean Timmy would have been maybe twenty-four today?"

Greg asked.

"Yes, that would be correct" she replied.

"I'm sorry to get so personal, Priscilla but there is a reason I'm asking all these questions. How long ago did your mother pass away?"

"It's coming up on eight years. It was the on the anniversary of Timmy's disappearance."

"Would you have anything around that belonged to your mother, like maybe a hairbrush, comb, or a toothbrush perhaps?"

"I'm sure there is something in Daddy's room. He hasn't been able to part with any of it. I'll go check for you."

Greg's mind was working overtime but he knew it was a longshot. He wasn't even sure why he was entertaining the thought except that it would answer a personal question for him.

Priscilla returned with a hairbrush in her hand.

"I'm sorry, the brush still has Mama's hair in it." She was trying to pull it out.

"Oh, don't do that, Priscilla," Greg said excitedly, "It's better just the way it is. Would you mind if I borrowed this for just a while?"

"I wouldn't mind at all but can tell me why you would want it?"

"Priscilla, I have some friends in the FBI who may be able to get your mother's DNA form the hair and run it through their database of missing children. It's a very long shot but stranger things have happened.

We have technology today that didn't exist when Timmy went missing. It wouldn't change things but it may give you and your family an answer to what happened. It's okay for you to say no."

She handed him the brush. "It's worth a chance to find out," she said.

"Thank you, Priscilla, I'll make sure you get the brush back."

"I am supposed to meet him Tuesday night. I don't think he'll show now, do you?"

"He must know the police are looking for him so I doubt it. If I were you, I would make sure he doesn't find you. You need to take precautions, Priscilla and I mean that. He is considered extremely dangerous. You also know that if he tries to contact you, you must notify the police, right? I'm going to give you my phone number and I want you to contact me if you ever need anything. Tell me you won't hesitate to call."

"I won't hesitate, I promise," she said.

Greg hugged her and thanked her for her time. "You are an amazing young lady, Priscilla and I am better for having met you." He walked out with the brush and a bad feeling in his gut. It wasn't the milk.

Chapter 73

Charis was on the ground at 7:32 am. She was met at the airport by Agent Art Mansfield of the Boston Bureau. They had worked together just a couple years prior at the marathon bombing. Art was probably close to her father's age, in decent shape and a true gentleman.

Art picked her up at baggage claim and they drove directly to the apartment building where the bombing occurred. They would check out the warehouse as well but a body was found in the apartment which made that scene the priority. It was a nice building in a decent neighborhood. After touring the damage, they were to meet with the landlord which was really a management company executive.

The outside of the structure handled the blast quite well. The southern facing windows of the unit were blown out but structurally, the rest of the building was sound. They entered through the parking garage underneath the apartments and took the stairs to the third floor.

There were several local police officers still at the scene. Some were assigned to traffic control while others were gathering evidence and taking photos. The body had already been moved to the city morgue.

Mansfield flashed his badge and asked who was in charge. "I guess you are now," stated a middle aged man in a dark suit. "I'm detective Kroyer, Homicide."

"We're Special Agents Mansfield and Andrews. What do you have?"

"It looks like the blast came from under the bed. The mattresses cushioned some of the blow but the resulting fire is making it difficult to identify the victim." Kroyer said.

"Did you find any fragments?" Andrews asked.

"We found some larger fragments of white PVC plastic that melted to the underside of the box spring. We also found this in the refrigerator." He handed an evidence bag to Mansfield.

"Suicide note?" Mansfield asked.

"You got it."

"Detective, could you tell if the body was male or female?" Charis asked.

"Definitely male. About six feet tall, dark hair, slender, and maybe twenty-five to thirty years old based on muscle mass."

"What did the note say?" Mansfield asked.

Kroyer pulled a note pad from his jacket pocket. "I thought you might ask," he said.

"This was written on a piece of stationary with the heading 'ReadiMed Scientific Supply Co.' We didn't find the pad in the unit. Here is what he wrote:

"If you're reading this, I'm already gone. While I am not sorry about the things I have done, I can't live with the thought of imprisonment. I would rather die young and free than old and locked up. As for why I did what I did, I'll leave that to you to figure out. Good luck! B.K."

"Do you find it peculiar that he doesn't mention any family? I mean not as much as a goodbye, Mom, or a note to a girlfriend?" Mansfield asked no one in particular.

"Maybe there isn't anyone to say goodbye to," Andrews added. She walked around the other part of the apartment. It was scarce and neat, compulsively neat once you got past the dust from the blast. Were any personal belonging found?"

"A few articles of clothing, some cologne, not much else," Kroyer responded.

"What about a wallet?" Andrews asked. "Any car keys found? A bus pass?"

"Nothing like that. We did find a couple ticket stubs from Fenway from early in the summer."

"We will need to see a copy of those as soon as you can get to it, Detective. No car and no wallet yet he has driven all over the northeast. It doesn't add up," Charis said.

"Kroyer, you said the property manager is around somewhere? We would like to speak with him."

"We're holding him downstairs, follow me," Kroyer said.

As they followed Kroyer out of the building Charis turned to Mansfield and said, "After the warehouse, we need to go to the morgue."

Waiting next to one of the Boston P.D. squad cars was a man dressed in expensive athletic attire. He seemed to be late forties, maybe fifty tops. He seemed a little agitated.

"Mr. Baldoni, this is Special Agent Andrews and Special Agent Mansfield from the FBI," Kroyer said.

"It's about time, do you know how long I've been waiting here? It's going on two hours! I've got things to do, like getting this place fixed and rented for crying out loud."

"Mr. Baldoni," Art said, "this building is a crime scene, you'll be lucky if you get so much as a hammer near this place in the next two months."

"Yeah, that's what you think. I've got lawyers that will get me in here next week!"

Art took the man gently but firmly by the arm and walked him ten steps away from everyone. In a controlled, gentlemanly voice he said, "I don't care if you have F. Lee fucking Bailey as your attorney, you raise your voice or say anything unkind again in my presence or in the presence of any of these law enforcement officers and I'll arrest you for contempt and it will be two months before you see daylight." He brushed the man's sleeve and said, "I hope we understand each other." They walked back to the group.

"Mr. Baldoni here was just saying he is ready to answer any questions you have for him."

Charis had all she could do to hold back a smile. She knew exactly what just transpired. "Mr. Baldoni, whose name was the lease in?"

"I already told the other…" he stopped when Art coughed. Baldoni started again, "as I told the other officers, the lease was held by Ben Kovak. I have never met the man."

"Is it customary that you never meet the people you rent to?" Charis asked.

"No, most of the time either I our one of my associates meet face to face with a potential tenant."

"Why was this different?" Charis drilled him.

"We received a personal reference from the dean of Harvard medical school. We also received a background check and two years rent and security all paid upfront."

"When did the lease begin?" she continued.

"It was two years ago this past August."

"Have you ever had any complaints about the tenant? Has he ever called about fixing a leak or patching a wall?"

"No, never." There has been zero communication between my office and this tenant."

"Do you usually perform routine inspections?"

"We change the filters on the air handlers every three months and an exterminator comes every six months."

"How was the rent paid and by whom?" Charis again, as she was controlling this part of the interrogation.

"The rent was paid by electronic transfer from an oversea account. One transfer of fifty-two thousand and five-hundred dollars which included one month's security."

"Do many of your customers pay two years in advance, Mr. Baldoni?"

"None that I remember."

"Did you think it odd that a college student could come up with that kind of money?"

"No, that's not even one year's tuition at Harvard. The truth is, the money came in, he had a clean background check and I signed the agreement. That's what I get paid to do so that the owners of this building along with several others can send their kids to Harvard and pay cash. It's business."

"Mr. Baldoni, we will need a copy of that wire transfer and a copy of the background check. Detective Kroyer will pick that up from you in the morning," Art advised him.

"What time in the morning? I won't be in the office until eleven."

"He will be there at nine, and so will you, We appreciate your cooperation, Mr. Baldoni."

Andrews, Mansfield and Kroyer walked away.

"Detective Kroyer, would you be so kind as to escort us to the warehouse please?" Charis asked.

They hopped in Kroyer's car and headed toward the warehouse.

"What did you say to that nice man back there, Agent Mansfield?" Charis asked.

"I just reminded him of his manners." Art replied.

"Did you tell him two or three months?" Charis asked again.

"Two." He responded.

"You're a cupcake," she said with a smile.

"Tell us about what we're going to find at the warehouse, Detective," Art said.

"Similar bomb but not a lot of damage. A couple new doors and this guy's back in business. I think the bomber took it easy on him."

"Why do you think that, Detective?"

"He left another note. He apologized to the owner saying he had a great time working there and he was sorry he had to mess the place up. He said he looked up to Mr. Willett like a son would to his father."

"We should all have sons like that," Art said.

Chapter 74

He was already bored out of his mind. Ben hadn't been home for twelve hours yet and he was so restless he thought he would tear his own hair out. Mother was no help of course, she was still pissed that he went away again. He tried telling her that it was a productive trip and that he wouldn't be going back again. He was done with Boston.

Then he realized that his flight was leaving from Boston in just a few days. He thought about the risks of going back there. They knew who he was but they didn't know the vehicle and they wouldn't recognize him in his disguise.

He thought about changing his tickets. He could fly out of JFK or La Guardia but he hated driving through the city. Newark would also work and that airport didn't seem too difficult to get to. He had one last thought, Philadelphia. He found that to be an easy ride. *Would they still be looking for him there,* he wondered? *Not as much as they would be in Boston,* he answered himself.

He pulled the information up on his phone and dialed the reservations desk for Lufthansa. Then he quickly hung up. He remembered that he had made those reservations for Ben Kovak and Martina Kovatikova. He couldn't change them now, that would draw attention to himself. The police were probably already screening reservations in his name. *This will work out perfectly,* he said to himself, *I'll make a new reservation in a different name. Let them chase Ben Kovak all over the world if they want. He won't be flying!*

He would need a new alias. He would also need a new credit card. All of his current ones would draw scrutiny. He had tons of credit card information from the hardware store. He went to retrieve a shoebox from his room.

He began looking through the reams of information. It would need to be recent to minimize the chance of expiration and it would have to be somebody with a high credit line. A round trip ticket at the last minute would be expensive. He only needed to look at a dozen accounts before he found it.

He would be traveling at the generosity of Gregory Webster. *This is perfect*, he thought. *We're about the same size, same color hair and I could easily make a fake driver's license and passport.*

He was no longer bored because now he had work to do. He had a mission. His mother was always saying something about idle hands and the devil. He would need to book the flight last minute to be sure the credit card charge didn't show up before he took off.

He also needed to pack and prepare the house for his departure which included changing all the batteries in his toys. *You see mother, if you had let me play with regular toys and other kids I might not be making bombs!* The house was secondary, his primary task was making the documents. *The devil is in the details*, he could hear his father saying. He shouldn't have listened to his father so much when he was young and he definitely shouldn't have communicated with him while he was in prison.

He always went as Timmy Schmidt when he visited the prison. He couldn't go until he was eighteen so it was just the last four or five years. He looked so old and fragile toward the end. He would always ask how Ben was doing and Ben would always lie.

At his last visit, his dad opened up about his mistakes in life and his failures. He said his biggest of both was not being the father he should have been. It was nice to finally hear but it was too late to change who Ben had become. He thanked his dad for admitting that.

It was there in that cold hard visiting room where his father told him how life had changed. He was destined to be a great surgeon. He had planned for that his entire early adult life. He had a few issues with some of his instructors at Plattsburgh based on their knowledge being less than that of some of the students. He received good grades because they couldn't deny the fact that he was brilliant even if they didn't like him.

It was no different at The University of Vermont. His early medical training seemed almost juvenile at times. He tried to suffer through it but at times became impatient. The professors saw that as a character flaw, one that would not serve him well in his chosen path.

When it was time for graduation and receipt of his medical degree, he realized he had not been accepted to any of his chosen surgical residency programs. He was devastated and questioned some of his mentors.

They were forthright in telling him that they wrote mediocre reference letters on his behalf. They didn't believe he had the unshakable temperament required of great surgeons. He told Ben he wanted to reach out and strangle each one of them. As far as he was concerned, those schools could have disappeared off the map.

That late in the game, his choices of residency programs was limited. The one glowing reference he received from both schools was from the dissection anatomy professors. He knew he had a talent for it and he was frequently praised for his work. Because he was good at it, didn't mean that's what he wanted to do. But, he played the cards he was dealt and applied to Albert Einstein in Philadelphia.

That was the beginning of the end he would tell Ben. It was important work but not worthy of recognition and reward like surgery was. He made far less money than that of a surgeon and dealing with death every day, all day took away his passion for life. By the time Martina arrived and then Ben, he was already down the rabbit hole. He began to take more interest in the dead than he did the living. Everything in his life became cold, just like the tissue he encountered every day.

Ben felt something for him, some connection that he hadn't felt before. He didn't know how to classify the emotion or even if it was an emotion. If anything he felt a little bad for him. He wasn't sure he loved his dad or his mother for that matter. For as long as could remember, he felt out of place there.

There was something that he missed at a cellular level but could never understand it. He surmised that it was because he didn't feel loved or cared for although he was taken care of. Like dad took care of his mother, like he takes care of his mother, like pesticides take care of insects. Taking care of and caring for were not the same thing. At least he didn't think they were.

So at their final visit, Ben took care of his father. He had brought what was asked of him and he promised he would take care of his ugly scholastic past. That's what Seike's do, they take care of each other. Ben passed the plastic bag containing 50ml of propofol under the table to his dad. His father assured him that obtaining needles in prison was the easy part.

Chapter 75

"Charis, it's been a long morning for you. How about if I drop you at the hotel and let you check in? You can have a leisurely lunch and rest for a while before we reconvene mid-afternoon."

"That sounds great, Art, I appreciate that. I have a few phone calls I can make as well." Art dropped her off at the Hilton Boston Back Bay. He helped her with her bag and told her he would be back around three. They would work awhile and then have dinner.

Check in was smooth and quick. She rode the elevator to her room on the fourteenth floor and let herself in. She did a sweep of the room and double locked the door. She thought she would take a hot shower and try to revitalize. She considered a workout first but she had some thoughts she needed to flush out. By the time she had her clothes off, her phone was ringing.

"Andrews," she answered.

"Webster," he replied, "I think I'll answer my phone that way from now on."

"I'm naked, what do you want?"

Greg thought about it but refrained from saying it.

"Turnabout is fair play," he said.

"I said I was naked, not in the middle of it," she said.

"Then what's the point of being naked?" he asked.

"Soap seems to be more effective without my clothes on."

"You do realize it's noon, right?"

"Busy morning, I'm in Boston."

"When did you go there?" he quizzed.

"I left at 6:00 am this morning. Started investigating at 7:30 and just took a break before getting back out there. Is that okay, dad?"

"Hey, if you're going to dad me then I'm going to lecture you about being naked in a hotel room at noon!"

"Are we going to talk about anything productive during this call? If not, I'm going to set the phone down while I shower and you can lecture all you want."

"Do you sing?" Greg asked.

"What?" she replied.

"Do you sing in the shower? If you do, that may be worth holding on for!" He joked.

"I'm hanging up now," Charis threatened.

"No, don't do that, I have something important," Greg pleaded.

"What is it?"

"A hairbrush. A hairbrush with hair," he stated.

"I'm listening," she said.

"I met with Priscilla Chalmers this morning. What a delightful young lady. Anyway, she had a brother disappear when she was just a baby and the brother was two years older than her. The boy was never found."

"So you want me to take on a missing persons case that went cold more than twenty years ago?"

"Yes! Sort of. My gut tells me there's more to it than just a missing kid. She described her meeting with Ben for me and there was this instant chemistry between them. She said he was polite, thoughtful, and easy to talk to. She said she felt like they knew each other forever."

"And you think he may be the long lost brother? Tell me she slept with him and I'm going to throw up."

"I know it's a really long shot here, but I felt something and it wasn't the milk." Greg emphasized.

"Yeah, I'm going to let that last one slide" she said, "I can have forensics check the hair. Where is it?"

"It's in a bag."

"A little more information would be helpful," she responded.

"I have it at home, how do I get it to you?"

"I'll send a courier to your house. Will you be there for an hour?"

"I'll be here, and if for some reason I'm not, someone else will be. Do I need to package it somehow?"

"The courier will take care of that."

"How will we know it's them?" he asked.

"How many people come to your door asking for a hairbrush wearing an FBI jacket?"

"Got it. Do you have anything for me?"

"What do you want? I could trade you a lipstick or eyeliner," She replied.

"I could use a new eyeliner but I would settle for some information."

"You know you're a little strange, right?" Charis asked.

"Who is the naked one talking on the phone!" he joked.

"Touché. There was a body in the apartment, along with a suicide note signed by Ben Kovak. He also left another note in the office at the warehouse. This one was an apology to his boss who felt like a father figure to him."

Greg was silent for a moment. "Do you think it's him?"

"I have no reason to think it isn't him. The size is right, the age is close, and the hair is good. The body was in Ben's apartment, in his bed in fact, and the bomb was one of his. We went by the morgue to get some prints and dental impressions. Hopefully, we will find something to compare them to. The apartment was clean of fingerprints."

"There must have been hair somewhere, right?" Greg responded.

"You would think so wouldn't you? The place was pretty clean."

"So, you're telling me that the guy does the most thorough housecleaning in the history of houses and then kills himself? Because he doesn't want to be remembered for keeping a dirty house!"

"Do you want to hear something else strange?"

"Are you still naked?" Greg asked.

"Yes," she replied.

"That's strange enough," he laughed.

"I'm getting used to it, wise guy. Anyway, we didn't find a wallet in the place."

"How about in the car?" Greg guessed.

"No car keys either," she said.

"That trumps nakedness!" Greg said.

"You are fixated on this nakedness! Is there something wrong with you that you're not telling me about?"

"Yes, I have a serious lack of filters!" He replied.

"You think?" she said. "I'm going to the shower now."

"Good, call me when you have some clothes on."

Charis climbed into the shower. "What a character he is," she thought of Greg. He was smart, intuitive, and much of the time, childlike but she had a good feeling about him. He felt like an older brother from different parents. She was curious about his gut feeling. She learned in her class at the academy that his reliance on instinct made the difference in the City Hospital case.

She went about business the same way, remembering everything she was taught about tactics and discovery but blending in a good portion of instinct. She started making a mental list of outstanding tasks surrounding the Kovak case.

She would check the hairbrush evidence against the hair DNA from Kovak's Philadelphia haircut. She needed to ring somebody's bell at the cell phone company to get the data she requested. She needed to call Veronica Sweet, the young girl in Vermont that Agent Taylor Summers was hooking up with and she needed more information on Martina Kovatikova. Her gut told her Kovatikova was linked closely to the case but she wasn't sure how.

She had time to follow up on most of those items before she left the hotel at 3pm. She made the water a little hotter and leaned back into it.

Chapter 76

Bill and Richard were having coffee at the Gerardi's in Palatine Bridge. It was a half hour east of High Falls but made the commute easier for the guy from Gerardi's headquarters in Ballston Spa. "No pastries today, Richard?" Bill asked.

"No, I'm trying to cut back a little bit."

"That's good. It must be hard cutting out smoking and sugar at the same time." Bill sympathized.

"I just realized that I was doing all those things out of boredom. I don't need donuts every day, and I can certainly do without the smoke. I decided to start walking more and doing everything else less. I feel better already!" Richard explained.

"How are things at home," Bill asked.

"Things are good. The walking gets me out of Marilyn's hair for a while and she is responding favorably."

"You're a lucky man," Bill said.

"That I am," Richard agreed.

"What about you, Bill, are you alright?"

"Yes, I'm fine, I still miss my wife everyday but it does get a little easier over time."

"Have you thought about dating, Bill?"

"I haven't had a date in over sixty years, Richard. I wouldn't know the first thing about it. Besides, I don't think I'm ready yet."

"Not ready yet?" Richard asked. "Do you think waiting another ten years is going to make you more attractive to women? You have to saddle up while there is still a chance you can get on the pony!"

"And where do you think I would find a woman?" Bill asked.

"Take a look around," Richard said.

Bill turned in his booth and glanced in both directions. The store only had five booths inside but there were several tables outdoors on the patio.

"I count seven women who are here with other women. That table of four over there, I'll bet at least half are widowed or divorced," Richard offered.

"Why would you think that?" Bill responded.

"Because the law of averages dictates it, but also because they keep looking over here."

"Maybe they can't see this far and they're really just looking straight ahead," Bill said.

"Well I can assure you that the two with their backs to us who keep turning around, can see this far," Richard promised.

"Maybe they're the two at that table who are married."

"You need to have a positive attitude, Bill. I agree that they are probably looking at me, but I'm taken."

"Looking at you? Over me?" Bill questioned.

Richard stood up and walked over to the women at the table. "I'm sorry to interrupt ladies, please pardon me. My friend and I are having a conversation and we have reached a stalemate. We were discussing the difficulties involved in re-entering the dating game at our age. My friend doesn't think there are any available women out there and I disagree. Can you help me out?"

The women looked at each other. One said, "which one is his friend?" One of the others replied, "the table over there, the one we've been checking out. His friend is the handsome one."

"When was the last time you saw your optometrist?" Richard asked the woman. "It doesn't matter, the question is how many of you are single, widowed or divorced?"

"We are all single at the moment," one of them replied.

"That's great," Richard exclaimed, "how often do you come here?"

"Every Sunday," they replied. "The home takes us to church and then drop us off here for an hour." They were all smiling and giddy.

"Thank you, ladies, you have answered my question and resolved my dispute with my friend. I hope you have a wonderful day." Richard turned and walked back to the table.

"What did they say?" Bill asked.

"They said you're going to be single for a while longer."

Richard sat down just as the bus pulled into the lot. "Back to the Shady Rest, ladies."

At the same time the man Bill was waiting for walked in. Bill stood up to greet him.

"Hi Bill, good to see you again."

"Hello, Danny, this is my friend Richard, thank you for coming."

Richard put out his hand, "Richard Ingraham, good to meet you."

"Danny Scoville, the pleasure is mine," he said as they all sat back down.

"Richard, Danny is the guy who helped us find Kovak and the car."

"I was there, I remember," Richard said.

"Right, I forgot about that. Anyway, he has more news for us, isn't that right, Danny?"

"It is, I have been reviewing tape from all of our stores in this area and I have found some interesting things. We have videotaped your boy at several of our shops including the one we're sitting in. Some of the sightings go back several weeks but he has been around. It appears that he comes back to this area after every attack, including the one yesterday in Boston."

"He was in one of your stores yesterday?" Richard asked.

"Not in our store but at the gas pump. We have a store just west of Amsterdam on Rt. 5s. He pulled in just after dark. We were able to get a look at his face but we didn't catch a plate. We do know that he is driving a truck now. It appears to be an older

Toyota. Some of our cameras still shoot black and white so I can't tell what color it is. I have a flash drive for you." Danny held the drive out for Bill.

"Danny, this is great! Thank you," Bill said.

"There's more," Danny followed.

"I also have a credit card number for you. I have a printout of the details right here." He handed the paper to Bill. Bill opened the paper and looked it over.

"This card belongs to Martina Kovatikova," he said. "Do we know her?" He directed the question at Richard.

"It doesn't ring any bells with me" he replied.

"We looked back over the records and this card has been used multiple times in our stores and I can give you the dates and locations."

"This is exciting stuff, Danny, we'll make sure it gets to the FBI right away. I can't tell you how helpful you have been." Bill offered.

"I'm happy we could help. Ice cream anyone? I'm buying!" Danny said.

Chapter 77

Charis answered the phone. "Are you finished with your shower?" Greg asked.

"Yes, like two hours ago," she answered.

"Good, I have news for you. We have new footage of Kovak filling up his tank."

"Regular or premium?" she quipped.

"Sure, everything is funny when *you* want it to be," he returned.

"Where is this video from?" she asked.

"It was at a store just west of Amsterdam, about thirty minutes from High Falls. Here's the thing, Charis, this video was captured last evening."

"Are you sure, Greg?"

"I haven't seen it myself but it's from the same source that identified Kovak in Vermont. I'm about to upload it and send it to you. By the way, we also know he's driving a pickup truck but we don't know what color and they didn't see the plate. We know it's an older Toyota. I have more."

"I like more," she said.

"We have the credit card he's been using at several of these chain stores in the area. I'll email you the details but the card belongs to Martina Kovatikova."

"Holy cow, Greg, that was a lot of information. How did you come across all that?" she asked.

"My guys asked nicely."

"Why do I even carry a badge and a gun?" she asked. "All this time all I needed to do was ask nicely."

"You catch more flies with honey," he replied.

"Not the flies I'm after. I tend to catch more with a .38."

"Okay, your turn, what have you found out?"

"I have been looking into Kovatikova as well. So far I haven't found much. It's like she doesn't exist. How can a person not have medical or dental records?"

"Perhaps they use multiple identities," Greg replied.

"There has to be something that they can't do unless they have a valid ID," Charis said.

"Hey Charis, I have some ideas, let me do some snooping around on Monday when offices are open. In the meantime, I see that you sent me the permission to check for medical records so I will do that."

"Sure," she said "and if I find something in the meantime, I'll let you know. Now how about that video?"

"Uploading right now," he replied. In a matter of seconds, the video was playing on Greg's computer. "it's him Charis, I'm forwarding it right now."

Charis opened it the second the file arrived. "I guess we need to figure out who the stiff in the bed was because it sure doesn't like it was Ben Kovak. It also means he's back home, Greg, you need to be careful."

"We have taken some precautions already and we're meeting again this evening to finalize our strategy. By the way, your courier showed up right on schedule. The hand off was successful. He wasn't the most talkative guy."

"They're not paid to socialize, Greg."

"How long before you have the evidence in hand?" he asked.

"As long as it takes to drive from your house to Quantico. He won't be stopping for red lights or stop signs. He will also be using the express lane on I-95 without extra people in the car. Don't tell anyone."

"It will be our secret, Charis."

"Keep your head down, Greg."

"I will. We will talk soon."

Greg hung up and thought about whether he would tell the truth at the meeting tonight. He called John, Bill and Richard and asked them to meet him at the hospital an hour before the scheduled meeting with the family.

Charis hung up and made a call to Art Mansfield. "Art, we need to go back to the morgue. We also need to check missing persons."

Chapter 78

Priscilla was bringing the herd in from grazing in the field. By the time they were all in and given some grain, it would be time to make dinner. After the kitchen was cleaned up, it would be time for milking again. The schedule never varied and although she grew tired of it at times, she knew she had no way out so she wouldn't spent time worrying about it.

Her dad had been making some repairs to the grain silo but stopped to run to Smitty's for something or other. He offered to switch tasks with her but she couldn't face going to the store where magic happened one night and disappeared the next. She would rather have the muscle aches than the heartache.

She watched the cows come in slowly, following each other, inherently knowing that it was time to come home. Sometimes she would imaging seeing Timmy in the pasture. He was still two years old, encouraging the cows to move, imitating dad. The meeting this morning left her feeling unsettled. She enjoyed Greg's company and she found him sincere, kind, and trustworthy but she couldn't shake the topic.

Hearing the story about Ben on the news seemed detached somehow but hearing it firsthand from someone close to the case made it much more real. She still couldn't fathom how this sweet boy she had met could be committing unspeakable acts of murder and terrorism.

When the last lady was in, she secured them in their stalls and pulled the lever on the grain conveyor. It occurred to her that a dairy cow's life wasn't dissimilar to her own. She walked back to the house to clean up and start supper. She washed her hands and put a larger kettle of water on the stove to boil. She set the burner to a low setting so that she would have time to shower without it spilling over.

She pulled her tired body up the stairs and into her bedroom. She removed her soiled clothes, threw her bathrobe on, and proceeded back to the bathroom. She turned on the water and looked in the mirror. Her twenty year old eyes saw a much older woman staring back at her. She barely recognized her own reflection.

She turned away, not wanting to see the truth. She stepped into the tub and pulled the curtain around her. The water was warm and soothing and she could feel her tissue respond but as her muscles relaxed, so did her courage. She allowed her tears to mix with the warm water and flow down the drain because once she was out, there wouldn't be any more tears.

When Priscilla was dried and dressed she returned to the kitchen. She was still ahead on the water boiling so she got out the cutting board and began chopping vegetables. She found it odd that her dad wasn't back yet. She looked out front by the barn but didn't see his truck. She went about her business for another twenty minutes and checked again.

Now she was getting worried. She turned off the stove and walked back toward the barn. She passed the silo but he wasn't there. She walked around the front of the barn and didn't see any sign of him there either.

She went in the barn calling his name. "Dad, are you in here? Dad?" There was no answer. She turned back toward the door and felt the rag hit her in the face. The smell was awful and she tried not to breath in while she kicked her feet. They weren't landing at all and her arms were growing weary. Priscilla went to sleep.

Ben dragged her lifeless body to the side of the barn where he set her down easily. He quickly ran off through the field toward where he had parked his truck. It was just off the road behind a hedge of overgrown grape vine about two hundred yards before the driveway. He jumped in and started the engine, backed the truck over the ditch, into the road and headed toward the driveway. He turned into the drive and sped toward where Priscilla was laying in the clover. When he got there, she was gone.

Ben checked his location again. He was sure he set her down right there, he could see the imprint of her body in the clover. He walked back toward his truck and thought about leaving but he couldn't. He stepped into the barn quietly, bending to look beneath the bodies of the cows. He didn't see anyone.

He was moving toward the back of the barn when he thought he heard a noise. He stopped and listened. It seemed to be coming from the milk room. He approached the door and listened again. There was moaning coming from the room. He heard just the one voice, female, it had to be Priscilla.

He opened the door and found her sitting on the floor in the corner. She gasped when she saw him. He still had the rag in his hand.

"You have been a bad little girl, Priscilla, I thought you had gotten away."

"Why Ben? Why are you doing this? All the stories, they're all true, aren't they?" she said sadly.

"They are all true, and there are more that no one even knows about. Pretty impressive, don't you think?"

"I think you're sick Ben, I think you need help?"

"You have no idea who I am, Priscilla. Sick? No doubt. Fixable? Absolutely not. It's way too late for any of that. All I wanted was one short date with you, and you're trying to deny me. After all I did for you the other night, this is the thanks I get?"

"Why didn't you just call me, Ben, I would have met you and we could have talked."

"Talked? About what, Priscilla? All the people I've killed, then what, off to the fair for popcorn and cotton candy? No, it would have been 'hold on, Ben while I call the police.'

"So what were you going to do with me?"

"I was hoping to take you away from here, go someplace nice like Austria."

"You were going to kidnap me and take me out of the country? Do you think I would want that?" she asked.

"You would have grown to like it, maybe even learn to like me."

"I did like you Ben but this isn't the way things work. You don't just take someone away from everyone they love, against their will."

"I'm not really sure what love is but I think it's overrated," he replied.

"I'm sorry for you if you don't know what love is but I can tell you it is the greatest thing in the world. It may be the hardest thing and sometimes the scariest thing but it is worth every joy and every tear that comes with the package. Why don't you sit down and we can talk about it, Ben?"

"I'm done talking, Priscilla, I need you to come over here and let me put you back to sleep. I can take you to meet mother but you need to be asleep first."

"You know that's not going to happen, Ben. I'm not going anywhere with you. Let me call the police and they will get you some help."

"Like they did my father? he shouted. No thank you, I don't need help. All I need is for you to come with me." Ben slowly moved toward her. She struggled to get to her feet. He reached for her and the window behind Priscilla exploded inward sending shards of glass over her head and at Ben.

He quickly made his way out of the room and ran through the barn toward his truck. From behind him, he heard another gun shot. He ducked and ran faster. He made it to the truck and started it. He slammed it in reverse and put the pedal to the floor. He heard the gun go off once more.

Chapter 79

Charis and Art had just re-visited the morgue. Looking at the body again, closer this time, they noticed that the man had a double nipple on his right side. They were so close together that if you weren't looking for it, you would miss it. It would almost require intimacy to discover it.

The pathologist defined it as a supernumerary nipple. He said they develop in utero and are not uncommon. He estimated the frequency to be around twenty percent. They can be found anywhere between the arm pit and the groin. Not having a photo of Ben Kovak's body and short of discovering any medical records, there was nothing to compare to. Otherwise, there were no differential anomalies.

When Charis and Art returned to the car, Charis made a phone call. This one had been on her list anyway so maybe she could cast one stone and catch two birds. A young female voice answered. "Hello," the girl didn't seem too enthusiastic.

"Is this Veronica Sweet?" Charis asked.

"Yes." She sounded frightened.

"Veronica, my name is Charis Andrews and I'm an agent with the FBI. Don't say anything until I say it's okay." There was no response. "Is there another agent with you right now."

"No," she replied.

"Are you able to talk freely?" Charis continued.

"Yes, but he may be back soon," the girl said.

"Are you afraid of him, Veronica?"

"Yes, he won't go away." She sound scared to death.

"I'm going to help you, alright?"

"Yes, Please."

"Are you at your home?"

"Yes," Veronica answered.

"Do you have a car?" Charis asked.

"Yes, but he took the keys. I've been stuck here for several days."

"Alright, we are calling the local police right now and they will send a car to you. Is there someplace safe you can go to wait?"

"I have a neighbor on the backside of my apartment. I saw her car pull in just a few minutes ago."

"Alright Veronica, are you on a cell phone?"

"Yes,' she answered.

"Veronica, stay on the line with me and walk to your neighbor's apartment. Do not hang up. Look out the window, do you see his vehicle?"

"No."

"Go right now. Go fast and do not look back."

Charis could hear the door opening followed by footsteps. There was a knocking sound. The door opened and then closed.

"Veronica, are you in?"

"Yes," she answered.

"Good," Charis responded, "please put your neighbor on the phone."

"This is Lauren, what's going on?"

"Lauren, I'm with the FBI. There are police on the way to your apartment but until they get there, turn off the lights, draw the shades and don't answer the door. Someone will be there very soon.."

"Can you tell me what's happening?" she said.

"I promise I'll tell you everything but for your own safety you need to act right now. I will stay on the line with you until the police arrive."

There was silence for thirty seconds then, thirty more.

"I'm afraid," Veronica said.

"It's going to be alright," Charis replied, "just keep your voice down."

There was a knock on the door. "Don't answer it," Charis said, "just remain quiet." She looked at Art who was on the phone with the local chief. He shook his head no.

"Veronica!" a male voice shouted. There was banging in the door. "Veronica, if you're in there you had better come out!"

"Don't open the door, Veronica, the police will be there. Go to the back of the apartment and lock yourself in a bedroom. Get on the floor and stay away from the windows." Charis ordered.

She could hear shuffling and whispering. She could also hear the banging getting louder. Art raised two fingers.

"Veronica, they will be there in one minute, just stay down and stay still." The banging continued. She thought she heard the front door give way. Summers was now in the apartment. He was opening doors as he went down the corridor. He came to the last room and banged on the door.

Art gave a thumbs up.

"Police, come out with your hands up," Charis could hear from Veronica's phone in the bedroom. The banging continued. "Police! This is your last chance. Come out now or we are coming in."

"Stay down, Veronica. Get under the bed if you can."

"We are under the bed," she replied.

Charis gave Art the go sign. "Go!" Art shouted into the phone.

Summers stepped back and kicked in the door. The lunge threw him into the bedroom. Charis could hear gunfire and glass shattering. The velocity of the bullets striking him tossed him back into the hallway where another hail of bullets coming from the living room spun him around. He hit the wall and then the floor.

"Don't move, Veronica, it's over but stay where you are until the police ask you to come out. Are you both alright?" Charis asked.

"I think so," she replied.

"You did a great job, Veronica, Lauren too." Charis looked at Art. He nodded his head, it was over.

"Veronica, the officers will be coming to get you out of there. They will take you back to your apartment and ask a few questions. I'm going to call you back in fifteen minutes and ask you a few more. Is that alright?"

"Yes, thank you, Miss Andrews." Charis could hear the officers talking to her. She hung up and sat silently for a moment.

"How did you know?" Art asked.

"I didn't, I got lucky. I was calling to ask if she remembered if Ben Kovak had a third nipple."

Chapter 80

Ben didn't waste any time getting home. He pulled the truck into the first bay and closed the garage door. The farmer saw his truck and they would no doubt be calling the police. He would need to change vehicles again but he would wait until dark. He checked the front of the truck for holes but there weren't any. Had it been a rifle he may not have made it out of there. The shotgun was easier to outrun.

He set the keys down on the kitchen counter then went back downstairs to visit with Mother. She was in her usual place, watching TV. "Hello Mother, I told you I wouldn't be gone long. What's that? No, she couldn't make tonight, perhaps another time. I know, I'm disappointed too." He wasn't about to tell her he was shot at, that would just make her worry.

"I'm going to the work room, just yell if you need me." He left her room and went down the hall toward the back of the basement. He needed to make sure everything was ready for his departure on Wednesday. The bombs were already prepared but he needed to replace the batteries in the detonator. The long bench where he usually worked was cleaned off so that he could spread out the maps.

In the adjoining room, which his dad had referred to as O.R. 1, would need to be set up as well. The tilting table and straps would need positioning and the autopsy and embalming equipment required cleaning and positioning. "All in good time he thought." There wasn't any real hurry as he wouldn't be leaving until Wednesday morning and this was still Sunday afternoon.

He laid the maps out on the bench. The first was of his own property lines. The second was of the Syracuse campus and the third was a detailed map of Austria. His disguise would get him just so far, he needed to sound and act like a local. He had been studying the German language for some time. His father spoke it whenever he was around and his mother was also fluent in both German and Russian. I have smart parents. "Ich habe kluge Eltern," he said aloud.

He left the maps open and went to use the bathroom. When he finished, he moved to the sink and looked at himself in the mirror. He hadn't noticed before but he was bleeding from the left side of his scalp and the blood had dripped onto his left shoulder. He peeled the collar of his shirt back and realized the blood was coming not from his scalp but the shoulder itself.

He went back to O.R. 1 and looked for supplies. He gathered forceps, a scalpel, a medium gauge suture with a curved needle, and alcohol.

He positioned a large mirror in front of himself and moved the surgical light so that it was pointing at his scalp. He wanted to take care of the scalp first while he still had the use of both hands. He knew that he might have to dig in the shoulder some. His hair was in the way. He opened another drawer and pulled out electric clippers. He shaved his entire head as short as he could. With that out of the way, he went to work.

There were six small balls of shot under his skin. He sprayed some Novocain on his skin and let it sit until he couldn't feel the cold any longer. One by one, he spread the skin with the forceps and removed the shot with a tweezer. He wasn't sure if he needed to suture the wounds so he just bandaged them for the time being. If they were still bleeding by morning, he would suture them then.

He took off his shirt. There was slightly more damage there. A couple of the shot were so close together that they formed one wound. Nothing very deep and he got them out easily but the longer wound would require at least a couple sutures. He wiped the area down with alcohol and let it evaporate. Then he numbered it with the spray and opened the sterile package containing the suture. He hadn't done this in a while and wasn't sure how he would manage with one hand.

His father was so good at this. He would watch him open an artery in one of his subjects just to show him how to close it. His victim, or his patient as he liked to call them, was still alive at this time and he thought the blood pulsing from the artery was so cool. That was before he would clamp the proximal end of the artery so that he could see to sew it back together. "Good times," he remembered.

He pushed and then pulled the needle through epidermis and dermis layers only. He brought the forceps about halfway up, did a double hoop with the thread and then pulled the rest of the way. He tucked the needle into the other side of the opening and repeated the process. He watched the upper end of the wound pull together. He did this twice more until the laceration was completely closed. He wiped it again with the alcohol and placed a dry bandage over it. He put elastic strips over the lesser wounds.

He moved to the medicine cabinet and removed one of the bottles on antibiotic pills and dry swallowed two of them. "Twice a day for five days," he told himself. "That will be three hundred dollars."

He grabbed the trash container and picked up all the wrappings and waste. Then he got the broom and dustpan and cleaned up the hair. "The maps can wait," he thought, "may as well stay here and finish preparing the room." He held up his bloody shirt, "Mother is going to be upset about this. I don't think she'll like the haircut either."

Chapter 81

Greg was on his way to the hospital when his phone rang. He didn't recognize the number but it was local. "Hello," he answered.

"Mr. Webster, this is Priscilla Chalmers, I need your help." She was crying.

"What's happened Priscilla?" he replied.

"Ben was here, he tried to abduct me."

"Are you alright?"

"I will be, I'm just shaken now."

"Have you called the police, Priscilla?"

"Not yet, it just happened. You were my first call."

"Priscilla, I am going to send the police to your house and I'm coming over there too. Are you alone?"

"No, my father is here with me, he was here at the time. He saved me." She was crying hard now.

"Alright, Priscilla, listen to me. Lock all the doors and stay away from the windows. Turn off as many lights as you can. Don't open the doors to anyone except the police or me. Do you understand?"

"Yes, Greg. Please hurry."

"I'm on my way right now."

Greg ended the call and dialed the sheriff. He gave them the information. They knew where the farm was located and dispatched a car immediately. Greg didn't have much time. He was supposed to meet John, Bill, and Richard at the hospital in an hour. He called Charis. "Charis here. Hello, Greg."

"Charis, Ben just tried to abduct Priscilla Chalmers. I'm on my over there and I notified the police. I just thought you would want to know."

"Of course, thank you. Did she share any details with you?"

"Not yet, I wanted to get the ball rolling but when I find out, I'll let you know."

"Alright, Greg. Be careful. Oh, Summers is dead."

"What!" Greg said.

"I'll explain when you call me back."

It took Greg less than twelve minutes to reach the farm. When he pulled in the driveway, the Sheriff's car was already there and two officers were approaching to house. "Officers," he yelled, "I'm Greg Webster, I called this in."

They waived him up. He ran toward the house. As he approached he said, "let me talk to her through the door and she will open it for you." They agreed. "Priscilla, it's Greg, I'm here with the Sheriff's department. You can open the door now."

Priscilla, opened the door just far enough to see Greg's face. Once she saw him, she opened it wide. Greg stepped through and Priscilla nearly jumped in his arms.

"It's okay," he said as he held her. "You're okay now, everything's going to be okay." He reassured her. "Let's let the officers in so we can talk." She dropped her hug but held onto his hand. She led him to the sofa next to where her father was sitting and asked the officers to have a seat. When everyone was seated, the officers introduced themselves. One of them was familiar with her dad.

"Mr. Chalmers, I don't know if you remember me but you delivered dairy to my parents' home for a lot of years."

"You look like one of the Rector boys from over on Burwell Street."

"That's amazing! I haven't seen you in a good fifteen years," the officer replied.

"You haven't changed all that much, a little bigger is all."

"Who wants to go first," Rector said.

"I will," Priscilla said.

"It was about a quarter before four and I headed into the house to start supper. Dad had gone to the hardware store. I took a shower, got dressed and came back down. I was preparing some vegetables and realized Dad still wasn't back. I looked out the window and didn't see him or his truck so I went out to the barn. He had been working on the silo earlier and I thought maybe he went right back there."

"I couldn't find him so I started to walk back toward the barn door. The next thing I knew, I had a rag over my face and was being picked up off the ground. I kicked as hard as I could but I didn't make contact with him. The next thing I remember is waking up in the milk room, alone. I was barely awake and I felt awful. After a few minutes, he came into the milk room."
"Who did, Ms. Chalmers?" Officer Rector asked.

"Ben Kovak," she answered.

"Is he a boyfriend?" he asked.

"No, I just met him a few days ago at the hardware store. We had planned a date for Tuesday but that was before the police were looking for him."

"What happened then?" Rector asked.

"I'll have to let my father tell you." Priscilla said.

"Mr. Chalmers?"

"On my way home from the store, I caught just a glimpse of a red pickup truck behind the overgrown grapevine about forty yards north of the driveway. I had a bad felling so I pushed up the road a ways and walked back through the field.

When I reached the side of the barn, I saw Priscilla laying in the grass. She was unconscious. I looked around and I could see the truck moving out from behind the vine. I knew he was coming back for her so I picked her up and moved her to the milk room. I thought she would be safe there while I went to get my shotgun. I loaded it in the house, put a few extra shells in my pocket and came to the back of the barn.

He was in there, I could hear him talking. Priscilla was awake too and I could hear her voice. I just listened for a couple minutes while I thought about what my next move was. He raised his voice at one point and I thought I had better move quickly. I stood up enough to peak in the window. He was standing facing me with his back to the door. I heard him say he was going to put her to sleep and take her to see his mother."

"I didn't see Priscilla so I assumed she was still on the ground. So I raised the gun and fired. The glass shattered into the room and I could see him running toward the front of the barn. I went around the side and saw him running toward the truck. I stopped, aimed, and let another round go. I must have missed because he just kept running. He got in the truck, started it, and backed up in a hurry. I had reloaded and I fired one more round at the truck but he was almost at the end of the driveway. I don't think I hit him at all. He peeled off heading north."

"You fired three shots altogether, is that correct?" Rector asked.

"Yes, the gun is in the kitchen," he replied.

"Do you mind if I have a look?"

"Go right ahead officer," Chalmers said.

Rector sent the other officer to check out the weapon.

"What did Kovak say to you, Priscilla?" Greg asked.

"He admitted killing all those people with the bombs and he said they weren't the only ones. He said he wanted to take me to Austria with him. When I said I wasn't going anywhere with him, he said he was going to drug me again.

I told him he needed help, that I could call the police and they would get him help. He said, 'Like they helped my father!' He actually screamed at me. Right after that, the window crashed into the room."

"Did any of the glass hit him, or you?" Rector followed.

"A couple pieces fell on my head but I wasn't hurt. He ran out there so quickly that I didn't have time to notice if he was hurt."

"May we check out the milk room, please?"

"I'll take you out there, officer," Mr. Chalmers offered, "I don't want her leaving this house until he is caught."

"That will be fine." Rector replied.

"Webster, will you stay with her until I get back?" Chalmers asked.

"You have my word," Greg replied.

The officers and Mr. Chalmers went out the front door.

"Priscilla, you were great. Sit tight a minute while I make a couple calls."

She nodded her head in agreement. Greg didn't leave her side and called Bill.

"Hi, Bill, change of plans. Can you call the other guys and tell them we will meet at my house at seven? Yes, back to the original plan. I will explain later. Thanks, Bill."

When that call ended, he called Charis.

"Andrews," she answered.

"Charis, this was a scary situation here, is there any way you can arrange for protection for the Chalmers?"

"Did you talk to the officers at the scene?" she said.

"Not yet but I know things would happen a lot quicker if you asked."

"Is everyone okay there?" Charis asked.

"Yes, but I don't want them here alone. I would offer to take them home with me but they run a farm here and the cows can't wait until we catch this guy."

"I get it. Let me make a few calls. It may take me awhile, we're currently one agent short in the Albany office."

"I need someone here by 6:45 tonight, is that doable?" Greg asked.

"I can put some heat on the locals to cover until we get an agent out there. You do what you need to do, Greg."

"Thank you Charis. Can I call you after the meeting tonight?" he asked.

"I'll be around," she answered.

Greg made one more call. He wanted Mary to know he was going to be late. "I'm going to stay with you until an officer arrives to keep watch," he told Priscilla. "The FBI is sending an agent to watch the house tonight so that you and your dad can get some rest."

"That's very nice of you, Greg, I don't know what we would have done without you."

"How are you doing, Priscilla? This must be very difficult for you," Greg said.

"I think it actually brings some closure for me," she responded, "I'm not sure I would have ever fully believed he was capable if I didn't see it with my own eyes. He is a sick man, Greg, and he needs help."

Greg agreed and promised her that the authorities would make sure that happened once he was apprehended. Rector and Mr. Chalmers walked back into the house.

"We found some blood in the milk room," Chalmers said, "he must have been hit."

"We took some photos and a sample of the blood. We will get that off to Albany for analysis first thing tomorrow," Rector piped in.

I called my contact at the FBI," Greg interjected, "They will be sending an agent to watch the house tonight."

"I heard," responded Rector, "I already have my orders to stay until he or she gets here."

"Sorry about that," Greg said, "I tried to cut through the red tape."

"It worked," Rector replied. "I'm going to run my partner back to the station then I'll come right back. Thirty minutes tops."

"I'll stay with them until you return, officer," Greg offered.

"I appreciate that, Mr. Webster. I'll see you in just a bit then."

The officers left and it was just the three of them. "Mr. Chalmers, it occurs to me that we were never formally introduced," Greg said as he stood to shake his hand.

"You can call me Chas, Greg, most people I know do."

"It's nice to know you, Chas. This is one amazing daughter you have here."

"She sure is. I don't know how I would get along without her but one of these days we're going to find out."

"I don't plan on going anywhere, Daddy, you know that!"

"I know you want to stay to help me and I appreciate that, but life is short and uncertain Priscilla, and I want you to go out and make a life of your own instead of living mine. Besides, I wouldn't feel right bringing a date home with you around," he kidded her.

"I will leave when we are both ready, Dad. How is that?"

"As long as you keep an open mind, it's a deal."

"I would be willing to help you out when I can, Chas. I don't know the first thing about dairy farming but I'm a quick study." Greg was trying to keep the conversation lite.

"That's mighty nice of you, Greg but you might be a little old to start farming. Now if you had a son or two, I might be interested," Chalmers stated.

"I do have a son who is away at college but he could be looking for some work during his breaks as well as over the summer. I'm going to see him this week so I will plant the seed."

"A little farming humor, Greg?" Priscilla asked.

Rector was back in just over thirty minutes but that left Greg enough time to get home. He said his farewells and offered for them to call him anytime they needed to. They thanked him and promised they would.

Greg didn't have time to run by the hospital but he made a mental note to go in early the next morning and do his research. He passed Smitty's at the end of the road and wondered how a kid working at a hardware store got caught up in a mess like this.

Chapter 82

Greg pulled into the driveway just as the other members of the team were arriving. They greeted each other quickly and walked into the house. Mary and Sara had made desserts which were plated and resting on the dining room table. There were small plates, cloth napkins, beverages, and glasses as well. Jocelyn, Jillian, and Maria were upstairs.

Greg invited everyone to sit and help themselves to the food and drink. "Should I get the girls?" Mary asked.

"I would like to start without them if that's alright. We can bring them in shortly. Around 4pm, I received a call from Priscilla Chalmers. For those of you who may not know, she was the young lady who went to Smitty's after the announcement about Ben Kovak's probable involvement.

My FBI contact, Charis asked if I would question her about the relationship between the two. I met with Priscilla and then gave her my phone number and asked her to call me if needed. She did just that, this afternoon."

"Did she have more information?" Richard asked.

"That would be an understatement," Greg replied. "Kovak tried to abduct her."

"From where?" Mary asked.

"From her home," Greg replied. "She lives and works on a farm outside of town, just up the road from Smitty's. She was expecting her father to be returning from Smitty's while she was preparing dinner. When he was late, she went out to check the barn. Ben surprised her and held a chloroform soaked rag to her face. She passed out and he laid her next to the barn while he ran for his truck." Greg went on to tell the rest of the story. He answered the perfunctory follow up questions before moving on.

"Greg," Mary asked, "in light of this, will you be postponing your trip to Syracuse on Tuesday?"

"That's open for discussion but I would like to give you my thoughts first, if I may." No one spoke. "I don't believe any of us are targets. So far, he has struck out against the schools Seike attended and Pricilla whom he wanted to kidnap because he liked her. I don't see how any of us fit into that. He also has no way of knowing that we have been involved in his case."

"It still seems risky to me," John said. "Who knows what he really knows?"

"But aren't we playing the game on his terms if we change our lives out of fear?" Richard said.

"I agree," said Sara, "I think we should be careful but I'm not convinced we need to change our plans. Think about it, would we not send our kids to school? Not go to the grocery store?" she asked.

"I'm with Richard and Sara on this. However, I do think we need a plan for our own surveillance. Let's talk about what we can do to protect ourselves and each other without giving up our routines. I'll begin," he offered. "I will ask for police protection while I am speaking at SU. One call to Charis and she will have someone from her office or a local agency watching over me."

"I will be here to watch your children and the women," Richard restated.

John was next. "I'll need to be at work part of the day but I will be available late afternoon and evening. Until then, the girls can be over here with Richard."

"I'll be here with Richard and I will drive the girls back and forth to school," Bill offered.

"Bill," Mary said, "If you can drop all the girls off and pick up Maria and Jocelyn after school, I will pick up Jillian after field hockey practice. She is finished around 5:30."

"That's fine," Bill replied, "We will all meet back here then."

"Routine stuff, I know, but always lock doors and always know where everyone is. The girls are to remain inside after they get home from school." Greg advised.

"Does anyone have anything else?" Greg asked.

"Do you think he'll come out again, Greg?" John asked.

"No, I don't." Greg replied. "We know the make, the color, and the model of both vehicles now. Police are in heighted awareness mode and if he were to move, someone would pick up on him right away. I really think he will lay low for now. Shall we bring the girls down and go over the plan? You know, I just thought of this but is everyone available to do a run-through tomorrow?" Everyone nodded their affirmation. "Great! Let's call the girls."

Chapter 83

Greg called Charis to ask for another favor. He didn't think it was necessary but he couldn't ask everyone else to implement precautions while not exercising any himself. He really thought the kid was going to lay low until the temperature cooled down.

The meeting with the girls went well. They promised to be careful and observant and to spend all non-school hours at home, inside the house. They were in their rooms now and Mary was upstairs reading. He sat at his desk in the den and dialed Charis' number.

"Good evening, Greg," she answered. Greg could tell she was still in a car.

"It's kind of late to be driving around, isn't it?" he asked.

"I'm heading back to DC tonight to see if I can pull some strings to get answers to the myriad questions I have," she replied. "How about you? Did you have a productive meeting?"

"I think we covered the bases, we at least have a plan to watch out for each other. That is, all except me. Can I ask a favor?"

"Of course, Greg, what can I do?" Charis asked.

"I'm still on the schedule to speak at Syracuse University Tuesday at 11:00am. Is there anything you can do to arrange for a single officer to cover the event? I hate to ask but I can't very well expect everyone else to comply if I won't."

"That's very considerate of you," she replied.

"I really don't think it's necessary and I hate to waste resources," Greg responded, "I don't think there is a great likelihood that Kovak will show up anywhere. In fact, we have reason to think he is injured."

"Well, I think it's a good use of resources to have someone there. I'll call the western New York bureau chief to see if he can assign someone. I would call Summers but he's permanently off duty," she stated."

"So you said. What happened there?" Greg asked.

"It's a long story," Charis began, "I'll give you the short version. I had reason to believe Summers was sleeping with Veronica Sweet, the girl Kovak met at the Gerardi's Shop outside of Middlebury. It turns out that Sweet and Kovak didn't know each other at all. It was a totally impromptu meeting that resulted in very casual riverside sex. When Summers interviewed Sweet and she told him what had happened, he thought he was entitled to his personal time with this young lady, against her will no less."

"So you put out a hit on him?" Greg joked.

"Yes, that's current FBI protocol, uncover a bad agent and take him out," She said sarcastically. "These aren't the days of J. Edgar Hoover anymore Greg, we don't do it that way anymore. It was a serendipitous accident that I called Veronica that night. She was obviously distraught on the phone and being the supersleuth that I am, I detected the danger and had her go to a neighbor's place when he stepped out for a minute. Long story short, he was an asshole and got caught in the crossfire."

"So what made you call right then?" he asked.

"I was looking for a third nipple and no, I am not going to explain that!" she warned him, "We will save that conversation for another day."

"Good, he said, "that sounds weird and a little frightening," he responded. "Do you have any new information?"

"We know the body in the morgue doesn't belong to Kovak but I guess that's not news to you. I am still waiting on genetics results from the hair. Also, the phony suicide notes at the apartment and the warehouse tell me that the cadavers were sent to the universities from ReadiMed Scientific Supply Company. The owner has no knowledge of any of it but he did admit that Kovak worked there and he would have had opportunity. He also stated that Kovak was one of the best employees he ever had."

"The hardware store up here said the same thing," Greg replied. "What would make a seemingly good kid want to create all this carnage?"

"We will know after we catch him," Charis responded. "Were you able to find anything in the hospital records, Greg?"

"I never had a chance to get to the hospital. I was headed there when I get the call from Priscilla about the abduction. I am going in early tomorrow to see what I can dig up. I am also going to check county records for anything related to Martina Kovatikova. There has to be some evidence that this person existed."

"Alright Greg, let's talk in the morning. Maybe we will both have something new."

Greg agreed and hung up the phone. He leaned back in his chair and looked around the room. He was surrounded by memories. The walls were a pictorial history of his family. Mary was always good about keeping up with photos of the kids and she had a knack for displaying them. He couldn't remember the last time he had actually taken time to really look at them. He was in this room almost every day and he saw the photos but he was understanding the difference between seeing something and really noticing it.

As much as Greg reminded his family to be aware of their surroundings, he now realized he had failed to do the same. He was always coming from a safety perspective but missed the importance of what was going on in his own home, with his own loved ones. He told himself he could do better, and he would.

He turned off the light and went upstairs. The low glow of the bedside lamp told him that Mary was still awake. He surmised that she was worried about what was coming and he was prepared to attempt to alleviate her fears. Greg walked past the bed to the bathroom.

It appeared Mary had fallen asleep with the lamp on. He removed his clothes and went to wash up, careful to close the door quietly. When he opened the door, he could hear soft music playing, barely noticeable.

Mary was no longer in bed. The lamp was still on, casting a warm glow about the room. Mary was seated at her vanity with her back to the table and facing the bed. She looked beautiful in the warm light.

She wasn't wearing any of the sexy outfits she had recently purchased. In fact, she wasn't wearing anything at all. He approached her slowly wearing just his pajama shorts. She was sitting up straight with her legs crossed as if she were sitting at work somewhere. He moved closer.

"You have never looked more beautiful than you do right now," he said. "The dress-up stuff is fun sometimes but this is even better." Something about the nakedness, the total vulnerability made the experience seem spiritual. He knelt down before her and looked deep into her eyes.

There was no need for words. What he was feeling could not be defined. Staring at each other, tears of love and infinite appreciation were welling up in their eyes. Mary moved to the floor and faced her husband. They were both on their knees and they reached out and just held each other for a long time.

When the wordless conversation, the speaking of heart sounds paused, Greg stood and extended his hand to Mary. She held on as he lifted her to her feet. They moved slowly to the bed.

Chapter 84

In spite of the late night, Greg was up and out of the house by 7:00 am. He reviewed the plans for the day with Mary before he left. Bill would be picking the kids up to take them to school and Richard would be at the house by 7:30 am. Sara would join them then. Mary had left a voice message the night before at school to notify them they wouldn't need a pickup or drop off this week.

Greg checked in with Kathy upon his arrival at the hospital and asked her to find out when the county offices opened. He also requested a light schedule for the day. She promised to remove everything that wasn't urgent from his calendar.

He sat down behind his desk and fired up his computer. After accessing the medical records module, he entered in his first search criteria. Kovatikova, Martina. He left the search date field open so that the system would look back to the beginning of time. He also left the date of birth field open in case the document date was wrong or fictitious.

He pressed the enter key and sat back. He watched the wheel turning on the screen. Five seconds later, it stopped. *"No*

Results." He moved on to Kovak, Korben and entered the same search parameters as before. After a few more seconds, "*No Results*." One more shot, this time he entered the name Chalmers, Timothy. Leaving most of the fields blank again, he pressed enter and waited. The wheel turned a little longer this time. When it stopped, he received this message. "*Patient found, Record is Locked*."

Greg dialed the extension for Charlene Kuchar, the nursing director. He hoped she would be able to tell him why the chart was locked. In addition, she had been at the hospital for over forty years and had a great memory.

"Nursing Service, Charlene speaking," she answered.

"Good morning Charlene, it's Greg. Boy, am I glad you come in early too!"

"This sounds like work, Greg, I'm not liking it already," she responded.

"Look, you're going to be retired soon and you will miss my calls."

"Not much chance of that, but how can I help you today, Mr. Webster?"

"I need access to a locked chart."

"There are reasons why charts are locked, Greg."

"They're even locked from the hospital administrator?"

"Yes, Greg, even you. Why do you need access?"

"I'm working the college bombing case and I have a hunch about something," he said.

"Oh, a hunch, why didn't you say so?" she said jokingly. "Tell what you need."

"I'm trying to find information on a kid from more than twenty years ago. His name is Timothy Chalmers."

"I remember this case, he is a missing person file and his record is locked because it was labeled a sensitive case," Charlene said. "I don't believe the boy was ever found."

"I think I may have found him," Greg replied.

"Tell me what you need, Greg."

"I need something that will allow the FBI to test for genetic markings. Would we still have any blood or hair samples here?"

"I doubt it, but the police may have something in their evidence locker," she stated.

"But we do have information, I mean, the child was here for something before he went missing, right?"

"Yes, or we wouldn't have any record at all, hence nothing to lock," she replied sarcastically.

"Good point. May I see information prior to him being reported missing?" Greg asked.

"I don't see why not, let me see what we have. I'll bring it over when I find it."

"Thank you Charlene."

As Greg was hanging up, Kathy entered the office. "The county offices open at 9am today. Is there something I can assist you with?"

"Yes, if you have time," he responded.

"I will find the time. What do you need?"

"I need every county office to run the name Martina Kovatikova through their databases. Also, see if the New York State Department of Motor Vehicles has information. And Kathy, see if they can do it today."

Kathy left the office. Greg tried to think of anything he could be doing to move the investigation forward. Until something came to him, he decided to review his notes on the presentation at SU. He also wanted to check in with Jack. It was still pretty early but Jack always took it well when dad woke him up.

"What time is it," Jack asked.

"It's nearly eight o'clock," Greg cheerily responded.

"That would be morning, I suppose?" Jack asked again.

"Of course, Greg said, "I am not nearly this chipper in the evening."

"How about calling me back then," Jack tiredly joked.

"I'm sorry for calling so early but my day is going to explode and I wanted to touch base with you about tomorrow before it does."

"What about tomorrow?" Jack said.

"I'm coming out there, did you forget?"

Jack paused a moment. "No, I didn't forget, Dineen Hall, eleven o'clock."

"That's right, son, and what about lunch afterward?" Greg asked.

"I'm free for the rest of the afternoon and evening, Dad," he replied.

"That's great, Jack. So, how is everything out there?"

"Everything is fine here but I have a hunch something is bothering you. Dad, is something on your mind?"

"I'm just a little distracted I guess," Greg answered. "This guy is still out there somewhere, probably close by, and we can't seem to find him."

"Dad, do you think he may be targeting you or our family?"

"No, I don't, Jack. That doesn't make any sense. Even if he is Seike's son, why would he have a vendetta against me or the universities he attended? It doesn't fit his M.O. Anyway, I'll be there at least an hour early tomorrow. The presentation should be over in an hour, even if all four attendees ask questions," Greg joked.

"I wouldn't count on it, Dad, your program sold out. It's currently standing room only."

"Sold out?" Greg asked.

"Not for money, Dad, but all reserved seating has been taken."

"So that's like forty or fifty seats, right?" Greg asked.

"Try four hundred seats, Dad. You're like the Bruce Springsteen of whodunnits!"

Greg was both proud and nervous. "Then I guess I should go prepare a little more."

"You'll be fine Dad. At least you had better be or I'm going to be looking to transfer!"

"I won't let you down, Jack."

"You never have, Dad, I'll be proud one way or the other."

"Thanks, Jack. You can just call me Bruce, or maybe, 'The Boss.' Yeah, let's go with that."

"How about we just stick with Dad?"

"That works too. Take care, son, I will see you tomorrow."

Greg hung up and thought about how proud he was of his family.

His cell phone rang and it startled him. "Hello," he answered.

"Good morning Greg, it's Charis. Did I catch you at a bad time?"

"No, unfortunately," he joked. "What's up?"

"I have the results of the hair and blood analysis. Kovak is not related to Seike," she said.

"I guess I'm not surprised," Greg responded.

"There's more Greg, Kovak's blood found at the farm doesn't match anyone we have on file."

"That doesn't surprise me either," Greg said. "Charis, I'm waiting for some results of my own. Can I call you back in a little while?"

"I'm around," she replied and hung up. Greg dialed the extension for Charlene Kuchar.

"Hi, Charlene," Greg said without even allowing her to introduce herself, "I need to know if we kept a sample of Timmy Chalmers blood."

"I was just about to get back to you with some information on his case," she replied.

"He was brought in for a case of croup when he was only eighteen months old. Because of the young age, he was admitted for a few days and several test were performed. In children this age, it is not unusual to keep specimens around for a while. Once he became a missing persons case, we had the results frozen and sent to the FBI."

"That's great! Was that the Albany bureau?"

"Yes, it was," she replied.

"Thank you, Charlene, I don't think I will need any more information from that file.

Greg hung and dialed Charis. He spoke as soon as the ringing stopped.

"There is a sample of blood at the Albany Bureau that we need to check against Kovak's. I think I know who his real parents are."

"The number you have reached is no longer in service," she answered and paused. She could hear Greg swearing on the other end.

"Slow down," she said, "you should let people say hello before you begin speaking."

"Okay, you got me, but I need you to do this, and I feel like we are running out of time."

"I will take care of it, Greg. You need to take a few deep breaths. It sounds like you're starting to panic and that will work against you. Now, what can I do for you, Mr. Webster," Charis said very calmly.

Chapter 85

Bill Dillon was knocking on the door at the Webster house at 7:20 am. Mary answered the door. "Good morning, Bill, please come in."

"I know I'm a few minutes early, I apologize," he said.

"An apology is not necessary, Bill, come into the kitchen and I will get you some coffee. How do you like it?"

"Just black would be fine, thank you," he replied.

While Mary was pouring Bill's coffee, Sara came to the back door with Maria and Richard was ringing the front doorbell. Sara let herself in while Mary raced back to the front door.

"Good morning Richard, please come in."

"I was up early so I thought I would get started protecting my girls. I hope you don't mind."

"Why would I mind, Richard, you are doing us all a big favor and we appreciate it. Bill is in the kitchen. Will you join us for coffee?"

"Sure, I would love some."

"How do you take that?" Mary asked.

"Like my women," Richard responded, "tall, creamy, and sweet."

"Well that certainly describes Marilyn now doesn't it?"

"Wasn't who I had in mind, but it sure does," he agreed.

They walked into the kitchen and joined Bill and Sara. Sara had brought some fresh baked pastries which Richard walked right over to.

"These look great! Did you bake these, Bill?" Richard joked.

"No, but I could if I had a mind to do it," Bill replied.

"That's right, if you only had a mind," Richard returned.

"Go easy on each other boys, you need to stay focused today," Sara reminded them.

"We are super focused," Bill said, "we do this all the time."

Jillian and Jocelyn came thumping down the stairs. "What's for breakfast, Mom?" Jocelyn asked.

"Can you say hello to our visitors first?" Mary asked. They both said hello and gave everyone big smiles.

"Aunt Sara baked some very yummy things for us this morning," Mary said. "Pour yourselves a glass of juice or milk please."

"How about a little coffee," Jillian asked.

"As long as it looks more like milk than coffee," Mary said.

"What time do the girls need to be at school?" Bill asked.

"The bell rings at 8:20 but they like to be there a few minutes early so you have another ten minutes before leaving." Mary answered. "Bill, you will pick Jocelyn and Maria up at 3:15 this afternoon and I will swing by to get Jillian after practice at

5:30. The same schedule will apply tomorrow. Anyone have any questions?"

Hearing none, Mary said, "Alright girls, upstairs to brush your teeth and get your backpacks."

"Bill, feel free to come back after you drop the girls off. Richard will be here as well."

"I don't know, if he's going to be here, I may just continue on," Bill replied.

"I was hoping you would say that," Richard added.

Chapter 86

Ben had a restless night so he slept a little later than usual. It seemed strange not to be getting ready for work but he had other things to do today. He had prepared the last vehicle in the garage for the week ahead. His tools were packed and he put fresh batteries in the detonator.

He didn't move the new ride to the first bay as he had done in the past. He felt very exposed right now and didn't want the vehicles to be seen from the air just in case they were patrolling the skies.

Today was just some reconnaissance, nothing too taxing. He did need to change his bandages though so he went to the workroom to take care of it. Passing by Mother's room, he though he heard her stirring. He opened the door to find her staring at him. "Good morning Mother, are you feeling well today? You look a little pale, perhaps a fresh cup of formalin and a little makeup will make you feel better. I'll tend to that as soon as I change these bandages.

He opened the workroom door and was greeted by the smell of O.R.1. He wasn't sure that one could describe the smell as sterile, but that's what it was to him. Because it was at the back of the basement, which was built as an impenetrable fortress, the room could be completely dark.

Every once in a while, he would close the door behind him to experience the darkness of death. "Was it really so bad?" he thought. His father had taught him that death was just the final phase of life, something to expect and revere but not fear.

He closed the door behind him and leaned against it. There were no windows or doors to let even a crack of natural light in. There were no electronic gadgets with indicator lights to break the blackness. The human eye could never adjust to complete darkness. He stayed there for several minutes experiencing the absence of light.

He thought back to the time he accidently locked himself in the room. The walls were almost two feet thick and the door was six inches. He was told that this was the safe room of the house, as long as there was air coming in. His father had designed it with three redundant sources of air exchange. One pipe went straight through to the roof. The second went through the top of the wall just above the ground and the third was a feed from the spare bedroom on the second floor.

He didn't panic because he was taught not to. "Relax and slow your breathing down," his father advised, "if you panic, you will die." He was just eight years old at the time and despite what he was taught, he did fell a bit anxious. At least there was one light switch inside the room although the location wasn't obvious. The room was not designed for the comfort of its guests, nor did it allow for escape.

He was locked in that room for just over two hours until his mother finally figured out he was missing. "She did lose track of me sometimes," he remembered. She let him out but never apologized for forgetting about him for two hours. It was shortly after that incident that dad installed the remote lock release. He didn't trust Martina to care for him appropriately.

Ben opened the door and turned the main lights on from the hallway. He went to the counter and retrieved some bandages and a tube of antibiotic cream. Using the portable mirror and the overhead surgical light, he checked and re-dressed his wounds. He took time to admire his work. The sutures were nearly perfect and wouldn't leave a noticeable scar. There wasn't any indication of infection and the bleeding had stopped almost immediately as evidenced by the lack of blood on the gauze.

When he was finished, he looked around the room once more to make sure everything was in place. Content that he was properly prepared, he grabbed the supplies needed to make Mother presentable. "Mother, I'm back. Let's have a look at you."

Ben connected the bag containing the formalin to a catheter in her subclavian artery. He turned on the low pressure pump and let the two liters of fluid run through her circulatory system. The pressure would force the old fluid in her abdomen to drain into a urine output bag. It was a clever design that his father had come up with. This would hold her for a while but soon, she would need a complete transfusion using the embalming equipment. "Feeling better Mother? I thought you would. How about a little fresh makeup?" Ben found it to be a comfort to have Mother around even if she didn't respond. He didn't see the difference between Mother and another child's stuffed animal. They both required some imagination and they both provided comfort and companionship.

Now that his required tasks were completed, it was time for a little fun. He backed his new ride out of the third bay of the garage, closed the door behind him and drove toward the Webster place. It wasn't a very long drive.

Chapter 87

Bill dropped off the kids as planned, without episode. He was careful to watch them enter the school before he pulled away. He was on his way back to Greg's house when he saw a car coming slowly toward him. The vehicle slowed down as it passed the Webster address. Bill drove by the vehicle, taking care not to be noticed. He glanced without turning his head. The driver had a shaved head and a what looked like a few fresh bandages at the scalp line.

As soon as Bill rounded a bend, he turned around in the first driveway he came to. He proceeded slowly back around the bend and saw the vehicle come to a complete stop in front of the house. He stayed back and picked up his binoculars. He pulled a pen from his pocket and wrote down the plate number. He stayed back until the car pulled away and then followed it. At the next intersection, the car turned left on a country road and sped up. He followed from a comfortable distance but the driver kept accelerating.

When he left the Herkimer County line, he picked up his speed even more. He knew he was being followed. Bill backed off, turned around and headed back to the house. He found a wooded area across the street from the Webster home and backed his car in so he could keep an eye on the property.

He placed a call to Greg. "Hi Bill, what going on?"

"Greg, I think Kovak may have just driven by your house. I was returning from dropping the kids off at school and I passed this car moving slowly then almost stopping in front of the house. I turned around and fell in behind him. When he left, I pursued but he knew he was being followed and scurried off."

"Were you able to get a plate number, Bill?"

"I was, it's a New York plate Howard, Charlie, Thomas 4543. It a white Range Rover, maybe five or six years old."

"That's HCT 4543, correct?"

"Yes, what do you want me to do, Greg?"

"Can you stay and watch the house until the kids need picking up? I'm going to call this into Charis to see if she can help."

"I'm on it, Greg. If he returns, I will let you know. Richard is inside with Sara and Mary."

"Thanks, Bill, I will let you know how we are going to progress."

Greg dialed Charis once again. "Andrews," she answered.

"Charis, it's Greg again."

"I know, thanks for letting me answer this time," she said.

"Kovak just drove by my house."

"How do you know that, Greg?"

"Bill spotted a car driving slowly by and followed him. Once he knew he was being followed, he took off."

"Did he see the driver?"

"Yes, he is the right age but he has shaved his head and he has bandages on his scalp. He is driving a five or six year old white Range Rover, NY plate number HCT 4543."

"Wow, that is good work! Where do you find these guys?" Charis asked.

"I inherited them," Greg responded.

"Greg, we ran a quick check of the blood type as you suggested. The blood looks very similar. Both are A positive and a preliminary histology is comparable. It will be a few days before we can get the DNA results if they can do it at all. Even though Timmy's blood was frozen, too much time may have passed."

"We do what we can, Charis."

"Let me call this plate in and request surveillance for your home. I'll catch up with you later."

"Thank you," Greg said.

Greg sat back and thought of his next move. The county offices wouldn't be opening for another thirty minutes. He wondered if he should call home to fill them in or if that would just scare everyone unnecessarily. Bill was watching from outside and Richard was inside so he had some time. He would at least wait to hear back from Charis.

He decided to take a walk. He didn't know where he would go but he couldn't sit still. Sometimes, just walking made him think more clearly.

Chapter 88

Richard excused himself from the kitchen to make a phone call. "Would it be alright if I used the den to make a call, Mary?"

"Of course, Richard, I'm sure this girl talk is wearing you down," Mary answered.

"Not at all, I just need to follow up on some things, I'll be back in a few minutes."

He went to the den and closed the door. He sat in the comfortable leather chair facing the window to the back yard and dialed Bill's number.

"Yes, Richard," Bill answered.

"I will pay you to trade places with me," Richard begged.

"What are you talking about, Richard?"

"I can't stand listening to them anymore, I'm going crazy in here!"

"Richard, we are here to do a job. You can't protect them if you're not in there."

"Well, what are you doing?" Richard asked.

"I'm surveilling the house from across the street. Kovak drove by just a short while ago."

"No shit!" Richard exclaimed.

"I'm serious, Richard. I tried to follow him but I lost him."

"That's because you're a lousy driver, Bill, I've been trying to tell you that since our first trip. Let me change places with you."

"I don't think so, Richard, I told Greg I would stay out here. Besides, what makes you think I want to join in on the girl talk?"

"I said I was willing to pay you," Richard repeated.

"I'll tell you what you can do. I can only watch the front of the house, why don't you watch the back from the patio? That will get you out of the house for a while."

"That's a great idea, Bill."

"Richard, don't say anything about the drive by. Let's leave that up to Greg."

"Ten-four," Richard said and hung up.

He opened the door and re-entered the kitchen. Mary and Sara were in the same seats since he arrived at 7:30. "Listen ladies, I'm going to check out the back yard for a while. I'll make the rest of my calls from there. Richard is watching the front from across the street. If you need me, holler."

He opened the back door then stopped. I'm locking this behind me so please let me back in, okay?"

"Sure, Richard. Just knock."

Richard went out to look around. It was a good size yard, manicured for about 200 feet and then turned to heavy woods. He didn't see a fence nor could he see anything past the tree line. He envisioned an attack from the woods as quick and indefensible. He dialed Greg's number. "Hi Greg, sorry to bother you at work."

"It's alright, Richard, I was just finishing up a walk. What can I do for you?"

"I am in your backyard, Greg and I am concerned about how difficult it would be to prevent or even see an approach from this side."

"Bill spoke to you about Kovak snooping around," Greg said.

"He did but don't worry, I didn't say anything to the girls." Richard replied.

"I appreciate that, Richard. I spoke with Agent Andrews a short time ago and she is arranging for an agent to cover the house."

"Do you think one agent can cover all of it, I mean does she know your house sits on the edge of Sherwood Forest and doesn't have a moat or even a fence around it?"

"I see your point, Richard. What are you suggesting?" Greg asked.

"What about a safehouse? Somewhere he wouldn't know to look for you?"

"Are you offering?" Greg asked.

"I am absolutely offering but I'm not convinced that would be any safer. My geographic situation isn't much better than yours and he could have easily written down my plate number when he drove by. Who is to say he wouldn't find my address as well? The same is true for Bill. How do you feel about taking everyone to John's house?"

"His house borders the woods too," Greg said.

"Yes," replied Richard, but Kovak doesn't know he is involved. As far guarding the perimeter tonight, we would have you, John, Bill, me, and the agent. We could watch all sides."

"That's not a bad idea, Richard but that would force us to tell the ladies what's going on. I was hoping we didn't need to do that just yet. Hang tight until I speak to Charis. I'll run it by her and see what she suggests."

"That sounds good, boss. Let me know when you find out."

"Thanks, Richard."

Any clarity of mind that resulted from Greg's walk had just clouded over again. He usually had a gut instinct about these things but it felt like his gut was failing him now. He walked back into the administrative suite and Kathy greeted him at the door.

"I got through to the person in charge at the department of records for Herkimer County. It seems like you have an old friend there," Kathy stated.

"Really? Who would that be?"

"Does the name Lacey Meadows ring any bells?"

"My Lacey Meadows? Lacey from fourteen years ago?" Greg responded, surprised to hear her name. He had bonded with Lacey and her parents after the ordeal at the hospital. It took her nearly a year to recover from the attack which should have ended her life. They kept in touch for the first few years but then drifted apart. He had no idea she was able to work again. She was just a teenager then which would make her in her early thirties now.

"That's the one!" Kathy confirmed. "She is ready to give you all the help you need. "Would you like to call her back, I have her direct number?"

"Yes, I would," Greg replied. Can you connect the call for me please?"

"At once, Mr. Webster," Kathy said.

In under a minute, Greg had Lacey on the phone. "Lacey, is that really you?"

"It is me, Greg, How are you?"

"I am overjoyed right now! It is so good to hear from you."

"Thank you, Greg. It's nice to hear your voice as well. I'm sorry we fell out of touch, I guess we both got busy with our lives."

"I'm sorry too, Lacey. Can we catch up sometime soon?"

"I would like that, Greg but right now it sounds like you are in a hurry for some information."

"Yes, I am Lacey. Did Kathy explain the situation?"

"She did and we are already working on it. We are checking all of our databases as well as going through our property records by hand. Kathy said she was going to contact the DMV too but I told her I would do that for her. It's all here in the same building."

"That's wonderful, Lacey. How long can a search like this take?"

"The data searches should be quick, perhaps a few hours. The manual search for property records could take a little longer. I am committing every resource we have to this project."

"I owe you big time, Lacey," Greg said emphatically.

"It is I who owes you, Greg. I have never forgotten what you did to help all of us get through that difficult time. I am alive because of you. I am also very glad to help catch this guy. I told Kathy I would contact her as soon as we have something."

"Thanks again, Lacey. I can't wait to see you again!"

The call was over and Greg felt re-energized. He was reminded of the good work everyone did. How they all pulled together at a moment's notice to overcome a huge obstacle. They could do it again. They had to do it again.

Greg dialed the number for Charis again.

"You have reached Charis Andrews, personal assistant to Greg Webster, How may I help you?"

"Very funny, Charis."
"Oh, Mr. Webster, it's you! I am so sorry."

"I get it, Charis, I am a pain in the ass. I apologize."

"Just having a little fun with you, Greg. What's happening?"

"Did I mention that my house sits on the edge of Sherwood Forest?"

"Does it have a moat or Robin Hood and his merry men?" she asked.

"No." he answered.

She replied with one word. "Safehouse."

Chapter 89

Ben hung out in rural Schoharie County for an hour or so before hitting the road again. He was sure the old guy captured his plate number and that the police were probably looking for his already. He had anticipated this possibility and was prepared for it. He placed a real Connecticut plate in the truck. He also brought the necessary tools to change it. He even had the registration sticker for the window.

He used the GPS in the Range Rover to guide him on the least traveled roads back to High Falls. He had several hours to make it back there before school was out. Once he learned the routine, he could put a plan in place. It would be more difficult now that outsiders were involved but he trusted his instincts and he had been in tougher spots before.

It was coming to an end soon, at least in this country. A new life was waiting for him in Austria. He had purchased new tickets under the name of Wendel Lemke who was sixty-one years old had blonde, thinning hair and had blue eyes. He had the credit card, passport, and driver's license already. They matched the costume quite nicely. He didn't expect any trouble getting on the plane.

Wendel was generous enough to give everything to Ben. This included his car, credentials and even his life. He was a recluse so to speak although he did travel back and forth to Europe frequently. Not for business really, but mostly for pleasure.

He had no children to miss him or report him missing, no office to attend and remote houses both domestic and abroad. The odds that this guy would walk into a hardware store in rural upstate New York had to be a million to one. The fact that he and Ben had similar hobbies were probably ten times that.

Ben knew by what the guy purchased and the questions he asked that he was into something nefarious. Ben used the guy's credit card information to track him down. He lived further off the beaten path that Ben did. A smallish but nice home tucked deep in the wood near Laurel Reservoir, just south of the New York state border.

It was early June when Ben met the man and just a week later that he paid Wendel a visit. After two days of watching his routine from a little tent he set up on a knoll overlooking the house, Ben made his move.

Lemke had just returned from a hunting trip. It was just before dark but Ben could see he was not alone. He was carrying someone into the house. Ben watched as a dim light was turned on in the house and then approached silently until he could see in one of the windows.

Lemke was using the rope he had purchased from Smitty's to bind his catch to a chair. It appeared to be a male, maybe late twenties, or early thirties. Not well dressed and didn't look very clean. Ben guessed it was a homeless guy from the city. New York, Yonkers, and a few large Connecticut cities were all within an hour's drive. The man was obviously drugged and unconscious.

Ben continued to watch as Lemke cut the man's clothing off and proceeded to bathe him. The man started to come around toward the end of the bath and started to struggle against the ropes. Lemke pulled a syringe out his pocket, uncapped the needle and injected the man in the shoulder. He quickly went back to sleep. Wendel untied the ropes and moved his victim to the sofa where he bent him over the armrest and sodomized him.

This wasn't Ben's cup of tea but "who was he to condemn." He thought to himself. When it was over, Lemke gave the man another dose of the drug and pulled his naked body toward the back of the house. Ben had noticed the hole in the back yard earlier in the day.

It was large and deep, most certainly dug using the backhoe he found in the large shed. It didn't look like this guy was the Lemke's first victim. There were at least eight other fresh graves in the area.

The back door opened and Lemke dragged the body out and threw him in the hole. He then went to the shed to get the backhoe. He pulled it up to the side of the fresh grave and got off. He went back in the house and came out holding the man's clothes which he threw into the pit. I

t was then that Ben swung the shovel at Lemke's head. There was a dull thud as the shovel made contact. Wendel fell on his face, unconscious at the edge of the hole. Ben reached into his pocket and pulled out his own syringe filled with propofol.

He tied a small piece of rope around his upper arm, found a vein and injected 30 ml.. Ben then jumped in the hole with the remaining 20 ml. and shared it with Lemke's victim. Ben didn't like the thought of them being buried alive.

Ben crawled out the hole, rolled Lemke's limp body into it alongside the other man and replaced all the excavated earth. He rolled the Backhoe over the mounded earth to flatten it. He drove the backhoe to the shed and turned it off. He searched the house taking all the personal documents he could find along with the car keys. He couldn't take the car with him then but he would return by bus in a few days and drive it home. "What a blessing that Wendel Lemke showed up in his store during his shift," Ben remembered.

He wouldn't be able to take a partner as he had originally planned but he wasn't worried about finding one there. Push came to shove, he would follow in his dad's footsteps and buy a spouse. It seemed to work out pretty well for him, until it didn't. But the beauty of a purchased spouse is you can handle it like any other commodity. If it doesn't work out, you divest yourself of the asset. "You just bury your unwanted assets along with your ethics," his father would say.

"Good old Dad," he thought as he pulled his hat over his eyes to take a little nap.

Chapter 90

It was approaching noon when Kathy announced that John Shand was there to see him. "Come in John, thanks for coming. I wanted to talk to you about an idea I have. Please, have a seat." John took a chair next to Greg in front of Greg's desk. "John, Kovak's car was seen in front of my house today. Bill gave chase but was unable to keep up with him. I called Charis at the FBI to report it and ask for help. She agreed to provide an agent to cover the house but because we are bound by woods, she requested we all move to a safehouse. What do you think about your house?"

John thought about it for only a few seconds. "If you think that's our best move, you are all welcome of course. Did Charis approve that plan?"

"I haven't asked her yet. I wanted to make sure you were on board first," Greg responded.

"We share the same woods Greg, do you think that will be a problem?"

"I thought about that too and I'm not sure. I think the fact that he knows our address makes the woods a factor. I don't believe he has any information on you but we should run that by Charis," Greg stated.

"If she approves than so do I," John confirmed. "Are the girls okay now?" John asked.

"Yes, I've been in touch with Bill and Richard and so far there has been no further sign of him."

"Do Mary and Sara know?" John asked.

"Not yet, I didn't want to alarm them before we had a plan in place. As soon as I speak with Charis again, we should be able to bring them in."

"I plan to leave a little early today, probably by two. Let me know when you here from Charis?"

"Sure thing. Thanks, John."

Greg was getting anxious. He thought he would have some answers by now. Just then, the phone rang. It was Charis.

"Hello Charis," Greg said.

"You've been waiting by the phone I see," she answered.

"Not me, I've been busy doing other things. I haven't even thought about you this morning," Greg replied.

"I'm a cop, remember? I know when someone is lying."

"I remember, and you are a good cop at that!" Greg said.

"I found a safehouse for you and your family. I know nobody wants to pack up and leave home but it's the best way."

"I was thinking," Greg said, "maybe we can all stay at Dr. Shands place until this blows over."

"I thought you would think that and that's why I thought it through before calling you. John lives close by, right? And, you are best friends, right? And, he shares the same woods as you, right?"

"Yes, correct on all counts," Greg admitted.

"Too risky," she said. "We need everyone packed by 6pm today. You will drive your cars, one at a time to the diner on 5s. An agent will meet you all there at 6:30. Stay in your cars until he finds you. If anyone suspicious approaches any of your vehicles, Leave immediately and go in different directions. Are you following so far?"

"I'm following. Where are we going to stay?"

"I won't tell you that, you will know when you get there." Charis said.

"How will we recognize the agent? Greg asked.

"He will be the one wearing the red wig, lipstick, and clown shoes!" she joked. He will know you and he will approach you when the time is right. It will be at exactly 6:30. Don't worry about dinner, it has all been arranged. It will be waiting at the safehouse. By the way, Bill and Richard need to come along as well. We will need their help on that end. There are enough rooms for everyone."

"Will Richard's wife be safe on her own?" Greg asked.

"Absolutely. He doesn't need to worry," she replied, "but he does need to tell her he won't be home for a couple days."

"Greg, you may all be gone for a couple days. You can go to work and school but then you all meet at the diner at 6pm. You do not go to the safehouse until your agent takes you there. Understood?"

"Yes, the agent with the big shoes. You know what they say about agents with big feet, don't you?" Greg asked.

"Yes, they pay twice as much for shoes," she came back.

"Get the ball rolling. Just a change of clothing of two or three days and that goes for everyone. Everything else you can imagine will be provided for you. By the way, we intercepted the information for a flight to Austria in Martina Kovatikova's name. She is scheduled on flight out of the country Wednesday morning."

"So you have credit card information for her?" Greg asked.

"Yes, the funds are paid from a Swiss account and the home address is the cemetery, so we still don't know where she lives. I can guarantee she won't be getting on a plane. Any news on your end?"

"Any minute now," Greg said. Charis hung up.

Greg asked Kathy to have John join him again. Then he dialed the number for Lacey Meadows. "Lacey, Greg Webster. I'm sorry to keep bothering you, I was just wondering if you were able to find anything yet."

"It's no bother Greg, we are still looking at the land records but I did receive the results of some of the database searches."

"That's great!" he said, "anything we can use?"

"Well, I'm not sure. We know that Martina receives a monthly social security check for around seventeen hundred dollars each month that is direct deposited to an account at Valley National Bank. I checked with the bank and they verified the deposit and said the next day, the same amount is transferred to another bank overseas."

"A Swiss account, I'm guessing," Greg said.

"That's correct. Martina's home address as listed at the bank turned out to be fictitious," she continued.
"A cemetery," Greg interjected.

"Correct again, Greg."

"How about the vehicles, Lacey" he continued.

"The BMW and the Toyota truck are registered to Martina at the cemetery address, as is her driver's license. The Range Rover has an unregistered plate on it and no New York registration. We are searching for cars with a similar description reported as stolen in all fifty states."

"That sounds like it can take a while," Greg said.

"It can," she responded, "but sometimes we get lucky. By the way, I also ran everything on Ben Kovak but it's like this guy never existed. No birth certificate on file, no driver's license, no registered vehicles, no arrests, and no warrants. The only thing we do have is evidence that he attended Harvard Medical School in Boston until a few months ago. His home address was also listed as the cemetery."

"He doesn't have any health records that we can find either," Greg added. "I wonder where he got his transcripts from to get into Harvard," Greg pondered.

"That's out of my wheelhouse, I'm afraid," Lacey replied.

"That's alright, Lacey, I appreciate all your help."

"I'll keep working it, Greg, maybe the property maps will give us a clue."

"Let's hope so. I'll talk to you later, Lacey."

Greg felt dejected. He seemed to be coming upon one dead end after another. He sent Charis a text. "Nothing so far from the county. Accounts for Martina are held abroad. Address is always listed as a cemetery in town here. Nothing on Kovak either. He is the invisible man. I'm wondering how he got into Harvard. Fake transcripts?" He sent the text. A moment later he had one back.

"I'll see what I can find out. Is everybody packed?"

John knocked on his door. "Come in, John. It seems we are all going on a little trip. It's time to make some calls."

Chapter 91

Sara had just returned from delivering lunch to Bill who was still watching the front of the house from his car. Mary was on the phone. "Hold on Greg, I am going to get Richard and Bill for this. Give me a minute and I'll put you on speaker."

Sara went back out to get Bill and Mary called Richard in from the back porch. "Greg and John want to speak with us all." She placed the call on speaker.

"Hello everyone, I'm sorry to interrupt your afternoon but I have some news from the FBI."

"We're all here, Greg, go ahead," Mary said.

"Earlier this morning, Kovak drove by our house. Bill was able to get the plate number and a description of the vehicle but he wasn't able to apprehend him or keep up with him on the chase. I called Charis Andrews to give her the information. She is strongly, and I mean very strongly recommending we all move to a safehouse. She does not think relocating to the Shand's home is safe enough. I agree with her assessment."

"What does this move entail, Greg?" Sara asked.

"For starters, it means that everyone needs to pack a bag with three night worth of clothing. Charis was specific about clothing only. She said everything else will be provided for us."

"Where are you moving to?" asked Richard.

"All of us, Richard, you, and Bill included, and I don't know where we are going. We won't know until we get there."

"Why Richard and I?" Bill asked.

"Because the FBI needs your assistance. Charis assured me that Marilyn will be perfectly safe, Richard but if you want to bring her, that would be fine as well."

"As long as she is safe at home, I would rather leave her out of this," Richard replied.

"Greg, what about work and school? And what about your lecture tomorrow?" Mary asked.

"It's business as usual except we will be sleeping somewhere else. The FBI is not worried about Kovak attacking in public. I'm sure we will be guarded as we move about. Bill you will pick the girls as planned and bring them home. Mary, you will pick up Jillian after practice and bring her home.

I will be home by five and John will be there by three at the latest. John, Sara, and Maria can go back to pack up but Richard, I would like you to go and keep watch. When everyone is packed, we will meet back at our house. I will have further instructions by then."

"The girls are going to be scared stiff," Mary said.

"Reassure them that this is just a precaution and it's just a few days at most. Clothes and phone chargers only. Tell them it will be like a big sleepover for all of us. It could be quite enjoyable. We will all be leaving our house by 6pm."

"Should we feed the kids first?" Mary asked.

"They can have a snack if they need one but Charis said dinner will be waiting for us when we arrive. Any other questions?" Greg asked.

"Do you really need to go tomorrow, Greg?" Mary asked.

"It's too late to cancel now babe and besides, I need to talk with Jack about what's going on. I'm probably safer there than I am here and I will be back here with you by late afternoon. Wherever here is."

"If you're sure, Greg, I trust your judgement," Mary said.

"Alright then, let's put the plan in place and I will see you all shortly."

Greg hung up and looked at John. "That was too easy," Greg said, "what am I missing?"

Chapter 92

After Ben finished his nap in the car, he used the small tool kit he brought to change the license plate. He knew there were probably less than a hundred white Range Rovers in his part of New York but the Connecticut plate would buy him a pass, at least at first glance. Once he was finished, he headed back toward High Falls.

He had seen the old guy taking the girls to school earlier in the morning, before the man spotted him driving by Webster's house. He was sure he had called in the NY plate number but that was no longer an issue. He had called the school before he took his nap to see what time dismissal was. He planned to be in the area to get a feel for the traffic and security. He had plenty of time to get there and nose around a while. He thought it would be best to park a half mile or more from the school and walk it in from there.

He decided he would park in the Fairlawn Cemetery where there would be little to no traffic this time of day. The school was an easy twelve minute walk from there. He could take School Drive which started right across the street from the cemetery or he could walk through the sparse woods that paralleled the street. He thought he would be less noticeable in plain view.

He arrived at 2:45, parked toward the interior of the boneyard and began walking slowly. He was wearing a baseball cap and sunglasses with a light colored sweater which made him look almost school age.

It was a pleasant walk on a mostly sunny day. When he neared the building, he checked his watch. It was still a few minutes before three so he went to the baseball field where it looked like a group of young ladies were ready to begin a softball game. The home team had light blue jerseys with white piping around the sleeves and at the V-neck collar. The visiting team from Ilion were wearing maroon and white.

He walked toward the fence along the right field side to the end. From there, he could see the front entrance of the school. He would know when the old man showed up to pick up the kids because he knew his car and he knew the plate number. *The hunted becomes the hunter.*

It was 3:19 when the old man pulled up to the loading zone and shut off the engine. Ben was a good hundred yards from that spot but he could see well enough to make out who was getting into the car and when.

He leaned against the outfield fence and listened to the game going on behind him. At 3:25, the old man got out of the car and stood by the passenger door. At 3:31, two young ladies approached the car where the old man was holding the back door open.

He was expecting three but there were only two. He knew he saw three get out this morning which meant that one, the bigger one was either kept after school or had a different ride home. He stayed as the others drove away.

Now that the old man was gone, he could move closer to the building. He stationed himself halfway between the field and the building so that he could see people as they exited the front and the back of the school. In the front and to the far side was parking while in the back, there were two more athletic fields.

At 3:40, a group of girls exited the back carrying their gear. It looked like field hockey. He spotted the one he was looking for, she was lean but looked a little more mature than many of the others. She already had a woman's body, more defined calves and thighs and much fuller on top. She looked like her mother.

He walked between the school and the baseball field to a location closer to the field hockey field. He was far enough away that he wasn't worried about drawing attention. He found a little knoll of earth to sit on where he relaxed and watched both events.

He had never really played either but he was certainly familiar with baseball from his time in Boston. He missed his Boston life and he even missed Amanda. Things may have turned out differently had she not roamed from her relationship with him. He brushed away the anger that he felt rising within. If kept thinking about it, one of these young ladies would surely disappear today.

He closed his eyes for a while and listened to the sounds. He imagined himself as a child again but one with a normal lifestyle. One where he had friends and participated in sports or maybe learned to play an instrument. He could feel a softening within his core, a feeling that occurred so seldomly that he could count the times. He was drawn to it and frightened by it at the same time. He knew he couldn't change the past but he believed he could start anew in Austria. He would soon find out.

Cars started showing up around 5:15. Some were picking up softball players and other were waiting for field hockey practice to end. He didn't see the old man's car. By 5:25 the girls had gathered their equipment and headed toward the rear entrance to the school.

At 5:32 they started filing out the front door. He saw the Webster girl come out alongside another girl but they soon parted and walked toward their rides.

Webster was walking toward a late model SUV where Mrs. Webster got out of the car to greet her. Ben wondered how she felt about him now. Was she frightened or would she find the "bad boy" image more appealing?

After a brief greeting, the Webster women got back in the car and drove off. They were being followed by a sedan with another older gentleman driving. "There are bodyguards all around," Ben thought. He had what he needed to formulate a plan so he began his walk back to the cemetery to retrieve his car.

Chapter 93

Greg was almost home when his cell phone rang. "Hello, Charis," he recognized the number. "How is your day going?"

"It just got a little better, I have the results of a preliminary genetics test. It seems your instincts paid off again, Greg. It looks like Ben Kovak and Timmy Chalmers are the same guy."

"Oh man, that's one of those things you think you know but hope you're wrong." Greg replied. "So the blood from all those years ago still worked?"

"I don't know about that yet, but the hair sample you gave us from the mother worked with Ben's hair from the barber in Philadelphia. They were able to extract the DNA from both. There is .9995 percent reliability that they are mother and son," Charis stated.

"Do we let the Chalmers know?" Greg asked.

"I think we wait," Charis replied, "letting them know now will introduce a whole new set of emotions that may work against us. We can't risk losing this guy."

"I didn't think we had anyone to lose," Greg expressed.

"Maybe not, but he is as close as he has ever been and we need to make sure we get him. Let's hold off for now, Greg," she replied.

"Okay. Any other news?" he asked.

"Nothing solid. I'm working a lead from the cell phone companies to try and locate him but it's still open. We did find out whose body was in the bed in Boston. It belonged to a co-worker at the warehouse. The body type and size were a very close match. Ben may have gotten away with it if it weren't for the third nipple," Charis said.

"I don't even know how to respond to that," Greg said.

"It still weirds you out, doesn't it?" Charis replied.

"I know it shouldn't, but it does," he responded.

"We all have our breaking point, Greg."

"What's yours, Charis?"

"I haven't found it yet and I doubt I would tell you if I knew! What's new on your end? Is everyone ready for the getaway?"

"I hope so," Greg said, "I should know in just a few minutes. I'm on my way home now. I haven't received any more information from the county yet and they're closed now so I won't hear anything before tomorrow."

"Alright, try to have a good evening. Do you remember the drill for tonight?" Charis asked.

"I do. Should I check in with you when we arrive?" Greg asked.

"Not necessary," she replied, "the other agent will confirm for me. Just enjoy your time together. I think you will like the place."

"We will do the best we can, Charis. You do know how much I appreciate everything you have done, right?"

"The feeling is mutual, Greg. You and your friends have done more to expose this case than all of our police agencies combined. When it's over, maybe we will have a party."

"That sounds good, Charis. We'll talk soon."

Greg hung up just as he was turning into the driveway. He could see Bill's car tucked into the woods across the street and he waved as he walked up the front steps. He was surprised for a moment to find that the front door was locked. Surprise changed to relief as he realized his people were really paying attention. He rang the doorbell.

Mary pulled the drapes back to make sure it was Greg and then unlocked the door. He stepped in, closed, and locked the door behind him and took Mary in his arms. They hugged silently for several seconds then kissed each other. "I'm glad you're home," Mary said.

"Is everyone here and alright?" Greg asked.

"Yes, we are all here except the Shands, they went home to pack with Richard as an escort," Mary responded.

"Were there many questions?" Greg asked.

"Not really. The girls listened intently and then went to pack. I think they know more than we give them credit for," Mary said.

"You're probably right. I should get a move on it, I'll go up and get packed," Greg exclaimed.

"I have three suits in a garment bag for you complete with corresponding ties. I have also packed sox and underwear, pajamas, and a bathing suit. All you need is your kit bag."

"A bathing suit, do you know something I don't?"

"No, but we are going prepared," Mary said. "I have also packed a few lounge clothes for you and a few special items for me," Mary said as she raised an eyebrow. "Just in case."

"I hope we don't end up sharing a room with Richard or Bill!" Greg exclaimed.

"Or maybe both!" Mary replied as she raised the eyebrow again.

"You had all day to do that. Tonight, you are mine and mine alone," Greg said firmly.

They shared a smile and then Greg ran up the stairs to get ready. He put his head inside the girls' room and said, "the bus leaves in ten minutes."

He quickly moved to the master bathroom and packed his kit bag. When he was sure he had everything he needed, he ran back down the stairs. "Hurry up girls," he said as he descended.

"Have Bill and Richard had a chance to go home and pack?" Greg asked Mary.

"They wouldn't leave," she replied. "They are very dedicated."

Greg opened the front door and waived Bill in. Then he went to the back door and asked Richard to step inside. When both had arrived he asked them what their plan was. They both said they would return home one after the other once they all reached their destination safely. Greg approved and told everyone it was time to go.

Once the luggage was loaded and everyone was outside, Greg locked all the doors and set the alarm. He went back out and got in the car. "Are the Shands meeting us at the diner?" Greg asked Mary.

"That's the plan," she answered.

Greg motioned to Bill and Richard to get going. Richard led the way and Bill brought up the rear. "Hey Mary," Greg said, "won't you need your car tomorrow?"

"Yes, but not until it's time to pick up Jillian from practice. Richard said he would bring me by the house on the way to the school, then he will follow us back to the safehouse."

"Okay, good plan,' Greg responded.

It was less than fifteen minutes to the diner. John, Sara, and Maria were already there when Greg and his crew arrived. He backed in next to them in the parking lot. Bill and Richard flanked them on each side. Everyone in the front seats rolled their windows down so they could communicate across the four vehicles.

At precisely 6:30pm, a black SUV pulled up in front of the vehicles. The driver's door opened and a man got out. He was holding his badge up as he walked toward the vehicles. He knew to go to Greg's window.

"I'm Agent Sanchez, FBI, would you all follow me please?" He walked back to his car, climbed in, and pulled away slowly. He waited until traffic slowed enough that they could all make a left hand turn without getting separated.

They headed east on Rt. 5s toward Albany. In less than thirty minutes, they were in Canajoharie. They crossed the center of the village and made a right turn on to Carlisle Street. They proceeded up the hill for about a mile and made another right on to Cunningham Road.

In five hundred feet, they made another right onto a paved driveway. Set back another quarter of a mile was a huge old farmhouse that had obviously been spruced up and modernized. There were gas lamp posts that lined the driveway for the last six hundred feet. Between broad lawn to both sides, the drive continued under an enclosed overpass linking the main house on the right to the barn on the left.

The overpass appeared to be roughly ten feet above the ground, was at least forty feet long and had several small windows facing the drive.

When they reached the other side of the overpass, there was a parking area to the rear of the barn. The cars all fell in line next to Sanchez. They all stepped out and began reaching for their luggage.

"Please leave your belongings where they are and proceed to the house," Sanchez said, "Dinner is waiting for you. Someone will bring your bags to your rooms. Greg nodded to everyone and led the way.

There was a large, enclosed porch on the back of the house that could easily seat fifty people for lunch. There were several large tables each holding a unique Tiffany style lamp which were all lighted, washing the walls with a multitude of colors.

There was a forty-eight inch wide door separating the porch from the house and it was opened. Inside was a sitting room featuring several sofas and chairs in the Victorian style but appeared to be brand new. Here again, there was an absence of overhead lighting preferring to illuminate each section with tabletop lamps. The feeling was both old and opulent.

Through a large arched opening to the left was the dining room, holding a table that was a good thirty feet in length. Large buffet tables graced the walls on both sides of the table and still allowed six feet for people to pass even with chairs extended. The table was set for twenty with the head and foot open. There were old style chafing dishes under sterling silver servers keeping the mysterious dinner warm.

"This smells amazing!" Sara said.

"This whole place is amazing!" Greg responded.

A woman and gentleman appeared at the opening to the dining room.

"Good evening," the woman said, "we are Ellie and Patrick Millen, your hosts. Welcome to our home. We are ready to serve you anytime you are ready. Your bags have been delivered to your rooms so if you would like to freshen up before dinner, you are more than welcome. Don't be fooled by the décor, this is your home for the next few days and you should consider it as such.

You may dress as casually as you like. Your family is our only guests for the duration. The only other folks here are your staff who you will be introduced to at dinner. So please, either relax for a while or check out your rooms and freshen up.

Dinner will be served in shall we say, fifteen minutes? Martha will meet you at the top of the stairs to direct you to your rooms. This way please."

Patrick led them from the dining room to the hallway leading to the stairway at the front of the house. The stairs were off the foyer which was vast and open with a black and white tile floor.

The winding staircase began at the left wall facing the back of the house and curved gently to the center of the enormous foyer. The ceilings were quite high for a farmhouse allowing for a good twenty steps to the second floor. At the top. A large open balcony overlooked the entry.

Martha was waiting at the top. There was a long, wide hallway with four doors on each side. At the end of the hall, a left turn took you to two more room and a right would get you four for a total of fourteen bedrooms.

"If I may have your attention for just a moment please," Martha asked. "Jillian, Jocelyn, and Maria, you will be staying in suite number four, the second door on your left. There are three queen beds and an ensuite bath.

Mr. Ingraham, you have suite number one and Mr. Dillon will be in suite three. Mr. and Mrs. Webster will have number twelve, that's down the hall to the left and Mr. and Mrs. Shand will have thirteen, down the hall to your right.

All suites include ensuite baths which I think you will find to your liking. The exits are back this way through the front door and down the hall to your left past suite twelve which will exit from the back of the building. For your safety and the comfort of all our guests, we ask that you refrain from smoking indoors."

"While you are at dinner," Martha continued, "I will be settling your rooms. Before bed, we offer a turndown service. Do you have any questions for me? Very well, dinner will be served in ten minutes. You will meet the rest of our staff then." Martha turned and walked away.

They all took their keys and walked toward their rooms. "See you all in ten," Greg exclaimed and escorted Mary down the hall. Greg unlocked the door and pushed it open. They were staring at the magnificence of the room and they hadn't even entered yet. Mary walked through first. There was a king size poster bed with a canopy and silk enclosure curtains on all three side that were held back with silk rope ties. There was a sitting area straight ahead with windows but the curtains were drawn closed. They approached and took a peek. Looking below them, they could see the shimmering of an indoor pool and a large hot tub.

"Good thing you brought out suits!" Greg stated.

"Yes, it would have been a shame to have to swim naked," Mary hinted.

"I will if you will," Greg took the challenge.

Mary had already moved on to the bathroom. When Greg caught up to her, she was standing with her mouth open.

"My God!" She said. Greg stepped in and looked around at a room that was bigger than their entire bedroom at home. There was a private restroom, a double vanity with a large steamless mirror, a towel warmer and a sunken hot tub with rose petals floating on the water.

"Who needs the pool?" Greg said.

"Who needs dinner?" Mary answered.

"I think we all do," Greg said, "but hang on to that thought for later! We should round up the girls and head down."

"You're right, I'm getting carried away, in a few days we all turn back into pumpkins."

"Well, now that we know about this place, perhaps we could plan a romantic getaway," he suggested.

"That would be wonderful, Greg!"

She placed her arm through his and the left the room. "Should we lock it?" Greg said.

"Who are you, and what did you do with my husband?" she replied.

"I was just testing you. You passed."

Everyone converged in the hallway except for Richard and Bill. "How is your room?" John said to Greg.

"It's okay, I guess. Yours?"

"I would call it fair, wouldn't you honey?" Greg said to Mary.

"I could, but then I would have to call you crazy!" They all laughed.

"Who knew?" Sara asked. "A half hour from home and I didn't know this place existed."

"Maybe the FBI built it this afternoon," Jocelyn said.

"I hope the FBI is picking up the tab," Greg followed.

They made their way down the wide staircase, through the foyer and toward the dining room. Bill and Richard were enjoying a drink in the sitting room.

"Well don't you all look nice!" Richard said.

"We're all wearing the same clothes we had on earlier, Richard," Mary said.

"Oh really? I didn't notice anyone earlier," he stated.

"Some watchdog you are," Bill said.

Ellie was standing at the door to greet them. Inside the dining room, there were ten other staffers waiting to be introduced. She went through all of their names and their titles. There were room attendants, a barman, the groundskeeper, the chef, and his assistants. Agent Sanchez was in the room as well.

Ellie then introduced all of the guests by name as if she had known them forever. When she finished roll call, she asked everyone to have a seat. "The main meal will be served buffet style but you will be served your appetizers while we take your beverage orders. They all sat and still had enough settings to invite a half dozen friends.

They made it through the introductory session of several starters that would put most Food Network hosts to shame. Once the beverages arrived, the stiffness of the event loosened, inviting a busy but enjoyable flow of conversation.

Greg asked that the current 'situation' be left out of the otherwise routine discussion. Agent Sanchez left the room as the others sat down.

"Can you stay and join us for dinner, Agent Sanchez," Greg asked.

"I would love to, but my job is to look out for your safety and I can't do that effectively from here. Please forgive me," he responded and left the room.

"He takes his job seriously," Richard said.

"Yes, and we can be thankful for that," Mary responded.

They talked about school, sports, projects, gardening, vacations, and the fact that fall was just around the corner. Someone mentioned Christmas and it was shut down quickly.

Mostly, they talked about the meal and the service and the spectacular surroundings.

Their host talked about the amenities including the indoor pool and of course the kids were chomping at the bit to get there. They didn't admit it, but the adults were as well. "Dad," Jocelyn said, "May we go to the pool now?"

"Sure, honey, just let me make sure Agent Sanchez knows where you are. Go get your suits on and I will find him."

The girls quickly scrambled from the table and raced up the stairs to their room. Greg stood up to find Sanchez while the rest of the adults moved to the sitting room for an after dinner cordial.

Greg went out the back door and walked the circumference of the building until he found the agent near the front of the house.

"It was nice of you to let us have the time at dinner. I hope you know how much we appreciate this," Greg said.

"It's my pleasure, Mr. Webster. It is also my job. Agent Andrews thinks very highly of you. It's not every day that a citizen gets involved like you have. I understand you have a speaking engagement tomorrow. Is that a regular thing?"

"Not anymore," Greg responded. "After the hospital incident, I was asked to speak frequently but I turned many of them down. I enjoy the speaking and interactions with the listeners, but I also had a hospital to run and it was a new job for me so I felt I owed them a regular presence."

"It sounds like you are equally committed to your work," Sanchez replied. "It also seems that you watch out for everyone around you and that's a nice quality, I think."

"I'm not sure how people walk through this world and not pay attention to others sharing our space, Greg said."

"How did you get involved in this case? It's not like the bombings happened in your back yard," Sanchez offered.

"That depends on the size of your backyard I guess. Some people like to limit their boundaries and I must admit, it would be easier if I could do that. But when I listen to the news, there are times that I ask myself if there isn't something I can do, some way I can be proactive. Most of the time, I come to a reasonable answer rather quickly.

Sometimes I throw money at it because I don't have other resources to offer. But there are times when I feel like if I just fish around a while, I may discover a clue even if I'm not close to the issue."

"And that's what happened here?" Sanchez asked.

"I spent my early adult life going to work and coming home again. I always did my best and I did the job required of me. When I first went to City Hospital for what I thought would be a few hours, something changed. It was like I could sense that something wasn't right even without any real evidence.

The more people provided dead ends, the more I wanted to dig deeper. Maybe I was just looking for a fight. There were problems at home and the job at the health department was routine at best and perhaps even stagnant.

The hospital case offered a thrill of the pursuit, a desire to keep digging as if there was gold under the topsoil. That case lasted less than a week but it changed my outlook on life, family, and work and especially, community. Hey, before I forget again, I came out here to tell you the girls went to the pool."

"It's all good," Sanchez replied, "No one is going to find you here, at least not tonight. If someone lets the cat out of the bag tomorrow, it could be a different story."

"You mean if our people talk about it at school or work?" Greg asked.

"Exactly, It's especially hard for young ones to contain the excitement, particularly when they're staying at a place of this magnitude. Can you imagine being sixteen and keeping this a secret?" Sanchez asked.

"Then why would Charis choose a place like this? I'm not complaining, you understand."

"I know. Charis wanted a place that was safe and easy to monitor. This has all of that. Not many people know about it, the only way in is up that driveway and we have cameras all over the place," Sanchez explained.

"It seems like a lot of territory for one agent cover. Who's watching the cameras for example?" Greg responded.

"First, the cameras also have motion sensors which notify my phone if they are activated. Secondly, a few of our hospitality staff have other jobs."

"You mean some are agents." Greg said.

"Let's say they are in our employ, not necessarily full time agents."

"I see," Greg said. "How did the FBI know about this place?"

"Let's just say we found it during a previous investigation. Will that satisfy you?"

"It leaves a whole lot of reading between the lines but if that is all you can say, I will respect that," Greg said. "There were crimes committed here."

"There you go digging again! Don't make me take your shovel away!" Agent Sanchez said jokingly. "There were criminals associated with the property. That doesn't mean crimes happened here."

"So the federal government seized the property and it became this," Greg guessed.

"We seized it, but it was already this. "We wouldn't put that kind of taxpayers' money into a safehouse," Sanchez answered.

"So how often is it used?"

"Okay, digger," Sanchez said, "we have reached the end of this conversation. Why don't you go join your family in the pool and on the way, tell Ingraham and Dillon I would like to see them for a moment."

"Do you have a first name, Agent Sanchez?" Greg asked.

"I do," he said.

"That's it?" Greg replied.

"You didn't ask what my name is, you asked if I had one," he replied.

"Would you tell me?" Greg asked.

"Yes, I would," he replied.

"I get it," Greg said, "what is your first name Agent Sanchez?"

"Michael," he replied, "was that so tough?" he said with a big smile.

"Goodnight, Michael."

"Not yet, sir, I need to meet with everyone at 9:30 tonight, just to go over a few things. Let's meet in the sitting room, shall we?"

"Yes, Michael, See you then."

Greg made his way upstairs after he passed the message to Bill and Richard who were in the sitting room. He put his swim trunks on and walked to the overpass at the end of the corridor. He stopped in the middle of the overpass and looked out a window facing the backyard.

He found a beautiful view of the Canajoharie Creek below the steep drop, with the sun setting just behind it. He was always in awe of the beauty that surrounded him and in the vast amount of knowledge he lacked about his home area.

The Shands and the Websters had a great time in the pool. It caused Greg to remember how fortunate he was to have friends like them. He was glad they were all together and as much as he wanted the Kovak ordeal to end, he was thankful they would have more days to enjoy at the safehouse.

Everyone was seated when Sanchez entered the room. The staff had placed a few bedtime treats around the room for them to enjoy while they listened. The agent's mere presence commanded their attention.

"Thank you all," he began, "this will only take a few minutes of your time. From this point forward tonight, no one leaves the house. The front and rear doors will be locked and need to remain that way. In the morning, breakfast will be available in the dining room beginning at 7 am. There will be bag lunches available for the young ladies to take with them and for Mr. Ingraham and Mr. Dillon to get them through a long day of surveillance. There will also be coffee in to go containers." He stopped for a breath.

"How about me?" Greg asked.

"Yes, Digger, you will have provisions for your journey as well."

"Digger?" Mary said, looking at Greg. Greg just shrugged his shoulders.

"Continuing, I can't stress enough the importance of your discretion about this situation. Young ladies, it is vitally important that you do not mention this location to anyone. You will not talk about this place, your room, the pool, or the food you are enjoying. When this is all over, you are free to speak as you wish. Are there any questions?" he asked, making visual contact with all three of the girls.

"Okay, Bill and Richard, I will be guarding the exterior of the house tonight which means I will need you to keep an eye on things inside. The staff will be spending the night as well and they will be in the staff quarters on the north end of the home. I am requesting that you all lock your bedroom doors as soon as you return."

"There are bedside phones in each room and you can simply dial the room number to speak with each other. You will not have access to an outside line from your room but your cell phones will work. If you should need to dial 911 for any reason, you will identify your location as the Haven, that's all you need to say. Is that clear to everyone? Please repeat it to me. If you should call 911, your location is?" He paused for a response. They answered in unison.

"Young ladies, enjoy your day at school. For the other young ladies, if you need to leave the house, you do so only after alerting me and only if you have either Bill or Richard accompany you.

Dr. Shand, you should be safe getting to the hospital but if you see anything peculiar or if you feel you are being followed, call 911 and keep driving. Do not stop and do not return here until you are cleared to do so.

Mr. Webster, best of luck at your event and the same goes for you regarding being followed or anything unusual. Are there any questions? Alright then, you are dismissed. Enjoy the rest of your evening," Michael concluded.

The girls said goodnight and started toward the stairs. They were followed by the Shands. Greg went to take another cookie but Mary grabbed his hand.

"You won't be needing that darling, there is something sweet waiting for you upstairs," she whispered. Greg put the cookie down quickly and took Mary's hand.

"Goodnight fellas," he said as she led him away from the sitting room.

"Goodnight," said Bill and Richard. When they were out of hearing range Richard looked at Bill and said, "if the house is a rockin' don't come a knockin'."

Chapter 94

Greg was pouring his first cup of coffee at 6:15 am. Mary was still sleeping so he thought he would get coffee for the two of them. The house was quiet except for some small noises coming from the kitchen. The kids should be getting up soon especially if they were going to squeeze in three showers. He climbed the stairs and stopped at the girl's room. He tapped on the door lightly but there was no response. He knocked a little louder but still nothing.

He walked to the end of the hall and made the left turn toward his room when he saw a man dressed in dark clothing moving toward the overpass. He quietly followed behind him.

When the man approached the end of the overpass, he opened the door to the stairway that led to the pool. Greg turned and raced back to his room and unlocked the door. He set the coffees down on the table in the entry and moved quickly to the window.

He could see the man moving near the pool. He disappeared for a moment and then re-emerged holding a pool skimmer. Greg could see that he was wearing a shirt with a logo on the chest pocket. "Obviously, the pool boy," he thought to himself.

Inside the room, Mary was starting to stir. He picked up the phone and dialed the girls' room number. After four rings, Maria picked it up. "Hello," she said, still asleep.

"Good morning Maria," Greg said with a soft voice. "Are you girls getting up anytime soon? Breakfast is at seven and you have a half hour ride to school."

"Okay," she replied, "I'll wake the others up. These beds are so comfortable!"

Greg hung up the phone and brought the coffee to Mary who was just sitting up.

"What time is it?" she asked.

"It's 6:25," he responded. "I brought you coffee."

"I can see that, thank you."

"Breakfast is in thirty minutes so I am going to jump in the shower. Would you like to share some water?"

"I know what that is code for and it has nothing to do with water," she replied.

"Singing a different tune this morning?" Greg asked.

"Last night was great honey but I'm still asleep here. You get started and maybe I'll join you after I have some coffee," she replied.

Greg did as she suggested. He wanted to be on the road by 7:30 anyway.

They were both downstairs by seven. He was showered and dressed but Mary just threw on a bathrobe that was hanging in the closet. Sara and John were already in the dining room and

Sara had the same outfit on as Mary. Jillian, Jocelyn, and Maria came flying into the room just moments later.

"Everyone sleep alright?" John asked.

"Like the dead," said Maria. Those beds are so comfortable. Can I stay home from school today?"

"Nice try," Sara responded. "You girls need to hurry if you're going to make it on time."

"Where are Richard and Bill?" Greg asked. No one had seen them yet. Greg took his cup and a small pastry and walked toward the front door. He pulled it open to find Michael and the grumpy old men chatting.

"Good morning guys. Are none of you hungry?"

"Oh sure," Richard said, "we were just on our way in. Bill and Richard entered but Sanchez stayed outside to keep watch.

Entering the dining room Bill said, "Bus leaves in twenty, girls. We don't want to get behind the school buses, they stop at every driveway out here."

Everyone sat down for a few minutes and enjoyed a delicious breakfast. Afterward, the girls ran up to get their backpacks while Bill went out to start the car. When they came back in, they all grabbed a sack lunch, including Greg, Bill, and Richard. Greg kissed his daughters and then went to hug Mary.

"You be careful today, Greg. Call me when you get there and again when the lecture is over. I would like to speak with Jack if possible."

"I'll make sure that all those things happen, dear. No worries!" They kissed and Greg said, "I'll see you all tonight at dinner. Love you all!"

Sanchez was still out front when Greg exited the house. "Michael, there was a man in the upstairs hall early this morning. I followed him to the stairs leading to the pool. Do you know who he is?"

"Yes, I do," Michael replied.

"Here we go again," Greg said.

"Ask the right question and you get the right answer," Michael said.

"Who was the man in the hallway this morning?"

"The pool guy," he responded.

"The pool guy was in our hallway?" Greg said.

"Yes, he was."

Greg rephrased the question. "Why was the pool guy in our hallway this morning, Michael?"

"Because he is one of us. He slept down the hall, next to the Shands. A little extra protection at no additional charge, I might add,"

"Thank you Michael. Do you know how to reach me should you need to?" Greg asked.

"Yes! You see, a straight question and a straight answer."

"Have a great day, Michael!"

"Good luck today, sir!" Michael replied.

Greg smiled at him and walked to his car.

Chapter 95

Greg wasn't out of Canajoharie when his phone rang. "Good morning Charis!"

"Good morning to you, Greg," she replied, "How was everything at the flop house last night?"

"Flop house? Are you kidding? The place is more like Shangri La!" he replied.

"It may be as remote as the Shangri La but I'll bet the mattresses are better!"

"The mattresses and everything else. You went above and beyond Charis. How can I repay you?"

"First, we can catch this guy and second, we will send you a bill. Will that make you feel better?" she asked.

"I doubt it, but it would be worth it," he said.

"Listen," Charis began, "there will be an undercover state trooper at the college today. His name is Preston and you don't need to look for him, he will come to you."

"Is Preston his first or last name?"

"His last name," she replied.

"Does he have a first name?"

"Yes," she replied and waited.

"You too!" Greg exclaimed. "Is this an entire FBI thing or just a regional habit?"

"I don't know what you're talking about, Greg but you don't want to know his first name anyway."

"Sure, I do. What do I call him?" he asked.

"Well, you don't call him, he will call you and you are better off calling him Preston or detective," she stated.

"I don't know why knowing his first name is such a big deal," Greg followed.

"Alright, I will tell you," she conceded, "but you won't call him that."

"How do you know? I am a professional, I can handle all kinds of names," he assured her.

"Okay, smart guy. Are you ready?"

"Of course, I'm ready!" He could feel his frustration level rise.

"Charlton."

"That's not a bad name. Why is that a bad name?" Greg asked.

"Charlton Preston! Come on! You don't find that funny?" Charis asked.

Greg had to think about it. Then, it hit him. "Holy Shit! Like Charlton Heston," he said and began laughing uncontrollably. It took the two of them a good two minutes before they could speak again. He had just about gained control when she warned him.

"Don't think about thanking him from the stage. He'll probably put a bullet through your teeth!"

They started rolling again. Greg could feel the pain in his left flank from the laughter. "Charis, I have to stop before I pee myself!" he said.

"I'm surprised your eyes are open enough to drive!" she replied.

Greg just had a thought and it slowed his laughter immediately. "Hey, Charis, I just realized that unless you were sixty years old or a big movie buff, you wouldn't even get the joke!"

"Wow, you're right. That is a sobering thought." There was a pause and then they cracked up again. When it was all done, which felt like ten miles to Greg, they got serious. "You be careful out there today, Greg. I don't think you have anything to worry about but I don't like the fact that we can't find this guy."

"I think he may be in hiding now, Charis. We know what he drives and this is a small place. If he was around, somebody would see him. He must know the cops are looking everywhere."

"I'm sure you are right. Anyway, call me if you run into a snag. I'll be around," she said.

"Will do, Charis, and thanks again for everything. I mean it."

"I know you do, Greg. Watch your back!"

Charis hung up. She did not like the feeling she had in her gut. "Maybe it was the laughing," she thought to herself. In either case, she had to do something. She dialed the number for the cell phone provider she had talked to days ago.

"Hello this is Special Agent Andrews of the FBI. I requested tower information days ago and you said I would have the results in forty-eight hours. If I don't have them in the next forty-eight minutes, I'm getting a warrant for your arrest and I am going to deliver it personally. Do I make myself clear?"

Greg turned on the radio and drove to the first thruway rest area. He really needed to pee.

Chapter 96

Greg was a few minutes behind schedule thanks to the laughter and probably coffee induced rest stop. He knew he would arrive in plenty of time to meet Jack and prepare his notes but he liked being early.

He decided to try to avoid some traffic between the Thruway and the university by taking I-481 south to I-81 north and come up on the campus from the south. It was an extra three of four miles but a much prettier ride in addition to less traffic.

He was on the southeast side of Syracuse when the call came in. Greg saw that it was Lacey calling. "Good morning Lacey, how is my girl today?"

"Good morning, Greg, you sound very chipper!" she exclaimed.

"It's a beautiful day and I get to see my son today so I am chipper," he replied.

"That's wonderful, Greg. It sounds like you are on the road," she said.

"Just outside of Syracuse. My son is a student at SU."

"Well, I'm sure you will have a great time. Greg, I'm calling because we found a property report with Martina Kovatikova's name on it. It appears to be just wooded acreage and the deed goes back a while. We don't have any records of a dwelling having been built. There are no building permits and a request for information from the power company shows no requests and no activity."

"Lacey, you cut out there for a minute, did you say there is not a building on the property?"

"Yes, no building and no utilities," she answered.

"Do you have an address, Lacey" Greg asked.

"I have a plot number and the closest intersection. We don't issue an address until the property has a dwelling," she said.

"Could you send me an email or text with that information, please?"

"Of course. I'll send it over in the next few minutes, Greg. What is your email address?"

Greg gave her the information and they ended the call. He found a spot to pull off the side of the road and called Charis. He got her voice mail and left a message with the address of the property. He set his phone back down and continued to drive. He could see the white cover of the Carrier Dome up on the hill to his right. He exited the highway and began his accent to the campus.

Chapter 97

Ben hit the road around 9 am for an estimated arrival of 10:45. He was driving the white Range Rover with the Connecticut plates. A utility bag rested in the passenger's seat next to him. He made sure the house was ready for guests before he left so that he wouldn't need to worry about it later. He wasn't sure how long it would take to get home because he hadn't yet decided on his route back to High Falls.

He was taking a combination of NY Routes 5 and 20 to get there. Both roads went west and paralleled each other most of the way. Rt. 20 took him further south but by only a few miles.

He thought about taking I-81 north out of Syracuse and then moving back east along Rt. 31 following the southern border of Oneida Lake to Verona. From there he could work his way back down to Rt. 5 or 5s and back into Herkimer County. It would add an hour to the return trip but he could spare it.

He thought about his flight in the morning and his fresh start. He believed he still had a great uncle in Vienna but he wasn't sure. His father never spoke of him but the papers he came across at home made him believe it was still possible. He thought he may even have some cousins there. Time would tell.

Every now and again he would ask himself if he was capable of change. Was he running from his life here just to start the same one there? He wanted to believe that if he were surrounded by the right people, he could leave his current life behind for good. He had plenty of money to last him a long time. Work wouldn't be an issue but he could find something to occupy his time. He wondered what their hardware stores were like.

He would find out soon enough. He pulled his mind back to the task at hand. He had studied the map of the campus and he had called to confirm the location. He would have time once he arrived to find the best location to push the button. He was aware that it might take a few laps around to determine that. He also needed to time his exit from the campus to I-81 North. It would be well before lunch time so he believed most of the people would be inside at work.

He pulled into a small convenience store that also offered gasoline. He decided to fill the tank before heading on, knowing that he would have a better chance of being noticed after the project was completed. He also needed to empty his bladder.

Chapter 98

Charis left home early for the drive north. She had made several phone calls and conducted one conference call, making the trip thus far well worthwhile. She noticed that she had a voice mail from Greg. The time stamp indicated it had come in while she was in conference.

She selected the voice mail and pushed play. "Hi, Charis, it's Greg. I'm on the road to Syracuse and I received a call from my friend at the county offices. Here is an approximate location for a piece of property registered to Martina Kovatikova. It's lot number HF 3176.06 and it is near the intersection of D####roe on the bac######f course. Ch### t out."

His phone cut out and all she had were pieces of a puzzle. She dialed his number but it went straight to voice mail. She looked at her watch. It was 10:45 and Greg probably silenced his phone before taking the stage. She left him a message saying his message was breaking up and to return the call as soon as he could.

She figured she had a good hour and a half before she would hear back. The phone company had finally come through with the information from the cell towers but it couldn't pinpoint the location. The best they could do offer was a window of about eight square miles. If she had that lot location, she may be able to narrow it down a little more. She would do that as soon as Greg called back.

Charis decided to call Agent Sanchez to check on things at the Haven. "Sanchez," he answered.

"Good morning Agent Sanchez, it's Charis Andrews. How are things there?"

"Uneventful, Charis. Everyone got off to school and work without a hitch. It's nice and quiet around here," he replied.

"Good to hear. How is everyone else at the Haven?"

"Happy to have the company. It's been a while since they have hosted anyone but you would never know it, everything was as smooth as silk. By the way, your boy Greg is a piece of work."

"How do you mean?" she asked.

"He's full of questions that he doesn't know how to ask," Michael replied.

"You're not giving him the FBI squeeze, are you?" Charis asked.

"Just a little, you know. He is the kind of guy that walks right into it," he replied.

"I know," she responded, "but he is a great guy. Very smart and intuitive. I wish more of our own people were that savvy."

"I agree with you there. He is a nice guy. Actually his entire group of family and friends are good people. I like them," Sanchez said.

"They have been through a lot together. Something like that either binds you or breaks you. There's not much in between," Charis added. "Hey, Michael, make sure they have a room set aside for me in the staff quarters for the next couple of nights, would you please?"

"As you wish, Agent Andrews."

"Thanks, I should be there around dinner time but don't let anyone know I'm coming, I want to keep a very low profile."

Charis ended the conversation. Sanchez was her kind of agent. He was trustworthy, kind, and he had a sense of humor. She made one more call before setting the phone down.

"Detective Lawrence, how may I assist you?"

Chapter 99

Greg parked in the visitor's lot near the Administrative building and walked into the registration office. He introduced himself and received his guest pass as well as instructions on how to get to Dineen Hall. There was a parking lot closer to the hall but he decided to stay where he was and get a quick walk in. He thought it might get the blood moving to his brain and provoke thought.

He found the building and climbed the steps to the second floor as Jack had instructed. Sure enough, it was the first door at the top of the stairs. Greg opened the door into a vast and empty space. It was a beautiful theater with a slow sloping rake leading to a large stage. At the front edge of the stage stood a lectern with a microphone on what he assumed to be a squeaky gooseneck stand. He was used to it, they were all the same.

There were some lights on in the room but not all of them. It was just as well, if the audience found him boring, they should be allowed to sleep. He walked down the carpeted slope to the stage. There were stairs at both sides that led up to the stage level. He started up the stairs and heard his name being called from the back of the auditorium.

It was Jack. Greg stepped back down to the floor and jogged up the slope to meet him. As he approached, he threw open his arms to receive his son. Jack was just as excited to see his dad and reciprocated the intense hug. "It's great to see you, Son."

"It's good to see you too, Dad. How was the drive?" Jack asked.

"It was fine, a piece of cake really. Wintertime might make for a different opinion," Greg joked. "We have fifteen minutes, what would you like to do?"

"Gee, play a round of golf maybe?" Jack quipped.

"Still a wise ass, I see?" Greg said.

"The apple doesn't fall far from the tree," Jack replied.

"I guess you're right. How about a drink? I could use some water before we begin," Greg said.

Jack opened his backpack. "I thought that might be the case so I brought a few with me. There should be a shelf under the podium, I'll put a spare up there for you. He handed Greg a bottle then took the stairs two at a time to the stage floor. He crossed the stage to the lectern and placed the second bottle on the shelf. Greg followed him up.

"Do you ever think about getting involved with theater, Jack?" Greg asked.

"I'm not quite as comfortable in front of a crowd as you are, Dad. Backstage work maybe."

"I worked on set design in high school, Greg said. "It was a lot of fun as I recall."

"I never knew that about you. What else don't I know?"

"Probably more than you do know," Greg answered.

"He, Dad, are you using overheads today?"

"Nope, no visuals at all. Just a few notes and a lot of boredom. Why do you ask?"

"Because of that box over there. I'm in here twice a week for lectures and that box wasn't here a few days ago. There's a picture of an overhead projector on the box," Jack offered.

"Does anyone use overheads anymore, Jack?"

"I've never seen anyone use them here," he replied.

Greg looked at his watch, it was 10:50 and the room was filling up quickly. He walked toward the package asking Jack to stay where he was. He approached slowly and looked at the packing label on the top of the package.

It was addressed to him, care of the university. It also specified the room and the date of use. He looked at the return address and came immediately back to Jack.

"Son, I am one hundred percent sure there is a bomb in that box and if I'm right, it's going to blow in about nine minutes. We need to get these people out of here in an orderly fashion. You know where the exits are, right?"

"Sure, Dad," he answered.

"Go to the microphone, Jack, and tell the people they need to evacuate. Tell them the truth but after you tell them to remain calm and to follow your instructions. I am going to try to create less of an impact."

Jack didn't question his father. He walked quickly to the microphone, turned on the switch and tapped on it a few time to be sure it was live.

"Excuse me everyone, please let me have your attention." The room quieted.

"You are all here to listen to my father, Greg Webster speak about his experience and talents so you probably know a little bit about him. If you do, you will heed this information and respond accordingly." There was some cheers coming from the audience but Jack shut them down quickly.

"I need everyone to move in an orderly fashion toward the rear exits, Do not come back down the side hallway. Go out the rear doors and down the stairs to the first exit you see." No one was moving.

"You need to begin immediately. There is a bomb backstage and it will go off in eight minutes. I implore you to move as safely and as quickly as you can. The police and fire departments are on their way." People stood up and began moving. "That's it, keep moving safely but quickly."

Jack looked back at his dad who was grabbing anything he could find backstage that would cushion the explosion. Greg caught his eye.

"Jack, get behind the people and give them a little encouragement. I will meet you out in front as soon as I can. I called the police, they should be here any minute. Jack, do not come back here. Do you understand?" Jack nodded. To Greg, Jack looked like a little boy again.

"It's going to be alright, Jack. I will meet you out front. You have four minutes, Jack. Time to move."

Jack followed his father's instructions and got behind of the crowd that was left.

"Keep moving people, more quickly now. Please, keep moving." Jack was yelling now and people were responding, He could see the exit just a few feet ahead. "You're doing great, just keep moving." Jack looked back at the wall that his father had built around the box. He turned back around and pushed the people at the back of the line encouraging them to move. He finally reached the door and looked back around the auditorium.

He spotted a student in a wheelchair in the back of the auditorium but on the opposite side. He pushed the final people out the door and closed the doors behind them.

Jack ran across the back of the room toward the guy in the wheelchair. "Hi, I'm Jack. We are going to get you out of here." He unlocked the wheels of the chair and turned him toward the door. He looked at his watch, it was two minutes after eleven. He didn't think he had time to make it to the door.

"What is your name?" he asked the young man.

"Sam," he replied.

"Okay, Sam, here is what we are going to do. I'm pulling you out of that chair and we are going to lay on the floor. Are you up for that?"

"I would rather be out of here," Sam said.

"That makes two of us, but I think our odds are better right here."

Jack locked the chair and grabbed Sam under the arms. With one long tug, he lifted Sam and set him gently on the floor. He pulled him as close to the back of the last row of seats as possible. Jack took one look toward the stage. He didn't see his father. Then, he laid down next to Sam.

"Cover your ears, Sam.

Greg realized that he had neglected to call Mary when he arrived as promised. From his hiding place too near the bomb, he dialed the phone. "Mary, I'm sorry I didn't call sooner. I love you with all my heart!"

Chapter 100

Mary was walking back from the pool when her phone rang. It was Greg. "Mary, I'm sorry I didn't call sooner. I love you with all my heart!" Then she heard what she could only describe as the world coming to an end.

The sound was deafening and disturbing. She called his name repeatedly but there was no answer. She tried Jack's number but he didn't answer either. She ran down the stairs to find Michael. He was outside the front door.

"Michael, something is wrong!" she cried.

"Okay, easy does it," he said as he touched her arm. "Tell me what's going on."

"Greg just called and apologized for not calling when he got to Syracuse and then there was a loud noise in the background and the call disappeared."

"Did he say anything else, Mrs. Webster?"

"He said he loved me with all his heart." Mary broke down.

"Come inside. Let's find Mrs. Shand."

He picked up a phone and dialed Sara's room. "Mrs. Shand, It's Agent Sanchez, Can you come to the sitting room right away please? We have an issue."

Michael helped Mary to a chair and dialed Charis' number.

"Andrews," she answered.

"It's Sanchez, we have an issue. Webster just called with a disturbing message. It sounds like he is in trouble."

"Hold on," Charis grabbed her phone and pulled up the FBI alert page. "Son of a bitch!" she said. "Michael, there was an explosion at Syracuse University less than ten minutes ago. You need to keep everyone calm until we can figure out what's happening."

"I'll try. Keep in touch." He hung up.

Sara had arrived and was consoling Mary.

"Mrs. Webster, there was an explosion at SU just a few minutes ago. We don't have any other information yet. It will take some time before we know anything for sure. Just because there was an explosion doesn't mean your husband was near it. Cell phones can be affected by electromagnetic waves. It happens frequently."

"My husband was close enough to know what was happening and if he was close, so was my son. He's not answering his phone either," she was crying hysterically now. Sara was doing her best to comfort her.

"His phone is most likely affected for the same reason," Michael said, "we need to wait for further information. I'm sorry I can't give you anything definite."

"What about my girls? Are they in danger too?"

"There is no reason to believe that but I'll have someone go by the school just as a precaution." He stepped away and a made a call.

When he came back, he told Mary that the police were on the way to the school. He would get a call soon.

"It's that bastard Kovak, isn't it?" she screamed.

"We have no way of knowing that right now, we can't speculate. I'm sure we will have more information soon. I know it's difficult but we just need to be patient for a little longer," Sanchez said.

Chapter 101

Jack pushed the dust off himself and tried to move. There was something holding him down. Through the smoke and the dust, he could see that the wheelchair had landed on top of him. He pushed it aside and managed to get up on his knees. "Sam, are you okay?"

"I think so," Sam said. "I can't move my legs!"

Jack panicked for a second, then he said, "could you move them before?"

"No, I forgot. Sorry," Sam said.

Jack stood and looked toward the exit. It was covered with dust and debris but looked passable. "Sam, we need to get you up and out of here now. Are you ready?"

"I've been ready for a while now," he replied.

Jack stood the wheelchair up and helped Sam into a sitting position. He moved the chair behind him and lifted Sam from under the arms again. It was a struggle but Jack managed to get him into the chair. He unlocked the wheels and pushed him toward the door.

As he was moving, he looked toward the stage. He couldn't make out where things were. The stage floor had disappeared and the rest looked like fog at a rock concert.

Jack got to the door and pushed it open. The air was fresher out there and he could see better. He looked down the hall toward the stage end of the corridor. It was still mostly intact. Several police officers were on their way up the stairs.

"Are you alright, guys?" one asked.

"We're good," Jack replied. "Can you take Sam here, I need to do something?" The lead officer motioned to one of his assistants to take the guy in the chair outside. Jack started walking toward the stage.

"Where are you going, son," the officer asked.

"To find my father," Jack replied.

"I can't let you do that young man, it may not be safe down there," the officer said.

"That may be, but my father is down there. You can try to stop me if you want, but you'll have to shoot me to do it," Jack replied and started down the slope. The closer he got to the stage, the more debris there was. "Dad, are you in here?" Jack yelled. He didn't get a response. He move closer, climbing over things as he progressed. More cops were in the room now. "Dad, where are you?" Jack stopped and remembered. He was supposed to meet his father in the front of the building. He didn't know whether to stop and go out or keep looking. He decided to make it to the stage before he gave up.

"Young man," the officer yelled, "you need to stop and come back up here."

"As soon as I find my father. I could use some help," Jack said. He continued moving forward. A couple officers followed him down the slope. "Dad are you here? Dad!" he yelled again. From the left corner of the stage level, behind the partial wall where the curtains hide, Jack heard a sound. It sounded like a moan but he also heard some movement. "Dad, is that you?" He listened.

Again he heard some faint noises. He ran across the top of the debris and up the few steps to the stage landing. Tucked in the corner of the partial wall, there was a rolled up carpet standing in the corner. In the faint light, he thought he saw it move. "Dad, is that you?" He could hear the moaning again and it was louder this time. "Up here!" Jack yelled to the officers. They approached, crawling over the debris. "Help me get him out of there," Jack asked.

"Alright, be careful now. Leave the carpet rolled and turn it on its side," Jack said. We will carry him out to the hallway and unroll him there. "Dad, we're going to move you."

Jack could hear his voice from inside the carpet. "Be care, Son, I think I'm hurt," Greg's weak voice said.

"Okay, Dad, we will go easy but we need to get you outside. That means we need to turn this rug on its side to get you out. What hurts?" Jack asked.

"It's my upper back, I think?"

"Dad, can you move your hands?"

"Yes, my hands are down, they feel okay."

"Dad try to push against the carpet so that we know which way you're facing."

Jack pulled out his phone and turned on the light. He shined it over the outside of the rug. He could see the fabric moving in and out ever so slightly.

"Okay, Dad, I see it. This is the front he said to the officers. We need to lay the carpet down on the front to carry him out, then we will stand it back up to unroll it." Jack got in the corner and leaned the carpet toward the officers.

"Easy now, you take that end I'll take the feet. Most of the weight will be on your end, okay? Here we go." Jack pushed the top of the rug toward the officer until they had the full weight of the leaning carpet.

"On three, you guys will back up and let the rug settle. I will move forward and pick my end up.

"Here we go, Dad. One, Two, Three!" Just like that, the rug was parallel to the floor.

"Alright, I'm going first, out that exit door and into the hall." Jack backed into the bar handled exit door and pushed with his lower back. The door opened up and he walked backwards out the door. When they had cleared the doorway, Jack looked left and right.

"That way gentlemen," he said using his head to point out the direction.

He found a clear spot on the floor about thirty feet down from the stage door. Jack set his end down and stabilized it while the officers raised their end up.

"Get a medical team up here," Jack ordered. Jack and an officer held the carpet steady while the other cop called for medical.

"Where are all the other officers?" Jack asked, "There must be more than the two of you!"

"They're attending to the injured outside, Son. They will get someone up here as soon as they can," the officer responded.

"That may not be soon enough. We need to unravel this and see what his injuries are. We are going to do it standing up. Two of us will hold on to him and the other will walk the carpet around until it is off of him. Are we ready? Who is going to walk?"

"I'll walk," one of the officers volunteered.

"Let's go," Jack said.

The officer started walking with the open end of the carpet. It took four times around before he reached the final turn.

"Okay, hold it there, Jack said. Dad, are you okay?"

"Keep going Jack, just be ready to catch me when I fall," Greg said weakly.

"I won't let you fall, Dad."

Jack nodded to the officer and he slowly pulled the carpet away. Now that the carpet was extended, Jack could see a repeating hole about chest high. Something had pierced the fabric through all the layers, Whatever it was could now inside his father.

"Where are the medics, chief," he said to the lead officer. He got back on his radio and used some code to tell them they needed help. A few seconds later some men were climbing the stairs with a stretcher.

"Down here!" Jack yelled.

When they arrived, Jack said, "put that bed down as low as it goes. When we unwrap this last little bit, he is going down on his stomach. Something came through the carpet and pierced his back."

"Are you a doctor or an EMT?" one guy asked smugly.

"No, but I know what I'm talking about."

"What makes you so smart?" the guy continued.

Jack looked him in the eyes and said, "the man inside this carpet. Talk time is over, put the bed down!" Jack insisted.

"Listen to him," the chief said, "the kid knows his stuff."

The medics lowered the bed and stood by. Jack looked at the guy with the end of the rug. Then he looked at the medic.

"Get out some clean gauze to pack the wound."

The medic did as he was told. Jack looked back at the officer and said, "walk." The man walked, the carpet opened revealing Greg and Greg fell forward into his son's arms.

"Pull that bed under him." They did and Jack slowly lowered his dad onto the stretcher.

Greg was on his belly and the medic was dressing his wound. There was a lot of blood which alarmed Jack.

"Where will you be taking him?"

"Crouse is the closest," the medic said.

"I know where it is," Jack replied. "I'll meet you in the ER."

It was just a short ride but it was an even faster walk. "Dad," Jack said. Greg opened his eyes. "There are taking you to the hospital and I'll meet you there. You're going to be okay." Greg was whispering something but Jack couldn't hear him. He leaned down and put his ear near his mouth.

"I thought we agreed to meet out front," Greg said.

Chapter 102

Jack couldn't believe what he witnessed outside Dineen Hall. There were hundreds of people sitting and standing on and around the lawn. Some of them had minor wounds but the majority had escaped unharmed. There were plenty of law enforcement and rescue personnel outside in stark contrast to the noticeable absence of them inside the building.

Jack began walking quickly toward the hospital when he was approached by a man in a suit. "Jack Webster?" the man asked.

"That's me," Jack replied but didn't stop walking.

"I'm detective Mullins, I need you to stop walking so that I can ask you some questions."

"I'm happy to answer your questions, Detective, but you need to walk with me. They are taking my father to the hospital and I need to be there. Once I see him and know what's happening, I will give you all the time I need. I also need to call my mother so please bear with me for a few minutes."

Jack kept walking and he didn't wait for a response. Jack pulled his phone from his pocked and dialed his mom's number. It didn't ring once.

"Jack!" she yelled, "are you alright? Where is your father?"

"I'm alright, mom. Try to calm down and I will tell you what I know."

"Okay," she said.

"There was an explosion at the school, Mom. Dad was injured."

"Injured how, honey?"

"I don't know yet, he is in the ambulance on his way to the hospital. I am on my way there right now. I will call you back when I know more, Mom. Sit by the phone for now and I will call you."

"I am coming out there," she said. "Which hospital?"

"They are taking him to Crouse. It's only a couple blocks from here but Mom, wait for me to call. There is nothing you can do, plus it will take you two hours to get here. Let me get some information and I will call you just as soon as I know something. I have to go now, Mom. I love you!"

"I love you too, Jack. Tell your father..." He cut her off.

"He knows, Mom, but I will tell him."

Jack hung up and began jogging. "You look like you keep in shape, detective, try to keep up."

Detective Mullins did try to keep up but he was a good thirty seconds behind when Jack reached the Emergency entrance to Crouse University Hospital. He stopped to let Mullins catch up.

"I think we beat the ambulance here. It would still be parked out here, don't you think?" Jack asked.

"I do, Jack. They should be along any minute," Mullins replied.

Jack put out his hand, "I'm Jack Webster, I'm sorry I couldn't comply with your request immediately. You can begin asking now if you don't mind taking a break when the bus gets here."

"The bus? It sounds like you watch a lot of TV, Jack."

"Just enough, Detective. I have heard my dad call it that a few times."

"What does your father do, Jack?"

"You mean when he's not being blown up? He is CEO at City Hospital in High Falls."

"Was he here to visit you?" the detective asked.

"His primary reason for being here today was to deliver a lecture," Jack replied.

"A lecture on what, exactly?"

"He was asked to talk about the serial killer case that happened at City about fifteen years ago. I am surprised you haven't heard of him," Jack said.

"I think I have heard of the case but I am not familiar with the name. I transferred in from downstate just a few years back."

"You will be after today, Detective. My father saved about four hundred lives back there. He has a habit if being in the wrong place at the right time," Jack joked.

"How did he save lives, Jack?"

"He knew there was a bomb in the box," Jack responded.

"What box?"

"I met my dad in the auditorium about fifteen minutes before the lecture was to begin. I walked on stage to set a bottle of water on the lectern and I noticed a box on the stage floor. There was a picture of an overhead projector on the side so I asked him if was using overhead slides during his presentation. I thought it was odd because nobody uses them anymore.

He said he had no intentions of using one and went over to look at the box. That's when he asked me to go to the microphone and clear everyone out. Thank God we were early."

"Jack, do you know why he concluded there was a bomb in the box?"

"I don't know the exact reason. Maybe it was the return address? All I know is the man notices everything and he has supernatural instincts."

"It must have been hell being a teenager in his house!" the detective speculated.

"Let's just say I'm thankful for that now," Jack said.

Jack could hear the sirens in the background. In less than a minute the sirens stopped and the rig turned into the drive and up to the door. Jack ran to the back end of the ambulance. The doors popped open and two EMTs jumped out. They unlatched the stretcher and pulled it out. The legs flipped open automatically and they hurried toward the door. The electronic doors slid open ahead of their arrival. Jack was right behind them.

He moved to the unobstructed side of the gurney. "Dad, can you hear me?" Jack spoke. There was no response. "Dad," he said louder. His father half opened his eyes and closed them again. A nurse came to meet the stretcher. "Take him to trauma room eight," she ordered.

The stretcher was moving again and Jack followed. So did Mullins. It was a short walk to room eight. Once inside, the nurse and the EMTs slid Greg's body from the ambulance gurney to the hospital stretcher. When the ambulance crew exited the room, the nurse pulled the curtains closed and Greg disappeared behind them.

Jack didn't move. He could hear things happening on the other side. Soon, three others dressed in hospital attire entered the room and slipped behind the drapes.

"We need to cut his shirt off, check the wound and get him on his back for intubation." Jack could hear the beeping and buzzing of machinery and monitors powering up. The nurse stepped out from behind the curtain for just a moment.

"I'm Dr. Mehta, what is your relationship to the patient?" she asked Jack.

"I am his son," Jack replied.

"Your father sustained a puncture wound to his right upper back, probably from shrapnel. We can see it and we don't know how deep it is or what it is resting against. There is no exit wound so it is still in there. Once he is stabilized, he is going for a CT scan.

Then we will know what our next steps are. I need you to go back to the registration desk and provide some information. Then you should rest in the waiting room until I have more information for you. I promise I will keep you informed."

She went back through the curtain. Jack turned to go to the desk as instructed. He looked at Mullins.

"Go Jack, I'll be here." Mullins was no longer just doing his job. He imagined what it would be like if his son was in a similar situation. Probably far from home, no other relatives around and about to be faced with making some pretty serious decisions. He knew he was going to stick by this kid until there was some resolution.

Chapter 103

It had been thirty-five minutes since Ben pushed the button and he was just getting off the hill. Even though the timer was set for ten minutes, traffic around the university was heavier and much slower that he anticipated. He was so close when the bomb detonated that he could feel the percussion.

He wound his way down the west side of the campus making his way to I-81 north. Just ahead, Ben could see flashing blue and white lights which explained the slow moving traffic. When he reached about fourth in line, he could see that the university patrol was just trying to control the traffic.

When he approached, the officer didn't look in the car or check for identification. His role was strictly traffic control. Once

Ben did reach the ramp to I-81, the northbound traffic was moving well. He was hoping to get beyond the city before lunchtime and he did. Just barely.

He contemplated adjusting his route for the time he lost on the hill. He decided he still had plenty of time and would stay the course. He turned on the radio and scanned to a local channel. He entered the dialogue in the middle but it was clear they were talking about the explosion. He listened for a moment and then pressed the scan button again. This time he caught the beginning.

"Less than an hour ago, There was an explosion at Syracuse University. The center of the impact appears to be Dineen Hall, a lecture room building in the center of the campus. There are reports of injuries but no fatalities so far. We are awaiting a formal statement from authorities.. One eyewitness told WSAR he was in the building just moments before the explosion.

"The crowd had just started to fill the hall when a fellow student got on the mic and asked us to leave. We all thought he was joking before introducing the guest speaker. He was calm but authoritative and directed us to move to the rear exits in an orderly fashion. Once a few people responded, more and more followed. He told us without hesitation that here was a bomb on stage and that we had maybe ten minutes to get out. The kid was cool about it, very poised."

"Do you know the student's name?" the interviewer asked.

"No. I think I have seen him around but I've never actually met him."

"Do you know if everyone made it out before the explosion?"

"I'm sorry, I don't, but I know that there were a lot of people outside on the lawn when I arrived and I was toward the back of the pack."

Ben wasn't sure how he felt about that. If most people made it out, he wondered if Webster was one of them. He would find out soon enough. He still had a long ride home with plenty of time to listen to the news. Once he reached Rt. 31 near Cicero, he would lose the traffic and be able to just sit back and listen.

Chapter 104

Mary was worried out of her mind. It had been thirty minutes without any further word from Jack.

"Sara, I need to get out there. I can't just sit here any longer. What if Greg dies and I'm not there? I could never forgive myself," she cried.

"I'm sure Jack will call soon," she replied, It takes some time to get information from the hospital staff. I'm sure they are extremely busy taking care of everyone else involved in the incident." Sara was careful not to use the words bomb or explosion.

"Let's talk to Michael about it, maybe he has more information." She left Mary for a minute to find him.

She knew she would find him outside the front door.

"Hi Michael," he had his back to her and she couldn't see that he was talking on the phone. He turned and held up one finger to indicate he would be done soon. When he ended the call, he turned to her.

"How can I help you Mrs. Shand," he asked.

"Mary is adamant about going to Syracuse. Do you have any news?"

"I was just talking to one of our people in the Syracuse State Police, he confirmed that one person was taken to the hospital in serious condition but a name hasn't been released. He was on his way to the hospital to see what he could find out. That's all we know right now," Michael offered.

"We know it is Mr. Webster because of Jack's call to his mom. Perhaps we should get her out there."

"I think that would be a good idea. Perhaps Bill or Richard could drive her out there and I will go with the other to retrieve the kids after school. In fact, maybe we should ask the school to release the girls early today," Sara proposed.

"I would think about that for a minute. They are safe where they are and not knowing might be a better situation for them, especially with the limited information we have available. What would you want if it were you?" Michaels asked.

I suppose you're right. Can we at least get Mary on her way now?" Sara requested.

"Alright," Michael replied, "find Richard and bring him to me."

Sara was on her feet and back in the house. She believed she would find Richard out back, and she was right.

"Richard," she said, "Agent Sanchez would like to see you. He is out front."

"Sure, Sara. Do we have anything new?"

"Not yet, I think he wants you to drive Mary to Syracuse."

"Not a bad idea," Richard said.

Richard walked around the outside and Mary went in through the back door. She returned to Mary who was sitting in the same place holding her head in her hands. Sara resumed her place next to her and put her arm around her.

"We should go up and pack a small bag for you. Richard is going to drive you to Syracuse."

Mary's head shot up, "really?" She stood and headed up the stairs with Sara on her tail.

As they packed, Mary paused and said, "I can't go, I need to pick the girls up from school!"

"Bill and I will pick the girls up from school. I asked Michael about pulling the girls out early but he didn't advise it," Sara said.

"I think he's right, why let them worry all day. Just tell them I went to see Greg and Jack and that I will call them around dinner time. By then we should have some solid information and if necessary, we can hold them out of school tomorrow."

"How about Jillian, should we let her stay for practice?" Sara asked.

"I think so," Mary responded, "she loves it and there is nothing she could do here."

"Then I will stay here with the younger two while Bill picks Jillian up at 5:30."

"Perfect," Mary said, closing her suitcase. "Let's go."

Mary left moments later with Richard and Sara went to the sitting room to speak with Bill.

Chapter 105

Charis had reached I-81 south of Harrisburg when she got the call from Preston. He was observing Webster from the back of the auditorium, waiting for an opportunity to address him without interrupting his time with this son. Then his son asked everyone to evacuate.

He thought about approaching the stage but decided to assist in the evacuation. A quick calculation told him more lives would be saved that way than fighting the evacuees to get to the stage. Charis would have done the same thing.

She asked Preston to find out where they had taken Webster and to get over there. He promised to provide an update when he knew more.

She called the incident into the command center and asked for traffic monitoring on all routes from Syracuse to High Falls. She believed they were looking for a white Range Rover with NY plates but she couldn't be sure. The guy had already used three different vehicles and for all she knew, he may have three more.

She listened to Greg's last voicemail again but still couldn't decipher the missing words. She was hoping his details along with the cell tower results could pinpoint a location. She didn't know if Kovak would be going back to High Falls at all. She did know he had purchased a ticket for a flight out of the country the next morning. The FBI had a plan in place to thwart that possibility.

Listening to his voice again made her feel like she should have done more to protect him. She really didn't believe Kovak would go after him at the university.

The drive by his house was an indication he was keeping tabs on the Webster's but nothing pointed to a personal attack in public. She was having some difficulty maintaining the boundary between business and a personal affection for this guy.

He partly reminded her of a younger version of her father and she also envision him being an older brother. Mostly, he felt like a male version of her.

She was still over four hours away from High Falls even with her current rate of speed which was a little excessive even for her. She didn't have emergency lights on her car and being pulled over would just slow her down.

She felt an imminent need to be there ASAP. Charis always felt helpless when she was on the road and tried to think about what she could be doing to help the cause. She did have one idea.

Rather than waiting for Greg to call, she could make contact with the Herkimer County office. With any luck, she would be able to obtain the same information directly. She found the main number and dialed.

After explaining her situation, she was put in touch with the supervisor, Lacey Meadows. Within a few minutes, she not only had the information she needed but felt like she met a friend of Greg's. With this new information in hand, she could put a plan in motion to locate the spot.

Chapter 106

Jack had discussed at length his father's history and the events of the day with Detective Harold Mullins of the Syracuse P.D. Jack liked the guy. He was polite, not pushy and was supportive of his current situation. He was happy for the company.

Dr. Mehta approached the waiting room. Jack stood up to greet her. "Mr. Webster," she started.

"Please call me Jack. Mr. Webster is in there," he pointed to the exam room.

"Of course. Jack, we have the results of the scan. Your father sustained an injury to his right upper back, probably from shrapnel. The object is less than an inch wide and sharp, I'm amazed it didn't create an exit wound.

Anyway, it missed the crucial arteries in that area but it did collapse his right lung. We have put a tube in his chest to drain the blood and to reinflate the lung but he will need surgery to remove the shrapnel."

"Is he conscious?" Jack asked.

"He is sedated right now, Jack, but he has been awake. I think it's best if we let him rest before the surgery," she replied.

"When will the surgery happen, Dr. Mehta?"

"As soon as the surgeon finishes his current case. We will probably moving him to the OR in the next fifteen minutes. The surgeon will come by to speak with you before he begins. Do you have other family on the way?"

"Not that I know of," Jack replied. "They are waiting for an update from me. I will call my mom as soon as we're finished."

"Make that call. Your father is a lucky man, Jack. If that projectile had come out the other side, he may have bled out," the doctor stated.

"I think it was being smart rather than lucky. When he knew he couldn't get out in time, he rolled himself into a carpet on the floor. The carpet must have slowed the fragment down," Jack explained.

"That would explain the fibers we found in the entry would. That information will also be useful to the surgeon. I'll let him know. Good luck, Jack," Mehta said.

"Thank you for everything, Dr. Mehta."

She turned and disappeared.

"That's good news, Jack," Mullins offered, "It sounds like he will be okay."

"Yes, thank you Detective Mullins," Jack responded.

"Call me Hal, Jack, I think we know each other well enough now."

A man entered the waiting room and looked around. "I'm looking for Jack Webster."

Mullins answered for him. "he's right here. Who wants to know?"

"I'm Detective Preston, New York State Police," he said.

"Preston, I'm Detective Mullins, Syracuse P.D. This is Jack Webster."

Preston held out his hand to Jack. "It's nice to meet you, son. I was in the auditorium when this went down. I was in the back when you began the evacuation. I knew you were in trouble and I knew I couldn't make it to the stage so I helped get the people out. You did a remarkable job getting those people to move. You showed a lot of poise for a young man. I was impressed."

"It was my dad really, I was just doing what he instructed," Jack replied.

"How old are you, son?" Preston continued.

"I'm twenty, Detective."

"The twenty year old people I meet are either drunk or in trouble. Your father may have given the instruction but you made them move. Safely and quickly. You and your dad saved hundreds of lives today. You should be proud."

"I am certainly proud of my dad, Jack replied, but thank you for your kind words."

A tall man in hospital greens entered the waiting room. "You must be Jack Webster," he said, "I am Dr. Zilkins and I'll be taking care of your father today. The surgery should only take an hour but between pre-op and post-op care, you will get to see him In about three hours. Do you have any questions?"

"Make sure you get all the fibers out, he was wrapped in a rug," Jack replied.

"Yes, Dr. Mehta mentioned that. Your dad is a clever guy!" Zilkins said.

"You have no idea!" Jack replied. "Thank you Dr. Zilkins. "I will be waiting right here."

The surgeon did his vanishing act as well. A moment later, Greg's stretcher was wheeled into the hallway. Jack ran up to it. The staff stopped rolling long enough for Jack to take a look. Greg's eyes were closed so Jack just leaned over and gave him a kiss while he squeezed his hand.

Greg didn't speak but Jack could feel him squeezing back.

"You're going to be fine, Dad. I'll see you when you wake up. I love you, Dad and I am so proud of you." Greg gave another soft squeeze and the cart started rolling. Jack let go of his dad's hand and backed up. He couldn't control the tears any longer.

Hal Mullins walked up, put his hand on his shoulder and turned him back toward the waiting room.

Chapter 107

Mary picked up on the first ring. "Jack!"

"Hi, Mom, I have some news. It sounds like you are in a car," Jack said.

"I am, honey. I'm on my way there, to the hospital," Mary replied.

"That's good, Mom. Listen, Dad just went to surgery." He could hear his mother crying. "He is going to be alright, Mom. He was hit in the upper back by shrapnel from the explosion. He has a piece lodged in his right lung and his lung collapsed. They were able to reinflate it and he should be fine."

"Oh Jack, what about you, are you alright?" Mary asked.

"I'm fine, Mom, I wasn't hurt at all. Are you driving by yourself?" Jack asked.

"No, Richard Ingraham is driving. We should be there is a little over an hour," she stated.

"That's great, Mom, I can't wait to see you. Just check in at the ER desk when you get here. If I'm not in this waiting room, I will be in the surgical waiting room. Make sure you get the right hospital, it's Crouse Hospital, 736 Irving Avenue."

"Okay, dear, thank you! I will see you soon!"

"Jack, I'm going to the cafeteria. What can I bring you?" Mullins asked.

"I can go with you," Jack said.

"No, Detective Preston has a few questions for you. Stay and talk to him and I will bring some stuff back. Just tell what your beverage of choice is and I'll figure out the rest."

"Apple juice would be fine. Thank you!"

"No sweat, kid. Have a nice chat."

Chapter 108

It was nearly 3:00 pm when Greg opened his eyes. It was just for a second and he dosed back off. A few minutes later, he opened them again long enough to be able to make out the ceiling tiles and hear beeping and some distant chatter. When he woke up the third time, he was able to make some sense of his surroundings. He knew he was in a hospital but he couldn't remember why.

The last time he felt like this he had just had his appendix removed. He didn't have much control over his movement so he tried to survey his body. He closed his eyes again and took an inventory.

He could see and he could hear. He tried to wiggle his toes, first the left and then the right. They seemed weak but they responded. He did the same with his fingers. One of his fingers had a clip on the end of it. He could feel a prickle in the back of his right hand. He figured the clip was a pulse oximeter and the prickle was an IV.

He moved his head slightly, first left and then right. It moved freely but there was a tug on the right side of his chest and his back when he moved his head left. He did it again just to verify.

He knew that he was not lying flat because he could feel the weight on his bottom. He tried to think back to where he started this morning. He remembered leaving the safe house and talking to Charis on the phone. He remembered the drive to Syracuse and getting his guest pass.

Then, there was Jack but he was young, maybe ten or so. He tried to open his eyes again. He could make out images of people but they were blurred and their voices were not distinct.

He closed his eyes once more. He could feel Jack's hand in his and his lips on his cheek. He was hovering above him whispering that everything was going to be okay. Greg could see him on stage, telling people to go. Another glimpse of him, this time he was walking up the aisle behind the people. It was coming back to him. The stage, the people, and the box. He was moving everything he could find to put around the box.

There were exercise matts and cushions of some sort. There were walls on wheels, blackboards, or whiteboards maybe. There was a rug on the floor off to the side of the stage. He wanted to lay on it. It seemed odd to him but he needed to lay on the rug.

Then he was surrounded by cloth, like being swaddled, and noise. It was loud and percussive. He opened his eyes again and tried to move. Fire ripped through his chest and back and he immediately stopped. The beeping and the voices were getting louder and closer.

He suddenly remembered the box and the bomb. He could feel his anxiety escalate quickly. Jack. He wondered if Jack had made it out. He again had a vision of Jack hovering over him, telling Greg he loved him, that is was going to be alright. He suddenly had a horrible thought that Jack didn't make it, that he was speaking to him from the other side. "Jack!" he yelled. "Jack! Jack! Jack!"

He felt a hand on his arm. "Jack! Is that you?"

"Mr. Webster?"

"Jack!"

Mr. Webster, "I'm your nurse." Mr. Webster there has been an accident. You have been hurt. Mr. Webster open your eyes.

Greg did as he was told, The light was too bright and it hurt to keep them open.

"Where is Jack?" he asked.

"Jack is fine, Mr. Webster. He is waiting for you to wake up," the nurse assured him.

"I need to see him," Greg replied, "I need to see my son!"

"And you will, Mr. Webster, just as soon as you wake up. Take some deep breaths, You need to clear the anesthesia from your lungs," she advised.

Greg tried to take a deep breath. "It hurts," he said.

"I know, you had a little surgery on your lung but you are okay. The pain will subside quickly, I promise, but you need to try to breath as deeply as you can."

Greg tried again and again. The sooner he could do this, the sooner he could see Jack. He forced himself to keep his eyes open and he could see his nurse standing to his side. He could sense that his head was clearing gradually and his body movements were more controlled.

"I remember now," he said to the nurse, "I'm sorry for the outburst."

"Don't you worry about it, that's a normal part of coming out of anesthesia. My name is Gretchen and I have been your nurse here in recovery. You have been through a tough time it appears," she stated.

"Was Jack injured?" Greg asked.

"No sir, he's fine. Somewhat of a hero as far as I understand. That makes two of you!" she exclaimed.

"Others?" Greg asked.

"No fatalities, from what I've been told."

"Thank God," Greg replied.

"Amen to that, Mr. Webster. How do you feel?"

"To say that I feel like I've been in an explosion would be sort cliché, right?" Greg said, trying to make a joke.

"For most people," she replied, "but not you."

"It's good to see you have a sense of humor. That tells me you're going to be just fine." Gretchen said. "Now, I need you to have a sip of water and I need to check all your vitals before we can send you to your room."

"I suppose you'll also ask me to pee before you release me," Greg joked again.

"Oh no, we took care of that," she smiled.

"I've been catheterized?" Greg said with shock.

"Yes sir. That will come out later tonight or tomorrow," she replied.

"You must know how these things work. I hear you're a hospital administrator!" she quipped.

"I am, but I've never had direct patient care," he said. "I wish I had, it would make me a much better leader."

"The fact that you can admit that makes you a good leader," she returned.

"Alright, here are the details. You were hit in the back with shrapnel, which your surgeon successfully removed. Your right lung collapsed when the shrapnel struck but we reinflated it in the ER. You have a chest tube that goes through the wall of your right side into the lung and connects to a box that hangs by the side of your bed. That box keeps positive pressure on the inside of your lung and removes the pressure outside by draining any fluid that may accumulate."

"How long does it stay there," Greg asked.

"That depends on how long it takes you to pay your bill! You aren't the only one who can make a joke," she replied.

Chapter 109

It was 4:30 pm by the time Greg was in a regular hospital bed. When they wheeled him in, Mary and Jack were waiting for him. There were careful hugs and kisses, as well as a lot of tears. Soon after, two men in suits showed up at the door. Jack saw them and escorted them in.

"Dad, I want to introduce you to some new friends. This is Detective Harold Mullins of the Syracuse P.D.

"Call me Hal. Nice to meet you, Greg."

"And this is Detective Preston with the State Police. I'm sorry, "Jack said," I don't think I ever got your first name," Jack continued.

"You can call me Chuck, Mr. Webster." Greg knew his name and he was glad it didn't have to be said. He didn't want to laugh right now.

"It's a pleasure to meet you, Hal, Chuck. Are you drinking buddies with my son?"

"Dad," Jack said, a little embarrassed. "They helped me out while you were sleeping all day."

"I figured as much, Jack. Gentlemen, I thank you for your service, which seems like it went beyond your call of duty today."

"It was our pleasure, Greg," Mullins said, "This is quite a special young man you have here."

"Yes, he is. I couldn't be more proud of him."

Mary's eyes were filled with tears just listening to the gratitude being shared in the room and thankfulness she felt to still have them in her life.

"Listen folks," Preston said, "we are going to let you have some quality time to yourselves. We may be back to ask some questions tomorrow. You all have a good night."

Everyone thanked the detectives for their kindness and they left the room.

"I can't tell you how good it is to see your faces. Mary, I'm so glad you were able to come, thank you," Greg said with a shaky voice. "Before we continue, how are the other girls?"

"They don't know anything yet, Greg. We thought it would be best to have you call them after dinner, when they were all home. That way, they didn't need to worry all day and you can reassure them in your own voice that you're ok," Mary explained.

"That sounds like an excellent plan," Greg replied. "Are Bill and Richard making the school runs?"

"Bill and Sara have already picked up the younger ones and they are back at the safehouse. Sara will stay with the girls while

Bill makes the 5:30 trip for Jillian. Richard, that sweetheart, drove me out here."

"Where is he now?" Greg asked.

"He went to get coffee and to call Marilyn. He has been waiting patiently to see you," Mary replied. "Speak of the devil," Mary said as Richard walked in.

"Is he awake?" Richard asked.

"Come in, Richard, I hope you brought something to eat!" Greg said.

"You know better than that," Richard said, "You do run a hospital, right?"

"That doesn't mean I know anything about it!" Greg joked.

"I have thought that exact thing many times," Richard came back. "Do you know they have a soft-serve ice cream machine in the cafeteria? A sign of a good hospital."

"They also have doctors who know what they are doing!" Greg responded.

"I think the ice cream is more impressive," Richard said.

Chapter 110

Charis had arrived in High Falls and was driving the countryside behind a Sheriff's deputy looking for the location. They pulled over in front of a wooded lot. Walking back to her car the deputy said, "this should be it right here. We have been up and down this road several times already and this makes the most sense.”

“Well unless he lives in a tree, I think we have the wrong location.” Charis grabbed the county map that Lacey Meadows had left for her. She unfolded it and looked again.

“Alright deputy, why don’t you go about your business and I will keep looking around. I’ll call if I find something. Thanks for your help.”

Charis watched the squad car pull away. She wished the son of a bitch would just materialize in front of her. She would just run him over and be done with it. She thought about the absurdity of that silent statement and laughed a little. She just wanted this event over. Kovak could have his day in court.

She unfolded the map even wider and looked at the bigger picture. “What if the entry to the property was on the opposite side,” she thought. It was a large parcel and there was a road that ran parallel to this one. “Of course,” she thought. Charis drove to the end of the road and made a right turn.

When she hit the next crossroad, she turned right again. She measured her distance from where she had been to where she made the first turn. When she made the last turn, she measured again.

When she reached the same distance, she slowed down. It was a heavily wooded area but about fifty yards ahead, she thought she saw a small clearing. She approached slowly. There was a driveway. It wasn’t paved and it made an immediate turn so she couldn’t see down the length of it. There was no mailbox nor address post. She put her car in park and made a few calls.

Chapter 111

Ben made it back to town without being noticed. The news had told him he was wanted for questioning and warned people not to approach the vehicle. They gave a number for people to call if they spotted the car. Every hourly update included false claims of spotting him from places he couldn't possibly have reached in that amount of time. "These people are crazy!" he thought out loud.

The news had also stated that so far, there were no fatalities. That pissed him off at first but then he realized that a miserable life without his wife and daughter may exact an even worse fate than being blown up.

He originally had hoped to eliminate Greg, his wife, the son, and the oldest daughter, leaving just the youngest to fend for herself. "See how she likes it!" he yelled in the car.

"I guess sometimes you just have to settle for less." His dad knew all about that, settling for a life of performing surgery on stiffs instead of the living.

"All that death sucks the life right out of you," his father would say, "but you have to make the best out it, Ben. Crying about it won't do you any good."

"Neither will being an asshole to your toddler son, you bastard!" Ben yelled again. He looked at his watch. It felt like he had been waiting for hours. He was tired of looking around this cemetery. In a few minutes, it would be time to make the walk up the hill to the school.

He got out of the car to stretch his legs. They were cramped from all the hours he had been sitting. Between the drive out, back and sitting in the cemetery, he had been off his feet for almost ten hours. He couldn't wait to get home and stretch out for a bit before leaving for the airport.

He grabbed his tool bag from the car, locked it and began the half mile walk up the hill to the school.

Chapter 112

Bill was at the school a few minutes early. He thought he might as well watch the girls wind up their practice so he got out of the car and walked around the side toward the field. The softball team must not have had practice today. The field was empty and there was no one around. He walked to a small set of bleachers that was between the fields and took a seat on the lower bench.

Bill hadn't been sleeping well and he found himself dozing. He tried to stay awake but it was no use. Ben had recognized the car when he reached the parking area. It was the old man's sedan. The keys were in it. Looking around, Ben saw the old man sitting on the bottom row of the bleachers. He head was leaning forward as if he were asleep.

Ben approached from the back of the bleachers with his back to the softball field. He opened his bag and removed a syringe. He left his bag there on the ground and stepped quietly toward the bleachers. He slid onto the bench behind the old man trying not to wake him. He uncapped the needle and pushed the point of it into the man's neck. He made a quick motion and then slumped over in his seat. Ben looked at the field hockey field where the girls were gathering their things. He needed to hurry.

He pushed the old man's body onto the ground under the bench he was sitting on and then walked back to his bag. He picked it up and walked to the old guy's car. The front windows were open so he reached in and grabbed the keys. Then he slid into the back behind the passenger seat and got down on the floor. Hopefully, she would be one of the last ones out. He still had the syringe in his hand.

He could hear voices as the girls exited the front of the school. He listened as one car pulled up and then drove away. Several cars came and went. Finally he heard the girl's voice. "Mr. Dillon? Mr. Dillon, are you here?"

He heard her approach the car. She opened the front door and got in. He listened as one more car came and went. Then quietly, he rose from his hiding place reached around the headrest and stuck the girl in the neck. When her head fell forward. He got out of the car and re-entered in the driver's seat.

He put the key in the ignition, started it and pulled away. Down the hill he drove. When he reached the cemetery, he pulled up next to the Range Rover. He picked her up and put her in the back seat of his car. He closed the door of the sedan with the keys inside, got into his own car and drove away. He looked over at her. "You look just like your mother," he said.

Chapter 113

After parking her car on the back side of the lot, where she was earlier, she walked through the woods to find the dwelling. It was incredible. The color had to be named woods brown because the house disappeared into its surroundings. The windows were treated so that you couldn't see in from outside and the doors and windows were impenetrable, including the garage doors.

She didn't know how long she would have to wait there or even if he would ever return, but she had a gut feeling that he wasn't far away now. She was prepared to stay out there all night if necessary. She thought about Greg, hoping he was alright and wishing he could be there for the takedown. She believed he deserved it. The last she heard from Preston was just over an hour ago. Greg had made it through the surgery and was expected in his private room any minute.

At 4:45, a white SUV became visible from the house. Charis was anxious but stayed tucked back on the side of the garage making sure she wasn't seen by him as he approached. When he was twenty yards away she could hear the garage door activate. It was the closest door to her end of the garage so she reversed her position a little more. She had her service revolver drawn and ready.

Ben wanted to pull into the garage and close the door but he knew he wouldn't be able to open the door enough to pick her up and carry her to the house. So with the garage door open, he pulled up close to the opening and then stopped.

When Charis heard the transmission go into park, she moved to the passenger side of the vehicle in a squat position. She heard the driver's door open and then she heard the back door open. She couldn't see what was happening but she knew that if she waited, and the garage door closed behind him, she would not be able to get into the house.

Ben lifted the dead weight of the girl in his arms and backed out of the car. He moved to the open bay, just to the side of the car. He turned briefly back toward the driveway.

"Hold it! FBI. Put the girl down and come out with your hands up!"

Ben just stopped. He didn't move and he didn't speak. He was thinking. If he tried to get further into the garage, she might shoot at him. She would have an open shot at his head because he was supporting the weight of the girl near his waist. If he dropped her to run, the woman would definitely shoot. She was his protection.

Charis again ordered the man to put the girl down and surrender. "Kovak, we know everything about you. You must be tired of living this charade, why don't you set the girl down and we will talk."

Ben thought for a moment. "This house is loaded with explosives that are triggered to blow. I was going to wait until tomorrow but no time like the present, right?"

"We know all about that too, Ben. The flight to Austria, the Swiss accounts, all of it. It's over Ben. Sure you could blow us all up but what do you gain? Will a few more innocent lives get you anything? An extra level in heaven or a few more virgins maybe? Do the right thing for a change. Put the girl down and surrender."

"Do you really think I am a terrorist? Like the 911 terrorists? Do you think that's what all this is about? You're wrong. This is about blood, about a commitment to family. It's about accepting your destiny and committing to it. You don't know the first thing about me."

"Is that what Kyle told you? Is that what he taught you? Do you even know who you really are, Ben? Where is Martina, Ben? Do you know that she is not really your mother?"

"Of course she is my mother. She has always been here for me. You can leave her and my father out of this. I have the detonator right here, resting on this young lady's abdomen. Do you want me to push the button? I will!"

"No Ben, I don't want you to push the button." Charis could see that his arms were weakening, that he wouldn't be able to hold her for much longer. "Ben, put her down and let's talk. I have so much to tell you. I bet I have more to tell you than you have to share with me. We can have a nice long talk."

"I'm not much of a talker. I definitely don't want to talk to you." Now, move yourself back down the driveway or I am going to push this button. You get to choose whether she lives or dies."

"Ben, Priscilla said you were a great talker. She told us all about it. How nice you were, how much you had in common. Do you want to know the reason you had so much in common, Ben? I can tell you." Ben didn't say anything.

"Timmy, I mean, Ben, the reason you have so much in common is because Priscilla is really your sister. She is your sister, Ben, doesn't that interest you? I mean doesn't that excite you to think that you have a real sister? All these years alone and you have a sister. Not only that, but you also have a real father too, Ben. You had a mother as well but she passed on a few years back."

"Why are you telling me this?" Ben yelled. "It isn't true, I had real parents, my father died in prison and my mother is in the house. Why would you say such a thing?"

She could see his arms trembling from trying to hold the weight, and he kept shifting his weight from one leg to the other. "I know she's getting heavy, Timmy, just set her down gently and we can figure this all out. Just the two of us." Charis noticed something. The girl's arm which was just hanging down had moved. She was inching it up toward her torso. She was awake. "Come on, Timmy, that's your real name by the way, let's hash it all out. I think I can help you."

"You can't help me, you just want me to go away, just like my father. Didn't work out well for him being locked up all those years, the years that I needed him most. Do you want me to rot in jail like he did? I don't have a son who will put me out of my misery like he did. Good old Ben. Yes good old 'blood is thicker than water,' Ben."

"If it makes you feel any better, you didn't kill your father, Ben. Kyle Seike was not your biological father. Kyle and Martina stole you away from loving parents when you were just a baby. You met your real father recently, Ben. Your name is Timothy Chalmers. Priscilla's father, Ben, he is your real father."

"The man who tried to shoot me. There is a great father figure for you. How is he any different than Kyle?"

"You were trying to kidnap his little girl just the way you were kidnapped from him. He couldn't let that happen again. He loves her and he loves you. He may not love Ben but he sure loves Timmy." The girl's arm was right up near her chest now.

"You're lying to me, you don't know what you're talking about. My parents loved me, they just didn't know how to show it. My dad taught me everything I know. He taught me things, that's how he loved me. I'm ready to end this now. You can either move away or you can blow up with the rest of us. Your choice lady."

"My name is Charis, Timmy. I'm glad to meet you finally." *"Be ready"* she thought, *"please be ready."* "Timmy, you don't want to end it this way, just set the girl down, Timmy. Leave the weight of her and the weight of your past behind you. Aren't you tired of the weight?" The girl's hand was on her chest now. "Timmy, look at me! Look at me and tell me I'm wrong. Tell me you aren't tired of carrying this weight. Tell me!" she yelled.

"Your damn right I'm tired of it! Let's end it shall we? He moved to get his hand on the detonator.

"LOOK AT ME YOU COWARD!! Charis yelled and dropped to the ground at the same moment that Jillian rolled away from Ben and fell to the ground holding the small box. Ben reached for the detonator as the rifle shot cracked and echoed through the woods. Ben stopped and then slowly sat down. The bullet entered the top of his head and exited the bottom of his skull.

Charis quickly got up and ran to Jillian. "Are you alright?" she asked.

"I think so."

Charis helped her up and walked her away from the garage. "Don't look back," she said.

"Do you think you could have talked a little longer, Charis?" the girl said jokingly.

"Wait a minute, I know that sarcasm. You have got to be Greg Webster's daughter?"

"You know, you might be as good as my father thinks you are."

"That is high praise missy. Which one are you?" Charis asked.

"I'm Jillian, the oldest and the wisest."

"You are wise," Charis replied. "Let's get you home."

Charis could hear the sirens now. In less than a minute, the place would be swarmed by FBI, state and local police, Sherriff's offices, and reporters. They would know where to find her.

As she walked down the driveway, she looked up in the tree and waived, "nice shot, Detective Lawrence! Hey, pick up that detonator will you? Someone could get hurt."

Chapter 114

Charis and Jillian met Agent Sanchez at the front door of the Haven. "Good to see you Agent Andrews," Sanchez said. "And it's good to have you home Jillian. I hear you had a busy day."

"It was a great day, best day ever!" Jillian replied.

"Okay," Michael said. "I have something for you to do. There is a lovely lady in there who wants to check you out. Her name is Dr. Grady and she just wants to make sure you're alright. Can you do that?"

"I would be happy to," Jillian replied as she walked in the door.

"Do you need to be checked out as well, Agent Andrews?"

"Are you asking me out on a date?" she answered.

"I was asking if you wanted to see the doctor."

"Is that what we're calling it these days?" Charis joked.

"You do make things difficult, Andrews!"

"Just toying with you, Michael. You are doing a great job here. Thank you!"

"Just doing my job, but thanks."

Charis went inside and introduced herself to their guests. Sara, John, Jocelyn, and Maria were in the sitting room. "Hello, everyone, I'm Charis Andrews, FBI. I hope you are enjoying your stay here at the Haven."

"Thank you for calling earlier, Charis, we were getting worried about Jillian," Sara said.

"I'm sorry I wasn't able to call sooner but we had our hands full for a few minutes there."

"Greg called a few minutes ago and I told him Jillian was held up at practice and was running a little late. I don't like lying to him," Sara said.

"Let's consider it a slight exaggeration in the interest of the patient. If he knew the truth right now, he would discharge himself and that wouldn't be good for anyone. We will speak with him as soon as Jillian comes down." Charis offered.

"Do you have an update for us?" John asked.

"Yes and if it's alright with you, I would like to share it with all of you at the same time."

"Can you tell us where Bill is?" Mary asked.

"Yes, that I can share with you now. Bill was found semi-conscious by the bleachers at the school. He was taken to City Hospital for an evaluation and I anticipate him walking through that door any minute."

Jillian rejoined the group in the sitting room and sat snuggled up to Jocelyn and Maria on the sofa. The front door opened and Bill walked in right on cue. "Bill, welcome back!" Charis said.

"I am going to dial Mary's number in just a second but I want to make sure we are all on the same page. We are going suppress most of the details of today's events because we don't want to stress Greg anymore at this time. He should be back in a few days and we can share the whole story then. Agreed?"

"Agreed," they all replied.

"Alright, here we go." Charis dialed Mary's number.

"Hello, Charis, is everything okay there?"

"Hi, Mrs. Webster, yes, the chickens are all home to roost. Do you think you can put us on speaker phone so we can hear each other?"

"Yes, of course. Can you hear us?"

"Greg was the first, "Hello everyone, I miss you all!"

There was an unrehearsed and uncoordinated response of many voices speaking many words. Charis took the reins and spoke for the group.

"Greg, we all wish you a rapid recovery and a quick return to your family."

"Thank you everyone. I want you to know that I am fine. The surgery went well and I should be discharged in two or three days."

"That's great, Greg," Charis replied. "We would like to offer the Haven and all it offers to you for the next week. It will give you a chance to recuperate, enjoy each other and talk about the events that have transpired."

"That's very kind of you, Charis," Greg responded.

"Speaking for myself, that sounds both therapeutic and fun. Thank you!"

"It's the least we can do, Greg. The federal, state, and local law enforcement agencies appreciate you and your team's invaluable contribution to this case. Let me take this opportunity to update all of you.

Less than an hour ago, the saga of the university bomber has ended. He was taken at his home right here in High Falls. We regret that we were not able to bring him in alive but to do so, would have put more innocent lives at risk. It will take months or more to know the extent of his activities and to get a deeper look at what might have caused this young man to follow this destructive path," she continued,

"The intuition, the strength, and the dedication that this group of family and friends proves that citizen involvement with professional law enforcement is crucial to protecting our civil liberties. You are an example of what can and should be done by all of us.

You are heroes in my eyes and in the eyes of your community. I hope that you will all take opportunities as they arise, to speak to others about your experience and your participation. So Greg, Mary, Richard, and Jack, we look forward to spending time with you here and to discuss in further detail what transpired over the last few weeks."

"Thank you, Charis, for all you have done for us. I for one, can't wait to meet you. I am going to sign off and get a little rest. I will see you all soon. I love you all."

Mary took the phone, "children, please behave yourselves. I will be home in the morning, at least for a little while."

Epilogue

It was a rather nice day for mid-December with the temperature hovering around forty-eight degrees. Greg was outside breathing deeply, a function he used to take for granted. The pain was gone and everything seemed back to normal. He was excited but also a bit apprehensive about today's event. He had been speaking almost non-stop since that Tuesday in September that almost took his life. Mostly interviews with reporters in a one on one basis.

This would be different. This was big. His entire family was there as well as the Shands, the rest of his team and many others. Mary opened the exit door and told him they were ready to start. Greg said he would be right in. Looking around, he could see Dineen Hall, The Carrier Dome, and Crouse Hospital. It felt like yesterday and twenty years ago. He opened the door and found his place next to Mary and the kids.

He had his notes in his jacket pocket, just an outline of what he felt was important to cover. He was sitting in the front row of the auditorium between Mary and Jack. It wasn't Dineen this time as that was still being repaired. This was the five thousand seat main theater at SU and it was packed.

The Governor of New York was on stage to introduce them. He thanked everyone involved in the case and explained why this was different. The State certainly doesn't recognize people every time a crime is solved. Usually, crimes are solved by law enforcement officials he said who are performing their jobs. They get recognized in other ways, like promotions and pay raises.

When he was done laying the groundwork he introduced his first guest, Special Agent Charis Andrews of the FBI. There was a nice, welcoming applause, led by Greg himself.

Charis was poised and charming. She looked good on stage, a perfect balance of strength and femininity. She focused her speech to the role the FBI played in the investigation and subsequent apprehension. She covered the Kyle, Martina and Ben relationships including the details of what they found in the house.

A house which by the way, didn't exist on any land map or property tax record. The house was built by private contractors who were paid in cash to overlook license and permit requirements.

Charis explained that the house was built as an invisible fortress to facilitate the well thought out plans of Kyle Seike. She described it as a bomb shelter with bedrooms. She also confirmed that the house was loaded with explosive devices that were triggered to blow.

Ben was not issuing idle threats and if he had reached the detonator that day, the house along with her, Jillian and Ben would all be dust. She gave a special thanks and acknowledgement to Jillian for her bravery and intuition.

She went on to tell Ben's story of neglect, seclusion, and abuse. Seike and his mail order bride Martina Kovatikova kidnapped Timmy Chalmers as a toddler and kept him captive until he was an adult. Timmy was too young to know they weren't his real parents.

He didn't really have a childhood in the usual sense. There were no friends, no toys, and no sports. Ben's activities as a child and adolescent were human dissection, learning surgical procedures and making explosives.

At the age of nine, Ben watched as Kyle Seike killed Martina when he knew his criminal activities were coming to an end and he couldn't trust her to keep his secrets. Ben not only witnessed the murder but he watched his mother being embalmed. Then, he lived alone with her corpse for nearly fifteen years while his father sat in prison.

She was all Ben had and he talked about her in the present tense as if she was still breathing. Accept for an occasional stranger who would check on him periodically, Ben raised himself. He got on and off the bus to school, he did his own laundry and cooked his own meals. When Ben's father had had enough of prison, he asked Ben to end his life, and he did.

She wrapped up by saying Ben is what happens to a child in the wrong environment. Ben became a killer. Who knows what he would have become in a proper environment? Charis left the stage with a sincere thank you in the form of a loud applause.

The Governor then introduced Jack. He praised Jack for having the mindset to stay focused and said he performed well beyond what could be expected from most twenty year old men. He explained that Jack moved four hundred people from a space in under ten minutes.

He also lauded him for staying in the room, risking his own life to assist a wheelchair bound fellow student, lifting him from his chair and resting him safely behind the last row of seats. He even laid next to him to further protect his from the blast. After the explosion, Jack wouldn't leave the room until he knew what happened to his father. His efforts, according to police and rescue workers, saved his father's life.

Jack climbed the stairs to the stage while the audience showed their appreciation. Jack shook hands with the Governor and walked to the podium. The students in the room whistled and shouted as Jack began to speak. He raised his hand as he thanked them for the warm student welcome. The crowd quieted and Jack began.

He told the crowd that they should never underestimate their abilities and to trust their instincts. He gave thanks to the new friends he had made along the way including Sam, the EMTs and police. He called out detectives Preston and Mullins specifically. "I have learned," he said," that respect is the cornerstone of effective communication. It is the grease that allows differences to glide toward understanding and acceptance.

I couldn't heed the commands given me because I knew what was a stake but I was respectful in my refusal, and I offered a compromise. 'No sir, I can't do that right now but walk with me and I will give you all the information you require.' The officer walked with me. Not only did he walk with me, but he also stayed with me until I knew my father was going to be okay."

"My sisters and I have been told from an early age to be aware of our surroundings. Notice the things around you. There are times we wanted to rebel, there were times that we didn't want to be reminded and there were times we didn't want to look around, if for no other reason than defiance.

But we looked and we saw things without even knowing it. It is ingrained is us, as natural as walking and we thank God it is. I noticed the box on stage that day and I noticed it because I looked at that stage twice a week for two years. The box was nothing unusual but it's place on the stage stuck out like a pig in a horse race. I couldn't not notice it and when I did, I questioned it."

"I know what you're thinking," he continued, "that sounds like a compulsion, even paranoia perhaps but I see it as an awakening. When you truly look at the world around you, you will notice amazing things. Things that we take for granted every day.

We tell ourselves our lives are busy and that we don't have the time to look at everything but I'm telling you that it doesn't take any more time once you're used to doing it. The small commitment to paying attention comes with significant rewards like finding more beauty in life or like looking more deeply at someone or like saving lives.

Let me ask you a question. We have all been in this room for almost an hour. Without looking, who knows how many exit doors there are? How many of you have asked yourselves this question? If I had less than ten minutes to get out of this room, how would I do it?

There are five thousand people in this room. It took us eight minutes to clear a room of four hundred. Think about that. When that kind of thinking becomes second nature, it makes us all a little safer. I am grateful for my family, my friends old and new and I am thankful for all of you here tonight." There was a nice ovation for Jack including more hoots and hollers from the student body.

When the Governor approached the microphone once again, Greg knew he was next. He hoped he could be as poised as Jack was. He was so proud of his family that if he thought about it too long, he would break down crying with gratitude. He listened to the governor's words.

"Four hundred people came to this campus just two months ago to hear this man speak. Those four hundred people are still alive because he never got the chance to do it. While his son, Jack was safely directing people out of the building, this man was building a bunker around the bomb for those who might not be able to get out in time.

Using nothing but what he found backstage and using nearly all of that, Greg Webster directed the force of the explosion down into the floor because he believed that below him there would be reinforced concrete that would be capable of handling the impact. He was right."

"Two months ago," the Governor continued, "Greg would have been telling you about his experience as a Health Department investigator looking into one unexplained death at City Hospital in High Falls.

Tonight, while he may include some of that discussion, he will primarily focus on the recent events. Greg, you were a great investigator for the state and we miss you there but thank God you are where you are. Ladies and Gentlemen, please welcome Greg Webster."

There was thunderous applause as Greg rose to make the walk to the stage. He still felt mostly undeserving of the attention.

"Thank you, you're too kind. Thank you." He waited for the noise to settle. "Thank you all. I want to thank all of you for attending. I asked that the room lighting be dimmed for my portion of the program because I don't want to disturb your sleep should I be too boring."

There was a fair amount of laughter.

"Anyone who knows me will tell you that I try to maintain a sense of humor in every situation. I don't receive too many invitations to funerals.

I sincerely want to thank the Governor's office for this honor, Syracuse University for hosting in spite of the fact that I'm the reason Deneen Hall needs rebuilding, and Crouse Hospital for the five star care I received as a patient. I have been asked to speak at other colleges but now they require me to provide a certificate of insurance!" Again, many laughs.

"Rather than talk about the specifics of the cases which you have all probably heard on the news by now, I thought I would talk about the incidental positive outcomes that rise from the catastrophic ashes.

Volcanos lead to lush new lands and forest fires lead to abundant new growth and reduced risk of other fires. The are also silver clouds when it comes to what are often times heinous crimes.

Allow me to go back to 2001 for a moment. There are incidents that are foremost on my mind. One involved the death of a young, single immigrant mother. She had just given birth to a beautiful little girl."

"The baby's father had disappeared and she came to High Falls to live with relatives. She came to look for work and a new life for herself and her little girl but the relatives didn't have enough space for the new arrival and she was forced to seek financial assistance.

Because she looked like a social admission, which would mean an extended stay in the hospital for no additional reimbursement, greed turned to murder. The death of this young girl provided one of the first and most defining clues in the investigation. But here is the silver lining."

"Lorena Nunez told the social worker that all she cared about was providing a good life for her daughter. She wanted her daughter to have a better chance at happiness than she herself had. In her death, she got her wish. A local physician who volunteered to help with the investigation and his wife adopted this baby and vowed to provide the opportunity her natural mother was looking for.

Our family has since becomes best friends with their family. John, Sara, and Maria Shand." Greg pointed to the front row, inviting the Shands to stand up which they did proudly. Greg blew a kiss to Maria and she blew one back.

"The other story from that time is about a girl who was clinging to life even though she tried to end it. She was nineteen at the time. She was admitted due to a self-administered overdose of barbiturates. A far too common occurrence within our trouble teens and young adults. She had stabilized but her prognosis was uncertain and again looked like a lengthy stay. Our villain put her on his list of necessary casualties as well."

"One day, the nurse found her totally unresponsive and called a code blue. They were able to resuscitate her and move her to the Intensive Care Unit. No one thought she would survive. Her parents were holding on to hope and maintained a steady bedside vigil. If we had caught him just hours earlier, this girl wouldn't have been his victim.

She was next door to the room where our killer was caught and refused to cooperate with the authorities. Ultimately, he was shot and killed while attempting to inject an undercover state trooper decoying as a patient."

"When it was over, I went next door to apologize to her. She was alone and I approached the bed. I told her I was sorry that it took so long. I held her warm, soft hand in mine. I said, "I'm sorry Lacey, I wish I could have done more. She squeezed my hand, not tightly but certainly. I told her I needed to go but that I would check on her again before I left.

The next morning, I stopped before leaving town for what I thought was the last time. I made my way to the ICU and to Lacey's door. There were several people gathered around the bed and my mind went to the worst possible scenario. I made my way through the crowd to find Lacey sitting up in bed, eyes open and smiling."

"She wasn't able to talk but I knew what she was wanting to say. I held her hand again and she squeezed it much more tightly this time. I knew she had a long road ahead of her but there was hope.

Her parents introduced themselves and thanked me for my involvement. They were overjoyed to have their little girl back. Lacey and I kept in touch for a few years but then as life often does, it got in the way.

A few days ago, our paths crossed again. In fact, she is the reason Agent Andrews was able to find Kovak's house. It turns out that Lacey is the head of the records department at the county office building. She committed every resource available including many hours of her own time to provide us with the information we needed to catch this guy."

"Here is a young girl confused about life to the point of wanting to end it. When her attempt fails, someone tries to murder her by giving her ten times the dose of a perfectly good and useful drug at the normal dose, but almost always causes death at a higher one.

There is no explainable medical reason for her to still be with us. But, here she is, fifteen years later helping to save others from a similar fate. Destiny? Coincidence? I see it as the positive that can come from a negative. Lacey, thank you for letting me use your story." She held her hand up and people applauded.

"I know it's getting late so I will wrap this up and take a few questions. My last story is brand new. It is the upside of a horrific reign of terror and I am going to thank all of the parties involved for wanting to share this.

On his way home from detonating the bomb at Plattsburg, Ben Kovak made a stop to use the restroom. A young lady by the name of Veronica Sweet stopped at the same place for the same reason. Without going into detail, let's just say that this unattended meeting resulted in a pregnancy." There were a few subtle laughs.

"It was the only time the two would meet and they never told each other their names. This is late August remember. Veronica had more trouble. An FBI agent investigating the connection committed gross misconduct by an agent. Instead of questioning her and moving on, he held her captive for two weeks. If it wasn't for the unbelievable instinct and hard work of Special Agent Andrews, who knows where Veronica would be now."

"After a few months feeling different and a couple missed monthly cycles, Veronica purchased a pregnancy test kit. The results confirmed her suspicion. She figured she was either carrying the baby of a corrupt cop or a serial killer. For those of you who thought an unplanned pregnancy could be the worst thing, thank your lucky stars!" There was quite a bit of laughter then. Greg held his hand up. "The plot thickens!"

"We are having a stunned laugh at the situation. After all, we are human. But for this poor girl, there is nothing funny about it, right? A few days ago, our own suspicion, actually, it was more of a hunch, was confirmed.

Throughout the investigation, we could never link Ben with Kyle Seike or Martina Kovatikova. In the meantime, Ben met a young lady at the hardware store where he worked. They hit it off right away. There was an indefinable connection between them that could only be describes as kismet. They arranged to meet at the hardware store after closing.

Ben and Priscilla talked about everything under the sun. Now remember, this is Ben, the introvert, and Ben the Killer. He had no problem talking to Priscilla. In fact, when she showed up with a picnic lunch that evening, Ben converted one aisle of the store to a picnic area complete with a table, music, and glow in the dark stars. All they did was talk. Priscilla had to be up to milk the cows in the morning so she left by 10:00 pm."

"I think you will agree that this is a different side of Ben. Ben was obviously infatuated with Priscilla. So much so that he tried to kidnap her to take her to Austria which was his ultimate plan to leave the country. I guess the good side of Ben didn't last long.

Anyway, Priscilla's father caught Ben after he had put her to sleep with chloroform. Her dad found her lying beside the barn while Ben went to get his truck that he had hidden in the brush. When He returned with the truck, Priscilla was gone. He looked in the barn but she wasn't there. He moved to the back of the barn and found her in the milk room. In the meantime, Dad went to get his shotgun."

"Dad came around the backside of the barn and could see Ben through the window. He could also hear him telling Priscilla who had woken up by now that he was taking her to Austria. She disagreed and Dad backed her up by shooting at Ben through the window. I know this all sounds like a made for TV movie but stick with me and I will show you the power of the universe."

"Dad mostly missed and Ben ran off. Priscilla called me because I had already interviewed her regarding Ben. I called the police and we all met at the Chalmers' dairy farm. I spoke with both her and her dad as well as the police. Then I called Charis Andrews who set up police protection for them."

It was after talking with them that I had this feeling that I couldn't shake. The Chalmers had told me about Mrs. Chalmers who had passed a few years before. Priscilla told me the mother's room was just the way she left it. Mr. Chalmers wouldn't face moving on. On a whim, I asked if she had her mother's hairbrush. Well, she did and I called Charis. Do you see a pattern here?" more chuckles.

"Charis had an agent pick up the brush to compare with the hair Charis found in a Philadelphia barber shop where Ben Kovak had received a haircut prior to blowing up the hospital. Is everyone with me?

Maybe you know where this is going. I hope so, I have confused myself! A few days ago, we get the results. The part I'm leaving out that ties this together, you may have heard about. Over twenty years ago, a toddler was taken from his own yard. Authorities were notified and the search went on for years. There was never any trace of the lad. It became a closed case."

"The mother, devastated by the loss and holding herself responsible, never recovered from the trauma and died broken hearted a few years ago. The hairbrush belonging to her contained hair that was matched to the DNA found in the barber shop. Ben Kovak was born Timothy Chalmers to a loving family from High Falls, NY. He was abducted and raised by Kyle Seike and Martina Kovatikova." There was a lot of talking going on which Greg anticipated.

"The Chalmers had to be told. We knew it would open a wound that may never close but they deserved to know. Priscilla could now understand the instant connection. Dad didn't want to admit that he had a son who became a killer. It took a while but they agreed to see a counselor and I agreed to provide any help I could.

After a few sessions and a lot of talk as a family, the Chalmers decided to reclaim Timmy and bury him in the family plot next to his mother. Time has a way of softening us as well as healing us. The Chalmers allowed Charis, The Shands, and the Websters to attend the burial service for Timmy. I am happy to say that we are becoming fast friends."

"There is one last chapter to the story and then I promise I will let you go. Veronica Sweet is now four months pregnant. She has no family to speak of but she is a good woman and a grateful woman who loves the child she is carrying. She also witnessed a truer side, the Timmy side of Ben. When she looked in his eyes, she saw a sweet boy.

If you think about what Timmy endured growing up in a house where there was no love, no friends, and no toys, is it any wonder that he turned out the way he did? Picture a nine year old, totally on his own except for his deceased mother. Is there any wonder? We can hate who he became but shouldn't we grieve for the boy who had no choice?"

"Here is the universe working in mysterious ways. The Chalmers family has offered to adopt Veronica and raise their grandchild on the farm. Priscilla is excited to have a sister and Dad looks forward to having a little one to look after.

If that's not finding a light in the darkness, I don't know what is. I encourage all of you to look for the light in every situation. Oh, take the time to notice your surroundings. You will be amazed at what you will find. Thank you."

Greg left the stage to a standing ovation that went on for several minutes.

About the Author

Gerard Michael resides in the Mohawk River Valley of upstate New York with his best friend and partner, Marilyn. In addition to writing adult fiction, he writes and publishes children's books under the name Michael McAllister. He is also a musician, paintographer, saponier, gardener, partner, father and grandfather.

You can visit Gerard and Michael at www.gerardmichaelmcallister.com

Other Works By This Author

Deadly Ethics: Death May Not Be the End

Book 1 of the Greg Webster/Ethics Series.

Buried Ethics: Digging Up Bones

Book 2 of the Greg Webster/Ethics Series

Twisted Ethics: How Thin the Line

Book 3 and final book of the Greg Webster/Ethics Series

Children's Collection

A Tale of Two Fishermen *by Michael McAllister*

Why Do We Have To Move? *Co-written by Marilyn J. Keenan*